I0763358

Legends

The Prophecy of Heroes

By Russel Bush

Published in Las Vegas, Nevada

Published in the United States of America

Published By Turning Point International
3315 E Russell Rd Ste A4-404
Las Vegas, NV 89120

Legends: The Prophecy of Heroes
ISBN: 978-0-9882307-7-4
First Edition: June 2022

Cover Artwork: Rebecacovers
Layout: Jake Naylor
Illustrator/Photographer: Yulia of Ev36.com

In Loving Memory of

RUSSEL E. BUSH

For the Father who's mistakes fueled my ambition.

"Failure does not define greatness.
Perseverance through that failure does."
Russel Bush

Acknowledgements

I cannot express enough thanks to all who were involved in the completion of this book. It was a slow critical process that I never could have finished alone.

To my editor Judi Moreo. For one, thank you for believing in this book. Who knows where this book would be without you. Second, thank you for your continued support and encouragement while we edited the manuscript numerous times. Your knowledge in the field has been extremely helpful and has helped pave the way. Not only did you guide the transformation of an idea into a professional manuscript, you are aiding in its success. I am deeply grateful.

To my layout artist Jake Naylor. Thank you for doing such a great job. The book looks amazing! I could not have asked for anything better. Also, I appreciate you putting up with me while I harassed you during the weekends.

To my cover illustrator Rebecacovers. You brought this book to life. Thank you for your patience and ensuring the fine details. The scene you created gives the readers an accurate visualization of what is yet to come. You do great work!

To my illustrator Yulia of Ev36.com. You also brought this book to life. The scene you created demonstrates the beauty that exists in Legends. Thank you for your help.

Contents

Prophecy of Heroes

In the land of Legends, there are many myths set forth which foretell the coming of days. This is the telling of the Prophecy of Heroes…

Darkness will befall two worlds, and a Princess will be taken. This is the same darkness captured by a necklace from previous times. This necklace is named the necklace of Herana because it holds the soul of pure evil. If that evil is resurrected, the darkness might become too powerful to be stopped by the Heroes of Legends.

To save these worlds, the Leader of Heroes will arrive from Earth and band together with a group of lively and magical creatures to form the resistance who will defend against the oncoming evil. This group, the saviors of worlds, will be known as the Heroes of Legends. The leader from Earth will contain within him the ability to summon his power without a gemstone. As many inhabitants of Legends know, this ability is unheard of and will enable him to perform other astonishing feats that no one else has ever seen. The Leader of Heroes can be identified by his Earthen roots, his ironic sense of humor, and a mark on his left butt cheek.

The mystical creatures, Evos, created Mystics to defend against such evil by giving them immense power. The magic replenishing skills the Evos have will be essential to re-energize heroes during the coming war in order to not only save the Princess but save them all. If the heroes run out of energy, all will be lost. A combination of these magical forces and spirited creatures will forge the Heroes of Legends. Their powers will only strengthen once they find, earn, and bond with their weapons.

Countless mythical animals will help or hinder the heroes, including the sister of two sinister Nywolf brothers. Xena will become a friend and play an essential role during the heroes' journey.

Part 1

Searching for Priya

The World of Legends

Legends is the name of this world in which Aiden found himself. It is a world enriched by beauty, nature, and vibrant colors that include remarkable gemstones full of magical energy. Lush lands, abundant clear water, and clean air are many Legends attributes, not to mention the numerous types of Earth-like animals and other creature species. These creature species are called Roaks, Hairys, Grandars, Evos, Mystics, Devians, Gorgers, and more. Roaks are a human-like species born with extra strength and agility. Hairys are short and hairy dwarf-like creatures with feet like an ape which are used as hands. Grandars are eight-foot human-like giants. Evos are smaller than Hairys, furry, appear half human, half fox, and can replenish magic. Mystics are also human-like. They are born to wield magic and can tap into a higher strength of power. They are the strongest creatures on the planet of Legends. Devians are reddish, evil goblin-type creatures that Herana, the dark queen, initially created. Gorgers are greenish fourteen foot ogre-like huge monstrosities. Lastly, most of these creatures strive for status, and once they reach that status, they are considered Druids. Druids are any of these creatures, except Mystics, who have evolved to a state where they can wield magic. Mystics and Druids must have a gemstone in their possession to use their magic. Many of them place the jewels in their weapons.

There is something extraordinary about Legends. The world contains gemstones that hold elemental energy. These stones absorb energy from four elements of nature: Fire, Water, Earth, and Air. The stones are red (Fierna), blue (Watre), green (Dirte), and transparent like a diamond (Aire). Once a Mystic or Druid becomes a stone-wielder, that creature develops supernatural powers. A Druid can only bond with a specific type of gemstone and, once bonded, is the only one who can use that stone. Mystics can use any kind of gemstone and are the only ones who can use the Aire stones. The existence of these stones has allowed the emergence of many heroes over time, a few being God-like. Yet, the jewels also drove many insane from greed and an over-indulgence of power. There have only been a few, though, who went to the dark side and became powerful enough to pose an eminently dangerous threat.

In the past, there was a colossal battle of good vs. evil. Good prevailed as the prophecy predicted. Before any evil ever appeared upon the world of Legends, there was a human Druidess who foretold three prophecies. These prophecies describe three instances when evil tries to take over the land and the only way good could triumph. Ever since the creation of these prophecies, this world has been called Legends.

Foggy Memory

Aiden opened his eyes. He had a severe headache. He felt a wet sensation on his lips, so he wiped them. He looked at his fingers and saw blood. He tried to think about what had happened but couldn't remember. Then, he tried standing up but couldn't and realized he was chained to a post inside some building. Aiden looked to his right and saw three devilish-looking creatures bickering over some food and wine. They were Devians.

The first Devian, Juggy, looked at the other, Dagon, and complained, "Why do you always get to go first?"

Dagon gazed sternly at Juggy and responded, "Because I'm your boss."

Juggy looked confused, replying, "Who told you that?"

Dagon pointed to the third Devian, Kroni, "He did."

Juggy looked at Kroni, "When did you tell him that?"

Kroni answered, "Yesterday, dummy!"

Juggy grabbed his chin, thinking, "Oh, I don't remember."

Dagon and Kroni began cackling because Kroni had never said that. They were teasing Juggy since he had asked a stupid question. Dagon had been their boss for years. Juggy raised his eyebrows, still confused, while the other two grabbed food and wine.

Aiden looked to his left and saw Melia chained across the room from him. Melia is a Roak, a strong, human-like creature on this planet. She was unconscious, hanging from her chains in a sitting position. Suddenly, vague memories started flooding back. Aiden was with Melia trying to find Priya when he engaged in a fight with creatures from this world. It was imperative to find Priya, for Legends and Earth would be doomed without her. Magus, a ruthless Mystic and leader of his Devian army, had Priya held captive somewhere in this castle and was about to sacrifice her. Aiden, God-forbid, had to save the world, not only this world but the world from which he came as well. To do that, he needed to get Melia and himself out of these chains. Aiden and Melia against Magus and his army. How in the heck were only the two of them going to do this?

The sound of fighting, screams, and bellows howled, although faintly, from outside. "Someone's fighting out there, but it's not too close," Aiden thought. Then he remembered his friends and Magus's army were outside in a heated battle. There was another tremendous roar from what had to be an enormous creature. Aiden was immediately very concerned about his friends. He yanked on the chains, trying to break free. His wrists snapped back as the chains demonstrated their durability. He was stuck. At this moment, he flashed back to what had happened to him before someone put him in this precarious position.

....Aiden and Melia, in full battle gear and armed with swords, were running through what looked like a side passage from a courtyard. SLAM! They heard the sound of a catapult from way out in the field beyond the castle walls, followed by silence. Seconds later, they heard a thunderous crash. A large object hit the ground right outside the castle wall. Some Devians and two Grandars ran in the direction of the noise.

Aiden and Melia ran into another group of Devians investigating the noise. The Devians had axes, swords, and daggers. One Devian jumped at Melia, thrusting its sword. As Melia dodged the strike, another Devian lunged at her, swinging its ax. Melia deflected this strike while doing a spin kick, hitting the Devian who held the sword. It was sent flying. She turned and grabbed the Devian with the ax, and judo flipped it over her body, slamming it onto the ground. She followed this with a hard punch to the head, knocking it out. Simultaneously, the other three Devians attacked Aiden: one swinging its sword, one holding a dagger, and the third grabbing Aiden around his neck from behind. Aiden blocked the sword attack with his arm guard and punched the Devian, who had the dagger in its mouth, before it could lunge with its weapon. Aiden saw the Devian with the sword raise the blade to attack again, and as it did, he felt a surge of power. In slow motion, he jumped in the air throwing a roundhouse kick. He cracked the Devian in the side of the head, sending it flailing. In the same strike, Aiden's foot bounced off the sword-yielding Devian's head, moving backward in a hook kick, and nailed the dagger-yielding Devian in the face. The Devian flipped back onto its head. As Aiden came down from the jump, he grabbed the arms of the Devian who was still holding him from behind, and in one motion, thrust it over himself twenty feet ahead. Aiden looked up at Melia, who joked, "Okay! I never taught you that one!"

Aiden and Melia headed toward the end of the passage and found a haystack on a back wall of a large building. It seemed like the path was a dead end. They looked around, trying to find a way through. Melia placed her hands on the hay and felt a faint draft of wind. "That's odd," she said, then moved some of the hay. It revealed a large hole leading into the building. The duo went through the hole into an empty room lit up with torches.

Melia whispered, "We have to pass the Great Hall to get to the West Wing. Once we're in the West Wing, we can take the stairs that lead to the dungeons. I don't know where to go from there. Priya could be anywhere."

Aiden gave Melia a curious look, wondering how she knew so much about this place, then replied, "Okay, let's go."

They left the room and ran down a long gallery to the Great Hall. Hearing voices, they hid behind some plants in the gallery corner, but they heard more than voices. Aiden and Melia also heard something that sounded like panting and sniffing. It seemed to be two large creatures, and they were getting closer. They could smell the stink of the creatures, like wet dogs, super musty, and bloody.

"Nooo, not Nywolves!" Melia said under her breath, but it was too late. A large snout, sniffing, followed by enormous sharp teeth, poked around one of the plants. Aiden and Melia quickly moved to the other side of the plants, hoping they were undetected. At first, there was silence; then what sounded like grunting; then quiet again. They looked at each other, wide-eyed, and shrugged. Aiden peered through the bushes and saw the two Nywolves (Geri and Freki) sitting by the entrance to the Great Hall, staring in his direction. The wolf-like animals were snarling yet patiently waiting.

Geri and Freki were huge, about fifteen times the size of a normal wolf. These wolfish creatures each weighed about 2000 pounds. The Nywolves' heads were massive with huge fangs. Blood was dripping from their mouths and off parts of their fur. They had a muscular build and large paws armed with devastatingly sharp claws. The coat of both Nywolves was a dull brown color with black mixed in with a touch of white. The noticeable differences between the two were: Geri was slightly smaller, narrower in stature, had a sleeker look, a longer snout, and skinnier eyes; Freki was more muscular-looking and had some white patches on his underbelly.

"The Nywolves can smell us," Aiden thought, then he whispered to Melia, "So, what's the plan?"

Melia looked at Aiden matter-of-factly, then looked down at her boomerang blade, made from wood and reactive metal. Hidden at its ends were devastatingly sharp blades which armed when it was thrown and retracted when returning. Melia grabbed her boomerang and threw it around the plants at the Nywolves.

Geri ducked and rolled while Freki jumped and spun over the boomerang towards the area in the plants where Aiden and Melia were hiding. Freki landed next to a bush and lunged towards them. Melia dove to the left, catching her boomerang, and Aiden dove to the right. Geri pounced towards Aiden, and Aiden jumped in the air, pulled his sword, and sliced toward the incoming Nywolf. Geri slashed, hitting Aiden across the chest. At the same time, Aiden's sword slid across Geri's side.

Meanwhile, Melia had pulled her sword and was face-to-face with Freki. The Nywolf rushed her, and she jumped, flipped over Freki, and cut off his ear with her blade. Melia landed behind him as he growled in pain. He persevered and back-kicked her. She crashed into the wall and fell to the ground in a daze.

Aiden landed on his back with a thud and looked down at his chest. He was fine, thanks to his armor. Geri had landed on his side and flipped over onto his feet. The beast pounced again. Aiden thrust his sword in the air. The Nywolf landed on him, and Aiden's blade penetrated Geri's paw. Aiden watched as it went through the massive paw. As if in slow motion, the animal's paw slid down the entire blade. Geri's claws stopped an inch from Aiden's face. Geri howled in agony and bared his humongous canines. He opened his mouth wide, intending to bite and tear off Aiden's head. Aiden felt a surge of power again, but it was more potent this time. A flash of blue energy coursed through Aiden's body, and he punched Geri with both fists so hard the Nywolf launched up in the air and crashed into the ceiling. Debris fell from above. Geri bounced off the ceiling and fell hard to the ground.

"That's enough," came the voice of Regin from the background. Regin is one of the most feared evil and powerful beings in the land. He has caused havoc throughout the years working as one of Magus' army generals. At one time, he was a good man with a family, but that changed after an unexplained accident killed his family. Some time passed, and he fell to the dark side, joining Magus' onslaught. Regin is a Roak turned Druid who wears his jewel around his neck. His magic comes from the Fierna (fire) gem.

Aiden got to his feet and turned in Regin's direction, ready to fight. He recognized the evil Druid. Regin looked at Aiden, smirked, then turned toward Melia as his necklace started to glow. Miraculously, Regin's hands also began glowing as he made fists, and they erupted in flames. Regin thrust his hands in Melia's direction, hurling fire at her. The fire landed, surrounded Melia, and trapped her within a fire circle.

Regin spoke again, "What is your plan now, Aiden? What will you do to take on the strongest Druid in the land? Do you think I won't enjoy burning your friend to a crisp? It's been a while since I've had some fun. What do you say, shall we burn her?"

"Nooo!" Aiden exclaimed, "Leave her alone! If you hurt her, I'll kill you!"

Melia moaned, regaining her awareness.

"You're gonna kill me, are you?" Regin replied, "I don't think so!" Regin raised his hands and moved them closer, causing the fire circle around Melia to close in.

Melia jumped up, screaming, "Ahhh, it's hot!" as the fire enclosed around her.

Aiden yelled, "Alright, stop! What do you want?"

Regin spoke sternly, "All I want is for the two of you to listen and do what I tell you. We have a big evening planned, and the both of you will have front-row seats to watch the sacrifice. Now, put these chains on and go through there!" Regin motioned toward the Great Hall doors. Two sets of chains came flying in and landed in front of Aiden.

"Think again!" came a loud voice from within the fire circle, followed by Melia jumping through the fire, boomerang blade in hand. Melia's left sleeve caught fire as she soared through the air. She chucked her boomerang, landed on the ground, rolled, and whacked her sleeve to snuff out the flames.

The boomerang blade zipped through the air toward Regin. He created a magical red shield that blocked the boomerang, causing it to rebound and fly back to Melia. Melia ran over to Aiden, and they gave an "I'm okay" nod to each other.

Although Geri's side and paw were injured, he had gotten up and rejoined Freki. They stood in attack postures with their teeth bared, facing the two heroes.

Aiden looked around and assessed the situation. He saw the Nywolves on each side of him, ready to attack. Regin was standing about twenty feet in front with a condescending look on his face as if he wanted to glance at his wristwatch, if he had one, and say, "Time's ticking. You guys about finished?"

Aiden was infuriated. Blue energy coursed through his body as he felt his anger and strength building. He took off like a lightning bolt, running toward the evil Druid.

Regin saw the blue power surge through Aiden and was confused but reacted with a magical defensive block. BAAMM! A bright flash of red and blue energy followed a thunderous bang. Aiden flew backward and landed by Melia, unconscious and smoking.

Freki watched his boss fly backward and crash halfway through a stone wall. The bottom portion of Regin's torso lay in sight, also smoking. The blow hurt Regin, but after a minute, he was able to work his way out of the wall and stand up. The Nywolves nudged the chains in front of Melia, prompting her to put them on...

Aiden snapped out of his daze, perplexed at what he had been thinking. Realizing his situation again, he looked around for something he could use to pick the locks on his chains. He didn't see anything handy, but he could see the bottom of the keys dangling from Juggy's belt and thought, "Why would they give him the keys when he seems like the one you definitely wouldn't want to have the keys?" With his realistic perspective, he followed that thought with, "Maybe it's so the others can make him take care of the prisoners."

Dagon and Kroni walked out the door while Juggy finished getting his fill of food and wine. Juggy drank half a jug of wine in one long swig.

Seeing this, Aiden remarked, "I could use some of that wine. My head is killing me."

Juggy looked at Aiden and sneered, "You'd like that, wouldn't you, outsider! You don't deserve any wine, you dirtball. Anyone who smells like you doesn't deserve a thing. I could smell you from the stables!"

Aiden sarcastically replied, "Are you sure that wasn't the stables you smelled, genius? Or, maybe your butt?"

Juggy gave a weird smirk as if he almost laughed, then recovered and made an angry face. He walked closer to Aiden and leaned in. Fuming, he pointed his finger close to Aiden's nose, "You do not speak to me with such a tone. I will chop your hands off and feed them to our ogre, Drakkar."

Aiden lunged at Juggy's finger, caught it in his teeth, bit down hard, and took off half of it. Aiden spat out the piece of finger and tripped Juggy to the floor as Juggy screamed out in pain. Once Juggy hit the floor, Aiden heel-kicked him to the head, knocking him out cold.

At the sound of Juggy hitting the floor, Melia was startled, and her eyes shot open. She looked around, still in a haze, and could see a Devian on the floor next to Aiden. Aiden attempted to get the keys from Juggy's waist using his feet but couldn't reach them.

Melia spoke up, "Where are we? What happened?"

Aiden replied, "Well, look who decided to join the party! Um, I'm not sure. It's still fuzzy," he looked around, "I think we're in a bakehouse. Help me get these keys."

Melia suggested, "Why don't you use your powers? You've been getting better at controlling them. I mean, first, you did some spectacular kicks earlier. Then you double power-punched a Nywolf and then ran faster than the speed of light! What's next? Are you gonna teleport?"

"Wouldn't that be something!" Aiden responded, smiling, "I don't know. It just happens."

"Sooo, you can't bust outta those chains? Even after all our training?" Melia asked.

Aiden looked down at the chains and hesitantly answered, "I can try."

Aiden took a deep breath to calm himself and focus on his chains. He tried thinking about the chains, visualizing breaking out of them, and even thinking about getting revenge on Regin for putting him in them. After a moment, his hands started to shake, and the chains began rattling. Seeing it was working, he gave it everything he had. He was straining so hard a vein popped out on his forehead. There was a glimmer of blue energy that fluctuated in his hands but disappeared as fast as it appeared. Disappointed, Aiden laid his hands down and glanced back at Melia. "Nothing," he said, shrugging, "We need to get those keys."

"Hold on," Melia spoke sternly, "Are you ok? You and Regin collided and exploded. You were knocked out. I was really worried. I thought you might have, you know, died!"

Aiden acknowledged Melia's concern for him and replied, "No worries. I feel okay. Head hurts, but I'm okay."

There was a loud bang from outside and a faint thunderous roar at that moment. Next came loud voices from right outside the door. An upset voice sounding like Dagon said, "What the hell was that? Where is Juggy? Juggy quit drinking, and help us! Drakkar needs help!"

Dagon ran through the door, followed by Kroni, and they saw Juggy on the ground, knocked out, next to Aiden. Again, Aiden tried to reach for the keys. Dagon yelled, "Hey, what are you doing? Juggy, get up, you louche!"

Kroni looked at Melia and warned, "Don't you move!"

Melia responded, "I'm kinda stuck here, not going anywhere."

Dagon ran to Juggy, "I can't believe you passed out on the job again!" he exclaimed. He grabbed a jug of wine and poured it into Juggy's mouth.

Juggy's lips quivered at the taste of wine, and he started waking up. "Wha, what happened?" Juggy wearily said, "Owww, my finger! That bastard!"

"What did you do to his finger?" Dagon spouted at Aiden as he looked at Juggy's finger, "You bit it off? You bit it off! That's it! I will kill you!" Dagon stood up and pulled his dagger.

"We can't! The big boss wants them alive for now!" Kroni warned dubiously.

"Kill them!" screamed Juggy. Dagon raised his dagger with murder in his eyes. Aiden braced himself in a defensive posture. Subtle blue energy began to coarse through Aiden's body. Dagon held the dagger high, a second from plunging it into Aiden's chest. Aiden only hoped he could defend himself with another spectacular move. A pot came flying in and nailed Dagon in the head in the spur of the moment, knocking him to the ground.

"Hey guys!" exclaimed Gil, as he appeared in the doorway, smirking, satisfied that his aim was true. Behind Gil followed Cedric, both of whom are Hairies. Kroni turned toward Gil and pulled his sword. Gil had another pot in his hand and threw it, hitting Kroni in the head, as well.

"Damn, you're pretty good with those!" Cedric joked. He ran at Kroni, tackling him to the ground while throwing punches.

Juggy was still within Aiden's leg length, so Aiden kicked Juggy in the head, knocking him out again. Gil ran over to Juggy, grabbed the keys from him, and unlocked Aiden and Melia from their chains.

"Thank goodness you guys got here!" declared Melia, "What is our position?"

"Jack and Borak are fighting that huge ogre-looking beast!" Gil informed, "They need our help! We hit Drakkar with the catapult, but that son-of-a-gun is tough!"

Aiden got up and hurried over to Melia. "How are you feeling? Do you remember any more of what happened?"

Melia hesitated for a second, then stuttered a little, "I uh, I, uh, um, hmm. Yea, I feel fine. Wait, I remember you were lying there, on the ground, smoking. I was worried if you were ok, so I dropped my sword and tried to wake you. You didn't move, but you were breathing. Then, they made me put the chains on us."

...Melia reached over and grabbed the chains as Freki and Geri stared at her. She put the chains on herself, then on Aiden. Regin spoke, "Ahh, that's better. Great to have you on the team. If you will head through those doors now, please, there's something I'd like you to see." Melia picked up Aiden, slung him over her shoulder, and walked toward the Great Hall. Freki and Geri followed behind with their teeth bared. As Melia entered the Great Hall, she could see creatures up on the stage. She looked closer and could see female Devians giving another woman in shackles a makeover. The Devians were partially in the way, so, at first, Melia could not tell who was getting the makeover.

"Oh, doesn't she look beautiful! A little dab here and a little rub there and voila, we turned this hideous creature into a star," complimented one of the female Devians.

"Yes, she was so ugly when we first met her, and she's so beautiful now!" agreed the other female Devian.

Melia walked in further and could now see the woman in makeup. "Holy crap!" she thought to herself. Looking past the horrible makeover the Devians had given the imprisoned woman, Melia saw it was Priya.

Priya had on black lipstick and eyeshadow. Red paste covered the rest of her face. She wore a plain white dress and jewelry, including a crown, bracelets, earrings, and a perfect shimmering golden necklace with colorful gemstones in it. It had four stones: red, blue, green, and one that looked like... wait, one is missing.

"Priya!" Melia yelled out. Freki swatted her in the back, cutting her off. Aiden tumbled off her shoulder, and Melia fell to the ground.

"Conversations aren't allowed. I'll tell you if you can speak," instructed Regin.

The two Devian ladies, giving Priya the makeover, glared at Melia as she picked herself up.

Regin spoke again, "So as you can see, the beautiful Priya is looking ravishing for her theatrical debut. We have dressed her traditionally with makeup and jewelry. Did you notice the necklace she has on? That is the necklace of Herana. You know, the one that consumed Herana when Naru defeated her. Once the necklace has consumed a worthy replacement, it will release Herana. Priya will be the next sacrifice. She shall be the one to bring the Queen back!"

"All praise Herana!" chanted the lady Devians as they bowed.

"You will not hurt her! I will kill you! She will kill you!" screamed Melia at the evil Druid. Melia turned her attention toward the enslaved Princess and said in a softer voice, "Priya, why aren't you doing anything?"

Priya looked at Melia and Aiden remorsefully. Aiden was lying on the ground, unconscious and bleeding. She wanted to say something to Melia but, more importantly, didn't want to get her killed. Melia was ignorant of all the necklace's powers. The necklace of Herana can also allow the worthy entity who wore it the ability to communicate with the spirit world. Not only that, it can act as a magic dampener. When the necklace was missing a gem, it prevented anyone wearing it from using magic. Priya was a Druid like Regin and known to be as powerful as Regin, if not more powerful. Because the necklace was missing one of its gems, Priya was currently powerless.

"The sacrifice is ready, Master Regin," spoke one of the lady Devians.

"Good, take her to the dungeons. Don't worry, Melia. You won't miss any of the action. You shall have a front-row seat," Regin said wickedly.

Melia rushed the stage toward Priya as fast as possible in her chains. Regin reacted by whipping his hands around his head and throwing a red energy ball at her. The energy ball struck Melia in the side and tossed her to the left into some barrels, knocking her unconscious. Priya put her head down as the Devians guided her to a set of stairs that went into the dungeons....

Battle With Drakkar

"Okay, let's go! We've gotta help Jack and Borak!" Aiden said hurriedly and glanced over at Gil and Cedric, "Lead the way!" Gil ran out the door first and turned left, opposite the Great Hall and the dungeons. Everyone else followed. They were on the east side of the inner ward of the castle. As soon as they exited the door, they heard yelling and the sound of swords clanging against each other. Drakkar let out another monstrous roar.

They ran toward the battle. While they ran, they heard Drakkar growling and grunting. Then his deep and powerful voice challenged, "Come on, you cowards! Is that all you got?" They saw dust flying and the castle walls vibrating, causing bricks to fall. The ground shook periodically, imitating minor earthquakes. They tried to catch a glimpse of the horrid creature making all the noise, but a building was in the way. Finally, the four reached the building, giving them a view. Aiden saw the ugliest grotesque ogre beast of a creature he had ever seen.

"He's blocking their way in!" yelled Melia.

"It's Drakkar! What do we do? He's friggin' huge!" added Cedric.

Aiden took a second to think.

Drakkar, a fourteen-foot tall Gorger, stood in a gap in the castle wall that appeared to have been blown open by something. Borak was at battle with Devians in a field in front of the gigantic Gorger. The Devians were closing in on Borak. Off a little to the left in the field were three Grandars. Two of them seemed to have just finished combat. Jack was one of these Grandars.

He had injured the other one, who was on the ground with part of its arm cut off. The third Grandar was on the attack, making its way toward Jack.

Jack and Borak appeared to be injured. Jack clutched at his side, and Borak limped on his right leg. They both seemed to have lost their weapons. The Devians purposely flanked Jack and Borak to drive them toward Drakkar. By now, the two heroes were near each other and slowly backed up closer to the angry ogre. Drakkar salivated in anticipation of blood, absentmindedly inching himself toward them. The giant beast looked behind himself at the gap in the wall and took a step back into it. He didn't want to leave an opening for someone else to sneak through. The Devians yelled for reinforcements. A few who had fallen earlier rose to their feet. The larger group of Devians and the evil Grandar continued forcing Jack and Borak back until the heroes were only yards from where Drakkar was standing.

Aiden looked at Melia and shouted "Melia!" He shot his eyes at her boomerang. Drakkar stepped forward and reached to grab Borak but missed as Borak rolled out of the way. Melia quickly grabbed her boomerang and threw it. Melia's boomerang blade zipped through the air and curled towards Drakkar. Drakkar appeared to sense the boomerang and leaned back. The boomerang barely missed Drakkar's face and sliced across his arm, leaving a long gash.

"Let's go!" yelled Aiden. They all ran toward Drakkar.

At this time, Borak and Jack looked over and saw their comrades running to help. Jack's foot hit a sword, which he picked up, and Borak found a dagger on the ground. They held up their weapons and gave each other a slight snicker as if they had an inside joke.

"Thas' not a knife!" Jack joked. He gestured with the sword he picked up, "Now thas' a knife!" He smiled and added, "Here we go, aye!" No one could figure out exactly what Jack's accent was. It sounded Australian, British, or Scottish at different times. It was odd since he had never been to Earth to have heard those accents. Jack ran at the other Grandar, and their swords clanged together.

At the same time, Borak lunged at a Devian and stuck the dagger in its neck. Borak followed this with a back sweep, tripping another Devian to the ground and stabbing it in the chest. Meanwhile, Drakkar turned around to face the group running toward him, happy to have more adversaries to kill.

Gil and Cedric reached the wall first. They rapidly climbed up each side of the gap where Drakkar was standing. Hairies are very agile. At the same time, Aiden and Melia attacked head-on. Aiden jumped-attacked, swinging his sword. Drakkar swatted Aiden out of the air. Melia slid on her knees under Drakkar's legs and sliced his left leg with her sword. Drakkar hollered, in pain.

The two Hairies jumped on Drakkar's back and jabbed their miniature swords into his shoulders. They looked like two parrots holding on for dear life. "It's times like these. I wish I were a little bigger," joked Cedric. Drakkar roared, in pain, and smacked both Hairies off him.

Melia, still sliding, turned and sliced again with her sword. Her strike rattled off Drakkar's armor. Drakkar heard the clang and looked down, spotted her, then tried to stomp her. He missed. Then, he kicked her like a soccer ball. She shot through the air twenty feet before hitting and bouncing off the ground.

After going back and forth with their swords, Jack swung his weapon and threw a front kick knocking his opponent back. The other Grandar noticed Jack wince in pain as he did this. Remembering Jack's side was hurt, the evil Grandar attacked with its sword again. It punched Jack in the face and kicked his injured side. The pain caused Jack to fall to one knee. He grabbed his side, looked down, and saw blood. "You gotta go for me vulnerable spot, do ya? How admirable of ya!" Jack said sarcastically.

Jack had a stab wound from the Grandar he fought earlier. Thinking the fight was about over, the Grandar he was fighting now sliced downward with its sword. Jack dove sideways, dodging the strike, and rolled to the right. He started to get up but only made it halfway when the Grandar kicked him in his injured side again. "Ahhhh!" screamed Jack, in pain, as he fell onto his back.

"And now, it is your end," promised the attacking Grandar in a confident tone. It raised its sword and pointed the blade down toward Jack's chest, preparing to shove it through his heart. Before the wicked Grandar could complete its act, Jack thrust his sword up at his enemy's body. The Grandar released one hand from its sword and grabbed Jack's blade with a bare hand. Jack's blade stopped, and the Grandar's sword began its descent.

Suddenly, there was a thud. The Grandar on top of Jack hesitated, then screamed in pain. Blood dripped from its hand as it held onto Jack's blade. It looked behind itself to see Melia's boomerang sticking out of its back. Jack didn't waste any time and drove his sword, with the giant's hand still on it, up and into its stomach. The blade pierced through the Grandar's body and stuck out of its back. The enormous creature coughed up blood and fell sideways. Jack got to his feet and looked over at Melia, who was looking back at him. They gave each other a nod. As the severely injured Grandar lay on the ground bleeding, Jack pulled his sword out and yelled revengefully, "This is for my sista!" He plunged his sword into the Grandar's chest, puncturing its heart and killing it.

Borak dodged a sword by leaning back and watching the sword zip by his face. He then parried a dagger strike with a grab and flipped the Devian over his shoulder, throwing it into the Devian that had swung the sword at him. Borak's leg shot pain through it, and Borak winced but continued to fight. Three Devians ran at him. He side-stepped under the leftmost Devian's attack and sliced its neck with his dagger. He spun and swiped the next Devian's sword from it, pushed the creature back, and slashed down its chest, followed by an up-slice to the rightmost Devian's stomach and chest. Borak spun again, threw a back-kick to the next attacking Devian's stomach, and sliced through two more Devians. This left three Devians alive, two of them getting up from the ground. They all looked, hesitantly, at Borak.

"Are you sure you want to do this?" asked Borak with a smirk. "Raahhh," he yelled, running at the Devians. They all turned around and ran away.

Aiden landed in a pile of rubble by the wall. His head hit a rock and knocked him in a daze.

Drakkar grunted in annoyance, "Quit moving, you mangy pests!"

Gil and Cedric ran around Drakkar, throwing little knives and rocks at him. "Too quick for you, you big ope," teased Gil.

Cedric humorously replied, "I think one of my knives hit his..." He cupped his mouth and lowered his voice to almost a whisper, "....you-know-where." Gil laughed.

In the background, Aiden saw Jack throw Melia's boomerang blade to her. She turned toward Drakkar and threw the boomerang at him, nicking the side of his neck. Drakkar let out a thunderous wail in anger, grabbed a boulder, and threw it straight at Melia. She dove in time to avoid being crushed by it.

Drakkar turned quickly and grabbed Cedric as he was running under its legs. The hideous ogre picked Cedric up by his shirt and stared him directly in the face and sneered, "You think you're funny, do ya? Let's see how funny you are now!" Drakkar clenched Cedric in his hand and began squeezing.

Gil saw this and screamed, "Noooooo! Don't do it! Wait! Stop!"

Drakkar stopped squeezing and, in a treacherous voice, questioned, "Why should I? You two little pests deserve it."

Without thinking, Gil ran at the murderous monster. It was a desperate attempt to save Cedric because he was too far away. Drakkar started squeezing Cedric again.

Aiden watched helplessly as his friend was on the verge of being crushed alive. Suddenly, he was energized in blue light, jumped up, and ran at an incredible speed. He flew off the ground and super-punched Drakkar in the face. CRAACK! It sounded like a lightning bolt hit the ground, but instead, it was an explosion on Drakkar's face which sent the enormous ogre soaring through the air into the side of the castle wall. Cedric flew out of Drakkar's hand, flipping end-over-end, and landed in a horse carriage. A tower on top of the wall shook back and forth as the wall crumbled. The tower and wall came tumbling down on top of the ogre, and Drakkar disappeared. Everyone looked at Aiden, amazed.

"How in the world?" Gil pondered initially and then turned toward where Cedric landed in the horse carriage. He yelled, "Cedric!" Gil ran frantically to the horse carriage. There was no response, and Gil kept running. Now, everyone started running to the horse carriage. "Ceeddric!" Gil yelled again as he arrived. The top had caved in where Cedric landed, and the carriage was leaning on one side where a wheel had popped off. It was an old wooden carriage, so Gil had to pull wood and part of a tarp off Cedric to find him. Cedric's arm and leg were twisted awkwardly behind him, his eyes were closed, and he wasn't moving. Gil pleaded, "Cedric! Cedric! Get up, you little hairy bastard! I can't do this without you! I love you, man! Wake up!"

By this time, Aiden and the rest of the gang had arrived. Cedric didn't reply and only lay there in silence. Gil bent over Cedric and started crying. Aiden, Melia, Jack, and Borak looked at each other somberly, with little hope. The way Cedric was lying didn't look good.

After concluding Cedric must be gone, Aiden put his arm around Gil, "I'm sorry, man." Gil looked at Aiden and sadly nodded while wiping his tears and nose.

Then, out of the corner of his eye, Aiden saw Cedric's lips pucker and make a kissing sound. Everyone looked over at Cedric. Cedric puckered his lips again and made another kissing sound, then razzed his buddy, "You said you love me. Come kiss me!"

"You butthole!" Gil reacted, relieved, then grabbed Cedric and hugged him tightly.

"Ow, ow, ow, be careful! My arm is still twisted behind my head over here!" Cedric uttered in pain.

"Sorry, sorry," Gil responded and got off Cedric.

Now that everyone knew Cedric was, for the most part, okay, they realized the position his body lay in was quite comical. Cedric's twisted, dislocated arm was up behind his head. Also, behind his head was his right foot somehow sticking out of the wood, and his toes were wiggling. Everyone was looking at Cedric, not knowing whether to laugh or try to find a medic.

"A little help here, guys!" Cedric finally said in a self-evident tone.

Cedric was injured, but he's always been flexible and very pain tolerant. The group tried to help him out of the awkward position, but it hurt him more than it helped.

Cedric stopped his friends, saying, "Look, I'll be fine. I'm fine, leave me here. Go get Priya."

"No, I'm not leaving you here! Are you crazy?" Gil responded.

"Gil, I can't stand up right now, but I'll be fine! You guys have to save the world!" replied Cedric.

Melia touched Gil's hand, attempting to talk some sense into him, "We'll cover him up for now and come back. He's right. We have to move."

Gil put his head down, then nodded. At that, Melia turned to the others, and they all nodded in agreement.

After they covered Cedric with wood and the tarp, Aiden spoke up, "Is everybody else okay? We're almost there, guys."

"As good as I'll ever be!" replied Jack, clutching at his side.

"I'll manage," added Borak, who Aiden could tell was leaning on one leg to keep the weight off the other.

Aiden glanced at Melia, wanting to hear from her.

"I'm good. Let's go get our girl!" she responded.

"I'm gonna kill 'em allll!" Gil loudly declared, "Those sons of bii…."

Aiden quickly put his hand over Gil's mouth, then calmly told him, "We're all upset, but that was too loud. You need to focus." Aiden paused and noticed everyone was looking at him, so he continued speaking, "They took Priya to the dungeons. There is access to the dungeons by the Great Hall down the stairs. We know the Nywolves and Regin are down there, and I'm sure Magus is also down there. So we need to stay on our toes. We don't know who or what else we might run into."

"Magus," Borak scorned hatefully at the name.

The Forbidden Adventure

Borak, Melia, and Magus had history. Borak and Melia first met Magus when they were children in the land of Heirstone, where their parents, at that time, were King and Queen. The two were only preteens, and life seemed great. Their parents ruled the land, they were in line to be the successive rulers, and they basically could do what they wanted within reason. As the children of the King and Queen, they were obligated to train in martial arts and weapons combat. However, they were still children and didn't always do as they were told. One day, Borak and Melia skipped out of their training for an adventure in the woods, as they did from time to time. They weren't allowed to travel outside of the city's boundaries by themselves and had been reprimanded for doing so a few times previously.

...*"Where do you want to go this time, Melia?" asked Borak.*

"You know I want to go to the waterfall. I always tell you that, and you never want to go," replied Melia.

"Because it's too dangerous, and you know that. It's not a good idea. Everyone who goes into that cave disappears. Remember the traveler?"

The traveler was the last person known to go to the waterfall and disappear. Melia had seen him in the market a few months back. The traveler asked around about the waterfall and cave and ran into Melia. She told him the waterfall is said to have clear, beautiful water that sometimes turns different shades of red, blue, and green. She also warned him of the danger of the cave, telling him, "An old tale says, there is a treasure in the cave, but only the worthy can wear it. All others will be lost." The traveler wandered around the market a while longer and disappeared. Rumor has it; he went to the cave, which was the last time he was ever seen.

"We won't go into the cave. I only want to look at it and see the waterfall. I'm going this time with or without you," Melia told her brother sternly as she started walking in the direction of the waterfall.

"Wait! Melia, wait!" pleaded Borak.

Melia knew her stubborn brother would try and stop her, so she began running. All Borak could do was run after her and try not to lose her as Melia was very fast. When he finally caught her, they were at the waterfall. They could see the cave entrance about ten feet off the ground, directly behind the waterfall.

"Geez, Melia, what are we doing? This is not a good idea," stammered Borak.

"You always say that!" Melia said in a sort of irritated tone.

They both stared in awe for a minute at the cave entrance.

"Melia, we can't go in. I won't let you!" Borak finally spoke, knowing what his sister was thinking.

"I dare you to stop me!" Melia snickered, then grabbed the wooden baton she had on her belt.

Borak reached for his wooden baton, and Melia smacked him on top of his hand, causing him to recoil in pain.

"What the heck are you doing?" barked Borak, half-confused.

"I'm going in that cave!" replied Melia.

"No, you're not!" Borak proclaimed confidently, this time successfully grabbing his baton.

Melia let out a deep breath, knowing what was about to happen. She swung her training weapon downward at Borak. He countered by blocking her strike and tapping her on top of her head with his baton. Melia glared at her arrogant brother before following with a few more downward strikes, which Borak blocked again, and then attacked low, hitting him in the leg. Borak dropped to one knee, and she gave him a "got you" look.

Borak retaliated by sweeping Melia's legs out from under her. He then dove at his sister, swinging his baton. She rolled out of the way, and his baton hit the ground. She jumped to her feet. Borak spun backward, swinging his baton again. Melia blocked his spinning attack, then front-kicked him to the mid-section and threw a high-kick to his head. Borak blocked the high-kick, grabbed her leg, picked her up, and slammed her on the ground.

"You're not going in there!" Borak yelled, repeating himself.

Melia forced in some deep breaths trying to recover from the impact of the ground. It had knocked the air out of her, but she was attempting not to show it. Borak lay on top of Melia, taking deep breaths, tired from their fighting.

"Fine!" Melia said in between breaths.

As they lay on the ground, catching their breath, someone yelled from inside the cave, "Help! Please help me!" The siblings looked at each other, a little perplexed. Again the voice cried out, "Hello? Somebody help!"

"No, Melia!" Borak pleaded. But it was too late. She flipped her brother off her, got to her feet, and ran to the cave entrance.

"Hello? Hello? What happened? Who are you?" questioned Melia, cautiously standing at the cave opening.

The voice replied, "Oh, thank goodness! I'm stuck! Please help!"

"Why did you go in there?" Melia asked.

The voice spoke up, "I was looking for my brother. He was trying to find this place a few months back. He never came home!"

By this time, Borak was standing next to Melia. They looked at each other with sudden recognition. "The traveler is his brother," Melia whispered.

Melia took a step inside the cave, but Borak stopped her by grabbing her shoulder. She merely shrugged his hand off and continued. Borak didn't want to admit it, but he was extremely curious, too. He followed behind her.

"Wa-wwhere are you?" stammered Melia.

"Over here! Follow my voice," answered the voice which sounded in pain. Melia and Borak followed the voice down a tunnel that forked left and right. The voice was coming from the right, so they went that way. The siblings walked a little further until they came around a bend and saw a beautiful, colorful pond and a young man sitting along the front edge of it.

"Oh, thank goodness, you're here! I've been stuck for days! My foot is caught in the mud," the man said frantically.

At first, Borak could only see the man's leg disappear under the water's surface. After a closer investigation, it looked to him like the ground had swallowed the man's foot. Melia walked closer and saw the same.

"I don't know what this is, but my foot won't budge," pouted the man.

Melia could see a silky lining covering the bottom of the pond. The entire pond wasn't more than two feet deep except in the center of it. The color seemed to be coming from a deep hole in the center, but she couldn't tell what was causing it. The pond also formed into a stream that ran toward the waterfall.

"Hold on! We'll get you free!" Melia told the man.

Borak walked close to the trapped man with his baton in hand and jammed it in the mud next to the man's foot. His baton didn't wedge well and only slid around in the muck. Borak then tried pushing the mud out of the way to give room for the man to pull his foot out.

"Oowww!" the anxious man let out, "It's only getting tighter!"

Borak noticed the mud was merely maneuvering around his baton and, yes, becoming tighter.

"Do you see this?" Borak asked his sister, "It's like it's not even there. Like it's there, but not."

"Yeah, that's weird," she replied, "What are we gonna do?"

Borak thought for a second before speaking, "Well, it looks like the mud only has his boot. Maybe I can cut his foot out? Can you raise your boot any?" he asked the man.

"What? You're gonna do what?" the pinned man interjected, then said, "Um, I'll try." The man stood up on his left leg for leverage and yanked up on his right leg. His boot barely budged, but it did move enough to reveal the top of it.

"Hold on. Don't move," Borak said, ignoring the man's hesitance. He pulled his dagger and slowly cut backward, from a little higher than the toe, where the top of the silky mud was sitting. As Borak began working his way up the laces, the soil ever so subtly started rising.

"Crap, it's moving!" the man informed.

Borak quickly cut through the rest of the boot, and the man pulled his foot out. The mud overtook the boot and sucked it under.

"Holy crap, that was close!" the man expressed. "Aaaahh!" he moaned, grabbing at his ankle in obvious pain.

Changing the subject, Melia seriously asked, "Why did you step in there? You got really lucky!"

The embarrassed man answered, "I didn't know that would happen. I was trying to get the necklace."

"Necklace? What necklace?" Borak chimed in.

"What necklace?" scoffed the man, then he continued, "The necklace of Herana! My brother came here to get it and never came back. I hope that's not him over there."

The man pointed to the other side of the pond and gestured in the same direction with his chin. Melia and Borak looked over to see a body lying with its back toward them on the ground next to the pond.

"Oh no! Is he? He's dead!" Melia cried as she shoved her head into Borak's chest. Melia had never seen a dead body before. The body had an arrow sticking out of its neck.

Other arrows were lying on the floor. Borak could see holes in the cave walls above the pond from where the arrows must shoot out. The traps seemed to prevent anyone from climbing the walls and jumping to the center of the pond.

"It looks like there are other traps in place," remarked Borak. He stared

at the colors coming from the hole in the center of the pond, then asked, "Is that where the necklace is?"

The injured man nodded.

Melia was choked up but composed herself. Meanwhile, the man watched the young children intently and was impressed by how Melia built up the strength to shrug her emotions away. She confidently walked toward the body.

"Be careful," warned Borak.

Melia reached the body and checked it. There was no denying it was dead. She rolled the body over and asked, "Is this your brother?"

The man shook his head and answered, "No," then wiped his brow, "Whewww, I was so worried." There was a moment of silence, and then the man persisted, "We need to get that necklace."

Borak and Melia stared at the red, blue, and green colors flowing from the center of the pond. They couldn't see the bottom, but they could make out the luminescence of something beautiful, shimmering.

"That must be the treasure, but we need to get out of here," Borak insisted.

"Shouldn't we try to get it?" urged Melia, "Remember the story? It says you must be worthy or you'll be lost. What if that's why people disappear?" Melia thought about it for a second, then remarked, "You're right. Let's go."

At this moment, the man interrupted, "You are correct. The necklace is why people are disappearing, and I think it took my brother. We must retrieve the necklace to save him."

Borak thought, then replied, "I'm sorry, but it's too dangerous."

The man insisted, "Not only can we save my brother, but we can save all who the necklace has consumed. It says so in the story."

There was silence again, and Melia gave Borak a sorrowful gaze insinuating, "We have to."

Borak shook his head, disgusted, because he knew, again, he had no choice. He began contemplating, "How was anyone supposed to get over the magical death mud?" Borak looked at the walls and started talking to himself, "There must be triggers that set these arrows off. Maybe some type of motion detector." He grabbed a long stick and threw it across the pond. Two arrows shot out and bounced off the other side of the cave. "I knew it," he told himself. He threw another stick in the same area, and two more arrows shot out from the same holes. "Well, it looks like they somehow reload," Borak continued talking to himself. He then asked the others, "Any ideas, guys?

"Can you float?" the man asked.

"Hmmm, that might work, but the pond is so shallow," Borak replied, "What do you think, sis?"

"It has to be someone light. She is the smallest," the conspicuously helpful man pointed out.

"No, no way!" reacted Borak.

"That's what I was thinking. It's the only way," Melia agreed. She put her hand on Borak's arm until he turned, and they locked eyes before she reassured him, "I'll be fine."

Melia began walking to the edge of the pond. While she walked, she looked over at the corpse, then pushed away any disturbing thoughts.

"Let me help," demanded Borak. He grabbed her hand, and they walked to the edge of the pond together. Once there, Borak placed his hands, palms up, on Melia's stomach. Melia understood what he was doing and slowly laid down on her brother's hands. He lowered her, belly down, onto the water's surface.

Borak laid Melia flat in the water and waited for her to stabilize. Then he asked, "Are you ready?" His sister nodded, and he quickly slid his hands out from under her.

Melia dipped down in the water a little, and they all held their breath. She bobbed back up to the surface and appeared to be okay. Unknowingly though, a string from her pants hung down and touched the mud. Immediately, the mud seized the string and began tugging it. Melia couldn't move because she risked touching the mud herself if she did. The mud yanked harder, pulling her down. Borak grabbed the back of her shirt and was on the verge of pulling her out.

"Hold on!" urged the man while drawing his knife. He slipped the knife between Melia's stomach and the mud and cut the string. "There you go," he said.

Melia bobbed and settled on the surface of the water. She was relieved and grateful to still be alive. She slowly inched her way forward, doing all she could to keep her body parts on the very top of the water. If she moved too fast, she would dip down in the water and, inevitably, be seized and drowned by the mud. Slowly but surely, Melia made her way to the pond's center above the radiant colors and shimmer of the necklace.

The center of the pond was extremely deep. A large hole dropped down to what looked like over thirty feet. At the bottom was the necklace.

The man walked up next to Borak, oddly clenching his knife as if he was preparing to attack with it. Distracted by what Melia was doing, Borak didn't notice him.

"What do you see?" asked Borak.

"It looks deep," replied Melia, "But I think I can get it." She took some deep breaths, then dove down.

Borak and the man stood silently, waiting for Melia to reemerge. Borak was now slightly aware of the man's hesitant demeanor.

"Do you think she'll be okay? Does the tale say anything else?" Borak asked, becoming anxious.

"I'm not sure," answered the man.

Melia continued to dive, holding her breath. From here, the necklace seemed so close, yet, so far away. Kicking and thrusting her hands forward, she swam down with all her might. The bright colors from the necklace were blinding, so she couldn't hold her eyes open for long. Her lungs were beginning to burn, and her ears agonizingly felt like they were going to burst. Melia remembered she needed to pressurize her ears, so she grabbed her nose, pinched it closed, and blew out through it. "Aww," she thought as her ears pressurized, but her lungs were still burning. Thoughts of giving up and heading back to the surface flooded her mind, but she persisted and pushed those thoughts away. "Please let me make it, please," the young Roak child pleaded. Abruptly, her hand hit bottom. Melia opened her eyes. Blinded by the brightness, she tried not to panic. She peered, as best she could, through the light and saw the silhouette of the necklace. At arm's length, it was lying inside a hollowed-out rock to her right. Melia grasped the necklace, picked it up, and instantly, the ground began rumbling. Spikes followed, poking out of the walls encircling her.

"This is it. I'm done for!" Melia thought to herself. The spikes were closing in as they continued to extend from the walls, but she noticed the necklace was glowing even brighter. The necklace felt like it was pulling itself closer to her, wanting something from her. Now, the spikes were inches from her in all directions. She had no clue what to do. Melia put on the necklace in a last-ditch effort before the spike's points gorged her.

The ground shook, and Borak shot a worried look at the man. The suspicious acting man clenched the knife tighter in preparation to strike the boy.

"What is happening?" Borak cried out in concern as he stared at the man.

The man didn't say anything and only stared back.

Borak looked back at the center of the pond as the ground continued to shake. "Noooo, Melliiaaa!" he screamed and grabbed hold of the man, hugging him in desperation.

The man had a moment of compassion, then gritted his teeth and held the knife up close to Borak's neck. The man seemed to be having second thoughts. Suddenly, the ground stopped shaking. Borak pulled his head away from the man's chest. At once, the murderous man put the knife back down by his side. Both the boy and the man stood there, waiting for something to happen.

The necklace flashed a bright light, and the ground stopped shaking. The spikes retracted back into the walls. Melia had been out of breath for a while. She was on the verge of losing consciousness. Her eyes closed, and her head and body fell backward. The necklace began lifting her toward the surface. She hadn't lost total consciousness and could feel herself floating upward until she broke the surface of the water. Miraculously, Melia's eyes opened, and she gasped for air. She floated on the water, not moving, while her brother watched in horror.

Borak was screaming for her, "Melia! Melia! Are you okay?" He was beside himself.

The man seemed to be pleasantly surprised and encouraged, "Quick! Help her in."

Interestingly, the silky nature of the mud had disappeared. Borak grabbed his baton and stuck it in the mud. Nothing happened. Not taking a second longer to think about it, he ran into the pond to get his sister. He grabbed her while she was coughing up water, so he patted her back as he pulled her to shore. He reached the side of the pond and pulled her up on the dirt. She coughed up more water. Melia took a minute to catch her breath and then realized the other two were staring at her. The necklace was glowing radiantly around her neck.

"What happened, sis? Why is that necklace glowing like that?" questioned Borak in amazement.

"She is worthy!" exclaimed the man, then continued, "Only the worthy can wear it! All others will be lost!"

"What does that mean?" asked Borak, still in awe.

The man eagerly answered this question, "That means she can wear it and wield its power. The tale says the necklace can provide a pathway to communicate with the Spirit World and even resurrect from the dead. Which means you can summon uhhh, um..." The man stopped talking.

"You can summon what?" Melia asked in a raspy voice, pushing herself up to her feet.

"Um, you can summon spirits, uh, who you once knew... was what I meant," the man uttered, trying to recover.

Both siblings looked at the man a little suspiciously. What Borak and Melia didn't know was the man meant to say, "You can summon the Dark Queen, Herana, and resurrect her body." Not only would that have suggested the man was up to no good, but it also would have suggested Melia was a potential sacrifice for Herana's resurrection. For the resurrection to succeed, someone would have to take Herana's place in the Spirit world.

"By the way, I never introduced myself. My name is Magus," the man said......

Acquiring Disguises

"What is our plan?" asked Melia. "You hurt one of the Nywolves, Aiden, but they are a lot to handle. And how are we going to fight Regin and Magus, the two most deadly sorcerers in the land?"

Aiden thought, then answered, "You're right. We need a plan." He pondered some more and came up with a good idea, "We need disguises. Let's find a group of Devians and take their armor. Once we have the armor, we can sneak in and grab Priya."

The whole group nodded in agreement, except Jack. "One problem there, mates. How am I supposed to find armor that fits me, aye? Eight-foot-tall giant, rememba?" Jack remarked in a smart-ass tone, pointing toward himself.

"Why don't you try some of that big ogre's clothes?" joked Aiden, glancing at the pile of rubble on top of Drakkar.

The group chuckled.

"Well, for one, he's unda a bunch of rubbish, and two, I'm not that big, ya funny bloke," Jack teased back, continuing, "I betta go grab some of that Grandar's armor. I'll catch up with ya guys." He ran off toward where he fought the other two Grandars.

Aiden and the rest of the group heard voices coming from around the building. The group quickly crouched down next to the building. Aiden peeked around the corner. He could see a group of Devians and two Hairies. One of the Devians was directing the group to search around the area. The lead Devian was Dagon. Kroni and Juggy were with him.

Melia didn't think twice, snuck around the other side of the building, and stopped behind a pile of wood. She heard a Devian slowly walking closer. The Devian stuck its head around a corner. It was Kroni. He directed someone else, "You check in there. I'll go this way." He pointed toward the woodpile. The other Devian, Juggy, headed inside the adjacent building to the left. Kroni started walking straight toward the woodpile where Melia was hiding. Wearily, he crept up to the woodpile while Melia was still deciding what to do. When he reached the pile and looked on the other side, Melia was gone. She had snuck around the opposite side, behind him. He never knew she was there. Melia bonked him over the head with a rock and knocked him unconscious. She quickly stripped off his armor.

Aiden saw Dagon order the two evil Hairies to search in their direction. Dagon then began walking toward the horse carriage where Cedric hid. "You guys take out those Hairies. I'll go after Dagon," Aiden told Borak and Gil. Aiden then ran inside the house.

Borak and Gil remained hidden where they were. As the two Hairies approached, Gil accidentally bumped a broom leaning against the wall. The broom slowly started to fall, stopped for a second, then fell to the ground with a smack. Borak put his head down, shaking it in disappointment, and Gil clenched his teeth, hoping their enemies hadn't heard. It became quiet. The two waited. Borak looked around the corner and saw the Hairies were gone. Not sure what to think, he glanced at Gil and shrugged his shoulders.

Very faintly, there was a slight creaking noise coming from the roof. The two hidden heroes looked up. Both evil Hairies attacked at the same time, jumping from the roof. One Hairie held onto the edge of the roof while it swung down and kicked Borak in the head. The other Hairie did a front flip in the air and landed in front of Gil.

"Hey, Gil, how you been?" the Hairie in front of Gil exclaimed.

"Benny?" Gil remarked, "I see you're doing well! I mean, working with an evil sorcerer and all. Are you happy with your decision?"

Benny previously lived at Heirstone with Gil and Cedric. They were good friends until he met his sidekick. No one knew his real name, so everyone called him "Sidekick." Sidekick became part of the group for a while, but there always seemed to be something off with him. Eventually, he showed devious motivations, so Gil and Cedric wanted him gone. Benny was caught in the middle and had to make a choice. Benny chose Sidekick, and they left Heirstone. Gil hadn't seen them since.

"I see you still have your Sidekick," Gil observed, motioning toward the Hairie fighting with Borak.

"Oh, yea, we're doing great! Sidekick's still disturbed, but we have it pretty good here. It's nice to be the one in charge for once," Benny said with an insinuating tone.

"Is that what the problem was? You wanted to be in charge?" Gil replied.

Benny thought for a second before he answered, "Maybe, but we have many coins and all the food we can eat here. We were dirt poor at Heirstone, running around like hooligans pickpocketing."

"I see," Gil replied, then reminisced, "Do you remember the good times we had? Like when Cedric got caught cheating at poker? When he knew he was caught, he got up to run out of the room and ran straight into a wall. Then we had to have Sidekick distract everyone while we pulled Cedric outta there!" Both Hairies started chuckling. Gil finished the story, "After that, we saw Sidekick running down the street, being chased by the guys who were at the poker table, and we didn't see him again until the next day! When he came back, he had the coins from the table and a big bowl of beef. We had no idea where he got it!" Now, the Hairies were laughing out loud, and Benny added, "That beef was good!" Borak and Sidekick stopped fighting to see what was going on.

"Funny, what funny?" Sidekick asked, confused. Sidekick spoke in broken English and had a raspy voice.

Borak looked back at Sidekick and followed with a punch to the face and a judo throw to the ground.

"Oh, I see, you distract Sidekick. Well, you haven't won yet!" the Hairie proclaimed. Sidekick grabbed Borak's arm and threw his leg over his combatant's shoulder, putting him in a triangle hold. Borak tried but couldn't free himself and dropped to his knees, beginning to feel faint.

Gil and Benny snapped out of their reminiscent daze and went after each other. Benny jumped at Gil with a superman punch, nailing him flush in the face. Gil took a step back and blocked the ensuing punches. Gil countered Benny's arduous attacks by dodging a punch and jabbing Benny to the face, followed by a roundhouse kick. Benny checked Gil's kick, then threw a front kick and right punch to a spinning back fist. The back fist cracked Gil in the face. He shook his head, spitting out blood. The two went back and forth...punch, kick, block, punch, dodge, counter, check-kick, punch, block. Gil dodged a punch, ran up the wall, and did a backflip kick. It hit Benny on top of the head and knocked him to the floor.

Borak fought the faintness and tried with all his might to stand up. Slowly, he lifted his knee and got one foot on the ground. He was on the verge of passing out. Pushing down hard with his foot, he lifted himself and got his other foot under him. Standing in a crouched position, he wrapped his arms around Sidekick's legs. The last thing Borak remembered was lifting Sidekick in the air and slamming him on the ground.

Gil looked over to see both Borak and Sidekick lying together asleep.

Benny was still lying on the ground seeing stars and spoke up, "Look, just go. Wake him up and go."

Gil hesitated before he replied, "For what it's worth, you're still my friend." Gil then grabbed a small bottle of liquid out of his pocket, opened it, and waved it under Borak's nose.

Borak's eyes immediately shot open, and he cried out loud, "Mamma!" Borak looked around, unsure where he was, trying to recover from being woken up so suddenly. He spoke quieter, "Maammaa?" Still confused, he looked around until he met Gil's eyes, looking at him curiously. Borak realized where he was and quietly sang, "Maaammaa, I'm coming hoooooooome!"

Gil cracked up laughing and said, "Nice, try! You were not singing that song." He then prompted Borak to get up, "Come on, we gotta go!"

Melia looked good in the armor. She contemplated whether she should go back to the others or go after Juggy to get his armor. She decided to go after Juggy. She stealthily crept along the next building's backside. She could hear rumbling and banging coming from inside. She looked through a window and saw Juggy rummaging around loose items in the living room.

"There's gotta be something valuable in all this junk," Juggy muttered to himself, "Junk, junk, oowww, arrrrgh, and more junk!" He continued muttering to himself, "Oooooo, what's this?" He was still getting used to having a freshly bitten half-finger.

Melia looked closely and could see Juggy holding up something shiny.

"Scooore!" Juggy exclaimed and put the shiny object in his pocket. The happy Devian looked to his right and saw some jugs sitting on the table. "Scooore again!" he yelled, this time even louder. He ran to the table to find two of the jugs empty, but the third jug was half full of wine. Salivating, he picked up the jug and guzzled it. After finishing the wine, he turned and walked to the front door.

Melia climbed through a window and threw a pebble to the other side of the living room as Juggy walked out the door. Quietly, she hurried and hid behind a wall. Juggy popped his head back inside the living room curiously, then walked inside, looking around toward where the pebble hit. He reached the spot where the pebble hit and picked it up. He said to himself, "Well, what do ya make of that? Elementary, my dear Watson. If the rock hit the wall here, somebody must have thrown it from..."

The curious creature put his hand on his chin, thinking for only a second before quickly spinning around. Melia's fist was already inches from his face. WHACCKK! She hit Juggy perfectly on the chin, and he went down like a sack of potatoes. She stripped Juggy of his armor and headed back to find the others.

Aiden ran through the building and stopped to look out a window. He could see Dagon was almost to the horse carriage, but he had to be careful the Hairies didn't see him. He looked through the window and saw the Hairies had stopped as if they heard something. One of the Hairies pointed up toward the roof. They swiftly hopped onto the roof, making it look like child's play. With the Hairies out of sight, Aiden saw his chance. He slipped through the window and ducked behind a bush.

Dagon made it to the horse carriage and moved broken pieces of wood and rubbish. Continuing to search, he saw the tarp and grabbed it. With Cedric about to be discovered, Aiden had no time to spare. He bolted, running full speed at the rummaging Devian. Dagon started to move the tarp, then hesitated and turned his head sideways as he sensed something coming his way. Aiden jumped in the air and slashed with his sword. Dagon quickly turned and blocked the strike. Aiden's sword ricocheted with a spark off Dagon's armor. Aiden landed on the evil Devian leader, and they both tumbled to the ground. The two rolled apart and got to their feet.

"Aw, yes, if it isn't twinkle-toes himself. I've been looking for you, dear boy. Finally, I get to put you where you belong.......in the spirit world!" Dagon snarled.

"Good luck with that, you little twerp! You'd probably have a better chance of getting Juggy to AA," Aiden replied sarcastically.

Dagon chuckled for a second, then stopped and asked, "Wait, what is AA?"

Aiden replied, "Alcoholics Anonymous. It's where people go to stop drinking."

Dagon chuckled again and tried using his wit, "You have a better chance of going to AA. You know, because you drink too much wine!" Not being good at humor, his joke fell flat. The Devian now felt unsure of himself.

Aiden replied in a bewildered tone, "Is that your best comeback?"

Dagon drew his sword and lunged at Aiden, swinging it downward. Aiden leaned backward, dodging the strike. Dagon followed with another downswing. Aiden used his sword to deflect it, then countered with his sword attack. Clang, clang, the blades continued connecting. Aiden faked a strike, dodged Dagon's sword, then quickly sliced across Dagon's cheek.

Dagon shook his head in disbelief. The embarrassed Devian bent over with his hand on his cheek and scoffed in anger, "I'm done playing with you! Get ready to die!"

"Good luck with that one. Let's hurry this up, though. I've got a Princess to save!" Aiden mocked.

Suddenly, Dagon pulled a dagger and threw it with ninja-like speed at

Aiden. The dagger hit his shoulder. "Ahhhh!" Aiden screamed in pain and slumped over. Seeing an opening, Dagon rushed forward. Aiden quickly reacted and jumped-kicked, performing the attack completely horizontal. Dagon swung his sword, barely missing Aiden's side. Aiden's kick hit Dagon square in the face with a solid impact. Dagon did a backflip with his momentum still going forward and landed on his stomach. The evil Devian leader moaned in pain as Aiden grabbed hold of the dagger sticking out of his shoulder. "Nice throw," he admitted. He pulled the dagger out with a grimace, adding, "But I'm sorry, buddy, I'm going to need that armor!" Aiden cracked Dagon in the back of the head, rendering him unconscious.

As Gil and Borak were getting ready to leave, Melia ran around the corner of the house with the extra suit of armor in her hands. "Here, brother put this on," she asserted.

Gil, reminded he needed one of the Hairies' armor, looked over at Benny.

"Oh, for goodness sake. Take Sidekick's armor. It's his fault for getting knocked out," Benny clarified.

"Okay," Gil replied, nodding in acknowledgment.

A minute later, Aiden ran up to the group. He could see everyone had on the enemy's armor and were now in good disguise. "Wait, where's Jack?" Aiden thought to himself and looked over in the direction Jack had run.

Jack made it to the area where he killed one of the Grandars. He found the live Grandar knelt over the deceased one in grief, crying. The live Grandar had lost a lot of blood and looked very weak. Jack approached the grieving Grandar warily. The giant creature heard him and looked up. "You killed my brother!" the Grandar attested, "And, you dare to come back? I will kill you where you stand."

The Grandar stood up, staggering back and forth, then tried to run at Jack. Jack pulled his sword, but the Grandar took two steps, lost his balance, and fell to the ground. The Grandar had tears rolling down his cheeks. Yet, he was strong and said, "Kill me. My brother is gone. He was all I had. Just kill me so I can be with him."

Jack looked at the Grandar and nodded, then raised his sword in the air to honor the giant's last wish. Jack paused with the sword still raised. Something stopped him from driving the sword through his willing enemy's heart. "Why did he not feel like doing it?" he thought. Jack felt sorry for the Grandar and put his sword down. He told the sad Grandar, "You will join him one day, mate, but not yet." Jack walked over to the dead Grandar brother, stripped him of his armor, and jogged back to the group.

Aiden could see Jack running toward them, so he spoke up, "Okay, here comes Jack. Are we all ready?"

"Ready as we'll ever be," replied Melia as she ran off into another building.

"Guess we're following her," shrugged Gil, and the group followed.

Melia tried to find her way back to the Great Hall from this building. This area was close to where she and Aiden had initially entered. "There it is," Melia said to herself. She had gone through a room and found the hallway that led to the Great Hall. The group caught up with her at the end of the hallway, and they entered the Great Hall together. The large room was empty this time.

Aiden saw what they were looking for and whispered while he pointed, "There are the stairs."

The heroes felt themselves closing the gap on Priya. They made their way to the stairs and ran down them into the dungeons.

Xena

The stairs spiraled down into a poorly lit, dingy, moldy corridor. The walls were greenish-yellow, and everyone could hear water dripping somewhere in the vicinity. They walked a little while until the passage forked into two directions.

"We're gonna have ta split up, aye," Jack noted.

Aiden nodded and pointed to the right corridor, "Okay, you three go that way," speaking to Jack, Borak, and Gil, "And we'll go this way. If you need help, yell." Aiden wasn't sure how else they could communicate. Jack, Borak, and Gil took off down the right corridor and disappeared.

Aiden and Melia went down the left corridor. It was very dark and surprisingly warm. From time to time, they stepped in water on the ground. As they moved deeper into the cavernous hallway, Aiden and Melia started to hear faint sounds and voices but couldn't tell what was said. A few turn-offs led to dead ends. They saw many small rooms which must have held prisoners. All of these prison cells were empty until they got further inside. At that point, the cells began containing a variety of creatures, including Roaks, Hairies, and Grandars. One cell even had a sad Devian inside. Melia stopped for a second to gaze at the Devian. It appeared depressed as it looked back at Melia, then it turned away and put its head down. "Why would a Devian be locked up?" she said aloud.

Melia and Aiden continued down the passage and found an enormous cell that gave the impression it was occupied by something big. They scanned the dark cell curiously and saw bones lying around and a big bucket filled with water. There were also many massive turds; some looked fresh. Aiden and Melia continued searching the cell but couldn't see anything else. They heard a low growl and immediately looked in that direction. While they searched, the growl became louder and closer. In the shadows, Melia caught a glimpse of a creature creeping closer. It was a Nywolf.

"Whoa, Aiden! Do you see that? Wait a second! I think I know who this is!" Melia exclaimed.

There were not very many Nywolves known to exist anymore because most were killed due to fear, yet here, right in front of them, was the third one they'd seen today. Freki and Geri had a sister, but she was cast out because of her disobedience against the dark cause. The Legend of Heroes mentions this third Nywolf. It says she will become a friend and join the fight for good. The third Nywolf's name is Xena.

"Xena?" Melia tried the name.

The Nywolf seemed to respond. She stopped creeping forward and looked at Melia curiously with her ears up and head sideways.

"Xena, is that you?" Melia tried again. She put a hand close to the bars of the cell so that the animal could smell her.

The Nywolf stared a little longer, then cautiously came forward. It kept its attention on Aiden while it sniffed Melia's hand. Melia remembered she had some jerky in her pocket and said, "I'm gonna grab you a snack, okay?" She reached in her pocket, grabbed a piece of jerky, and stuck it through the cell bars. The Nywolf sniffed the jerky, then delicately took hold of what now looked like a tiny morsel in its ginormous canines. The huge wolf inhaled the food like it was air, then sat there waiting for more.

"Xena, it is you!" Melia proclaimed and turned to Aiden, "We should let her out!"

"Are you crazy? No way! We have enough Nywolves to fight!" Aiden replied.

"It's foretold in the Legend that Xena will help us defeat Magus. The Legend also describes Xena as the strongest Nywolf of the siblings. I remember hearing how Freki and Geri would always have to team up to fight her," Melia explained.

Aiden looked perplexed, then asked, "Why were the brothers always fighting their sister?"

"Xena would fight against her evil obligations. She wanted to be good, so she and her brothers would fight. One day she disappeared. Magus must have locked her up in this cell," Melia answered.

Aiden could tell there was nothing he could say to stop Melia from letting the Nywolf out of its cage. So, he gave in, remarking, "Okay, you better be right about this." As Aiden said this, he reached back and grabbed his sword in case he needed to draw it.

On the other hand, Melia drew her sword and swung it at the chain lock on the cell door. CLANK! The lock broke open and fell to the ground with the chain following it. The door slid open slightly. Xena tilted her head and looked at them curiously again. She then changed her posture, lowered her head, and stared straight at Aiden. Slowly, she stood on her feet, pushed the door open with her nose, and walked out of the cell heading directly for Aiden.

Aiden tightened his grip on his sword as Xena approached. This Nywolf was smaller but was still an intimidatingly giant 1700-pound creature. Xena edged her way toward Aiden, watching him closely until her nose was literally on his face, sniffing him. After Xena got her fill of Aiden's scent, she turned to Melia and used her huge tongue to lick Melia's entire body.

The Last Remaining Royal Mystic

Jack led Borak and Gil down the right corridor. This path was narrow and steadily went uphill. The group passed many prison cells with various creatures, and Borak noticed the prisoners staring at him with hopeful eyes. One prisoner asked, "Are you here to save us?" Another prisoner reached through the bars trying to touch Gil.

"We've got to release them," insisted Gil.

"Yes, we will. First, we have to save Priya," assured Borak.

In the distance, they could hear something that sounded like a ritualistic ceremony. Although it got louder further into the cave, it sounded like the ceremony was below. As the three reached the top of the path, it leveled out to a flat spot. There was a large cross with something hanging from it.

The path ended at a cliff in a humongous cavern. They looked down below and saw thousands of Devians and creatures gathered in front of a stage. Steps encircled the stage, and two large torches were on top of it. Magus was on the stage, speaking to the crowd. Priya was standing behind him with her hands bound and head down. Behind Priya, there was an open coffin with a body in it.

"Holy crap, fellas!" Jack quietly exclaimed, "A woman is hangin' on that cross."

Borak ran over to the woman hanging from the cross, hoping she was alive. She had a sack over her head and was tied to the cross with rope. Borak cut the rope and brought the woman down. Even though the crowd was distracted, they had to be careful because the cross was in plain view.

Borak grabbed the woman's wrist, then shook his head, and said, "There's no pulse."

Gil untied the sack and pulled it off the woman's head. "Oh, my goodness. Do you guys see who that is?" he said, stunned. After taking a peek, Jack and Borak looked curiously at each other, then back at Gil.

"Look again," Gil told them.

Soot covered the woman's face. She was emaciated, changing her appearance. "Is that who I think it is?" asked Jack. Borak stared at the woman, speechless, not believing what he saw.

Gil continued, "Yes! It's Sen! The last remaining Royal Mystic! We have to save her!"

Jack was coming to grips with the discovery, "I can't believe it, mate! I thought for sure Magus did her in, aye!"

"It is her! We must bring her with us. There must be a way to save her," Borak added.

At that, Gil tried picking Sen up. He struggled since he's a Hairie and only about four feet tall. "Um, a little help here, guys," he told the others with a grunt while still trying to pick her up.

Battle of the Nywolves

Xena sat waiting, staring at Aiden and Melia.

"Wow, you were right! I think we have a new friend!" said Aiden excitedly.

"Yea, isn't it awesome!" Melia replied, every bit as excited.

Aiden nodded, and the three of them began moving down the corridor. They could tell the sounds they heard were chanting. They also heard one prominent loud voice as it became more audible. Aiden recognized it was Magus' voice. The corridor opened into a large cave room. There they found skeletons that had weapons in hand. One of the skeletons had a shield, and Melia picked it up.

In the distance, Melia saw an entrance to a massive cave. The chanting was coming from inside. This was it. Aiden and Melia needed to walk a little further, blend into the chanting crowd, and somehow grab Priya unnoticed. Just as Aiden took a step, he started to smell that dirty, wet, bloody odor again, which he had smelled back at the Great Hall when he ran into the other Nywolves. Xena stiffened into an attack posture and started to growl. At this point, Aiden knew they had found her brothers.

Geri and Freki appeared out of a dark corner which must have a different entrance. Geri was limping on his left paw, and Freki had a clump of blood on his head where his ear used to be. Behind Geri and Freki, Regin strolled arrogantly, as if he knew the outcome of what was about to happen. Geri and Freki looked extra vicious with their teeth bared, growling, and frothing at the mouth like they had rabies and wanted revenge.

Aiden looked over at Xena. She not only looked vicious but down-right enraged. It wouldn't be a stretch to say she appeared straight-up pissed off. Xena stared at her siblings as if they had done something unimaginable and unrepairable to her. It was apparent she had decided to kill them long ago. Xena's hair was standing up, and she was growling, displaying her supremely sharp canines as saliva dripped. Aiden noticed something else about her. Something about her stance felt reassuring, almost like she knew martial arts.

Aiden quietly mumbled, "I wouldn't want to be those two."

Geri and Freki had stopped about twenty feet in front of the heroes, led by Xena. Regin lingered like a spectator for a second behind his Nywolves, then walked into view.

"Well, well, well...look who decided to come out and play," Regin taunted, "Been a while, Xena. How long were you in that cage? About ten years? Look, I know you're a tad upset, but what do you say? Bygones?"

Xena turned toward Regin and snarled, on the verge of attacking.

"Okay, okay, didn't think that would work," Regin continued, "Nice threads, guys. You all look good in our armor. Let's be honest here, though. You're all outmatched," Regin pointed at the Nywolves, "Two Nywolves," then pointed at himself, "Most powerful Druid in the land. It's probably in your best interest to cut a deal?"

"Riiigghhht," Aiden answered, "So you can kill Priya and make us your prisoners? Sounds amazing! Sign me up!" Aiden couldn't help his sarcasm.

Regin let out a sinister laugh, then replied, "I understand. I don't have a good offer here. I figured any offer would be better than certain death."

Xena looked back at Aiden and scoffed, then stomped the ground. She seemed to be asking Aiden for permission to attack.

"You know, Regin, is it? I'm pretty sure we're not the ones that should be worried," hinted Aiden, gesturing toward Xena.

Xena scoffed again.

"Go get 'em, girl!" Aiden commanded, and Xena bolted toward her brothers.

Geri and Freki braced themselves, but Xena veered off to the right and ran toward the wall. She ran up the angulated wall and came back down using the rounded angle for momentum to gain more speed. The angry, betrayed sister Nywolf jumped at Freki headfirst with her mouth open wide. Freki turned to block the attack but was too late. Xena bit down hard on his neck, grabbing and twisting as she flew over him. She held on with all her might as her body sailed over his. She flung him through the air and slammed him into the wall, landing on her feet directly in front of Geri. They stared at each other for a second before they pounced on one another. The two Nywolves hit the ground rolling together, biting and clawing.

Aiden and Melia tried using the Nywolves' distraction to attack Regin, but he was waiting for them. The evil sorcerer's hands began glowing as the two ran full speed at the wicked Druid. Regin shot fire in their direction. Aiden and Melia jumped out of the way, dodging the fire, Melia going left and Aiden going right. Regin continued throwing fire at the duo. Aiden and Melia continued to evade the attacks, crossing paths as they jumped from one side of the cave to the other. Melia blocked a fire blast with the shield she picked up and threw her boomerang blade while running. Regin shot it out of the air. Melia's blade fell to the ground halfway between Regin and herself. Aiden was trying to tap into his blue energy to run faster, but he still didn't have control of it. All he could do was try to get within striking distance, which was much easier said than done. Regin was quick, constantly shooting fire at both Aiden and Melia, keeping them at a distance. Melia finally worked her way close enough to pick up her blade by flipping forward and blocking another attack with the shield again. She then jumped over a fire blast and threw the boomerang, this time slicing Regin's arm. Regin yelled in pain and took a step back, giving her enough time to reach him.

They jumped at Regin with roundhouse kicks simultaneously. Regin blocked both kicks, throwing punches and kicks back. The three went back and forth punch, block, kick, punch, block, counter. Regin caught Aiden with a jab, then Melia with a sidekick. Regin blocked their attacks, even using a magical shield when he ran out of limbs with which to block. Again, Regin hit Aiden, this time with a right cross, then spun around, blocked Melia's punch, and countered with a punch to her midsection. Although it hurt, Melia caught Regin's punch. Aiden immediately took the opportunity to high kick the evil Druid to the head. Regin was stunned, and the duo continued with a barrage of punches and kicks. The once arrogant sorcerer covered himself, becoming dazed. He yelled, "Rraaahhh!" Regin began glowing red. BAMM!!! He hit Aiden and Melia with a defensive energy blast knocking them ten feet away. Aiden hit the ground, and Melia hit a wall dislodging huge loose rocks. She flailed and bounced to the ground. The rocks fell down the wall and trapped her beneath them.

Xena and Geri rolled to a stop with Xena on top. Xena slashed at Geri's face, clawing. Although the strikes were slashes, they also looked like punches. Xena followed her tear with an intense bite on Geri's neck. As she was about to crush Geri's throat, Freki flew in and landed on Xena's back, biting down on her. Yelping, Xena let Geri go and maneuvered from Freki's bite, quickly rolling out from under him. When Xena got up, both of her siblings stared her in the face. She felt hot blood dripping from her back.

Xena looked more closely at her brothers. They were also bleeding, and it was coming from their necks. All three Nywolves were baring their teeth and growling, but they were also half-panting from the pain. Geri looked weaker, so Xena tried to bite him. At the same time, she kicked backward, hitting Freki in the mouth. Even though Xena was hurt, she was still faster than the other Nywolves. She was able to bounce back and forth, blocking, slashing, biting, and even sliding under the other Nywolves to claw at them. Freki and Geri were getting worked over by Xena until she finally made a mistake. She lost awareness of her surroundings and allowed herself to get backed into a corner. She tried to jump up the wall and out of the corner, but Freki caught her in the air. He slashed her across the face and knocked her to the ground. Xena got to her feet as Freki and Geri closed in. Her backfoot hit the wall, leaving her nowhere to go.

While he lay on the ground, Aiden saw Melia trapped under many rocks. Hearing a thump, he looked in the other direction and saw Xena getting up from the ground. The other two Nywolves cornered her.

"Dire situations cause selfish decisions. What do you do, Aiden?"

Aiden grimaced at the sound of his arrogant voice. He looked at the wicked Druid. Regin's hands were glowing while he aimed them at Melia.

"Should you try to save Melia or try to save your new Nywolf friend over there, who has already risked her life to save you two?" Regin went on.

Aiden looked at Melia and yelled her name, "Melia!" All he heard in response was weak groaning. He turned back to Regin, demanding, "Leave her alone! Don't you do it!"

Cedric in the Horse Carraige

Cedric nodded off a few times after the rest of the crew left. He had a slight concussion, causing him to drift in and out of consciousness. At one point, he thought he heard someone rummaging through the rubbish. At another point, he thought he heard Aiden fighting with some tough Devian. He wasn't sure because everything seemed like a dream. When he fully regained consciousness, he heard nothing and worried about how long he had been out of it and if his friends were okay. The resilient little Hairie was still in pain but felt better and decided he would attempt getting up. His foot and arm hadn't moved from their positions, still twisted behind him. One of his toes, wiggling by his face, itched. Since Cedric's arm remained twisted next to his toes, he scratched it with his fingers and said to himself, "There we go." He took a breath, "Now, it's time to get my butt up."

As Cedric tried moving, a sharp pain shot through his arm. "Ooowwww!" the pretzeled Hairie cried out. "What the heck am I gonna do?" he said, continuing to talk to himself. He scanned the area and saw a metal bar. "There, that'll do it!" he thought aloud. He grabbed the bar with his free hand, put it under his contorted arm, then placed the bar's middle on his shoulder for leverage. Preparing to endure some pain, Cedric took a deep breath and held it, cranked down on the bar, and his arm flipped out from behind his head and landed on his chest. "Aahhrrrrrr!" he moaned and waited for the pain to subside.

After a minute, Cedric tried to move his arm, and it barely budged.

Having happened before, he knew it was out of the socket. Regretfully, he also knew what he had to do. The wounded Hairie wanted to get it over with, so he didn't delay. He put a broken piece of wood in his mouth on which to bite down and grabbed hold of his wrist with his good arm. Cedric paused for a second, almost changing his mind, then yanked down hard on his arm. There was a loud crunch as it popped back into place. "Ooowwwwwwww!" he whimpered. The pain reduced, and he sighed in relief.

The relief didn't last long as Cedric remembered he had another problem. He looked above his head to see his toes wiggling in his face. "Great!" Cedric remarked to himself, "I'm trying to save the world, but instead, I'm stuck forced to smell my toes."

The hairie hero could move his arm now, with only a dull pain. It didn't matter to him what he had to go through to get to his friends, so he was moving forward and not thinking about the consequences. It was reckless but also impressive. Cedric raised both arms, balled his hands into fists, and placed his knuckles on the rubble. He pushed as hard as he could and lifted his body, making a grunting noise, "Mmph baaaah!"

He did it! Cedric's upper body raised off the rubbish, and he felt some tension in his body lessen. The Hairie smiled arrogantly, bragging to himself, "Hah ha! Nothing can stop you, Ceed! Ha!"

Suddenly, his back cracked, POP, and his smile turned into a grimace. The previously arrogant Hairie fell face-first into the broken wood debris. "Ooowwww!" he groaned, "I think I'm okay." Cedric lifted his head. A large splinter was sticking out of his forehead. He pulled it out. Next, he carefully moved his neck and body back and forth. A succession of cracks sounded off like firecrackers. "Oh boy! I needed that!" the Hairie acknowledged. He lifted his butt out of the rubble and rolled out of the horse carriage.

Out in the open, Cedric searched the area for any danger. He looked to his left and saw a Devian lying, unconscious, without its armor, then looked to his right and recognized some familiar faces. It was Cedric's old friends turned enemies, Benny and Sidekick. Sidekick didn't have his armor either and sat up, rubbing his head. Benny sat next to him, disappointed. Cedric cautiously made his way over to them and asked, "What are you guys doing here?"

"Huh," reacted Benny, then saw who it was, "Oh, I was wondering where you were."

Cedric ran and somersaulted, landing in front of Benny in a fighting stance. A sharp pain shot through Cedric's hip and leg. His leg felt as if it were going to give out under him. He regained his stance and questioned, "What do you care? You both are traitors."

Benny hopped up, revealing a fighting stance, and paused, staring at his old friend. After a moment, Benny sighed and dropped his hands. He spoke up, "Look. Your friends went that way. Here, you better take this." Unexpectedly, Benny unstrapped his armor, took it off, and handed it to Cedric, not saying another word. Cedric didn't say anything either, but he could guess what happened by seeing the others without armor. The rest of the crew must have grabbed the enemy's armor for a disguise. Cedric glared at Benny warily, then took the armor and disappeared, limping off after his comrades.

As time passed, his pain continued to lessen. He figured it was due to the adrenaline coursing through his veins plus the fact he hadn't broken anything. The Hairie wasn't sure where to go but figured he would start at the Great Hall. He cautiously made his way past a few rooms and through a hallway. He found the room he was looking for at the end. This room was usually associated with important events. Now, in the Great Hall, Cedric was at a standstill. No one was in the room, and the quiet was chilling. He searched around the area and came across some stairs. The stairs were lit up, looked peculiar, and seemed to scream, "This way!" Cedric didn't see another choice, so he went down the stairs.

The stairs led to a dingy corridor. Cedric followed the corridor until it came to a fork in the path. He thought he heard the voices of his friend's to the right, so he went that way. He was correct. The voices were those of his friends, Jack, Borak, and Gil, but they had gone down the left path. The voices quickly faded and turned into chanting. The chanting sounds were ominous, and the Hairie could only guess what it meant. He continued following the right path uphill, passing many occupied prison cells. Noises of fighting from openings in the hollow walls caused him to stop. It sounded like two different fights: a battle between large creatures and another close-combat battle. "That must be them!" he said to himself anxiously. Cedric heard a crash from the large creature battle and an explosion from the other fight. He stuck his head through an opening in the wall to see what was going on.

Sure enough, Cedric could see Aiden on the ground next to the sorcerer, Regin, of all people. Regin's hands were glowing red as if he was about to attack. From his vantage point, the concerned Hairie couldn't see anyone else but knew his other friends mustn't be too far. He was positioned up high, almost right above Regin, but the hole he was peeking through wasn't big enough to fit his body. Cedric frantically pulled his head from the wall and searched for a larger opening. BINGO, he found one right next to him. With complete disregard, he pulled his dagger and launched himself through it.

In the Nick of Time

Seemingly out of nowhere, a yell came from above, "Ahhhhhhhh!" A body landed on top of Regin and jammed a dagger into his shoulder. The unsuspecting evil Druid bellowed in pain.

Aiden couldn't believe his eyes. It was his hairie friend, Cedric, who he'd thought was badly injured hiding back at the horse carriage. Unbelievably, Cedric was okay! Aiden flashed blue, hopped to his feet, and rushed Regin faster than the speed of light. He dove into the evil sorcerer and smashed him into the wall, knocking him out. He grabbed Regin's glowing necklace and broke it off.

"Cedric, you're alright! Man, I'm glad to see you!" Aiden excitedly said as he hugged his little buddy. Aiden remembered Xena was in trouble and turned to run that way.

"Did ya blokes call for reinforcements," hollered another voice. Jack emerged from the corridor over by where the Nywolves were. Borak and Gil came into view, and they all charged the Nywolves.

"Ahhhhhhhh!" Borak and Gil yelled as they ran toward the Nywolves.

"Let's get 'em, boys!" shouted Jack.

Geri and Freki turned their heads as the trio reached them. Jack ran behind Geri, sword drawn and sliced Geri's leg, while Borak hopped on the back of Freki. Gil tried jumping on Geri but could only grab Geri's tail as Geri whipped around to face them. Geri felt Gil on his tail and kept waving it in the air, trying to shake him off. Gil flailed back and forth, hanging on for dear life.

"What was I thinking? I'm getting dizzy!" the Hairie complained while he was being yanked around in the air.

Geri stood half-facing Jack and half-facing Xena, still waving Gil around on his tail. Jack and Xena glanced at each other, then both attacked Geri simultaneously. Xena pounced at Geri and slashed him in the face while Jack rushed forward, slicing his shoulder. Geri swatted at Jack, knocking him across the room, then jumped at Xena, all in the same motion.

"I'm gonna puke!" warned Gil while he flew by, still hanging onto Geri's tail. Xena jumped toward Geri. They collided in the air, and slashed each other. Still grasping each other, they landed on their sides, hitting with a thud and sliding. Gil flew off Geri's tail and rolled right in front of Cedric and Aiden, who came running from the other side of the large cavern. Gil looked at Cedric dizzily and said, "Heeyyy!" then leaned over and puked.

Borak held on tight, riding Freki as he ran around the cavern. Freki was whipping around, spinning and jumping, trying to get Borak off him. Borak pulled his sword and stabbed Freki in the back, causing Freki to jump around more. The panicked Nywolf rolled on the ground. Although it looked like the ground should have smashed Borak, Freki's coat was thick, and Borak tucked down into the fur until the roll had finished. Freki spun around to see if Borak was still on him. The Nywolf felt another shank from the agile Roak on top of him, stabbing him again. This time the Nywolf yelped in pain and started spinning around faster and running into the walls. Freki jumped in the air, aiming for Borak to hit stalactites hanging down from the cavern ceiling. Borak didn't see the stalactites in time, and they smacked him, knocking him off the beast. The crazed Nywolf saw Regin lying over on the other side of the cavern, then looked back at a dazed Borak on the ground, holding his head. Freki salivated at the perfect chance to sink his ginormous death fangs into the annoyance he had knocked off him, but he also needed to save his master. Freki made his decision. This time self-preservation outweighed the importance of vengeance. He ran over to Regin, picked him up, and ran out of the room.

Geri and Xena got to their feet. Geri looked around to see Xena, Jack, Aiden, and Cedric staring him down, ready to fight. Gil was there, too, but still on the ground, throwing up. In the corner of his eye, Geri saw Freki run out the cavern holding Regin in his mouth. Geri thought for a second, then jumped on the cave wall, bounced, landed behind Aiden and the rest of the crew, and ran out of the cavern.

"Melia!" Aiden exclaimed and ran over to her, "Melia, are you okay? Melia?"

"Yea, ugh, I'm okay. I'm stuck. My legs are wedged," Melia replied, coughing, "And maybe some ribs are bruised. My chest hurts." There were some huge rocks on top of her.

"How are we going to move these rocks, guys?" asked Aiden.

"Maybe Xena can do it," Borak suggested.

"If Sen were awake, she'd do it," murmured Gil as he walked up behind everyone, wiping his mouth.

"Sen?" Aiden repeated, then asked, "What do you mean, Sen?"

"We found her up the other corridor on a cross. I don't think she's alive, though," confided Gil.

"Oh, my God! Are you serious? Where is she?" Aiden replied in shock.

Jack ran to get Sen and brought her over to the group.

"I, uh, oh, my goodness," stammered Aiden, still in shock, "I can't believe it's her. I thought Magus killed her, for sure. Um, I don't feel a pulse, but she doesn't seem to be dead. Her body hasn't gone through rigor mortis."

"Riga motis?" asked Jack.

Aiden smirked and explained, "When the body stiffens after being dead for some time. And her's hasn't, so I don't think she's dead," Aiden shifted his gaze to Gil, "Did you say Sen could move these rocks? So, maybe I could?"

"Yes, yes, I think you could with your powers. You've been using them more, but I don't know. Those are some pretty big rocks," replied Gil.

"Well, I have to try," Aiden stated confidently and put his hands on one of the rocks. He closed his eyes. He strained, hands shaking, trying to will the rock to move. At first, nothing happened. Then little blue flashes pulsated through his hands. The rock started vibrating. Aiden gritted his teeth and began making a growling sound as the rock shook more violently. The rock rose in the air slightly. It was too much. Aiden ran out of steam and had to give up. He gasped, breathing in and out, releasing the tension from his body. He kept breathing and caught his breath. Aiden was tired from the ordeal and put his head down, embarrassed. The rock had fallen back in its original place, and the hero felt like a failure.

The others in the group looked astonished.

"Whew, that took a lot out of me," Aiden admitted, then looked up at the others while he continued to talk, "I don't know what happened. I thought I had it, but I ran out of juice." He shook his head, disappointed.

"You were close," Borak said, putting his hand on Aiden's shoulder, "Aiden, we don't know how you've been doing this stuff lately, but that was impressive. All you have to do is try again. You can do it." Borak stared Aiden directly in his eyes and gave him a reassuring nod.

Aiden heard a faint, familiar female voice in his head. It was beautiful and enchanting. The voice mentored, "Focus on your pain. Focus on your motivation. You control your powers when you control your emotions. Find your pain, then calm it." The voice disappeared. Aiden's face changed from looking defeated to looking confident, and he nodded back at Borak.

Aiden's Earth Family

Again, Aiden placed his hands on the rock, closed his eyes, and strained in concentration. His thoughts took him back to his days on Earth, to the family he had there. The first thought he had was of his son.

...... "Dad! Mom's hurt!" hollered Chase weeping.

"It's okay, son!" Aiden reassured, then asked, "Where is she?"

"Over there!" Chase replied and pointed to the other side of the building. Aiden looked around to see he was in some large office building. The building was severely damaged, leaning to one side with holes blown out of its sidewalls. Loud explosions and gunshots echoed from down below, mixed in with the sounds of people screaming. Aiden looked through a window and saw he was very high up. He also saw fire and devastation because of a battle occurring on the street. A jet flew by, shooting at a group of Devians, a Grandar, and an enormous Gorger. The Grandar pointed a missile launcher at the jet and fired. The missile hit the jet dead center, and it exploded, sending fiery debris dispersing through the air.

When the jet exploded, Chase started running, yelling from fright. He ran in the direction of his Mom. Aiden followed. When they got to Sasha, Aiden's wife, she had been stabbed in the leg.

"Hey, handsome, thought you'd never make it," Sasha confessed, looking concerned, yet stoic, in her mysterious way.

"Hi, honey. Oh, we both know who the good-looking one is here," Aiden lovingly teased with a smile, then asked questions in concern, "How do you

feel? What happened?"

"I was stabbed, but I'm okay. I can't walk very well, though," Sasha confided.

Aiden looked at Sasha's injury and saw the bleeding had almost stopped, which meant the stab had missed her artery. "Okay, I'm still worried, but I feel better," he told her. Aiden took a deep breath and let it back out, then wiped the sweat off his brow, relieved his wife didn't appear seriously injured. "We gotta get outta here! Hold on. Here," Aiden continued. He ripped a sleeve off his shirt and tied it around Sasha's leg before he coaxed, "Come on, I'll help you up. Let's go!"...

Aiden's thoughts jumped to his son, weeping again.

..."Noooooo! Daaaaaad!" Chase screamed with both hands reaching in his father's direction.

Aiden was knocked backward and fell out of the large hole in the side of the building. As he fell, he looked to his left and saw Magus with his arm outstretched in a fist like he was posing after punching Aiden in the chest. Aiden could also see Siren, another evil Druid, standing to Magus' right, holding Chase. Siren looked at Chase and sneered, then threw him to the ground. As Aiden continued falling, the side of the building blocked his view from seeing anything else. He was falling to his death. All he could think of was what would happen to his family......

Aiden's hands lit up solid blue this time. The rock started shaking again. It was vibrating rapidly, but it was cumbersome and wouldn't lift off the ground.

Everything went silent. Aiden heard the voice again, "Find your pain, then calm it." Losing his family was his pain, but where were they? Was that a memory? Were they back on Earth, or were they dead? Aiden couldn't remember. Anxiety flooded in, and he thought he would have to give up on the rock again.

The Legend is True

Aiden took a deep breath and thought, "I may have lost my family. I don't know. But I have more family in front of me. Melia is my family, and I have to save her!" then he exhaled. At that moment, he felt at one with the rock.

Somehow, he felt at peace, and everything remained silent. The rock had stopped vibrating. Not aware of what happened, he had picked up the giant boulder and was standing there holding it. His comrades were all staring at him in awe. Seeing he had accomplished the task at hand, Aiden dropped the rock to the side. It hit the ground with a crack. He looked down and saw not only that his hands were glowing, but his entire body was lit up blue.

"The Legend is true, Aiden. You have come here to lead us and save our world. You are the Leader of Heroes!" Melia said proudly, "Now, finish the job and lift these other rocks off me. I'm still stuck!"

Aiden smiled and quickly grabbed another rock. Still glowing, there was strength surging through him. He could feel it. Aiden lifted the boulder with ease and threw it to the side. He repeated this with another huge rock for good measure. Briefly, he thought again about the voice he had heard and could have sworn he knew it, but it escaped his memory. He turned his attention back toward Melia.

"I think I'm okay, guys," Melia informed as she started to move, "A little scraped and bruised, that's all." She got to her feet.

"You are a lucky lady, madam. Please be a little more careful next time,"

Cedric requested with a stern look.

"You got it, and right back at ya," Melia replied with a wink.

On the other hand, Gil was still surprised to see his friend. "How are you okay?" he asked his buddy, Cedric.

"Oh, I uh, cause I'm a maanniiaaac, maanniiaaacc!" Cedric sang, and both Hairies shouted in each other's faces, "Arrrrrrrrr!"

"You sure you're not both pirates?" Aiden cracked.

"Haha! I'm double-jointed, remember? I worked my way out of the pile and popped my joints back in place. It hurts a little, but I'm fine!" Cedric added and turned back toward Gil.

"Arrrrrrrrr!" both Hairies shouted at each other again.

Jack heard a humming sound, looked down, and noticed something by his foot. He spoke up, perplexed, "Crikey! What have we here, aye?" Everyone looked to see what he was talking about and saw a glowing turquoise stone lying on the ground by his feet.

"It must have come out of that rock. It's a Watre gem!" Borak insisted.

Jack glanced over at the rocks Aiden had moved to see one was broken and crumbled at the bottom. A second later, there was a bang in the background where the skeletons were. Something had fallen from the giant skeleton, the Grandar skeleton. It was a giant's weapon, a double-bladed battle-ax, to be exact.

The Watre gem lifted in the air and instantly floated in front of Jack's face. It acted like it wanted something from him, hovering back and forth and pulsating with light. Again, they heard a sound coming from where the battle-ax was. It sounded as if someone was dragging the ax closer.

"It wants you to grab it," Aiden guessed.

Jack instinctively stuck out his hand and placed it over the gem. He could feel the power onto which he now held. He let go of the gem, and the ax, defying its weight, shot in his direction. The ax stopped midair and hovered with the gemstone directly in front of him. The two floating items spun in circles, slowly tightening together. Bright light flooded the room, blinding the group.

When Jack opened his eyes, he saw the gem had miraculously melded itself into the weapon's handle. While it hovered in front of him, he grabbed his new weapon and raised it high in the air. He felt a surge of power, solidifying the bond.

For the second time in a matter of minutes, the group of heroes stared at each other in awe. They weren't sure what to make of these spectacular events.

"Whoa!" reacted Cedric and Gil simultaneously.

The heroes were quiet for several seconds. Aiden tried to refocus the team, "Um, so I don't know what to make of everything that's been happening and not to take away from how awesome that was; but, uh, we've got more work to do. We need to sneak into the next room over there," he gestured toward the massive cave from which the chanting was coming, "And figure out how to save Priya."

Battered and bruised, the heroes were still in the fight. Everyone nodded in agreement. At that, Aiden led the way to the entrance of the massive cavern where thousands of evil creatures gathered for Priya's sacrifice.

Saving Priya

The group reached the edge of the entrance and peeked in. The cave was insanely huge. It had to be a hundred feet tall. They could see a cross standing by itself on top of the wall on the right side. Torches lit the cavern, and stalactites covered the ceiling. There was a large crowd of thousands of evil creatures, mostly Devians, but also included Grandars, Hairies, another Gorger, and another Druid, by the stage. Most of the creatures were in the middle of the cavern. The stage was at the other end. Two paths formed around the large gathering; one went left, and the other right. Outside of the large centralized main crowd, there were stragglers all around the perimeters of the cave. Aiden recognized the Druid by the stage. The Druid was Siren.

"Xena, stay here unless we need help, okay?" Aiden looked at Xena for confirmation after he said this. Xena, unsure, looked back at Aiden. "Xena, stay here, okay?" Aiden repeated, pointing over by the wall. The sleek-looking Nywolf stared at Aiden for another moment, then she licked his face, walked over by the wall, and sat down.

Aiden picked up Sen and brought her over to Xena. "Watch her with your life," Aiden commanded in a friendly tone. Xena looked at Sen, sniffed her, and then looked at Aiden, unsure.

"Guard," Aiden tried a different word.

Xena stamped her feet in recognition, and Aiden replied, "Good girl." Aiden was worried about Sen, but he thought she was safe with Xena. It wasn't as if they had a choice anyway.

"Any suggestions, guys?" Aiden asked the group when walking up to them.

Jack was the first to speak, but he responded to what the two Hairies were talking about, "Ha! Why in the heck would we do that, ya fools? We already have disguises!" He turned and spoke to the rest of the group, "These two bumblin' boneheads wanna jump on my shouldas and cover us up with a sheet or somethin' to look like the Gorger ova there."

"Yeah, so we can get close to the stage," Gil added.

Aiden rubbed his chin and replied, "That's not a bad idea."

"Whaaaat! Did you guys smoke some of that wacky tobacky when I wasn't lookin'?" Jack objected.

"Look, Jack," Aiden tried to explain, "Look at that Gorger. He's standing right by Priya, and he's got a robe on for the ceremony. What we need is that robe."

Jack looked at Aiden, trying to put together what he was saying, and asked, "We need the robe for what?"

Aiden continued, "If we can take out that Gorger and get the robe, you guys can get right next to the stage to grab Priya, hide her and get her out of there."

"Hmmm, a heck of a plan, chap! Okay, fellers, let's do it!" Jack asserted optimistically.

"Ummm, that sounds great, guys, but, uh, how the heck are we gonna do this?" Borak pointed out.

"You guys, go left, and we'll go right," Melia answered quickly and ran into the cavern.

"There she goes again," mumbled Aiden. He was getting used to Melia's recklessness.

Melia slowed down to a fast walk and went to the right, Aiden following. The rest of the group went left, trying to blend into the crowd. Aiden wondered where the heck Melia was going and why she would run off the way she did again. She was always running off, which could put the others in danger.

There was something Melia hadn't told the group yet, but there wasn't enough time. She had to hurry up and get to Priya. Melia walked toward the stage, following the long looping path. She maneuvered past many enemies unsuspectingly. Most of these evil creatures were in the massive crowd in the middle of the circular path, chanting, "The Queen will rise. The Queen will rise." Magus was on the stage, performing a ritual reading from an ancient book.

To Melia's right, some straggler Devians and Hairies were having odd discussions.

"Do you think the Queen will think I'm cute?" said one Devian.

The other replied, "How much wine have you had?"

"What do you think our master will do with her casket?" asked a Hairie.

The other replied, "Probably put you in it," then looked at Melia.

Caught off-guard, Melia hesitated to look back at the two Hairies before responding, "What? Her casket? Um, yeah, I'm sure there's enough room for the both of you!"

The Hairies were taken back, at first, and then erupted in laughter. "Hahaha! That was a good one!" Melia heard as she walked away at a fast pace. She was finally almost to the stage, but before she reached it, Siren stopped her.

Siren stepped in front of Melia abruptly, demanding, "And where might you be going in such a hurry?"

"Oh, uh, I was trying to get a better view," Melia replied.

Siren stared at her suspiciously and asked, "Hmmm, do I know you?"

Melia searched for something else to say and babbled, "Huh? Um, no. Everyone's big heads were in the way, and I wanted to glimpse the Queen's beauty. I thought I could...."

"Enough!" barked Siren, "You broke form from the chant." Siren looked over Melia intently as she continued to speak, "It is unlike a Roak to join us. It is against their cultural beliefs," the evil Druid paused for a moment, "Why are you here?"

At this point, Melia knew Siren was testing her and remembered something from her past with Magus. Before Magus had shown his true colors and when Melia and Magus were "friends," she had overheard him answer that question saying, "To walk in the darkness of the chosen one." Melia repeated the phrase, "To walk in the darkness of the chosen one." Siren only stood there squinting her eyes. After an awkward stare, she seemed to be satisfied and walked away. Siren walked over and stood in front of the stage, keeping her eye on the peculiar Roak. Melia looked away and acted as if she was chanting.

Borak, Jack, Cedric, and Gil were walking as quickly as possible in the direction of the Gorger around the left side of the path when Borak noticed an evil Grandar curiously walking toward them.

"Hold up, guys," Borak cautioned, holding his arm in front of everyone.

The group saw the Grandar and quickly turned toward the stage in the same direction as the other creatures. "The Queen will rise. The Queen will rise," the four of them repeated.

"The Queen will fart," Cedric snuck in.

"What? Shut up, Cedric," snickered Gil.

"The Queen has gas," Cedric joked again.

"Why can't you be serious," Gil said, holding in laughter.

The Grandar walked right behind the four heroes, glanced over in their direction, and kept walking past them.

"Whew! That was a close one, mates," Jack whispered.

"You guys see that tablecloth on the huge table? It's the same color as the Gorger's robe. Let's get it," Borak insisted and headed in that direction.

"What did she want?" asked Aiden as he walked up behind Melia.

"She was nosey. I took care of it," Melia replied.

"Okay, what are we doing here?" Aiden asked.

"I have a plan," Melia responded.

Previously, when Melia knocked out Juggy, she picked up the shiny object he had found. Up close, she could tell it was part of a latch or clasp, and then she noticed an H etched on it and knew it was from the necklace of Herana, the necklace around Priya's neck. Melia would tell the group, but since everything was happening so fast.

Melia saw Priya. Her beauty was undeniable. Even with all the red paste on Priya's face, she still looked amazingly beautiful. Many men regarded her as the most beautiful woman in all the land. Priya was in shackles on the stage, facing the crowd. Magus was in front of her, also facing the crowd, reading from an ancient text. Behind Priya sat the coffin with Herana's body propped up at an angle so the crowd could see their evil Queen.

Borak and the gang made it to the table with the tablecloth they needed. On the table were celebratory odds and ends, including candles, an assortment of food, silverware, jugs of wine, cups, and peculiar bone decorations.

"Why do we need this tablecloth again?" Jack asked, bewildered.

"We need to lure the Gorger away from the stage. We can do that by acting like another Gorger," Borak explained, "Maybeee, a woman Gorger?" he hesitantly added, shrugging his shoulders.

"Yeah, that's what we were thinking!" Gil spoke up, acting as if that was Cedric's and his idea all along.

"Woman Gorgea? You want me to act like a woman? What makes ya blokes think I can do that?" Jack inquired with an awkward smile.

"I'm sure you can pull it off," Borak answered, insinuating it would be easy for Jack.

"What ya mean by that, aye?" Jack replied. Borak didn't answer.

"Don't worry. I got this, guys!" Cedric assured everyone. He rubbed his hands together, staring at the table.

"Wait, don't do that!" Gil cautioned, "I've seen you try that trick dozens of times, and you always fail!"

"What trick?" Jack chimed in.

"I can do it now. Relax," Cedric replied.

"Cedric, are you sure?" Borak double-checked.

"Let's take everything off the table," urged Gil.

"There's way too much stuff on top. Let me focus," contended Cedric. He closed his eyes, continuing to rub his hands together. Slowly, Cedric put his hands on the table and grabbed the cloth. He rubbed the fabric in his fingertips in what appeared to be a meditative gesture. Abruptly, he opened his eyes and yanked the tablecloth out from under everything. Surprisingly, all the items only moved slightly and wobbled a little.

"Wow, how in the heck?" marveled Gil.

Just when they all thought Cedric pulled off this impressive trick, the four of them noticed a candle tree wobbling on the edge of the table. The candle tree slowed down and looked like it was about to stop, then spun one more time and fell off the table. It bounced around, CLING, CLANG, CLANK. The Grandar, who walked by them earlier, glared in their direction and began heading straight for them.

Luckily, only the Grandar was alerted by the noise. As the grotesque giant approached, Gil improvised, "Haha, you owe me 100 gold coins! Pay up, buddy!" He held his hand out to Cedric.

The Grandar reached the four of them, flipped its sword around, and smacked Gil on the head with the handle. "Get into formation, you bunch of louches," it sneered.

The giant turned to Cedric. Cedric was already in position, chanting, "The Queen will fart. The Queen will fart." The Grandar looked at Cedric weirdly, but before it reacted, Borak threw the tablecloth over it. Jack hit the large creature over its head with the same candle tree that had fallen on the ground, knocking it out cold. Borak and Jack immediately pulled it behind a boulder on the side of the cavern.

"We don't have much time, blokes! We gotta do this now!" Jack warned, looking at the two Hairies. Gil and Cedric jumped onto Jack's shoulders, and Borak threw the tablecloth over them.

There was no head. Borak looked at them and laughed. He told the others, "Hold on, guys, it's missing something." He looked around and saw a large basket of fruit and said to himself, "Perfect!" He dumped the fruit out and threw the empty basket at the transformed trio. Gil and Cedric caught the basket and placed it between their heads to help form a circular shape where a Gorger's head would be. For the final touch, Gil pulled the front of the tablecloth down over the basket to create a hood.

"Not half-bad," Borak complimented.

They walked out from behind the boulder toward the stage. Jack had a little trouble figuring out how a Gorger walked, but he was pulling it off well enough. As they made their move, Jack and the two Hairies on his shoulders caught a couple of glances from the crowd, but nothing stirred any commotion. The crowd was too entranced by the ritual.

Borak slapped his forehead as he noticed something while watching the undercover Gorger walk. They had all forgotten about the arms. He needed to tell them.

Borak caught up to his friends and loudly whispered, "There are no arms! Hurry up!" Jack, Gil, and Cedric heard their comrade and made "Oh crap" faces. Resembling the goofiest-looking Gorger anyone had ever seen, Jack sped up. The disguised Gorger's body swayed one way then the other, unorthodoxly. A Devian watched them hurry by and looked very confused.

They saw part of the wall jutted out not far from the stage where the other Gorger stood guard, so they went for it. They made it, and no one seemed to notice. Borak positioned himself in the crowd, so he had a good vantage point and watched.

Jack and the Hairies were within talking distance of the Gorger from where they stood.

"What now?" Jack whispered.

"I don't know. We have to call him somehow," replied Gil.

"How the heck are we gonna do that?" Cedric asked.

"Uh, ehhmm, ehhmmm," Gil made sounds, trying to get the Gorger's attention.

"What the heck are you doing? Clearing your throat?" Cedric questioned more.

"Sshhhh," Jack tried to quiet the Hairies so he could think, but it was too late. The Gorger heard them and was looking over.

"It worked! He's looking," said Cedric.

"Quick, move the basket and duck down," Jack demanded, then called out flirtatiously, "Yoouu-hoooo!"

The Hairies ducked down, and Jack grabbed the tablecloth holding it in a makeshift hood around his eyes. Jack leaned forward, which helped conceal his actual size since the Hairies were hidden inside the robe. He batted his eyes at the Gorger as it looked over at them curiously. He turned sideways and wiggled his butt at the Gorger, still batting his eyes, and walked out of view.

"You guys think that worked?" asked Jack.

"Um, I don't know what to say about that," confessed Gil while both Hairies looked at each other oddly.

"Is that how Grandar girls flirt with you, Jack?" Cedric made fun. Gil was doing his best to hold in his laughter.

"Shut up. I think I hear him coming," Jack responded, a little embarrassed.

Sure enough, they could hear the Gorger coming. The four hadn't thought this far ahead. How would they take out this huge Gorger and not make a scene? The Gorger, very interested, peaked its head around the cave wall. Jack batted his eyes again and wiggled his butt. The Gorger's cheeks turned flush red, and he smiled bashfully.

"Have you done this before?" Gil joked, leaving Cedric to hold his laughter this time.

"We're gonna lead him outta here, mates," Jack whispered, ignoring Gil's teasing.

Jack started walking quickly back where they came from, hoping the Gorger would follow. The Gorger followed. Whatever Jack was doing was working.

"Why are we shaking while we're walking?" questioned Gil.

"Because he's shaking his butt, hahaha," Cedric answered, laughing almost too loud.

"I'm tryna do me sexy walk, shut up," Jack responded, chuckling to himself.

The trio could hear the loud thud of the Gorger walking behind them. The thud began getting louder and closer until it sounded as if it were right behind them.

"Geez, is he running?" Jack thought out loud.

Cedric looked through a hole in the back of the tablecloth and replied, "Um, might as well be. He's walking fast, and his tongue is hanging out. What did you do to him?"

Jack dropped the "sexy walk" and started walking as fast as possible. He saw the back exit to the cavern ahead. They were getting close.

"Almost there! Almost there!" Jack said to himself.

They heard a low grumble behind Jack and the Hairies, "Ouch!" The Gorger must have run into something, slowing him down.

"Yes! We made it, fellas!" Jack exclaimed as they exited the cavern.

"Didn't realize this was gonna take us outside," Gil mentioned. Cedric was thinking the same thing. Looking around, Gil saw a dead tree leaning sideways over the opening to the cave. "Let's go, Ceed," Gil said, pointing at the tree.

"Already ahead of ya," Cedric replied. The two hopped off Jack's shoulders onto the tree's trunk and started jumping on it.

"What the heck are they doing?" Melia sounded like she was making more of a statement than asking a question.

Aiden looked over and saw the funniest thing he'd seen in a long time. A smaller Gorger in a raggedy robe shook its butt and batted its eyes at a larger Gorger. The smaller Gorger walked in the other direction, and the larger Gorger followed.

"Oh, my goodness," Aiden did his best to hold in laughter, "Those guys are somethin' else," he said, shaking his head and smiling.

"It worked," pointed out Melia.

Aiden looked over at Siren and saw her curiously watching the two Gorger's walk toward the back of the cavern. She glanced at Aiden, and he looked away quickly, hoping she didn't notice.

The seduced Gorger walked out the exit and saw the smaller Gorger on the ground, crying.

"Ow! Oh no, I think I broke my leg!" cried Jack in a rough woman Gorger-like voice.

The larger Gorger looked concerned, although a bit suspicious now that the presumed woman Gorger ran away from him and seemed even smaller since Cedric and Gil were no longer inside the disguise. Jack looked up at the Gorger with only his sad eyes showing and batted them again.

Meanwhile, Cedric and Gil had stopped jumping on the tree.

The giant ogre walked closer to Jack, asking, "Are you okay?" in a low, gruff voice, and reached out to him.

Jack quickly jumped up on the Gorger and said, "Kiss me, ya ugly bloke!" He stuck his head out of the make-shift hood, puckered, and kissed the surprised creature.

"Ptuu! Ptuuwee! Ewww!" the ogre spat, protesting in disgust, realizing it wasn't a woman.

Immediately, Cedric and Gil started jumping as hard as they could on the dead tree and heard it crack. They kept jumping, CRACK, CRRAAACK! The Gorger looked up to see what the noise was just as the tree whacked him in the head and knocked him unconscious.

The two Hairies fell with the tree, leaped to the side, and rolled.

"Uhggggg," moaned Cedric in pain as he rolled on the ground. When he stopped, he said, "Remind me to take a vacation."

"Great job, buggas, but we aren't done yet! Come on, let's get the robe and get back in there, aye!" Jack hollered enthusiastically.

Cedric looked at his Grandar buddy and rolled his eyes, responding, "Alright, alright."

Aiden and Melia saw the Gorger in the robe return, knowing it was Jack and the Hairies. "Thank goodness they got that robe. The tablecloth would never have fooled them," Melia commented.

Siren watched as the Gorger walked up and again stood guard at the stage. She glanced over at Aiden and Melia, who were watching the Gorger. "Something is up with those two," Siren thought. She decided to walk their way.

"Shoot, here comes Siren!" Melia said discreetly, jabbing Aiden in his side with her elbow. With her arm drawn back, Siren headed straight for them, holding onto her sword handle.

Magus had finished the incantations he was reading and looked up at the crowd. "Now, it is time to relinquish her soul and replenish this vessel with our Queen," Magus proclaimed, referencing Priya, "You will all be witness to the rebirth of Herana. Praise this day! Praise Herana!" Magus placed his hands together and bowed toward the crowd.

The crowd of creatures bowed back and, in ritualistic unison, replied, "Praise Herana!"

Magus proceeded by turning toward Priya. His hands began glowing white. Melia knew it was now or never, so she threw the broken clasp from the necklace of Herana at Priya. "Priya!" she yelled.

Priya had seen her friends were there to save her. She saw Melia and Aiden move up by the stage. She also saw the others lead the Gorger out and come back disguised. Even though she was in a dire circumstance, she had a tough time trying not to laugh and blowing their cover. Priya also noticed that Magus, absorbed in the ritual, hadn't seen anything. However, Siren seemed to be onto them and was walking toward Melia with her hand on her sword.

Suddenly, Melia threw something in Priya's direction. "What is that?" Priya wondered. There were glints of light flickering off the item as it twisted through the air almost in slow motion until it landed near her feet. "Wait, is that...?" Priya thought as she looked more closely, "It is! It's a piece of the latch from the necklace I'm wearing!"

Priya's magic comes from the Watre gem. Most of her captors didn't know that she had an internal gem located in her chest. They took her glaive when they captured her, thinking the weapon was the only Watre gem she had. Magus had ensured they placed the necklace on her to dampen her powers.

But, Priya had gone through a ritual called Completion for her coming of age. It is a secret ritual few in the world have ever experienced. A gemstone is inserted into a being's chest during this ritual, securing a complete bond and allowing unlimited access to the gem's powers. Magus was in Heirstone at the time and had instigated Priya's Completion for his evil agenda. Even though he knew of her internal gem, he didn't know how strong it made her.

Priya had been moved around a few rooms in preparation for the ceremony. In one of the rooms, she attempted to remove the necklace using her powers. It seemed like nothing happened, and this lowered her hopes further. Actually, though, the latch had broken.

Priya looked up at Magus, who was staring at her with murderous intent. His hands were still glowing white. She now knew the latch had broken, but what was she to do? She was out of time.

Standing in the crowd next to the stage, Aiden saw what was unfolding and felt stuck. It was all happening so fast. Magus raised his arms, and an electrical charge formed at the tip of an enormous stalactite. A lightning bolt streaked from the stalactite to the dark villain's hands. The evil sorcerer stood there with his arms up, ruthlessly charging up energy. Aiden watched the lightning gain in strength as Magus prepared to unleash it toward Priya.

The Leader of Heroes was at a loss for how he could stop the inevitable.

Part 2

Earth

The Beginning

"Dad! Daaad!" Aiden's son was calling him. "Dad, where'd you go? There are a bunch of military Hummers driving by and a lot of smoke over in the city! Dad, what's going on?" The longer his dad didn't answer him, the more worried Chase became.

Chase was twelve years old, in seventh grade, and up until today, was only worried about homework, what his friends were doing, and how to talk to girls. Aiden picked up Chase from school because of a national emergency. "Los Angeles was under attack by terrorists," was the announcement on the radio. Parents were to pick up their children and take shelter in their homes until further notice. All anyone knew was that the military was on the way. Everything was occurring rapidly. One second, Chase was at school where he heard about terrorist attacks that most of the other kids thought was a prank, and the next, his dad was picking him up. Now Chase and his dad were home, but Aiden had disappeared without saying much.

"Daaaad! Where are you? Where is Mom?" Chase kept calling.

Aiden slipped into the garage while he was on the phone. After numerous calls, he had not tracked down his wife, Sasha. She was not answering her phone. No one at her work nor her parents had heard from her for a while. The most troubling thought was that she worked in the city, which was under attack.

Aiden heard his son calling him. "I'm in the garage," he answered, "I haven't found your mom yet. Don't worry. I won't stop until I do."

Chase walked through the garage door as Aiden said this. The boy had tears in his eyes. He grabbed his Dad and hugged him. "You promise?" The way Chase looked when he said this made Aiden want to cry.

The phone rang. "Sasha!" Aiden exclaimed, answering the phone.

"Um, sorry, is this Aiden?" asked a raspy voice on the other end of the line.

Aiden sighed slightly and responded, "Yes, yes, who is this?"

"Hello, sir. My name is Dunagan. They call me Captain Dunagan. I think we may have found your wife, Sasha." Dunagan informed.

"Yes, sir! Captain Dunagan?" Aiden replied, startled at the name, "Yes, that's my wife! You found her? Where is she? Is she okay?"

Aiden was pacing back and forth in the garage. The entire situation was nerve-racking. Captain Dunagan was renowned in the military field and presumed dead, the last Aiden knew. Dunagan remained calm and answered, "Yes, sir. She is okay. She was in a car accident, and well, there were some other circumstances; but she is okay. I..."

Aiden cut him off, not concerned about who he was speaking to any longer, "What, what other circumstances? Tell me what happened?"

"Your wife is okay, but we could use your help. It would be best if you came down here, so she can explain to you what happened. We have a temporary hospital set up at a secure location. I'll text you the coordinates. I have to go." Dunagan hung up.

"Hello? Hello? What the fuck!" Aiden shouted, almost throwing his phone, but stopped himself. Chase was staring at his dad with wide eyes. "Sorry, dude. Your Mom's okay, though, bud. We're going to go get her," Aiden reassured his son while also calming himself down. Chase nodded. Aiden's phone instantaneously beeped with the location of his wife.

Sasha was in town, a few miles from her office. It was dead center in the middle of the terrorist attack. He didn't want to bring Chase but didn't know what else to do. After quick contemplation, he texted the number, "What is the safest route? I have my son with me."

Dunagan replied in a text, "SW has the least activity. Let me know when you're almost here. I need to make arrangements."

"Okay," Aiden answered, then turned to Chase and said sternly, "We have to go get your mother. I can't leave you here, and there's no time to take you anywhere. Grab your bug-out bag."

Chase nodded and ran upstairs. The boy came down in no time with his survivor bag he already had packed. Aiden, an ex-Navy Seal, taught Chase many survivor skills. One of those skills is always having your bug-out bag packed. Aiden had a few bags of his own ready as well: one with MREs and water, one with essentials, and one with guns and ammo. Aiden grabbed his bags and asked, "Now, are you happy we packed these?"

Aiden and Chase ran outside, and reality hit. It was a madhouse. On the drive home from school, the chaos hadn't started yet, but now, there was military everywhere, neighbors running around frantically, and smoke rising from many spots over toward town. Off in the distance, the side of a building exploded, blowing flames and debris into the air.

"Holy crap!" Chase exclaimed.

"Get in! Let's go!" Aiden hurried his son.

The two passed countless military vehicles and ambulances on their way into the city. At first, they tried taking the freeway, but it was gridlocked on both sides. It looked like a parking lot because traffic was at a complete stop. People were either trying to leave the city or stuck trying to turn around since the road was blocked. Luckily, Aiden knew most of the side streets and took them instead.

As soon as they made it into town, Aiden swore he saw something out of the corner of his eye that he'd never seen before. A group of devilish-looking creatures ran around a building out of view.

"Did you see that?" Aiden asked.

"See what?" Chase responded, looking the other way.

"Nothing, nothing," Aiden mumbled, not believing what he saw.

Aiden kept driving. They could hear gunshots in the distance. After a few blocks, they reached a road that looked like a battleground. Many stores had chunks blown out of them, gun holes in the walls, windows smashed, and were on fire. The street had huge cracks and an enormous hole where something must have exploded. There were also cars flipped over, dented, and a burning vehicle. The carnage worried Aiden even more. He looked at his phone and saw they were still eight miles from his wife's location.

Gunfire erupted, sounding like it was coming from right around the corner. Aiden saw two marines backing up from behind one of the buildings. They fired machine guns, then turned around and ran to avoid enemy fire. The soldiers took cover in the same building, but they were still exposed since part of the front of the building was blown off. A large group of Devians and a huge Grandar came charging around the building, looking for them.

"Oh, my God! That thing is huuuge!" proclaimed Chase in awe, "What the heck are those things?"

Aiden replied, shocked, "I have no idea, dude."

They were sitting in their car in the middle of an intersection, and thank goodness, no one noticed them. Aiden reached in his bag and grabbed the 6.5 Grendel, which he had modified with a Hellfire trigger and Leupold scope. He opened the door quietly and got out of the car. Using the car door as a gun stand, he placed his gun through the window.

The creatures made their way to the building entrance where the marines were. The marines unloaded on them. It was odd to see, but the Devians also had guns and started shooting back. A couple of the Devians went down. One of the marines was hit and screamed in pain. The other marine was cornered and held her hands up.

Aiden knew he had to act now and quietly cautioned his son, "Get down!" He aimed and shot one of the Devians in the head. The remaining three Devians and Grandar reacted quickly, turning toward Aiden. The marine dropped her hands and unleashed automatic gunfire. Aiden released a barrage of bullets, and the two of them dropped the remaining Devians. He shifted his aim back to where the Grandar was, but oddly, it was gone. Then he heard a stomp, stomp, stomp as if something big was running at him.

"Daadddd!" Chase yelled.

Aiden shifted his aim a little more to the right, and there it was. The Grandar was running full speed at him. The giant was halfway to them, so he needed to hurry. Aiden's first shot ricocheted off the Grandar's helmet. His second shot grazed its cheek.

"Shit!" Aiden cursed under his breath.

The Grandar was closing the distance quickly. Aiden lowered his aim, pointing at the ugly beast's chest, and unloaded his clip. The Grandar didn't slow down and kept running forward. The beastly creature continued rushing ahead as countless bullets entered its chest. Finally, it began slowing down. It stopped face-to-face with Aiden and fell to one knee. It stared into Aiden's eyes. The Grandar's eyes went blank, and it fell on its side, dead.

Aiden looked back at the marine and saw she was staring in his direction. He put his hands in the air as if to say, "I'm no threat." It appeared the soldier understood, so he started walking to her. The marine didn't overthink it and hurried over to the other fallen marine.

When Aiden reached the two marines, the woman held her comrade's hand, tearing up. "You're going to make it! Don't you leave me! We're gonna get you back to base!" she pleaded to the fallen soldier. She glanced over at Aiden and insisted, "Well, come on! Help me get him up!"

It didn't look good. There was blood everywhere. The marine had been shot at least three times, and one of the bullets must have hit an artery. A bullet may have hit a lung, as well.

The injured marine gasped for air while blood lightly poured from his mouth. "Sh...Sherri," the man struggled to talk, "You ah ah aaa...are a ahh a gooood partner. Th...thank you for your loyalty," the marine kept gasping for air as he spoke, "Na na nnn...now please be a guh gg...good partner and leave."

Sherri broke down, quietly weeping, "Noooooo! I won't!"

The marine was barely audible now, "Say goo...goodbye to my lit...tle girl for me." His mouth stopped moving, and the gasps for air ceased as his heart stopped beating. The brave marine's head fell to the side.

"Noooo! Help me! We have to get him to the base!" Sherri frantically pleaded.

Aiden calmly put his hand out until he touched Sherri's arm. At first, Sherri shook off Aiden's touch, but he tried again. This time, Sherri didn't shrug it off. Aiden pulled her into him, embracing her. She hugged him tightly, crying her eyes out.

After Sherri composed herself, she closed the marines' eyes, said a quick prayer, then asked, "Where are you guys headed?"

"We're going here," Aiden answered, showing Sherri the location on his phone.

"That's the base. Come on, let's go. I'll take you," Sherri offered, then took off running to the side of the building. Aiden and Chase didn't move, not sure they wanted to follow.

"But our car is..." Chase spoke up, pointing at their car.

Aiden looked over at his GMC Terrain. It was one of the most affordable and safest family vehicles on the market. He then looked at Sherri. She had stopped next to a military Humvee and held her palms up, looking at them as if to say, "What are you guys doing?"

Aiden glanced back over at the SUV. He said to himself, "I mean, it is a great vehicle," then nudged Chase forward, telling him, "Go wait with her. I'm gonna grab our stuff." Not a minute later, Aiden returned with their bags, and the three of them hopped in the Humvee. They headed toward the secret base.

It was a good thing they were in the Hummer because from here on out, the roads were mangled. They wouldn't have been able to make it without its all-terrain amenities. During the drive, Aiden strapped his Glock 21 to his leg. They saw a group of Devians, Hairies, and a Gorger while driving and had to change course. "What the hell is that?" was Aiden's reaction to seeing the 14-foot-tall Gorger holding a jet fighter rocket launcher.

Sherri had pulled onto a road and, luckily, was behind the menacing group of creatures, so she quietly backed up and took a different street. After some more quick-witted driving, dodging a downed telephone pole, and maneuvering through another fire, the trio made it within a couple of miles of the base. Sherri turned down another road and saw her usual route littered with debris. A fallen building had blocked their way forward.

"This was the only way through! We're gonna have to foot it from here," Sherri informed.

"That's what I was afraid of," Aiden answered and turned to Chase, "Grab your bag and stay behind us. Keep low, Chase."

"I got it, Dad," the boy responded, looking surprisingly poised.

It was eerily quiet. There were no gunshots in the distance or explosions like they had been hearing since arriving in the city. Sherri led the way through a few buildings, ensuring they stayed out of the open as much as possible. They quickly crossed a street and entered another building with huge holes in its exterior walls.

While traveling through the building, they heard something. It was a voice. The voice sounded raspy, deep, confident, and evil. "You all have a choice. You can either give up and do as you're told...or die!"

At first, they froze, thinking someone spotted them. The voice continued, "How 'bout you, Colonel? What do you say?"

After realizing the voice wasn't talking to them, Sherri looked through a hole in the wall and saw a large group of Devians, Hairies, and Grandars. She also saw their leader, Magus, who was the one speaking. They all stood about 20 yards away in a grassy area surrounded by buildings. The evil creatures stood around a group of soldiers. It appeared there had been a battle since dead bodies of soldiers and creatures lay everywhere.

Aiden peeked through the wall and saw what was happening. About ten captive soldiers were kneeling in front of Magus. "Shoot, what are we gonna do?" he whispered, "We have to save them."

"Yes, but how?" Sherri replied.

The Colonel answered Magus, "Well, let me see here. Fuck you!"

"Ahh hahaha," Magus laughed and kept talking, "I thought as much. You have balls, Colonel, but it seems you don't care about your life or the well-being of your fellow warriors."

Magus had taken a few steps away from the Colonel, pacing while talking. The warlock stopped and ignited his hands in a white glow. In an instant, the evil sorcerer turned toward the Colonel and hit him with a streak of lightning, electrocuting him. After a few seconds, Magus released the Colonel from his lightning grasp. The Colonel fell face first, hit the ground, and was dead. His head continued smoking.

"Oh, my God!" Aiden exclaimed under his breath, "I can't let him kill anyone else."

"Who is next?" Magus yelled out angrily while looking around, "Huh? Who wants to be next? You? You?" He was pointing at different people, "How 'bout you?" He stopped in front of another man who looked important.

"Shoot!" Sherri said to herself, seeing who it was.

Aiden looked over at the guy to whom Magus was addressing. The man not only looked important, but he also looked familiar. That's when Aiden realized it was Dunagan. He looked older, but it was Dunagan. Aiden also saw Dunagan messing with something down by his ankle.

"How about me, what?" replied Dunagan.

Magus leaned down close to the brave General, "You humans are tough guys, huh? Too arrogant to know what's best for you and your people." The leader of villains walked a few steps away like he had done with the Colonel before electrocuting him.

"Wait! Wait!" hollered Dunagan, "We'll do what you ask. We have put down our weapons and are on our knees. What else do you want from us?"

"Yeeesss, that's better, human," Magus sneered, "The sooner you all stop resisting, the fewer people will die. There's one problem though, tough guy. I don't need you."

Bunker Under Your Nose

Magus's hands lit up white again, preparing to electrocute Dunagan.

Aiden lifted his AR and shot as soon as he saw Magus' hands light up. It was a good shot. The bullet was in line with Magus' head, but the sorcerer sensed something. Instead of piercing his temple, the bullet stopped in mid-air and hovered. It was as if Magus had stopped time, but everything was still moving normally. Only the bullet had stopped.

Magus turned and saw that Aiden shot through a hole in the wall. "Aiden, there you are," he said, then plucked the bullet out of the air.

"What? How does he know me?" Aiden muttered under his breath.

Dunagan pulled a gun from an ankle holster and shot at Magus. That bullet also stopped mid-air but came closer to causing damage than the last one. Magus swatted this bullet out of the air and gave Dunagan a scornful look. Interestingly, before Magus swatted the bullet, Dunagan noticed that it moved ever so slightly.

The entire group of soldiers grabbed their guns from the ground and started shooting everyone who didn't look like they belonged.

The Devians, Hairies, and Grandars returned fire. Some attacked with swords and daggers. A Grandar lunged at one of the soldiers and sliced him in half with its sword. Aiden picked off a couple of Devians, saving a soldier. More Devians fell. A Hairie snuck up behind another soldier and stabbed her in the side with its dagger. Shots rang out from all directions.

Seeing his chance, Dunagan got to his feet and attempted to tackle

Magus. Magus grabbed him and spun 360 degrees, launching him straight at the building where Aiden, Sherry, and Chase were. Captain Dunagan crashed through the building and landed at Sherry's feet. He looked up and was glad to see who it was. Due to the pain, he could barely say her name, "Sheerrrry!"

Aiden and Sherry continued to shoot, picking creatures off. By now, three more soldiers had been killed. Another two soldiers tried to escape, but a Grandar cut them off. As the Grandar grabbed for one of the soldiers, Aiden shot him in the shoulder, halting the creature in its tracks. The giant reeled back, looking to see who shot him and saw Aiden. They stared at each other. Their eyes telling one another the other would die. The Grandar suddenly realized the two soldiers were gone and screamed in anger. It smashed the corner of a building.

Sherry was about to shoot at a Devian, but the building exploded, knocking everyone to the ground. Magus had nailed the structure with an energy blast, blowing it wide open.

"We gotta go!" warned Dunagan. Everyone got to their feet and ran.

Dunagan, Aiden, Sherry, and Chase ran for a mile ducking through buildings and hiding every time they heard something. They ran a little further and then went down an alleyway to find a dead end.

"Great, now where do we go?" Chase complained, finally losing his composure.

"Sshhhh," Dunagan hushed the boy and waved for everyone to follow him. The General led the group to a hidden door in a brick wall. Through the wall was a small area with a dumpster. Dunagan opened the dumpster and waved his watch in front of a sensor. The back of the dumpster opened into a room. Dunagan motioned to Sherry, saying, "Ladies first."

Once inside the room, it was obvious where they were. The foursome had entered the secret base.

"Welcome to Bunker Under Your Nose," informed Dunagan.

"Wait, for real? That's the name of the place? Under Your Nose?" Aiden asked, looking at Dunagan, smiling, waiting for a response.

Dunagan only smirked.

"Awesome, the government has a little inside joke at the expense of American tax dollars. That's not condescending at all," Aiden sarcastically joked.

The secret room was extremely white. Two soldiers were standing guard. The soldiers had their guns drawn until they saw Dungan, then welcomed the General. Dunagan greeted the soldiers, then walked past them to a set of double doors and waved his watch again. The doors opened, revealing they weren't regular doors but elevator doors. The group entered the elevator and went down what felt like ten floors. There was no way of knowing exactly what floor they were on or how far down they went because there were no buttons in the elevator. The elevator came to a stop and opened up to a long hallway with one-way glass windows, obviously set up as a safety measure for observation of those who entered. The group reached another door, and Dunagan waved his watch again. The door opened into a vast circular room filled with high-tech computers. Many agents typed vigorously on them.

Chase thought to himself, "Wow, this is amazing!"

When they walked into the next room, the group saw three considerable-sized monitors in the front with an open area that contained a unique flooring setup before each monitor. A marine with a headset holding a mini screen over one eye stood before the left monitor. The marine's monitor showed different camera angles, including a first-person view from an android robot that the agent was controlling. The robot appeared to be in another test room. The monitor in the middle had a different use. Agents on computers in the back of the room tracked the invading creatures. They were continuously informing the field troops of the enemy's position.

Aiden looked around the room and saw soldiers armed with guns, standing guard, and patrolling back and forth from other rooms.

"Nice set-up, Captain!" Aiden complimented, "So I noticed you're the General now."

"Yep, but I like the name Captain," Dungan replied.

"You'll have to tell me about that robot," Aiden continued, looking optimistically at Dunagan, then asked, "Where is my wife?"

"No worries! No worries! Please follow me," Dunagan replied and escorted the group to Aiden's wife.

"Oh, my God, honey! Are you okay?" Aiden asked as he ran up to his wife, lying in a hospital bed. He grasped her hand.

"Mom!" Chase yelled with watery eyes from behind his father.

Sasha was propped up in the bed and appeared to be okay. She looked alert. "Hey! Hey, you two! Oh, my goodness. I'm so happy you guys found me. I was so worried," Sasha replied, sounding a little frantic but happy. "This guy," glancing over at Dunagan, "Brought me here and forced me to stay in this bed."

Dungan smirked and responded, "Ma'am, it is for your own good."

Aiden chuckled a little, knowing his wife's stubbornness, then asked, "Honey, what happened?"

Sasha took a breath, preparing to tell the story. She began, "So I was driving back to work from lunch, and one of the buildings exploded next to me. A bunch of fiery debris hit the car, breaking out the window, and like... everyone wrecked. I hit the car in front of me, and the car behind me hit me. It was chaos, and I, uh, I was stuck, so like...I had to jump out of the car and run. There were guns shooting and people screaming. I ran as fast as I could, looking for a place to hide. I saw a subway entrance, so I ran for it. As I got to the subway stairs, the building next to them exploded! I think a missile or something hit it. I dove inside the stairwell and tumbled down the stairs. Thank goodness I dove because pieces of the building almost hit me! And then, I had to get up and run before the entire building fell on me! Luckily, I made it, but the subway entrance was caved in, so I didn't know what to do. I wandered around the subway for a while until a couple of soldiers found me and brought me here." Sasha was frantic now after describing the horrific ordeal.

"Oh, geez, hon. I'm so sorry! That sounds crazy! You didn't get hurt?" Aiden looked her over as he said this.

"No, no, only some bruises and scrapes," Sasha replied, becoming emotional. She stared at her husband longingly, searching for comfort in his eyes.

Relieved, Aiden lovingly looked into Sasha's eyes and placed his hand on her cheek. He grabbed her and gave her a passionate hug, and told her, "I'm so happy that you're okay!"

The doctor walked over. Dunagan introduced her, "Sorry to interrupt, but this is the doctor who is ensuring your wife's quick recovery...Dr. Thompson."

"Hello," the doctor offered her hand and continued talking, "I'm so glad you made it here unscathed. It's mayhem outside. Did you have any problems on your journey?"

"We did. We ran into an ugly evil-looking red-haired A-hole who can stop bullets in midair and has a large army," Aiden replied.

Chase added, "And he threw Captain Dunagan through a building! Crazy-looking creatures and bullets were flying everywhere!"

Chase kept telling the story to his mother while Aiden and the doctor continued their conversation.

"Wow, bullets stopping in midair? How is that possible? I heard Magus has magical powers of some sort, but I mean, that's something else. How do you stop that? Maybe we should give up before we all die," the doctor said, then hesitated, realizing she was talking too much, "I'm sorry. I'm a little stressed."

Aiden held his hand up, suggesting he understood, "It's ok. We're all under a lot of stress right now. I've seen things today that I thought only existed in fantasy novels."

The doctor quickly changed the subject, "As to your wife, she's going to be fine. We treated her scrapes and put some stitches in her leg. She needs to take it easy for a while."

"Stitches?" Aiden asked in concern.

"Not to worry, only five stitches. She'll heal in no time," the doctor responded.

Dr. Thompson walked over to Sasha, turning her attention to the patient. Aiden watched her, a little suspiciously, wondering why she was so eager to give up the fight.

Aiden and his family spent a little time together until Dunagan walked back into the room, motioning for him. "Come with me. I'd like to show you something," he said.

Chase and his mother were engaged in conversation. Not wanting to interrupt them, Aiden kissed his wife on the forehead and lightly rubbed the top of Chase's head before leaving with Dunagan.

"I want to show you our WAFU program. I believe you saw a glimpse of it when we were in the War room," Dunagan spoke intensely.

"Um, the robot? Yes, sir, I'd love to see!" Aiden responded. He then thought this was an excellent time to ask the General what was on his mind.

Dunagan saw Aiden hesitate and was on the verge of asking something. He already knew what Aiden was about to ask. He got this question a lot when he revealed himself since the military faked his death. Dunagan cut Aiden off, answering, "Imprisoned overseas. We saved many, but I was held captive. After five years, I escaped."

"Sooo...you're a hero, sir," Aiden replied, giving Dunagan his due respect.

"As are you, Aiden. As are you," the General reciprocated. At that moment, Aiden knew Dunagan was aware of his military background.

The two walked into another room that was, without a doubt, a test room for a weaponized Android robot. The room smelled like burning plastic. It was an unusually long room like an indoor target range, with three stations. A target at one of the stations was currently on fire. An agent ran over with a fire extinguisher and put it out. As Aiden looked around, he could see each station had targets set up to test different types of weapons. He heard a thud, thud, thud approaching and looked over. A robot walked up to him and stopped.

"Aiden, meet WAFU. The Water, Ammunition, and Fire Unit," Dunagan boasted proudly.

"Cool, he looks like a modern C-3PO," Aiden complimented.

Dunagan only looked at him blankly.

"You know, from Star Wars?" Aiden explained.

"Oh, oh, yes, but he can do way more. Observe," replied Dunagan, putting his arm out, prompting Aiden to watch the robot.

WAFU walked to the first station, where four targets were set up at different distances. The first two targets were circular shooting targets placed at 25 and 50 yards, the third target was a larger square placed at 100 yards, and the last target was tiny, placed up high at 100 yards. The second station had two plastic items placed at 25 and 50 feet, and the third station had a car hood standing upright.

A light in the back of the room turned from red to green. WAFU quickly went into action. It lifted its right arm and shot the first two targets. A display of its automatic capabilities followed by it unloading a barrage of bullets into the third square target. Then, the impressive robot aimed like a sniper and hit the last tiny target with one shot. WAFU ran to the second station and sprayed fire at the first target, then the second, incinerating both targets. Clumps of plastic were left burning.

"Nice! A flamethrower!" Aiden reacted, continuing to watch as WAFU ran to the third station. The awesome robot reached the car hood at the third station and shot it with a pressurized water jet stream. It cut with surprising speed through the hood like a stick of butter. The top half of the hood fell to the ground with a BANG.

"Well, what do you think?" Dunagan asked, already observing Aiden's excitement.

"Sold! I'll buy one! How much?" Aiden teased, "That thing is awesome!"

Dunagan smiled with satisfaction and said, "We're getting ready to launch three of them in the field a little later. Oh, I want you to meet the pilot." Dunagan held his earpiece and called for the pilot, "Pecko, Pecko, this is Captain."

"Go ahead, Captain," Pecko responded.

Dunagan, again on his earpiece, replied, "Come down here. There's someone I want you to meet."

As they waited for the arrival of Pecko, there was a massive explosion outside, then another.

Magus Arrives

"Shit! They found us!" Dunagan exclaimed and ran to the war room.

Aiden followed and saw the room had erupted into a frenzy. The agents used all three monitors: one showing a live video of Magus and his army outside the building under which hid the building; one showing a map of air traffic and incoming U.S. jets, and the other displaying correspondence with the White House.

"Shit! Shit! Shit!" Dunagan kept repeating, "How did they find us? Why would they come here?"

Aiden was trying to wrap his mind around what he saw on the first monitor. It was a massive army full of the creatures he had seen earlier.

"Ah crap, they're probably after that damn necklace. We're not sure why, but it started glowing when those creatures arrived. It's been stored here with some other alien artifacts for years," Dunagan divulged.

"Wait a second! You brought my wife to a place that has what those guys want?" Aiden snapped, pointing to the evil army on the monitor.

"Well, to clarify," Dunagan explained, "I didn't know, for sure, they were after the necklace. Not to mention, this bunker is pretty well hidden and fortified."

"Yeah, right under their nose, apparently," Aiden replied in a sarcastic tone, "It looks like maybe that wasn't the best place to put it."

KABOOM, another explosion outside, cut through the rising tension in the room. A long session of rumbling followed.

Dunagan spoke loudly across the room, "How many Wafu's we got online?"

A woman agent answered, "The only one ready is Pecko's, sir."

"Shit! Send it in! Send it in now! WAFU Team one, go!" Dunagan commanded.

"Yes, sir, sending in WAFU team one now," the woman responded, then spoke in her earpiece, "WAFU team one is a go. Repeat, WAFU team one is a go."

Aiden heard some commotion in the room behind him, then a door closed, and then there was silence. After a few more minutes, Pecko ran into the room and stood on the unique flooring in front of the middle monitor while agents attached virtual reality gear onto his torso, arms, and legs. WAFU came online. The central monitor now showed what WAFU saw. Pecko was ready for action and began directing the team. Everyone in the room watched on the monitor as the team ran out of the building and took a position to engage Magus' army.

The building on top of the bunker had been battered in an assault and was leaning to the left. It appeared to be about to topple over. WAFU, leading the team of thirty, approached from the rear of the building. They stayed tight to the walls and crouched behind large chunks of concrete that had fallen from the building. The team stopped, holding their position about a hundred feet from Magus' army. They saw the evil military had grown from around fifty to a few hundred in strength.

"There are too many!" remarked a team member.

"The enemy has grown in numbers. Requesting orders, sir," Pecko's voice asked through WAFU's speaker system.

In the war room, Pecko stood waiting for Dunagan to give him a command.

Magus began speaking, "People of Earth. Your fight is futile. I am rather impressed with your bravery, but you cannot defeat us. We have Herana on our side. You cannot withstand my power. Give us the necklace, and we will not kill you."

Dunagan ran over to Pecko and grabbed his headset to reply, "Your fight is futile! In route are jets on their way to blow you to hell!"

"You don't know what I'm capable of, Captain. Do you think a few little jets will stop me? Hahaha," Magus ranted, "I could set this world on fire if I wanted. Good thing for you, it looks like I don't have to."

"And why is that?" Dunagan asked curiously.

"Because Siren has already retrieved the necklace from... 'under your nose,' hahaha!" Magus answered and laughed at his joke.

The military team heard footsteps walking past them. It was Dr. Thompson leading Sasha and Chase in front of her. The doctor appeared different now. She had her hair down and wasn't wearing glasses anymore. Aiden recognized her. It was the same woman from his vision, the woman who threw Chase to the ground. It was Siren, and she was wearing the necklace of Herana.

Sasha and Chase looked as if they were drugged. Siren's hands were glowing green, somehow enticing Aiden's family to walk ahead of her. Siren continued walking past the military team, who, for some reason, only stared at her. She began walking past WAFU. Everyone watched, waiting for someone to do something.

"What the hell? Nooooo!" yelled Aiden while he watched on the monitor.

Pecko had his headset back on and used the robot to reach and grab Siren. Siren hit WAFU with a stiff arm throwing green sparks in the air. The robot flew twenty feet until it slammed into the ground with a clunk and slid.

"Really? That's it? I thought the robot was supposed to be tough!" Siren ridiculed.

"Ah, my beautiful, evil Druid Princess. So glad you could make it," Magus greeted Siren as she walked up with Sasha and Chase. "Who knew you'd be so good at this," he commended, then kissed Siren on the lips.

Aiden got a good look at the necklace around Siren's neck. For some reason, he felt a connection with it.

"WAFU, commence attack! Team, spray and clear out!" Dunagan commanded. He looked to his left where Aiden had been, only to find no one there.

WAFU got up from the ground and unloaded bullets into the crowd of creatures. Some of the bullets stopped mid-air in the vicinity of Magus, Siren, Sasha, and Chase, but the rest of the bullets ravaged the Devians, Hairies, and Grandars. The military team started firing. Siren quickly put her hands up and activated a green energy barrier in front of the army. The energy barrier protected the evil army from any more oncoming bullets.

The bullets hovering in the air by Magus dropped to the ground. He reacted, shouting in anger, "Aaaahhhrrrrr, bad move, robot!" The angry sorcerer glared at his soldiers and commanded, "Well, what are you all waiting for? Go get them!"

The evil army had now grown to over 500 strong. They yelled a battle cry, "Hail Herraannnnaa!" and ran toward the military team through the barrier Siren had created. The military squad continued to spray bullets, dropping their enemies by the masses.

"Finish your clip and fall back!" ordered Pecko through WAFU's audio. He then yelled, "Let's goooooooo!" as he blasted the creatures with his flamethrower and water jet. Devians and Hairies were immediately set afire and cut in half simultaneously. The military team began falling back as they emptied their mags. They shot the straggling creatures that had managed to get by WAFU's fire and water-jet slicing attack.

Siren had seen enough and charged up a sizable green energy ball. She flung it at WAFU. The energy ball nailed WAFU and sent him flying again. He rammed into a massive chunk of concrete.

"Fall-back!" hollered the military group. As they turned to run, a Humvee flew by them, heading straight for the army of creatures.

"Who the hell is that?" hollered Dunagan, startled.

WAFU's sophisticated sight identified the driver, and Pecko answered, "It's Aiden! Shit!"

WAFU got up, sparks flying from his back. He ran after the Hummer, heading directly toward the evil army. The creatures were climbing over the pile of burning, sliced, and shot-up dead bodies WAFU and the military team had created. BAM, CRAACK, BOOM, Devians bounced off the front of the Humvee. WHAM, the military vehicle ran into the pile of bodies, launching the vehicle through the air. The Humvee landed in the crowd, SMASH, THUD, and flattened more creatures. It continued ramming through the crowd, creating a path of dead bodies.

"Sashaaa! Chaaase!" Aiden cried out. He was almost there. CRACK, Siren nailed the front of Humvee with an energy blast. The vehicle stopped instantly, throwing Aiden headfirst through the window.

Following the path Aiden created with the Humvee, WAFU ran at high speed. He unleashed the flamethrower in one direction, leaving a wall of flaming bodies to one side and the water jet in the other direction, cutting everything in half on the other side.

Aiden did a front flip through the window and held his fist out, soaring through the air like Superman. He flew straight at Magus' face. Magus leaned back and barely dodged what would have been a spectacular punch. Aiden flew by Magus, hit a Grandar, and knocked it off its feet into a group of Devians. Sasha took the opportunity and attempted to hit Magus, but Siren stopped her mid-strike with some type of energy grasp.

"What!" exclaimed Sasha, confused, looking at the green energy wrapped around her fist.

Siren thrust her other hand at Sasha, hitting her with an energy blast that knocked her down. Aiden jumped up and attacked Magus. He threw a jab, right cross, and left hook. Magus dodged every strike with unreal speed.

While dodging, Magus teased, "Is that all you got, Legend?"

Aiden didn't have time to wonder why Magus called him Legend and continued throwing punches mixed in with a front kick and a roundhouse. Even though Aiden was a 4th-degree blackbelt, Magus continued dodging the strikes, seemingly without effort.

Distracted watching Aiden and Magus battle, Siren didn't hear WAFU coming. WAFU couldn't shoot his weapons at Siren since Sasha and Chase were near her. Instead, the robot leaped, performed a flying kick, and cracked Siren in the back. She tumbled to the ground away from Aiden's family. WAFU activated his flamethrower and ran at the wicked Druidess, who was still on the ground. Siren blocked the flames with an energy shield. WAFU tried to grab her. She jumped during the fight and flipped over the robot, landing behind it.

A circle had formed around the pair of fights as one would during a fight with a crowd. The problem was the ring was made up entirely of evil creatures. The outcome for Aiden and WAFU looked bleak, even if they won.

Magus caught both of Aiden's punches and pulled him face-to-face. The vile leader asked, "Are you ready?"

Aiden jumped and double kicked Magus in his chest. Aiden backflipped off Magus' chest, landed, and confidently responded, "Anytime, buddy! Are you?"

Magus zipped forward, seeming to transport himself through space, and jabbed Aiden in the mouth. He followed with a right cross. Aiden couldn't even see the punches coming. Magus threw a side kick and knocked Aiden off his feet.

WAFU sprayed Siren with bullets and flames at the same time. Siren held up an energy shield, blocking the assault. Slowly, Siren edged the shield close to the android's bolstering attack until she was close enough and transformed the shield into a circular forcefield that surrounded the robot. Bullets ricocheted inside the forcefield, and flames engulfed WAFU, causing him to shut down his weapons.

Magus walked toward Aiden and spoke theatrically, "You were supposed to be the hero that beat me! You were supposed to save the worlds! That's right, not the world, but worlds!" He held his hands up sarcastically, demonstrating exaggerated amazement, then walked up to Aiden and leaned down, sneering, "You're nothing but a weasel." Hands glowing white, Magus grabbed Aiden by the neck and picked him up. The evil warlock began to electrocute him.

Siren began collapsing the energy force field surrounding WAFU. It appeared to be the world's first android compactor.

Aiden shut his eyes. All he could think of was saving his family, but he didn't yet know how to control his powers. At this point, he didn't even know he had powers. He did know something felt different.

Aiden's body shook from being electrocuted. Blue flashes began pulsating through his body. Magus recognized the blue flashes and his eyes opened wide. He urgently told Siren, "Protect the boy! We need him! Hurry!"

Siren replied, "What? But..."

Aiden stopped shaking, instinctively calming himself. He put his hands together in front of his chest like he was praying.

"Hurry! Damn it, now!" Magus yelled. He was so confident a second ago but now highly agitated.

Siren released the force field over WAFU and quickly covered Sasha, Chase, and herself with a larger one.

Aiden's entire body began glowing blue. Everything was quiet. He couldn't feel a thing. Magus held him by his neck, but it felt like he was floating. He felt overloaded with power, and that power was begging him to release it. Who was he to deny the will of whatever had built up inside of him? Effortlessly, he gave in.

CRACK, WHOOSH, a massive energy wave discharged from Aiden. The surge destroyed everything in its path. Fortunately for Magus, he partly blocked it with a magical shield. The wave threw Magus miles away. The circular forcefield protected Siren and Aiden's family, and they flew in the opposite direction. All the creatures in the evil army were knocked down, most of them killed. WAFU's head and limbs were blown off his body.

Aiden fell to one knee. "What the heck was that?" he said to himself. He shook the cobwebs out of his head and stood up. He looked around to see most of the creatures lying dead on the ground.

There was a sparking sound. Aiden looked in that direction to see WAFU blown to pieces, shorting out.

"Oh noooo! Shiiiiit! Sashaaa...Chase!" Aiden yelled, falling to both knees, "Magus, I'll fucking kill yooouuu!"

The military team had successfully retreated to the bunker but ran back out to dispatch the still moving creatures. "Grab WAFU," one of the team members shouted.

"Aiden!" Dunagan called out, checking on him.

"Ahhhhh! Nooooo!" Aiden grieved, "My family!"

"We'll get your family back. I think they survived, but we need to get you back inside!" Dunagan assured. The General helped Aiden up to his feet, and the entire team ran back inside the bunker.

Magus' Dream

Magus was unconscious, flying through the air. He dreamed of the first time he put his hands on the Necklace of Herana, the necklace he so patiently and methodically pursued while performing the greatest ruse of his life.

......Previously, not too long after Melia had found the Necklace of Herana, Naru and the rest of the Mystics had arrived in Heirstone from another realm proclaiming they had been sent on a voyage of destiny. This happened more than five years after Naru had defeated Herana, so he was already renowned as the hero of the world and thought of in high regard by all. Naturally, Melia and Borak's parents, the King and Queen, stepped down in good faith as it is tradition for a Mystic to assume the position as King.

Years later, Magus remained in Heirstone and had become King Naru's trusted Commander-in-Chief and Melia and Borak's close friend. His deceitful plan had tested his patience on numerous occasions, but he persevered and waited until the perfect day to follow through with it. Today, once he got his hands on the necklace, was the day when his hard work was going to prove worthwhile. He reveled at the chance to demonstrate his worthiness to his Queen by being the one who revived her.

The community of Heirstone was distracted, celebrating another year of peace. During this time, Magus had convinced the Mystics to perform an ancient ritual on Priya to commemorate her coming of age. The ceremony must be carried out at the lake, so the King and the rest of the Mystics had to leave the castle to attend. Being the King's trusted Commander-in-Chief, Magus was in charge of protecting Heirstone while the Royal Mystics were absent.

While the Mystics were gone, Magus had one thing in mind. He walked with one other servant to the royal quarters, where a locked chest sat at the foot of Naru's bed. Naru had the necklace locked away when he became King. Since he was in charge, Magus had the key. He pulled the key out of his pocket as he continued walking. To add to Magus's mischief, he had an army outside the city walls waiting for him to give the signal.

The deceiving sorcerer opened the chest and saw the radiant glow of the necklace. Next to the necklace was something else. He picked that up first. It was an important-looking medallion with ancient writing on it that he didn't understand. He put it in his pocket and turned his attention back to the necklace. This was the moment he had been dreading. It was the moment he would find out if he were worthy of the necklace or if he would perish. Magus had brought a servant with him for this exact reason. He placed the necklace around the servant's neck as an initial test. At first, the servant was fine but then fell to his knees in pain. The servant looked at his arms and hands and saw he was becoming transparent. He reached forward for Magus to help, but Magus only, cold-heartedly, stepped away in concern for his well-being. The servant flashed white light. Mystifyingly, gray smoke seeped out of the servant's body and swirled. The necklace quickly consumed the smoke, and the servant's body fell dead.

Grinning anxiously, Magus felt unsure whether he wanted to put the necklace on after seeing what had happened. He knew the servant would probably die, but witnessing it firsthand was unnerving. The evil traitor scowled as he thought to himself, "Stop being weak." He snatched the necklace off the ground and put it on without further hesitation. Instead of feeling pain, he immediately felt the power of the spirit world surging through his body. Magus outstretched his arms, relishing the feeling as his body lit up in a pure white pulsating light. Lightning hit the roof above the room where the evil Mystic stood. The electricity conducted into the room through the chandelier and streaked in an arch into Magus' body.

"Aahhhhhrrrrr!" he growled while he powered up.

The army outside saw the bright flash of light and knew this was the signal to rush the gates and attack the city...

CRACCKK, SMASSHH, Magus crashed through a building on the 12th floor. The impact jolted him awake. He slid on the carpet, obliterating desks, dividers, and office supplies until he came to a stop. There were people hunkered down inside the room, shocked by what was happening. They were staring at him and not moving. The group of office workers watched while the man, who flew through a twelfth-story wall, sat up, shook the dust off, and stood to his feet.

Magus looked at the group of people and maniacally teased, “Boo!” Everyone gasped and ran out of the room. “Haha, run, you little cowards!” he snarled. He pulled a decorative compass out of his pocket and held it up in the air. The compass pointed exactly due east from where he was standing. He put the compass away and headed in that direction.

Siren, Sasha, and Chase

Siren, Sasha, and Chase hit the ground. They bounced off the road and crashed through a building. The ball-like force field kept bouncing, struck a car, demolished another building's exterior wall, and came to a stop inside the building. It had protected them, but they were bruised from being tossed around.

The force field disappeared, and Siren got to her feet. "Get up! Let's go!" she demanded as she dragged both Sasha and Chase to their feet. "Wait!" she barked again. Siren grabbed some twine off the ground and bound the two humans' hands together in front of them. She forced them to walk forward in the direction where they were to meet Magus.

Chase was tearing up, "Mom, what's gonna happen? I'm scared!"

Sasha grabbed Chase's chin, turned his head so she could look him in the eyes, and replied, "Honey, do what she says. We're going to get through this, okay? We're going to be alright."

Chase stared back into his mother's eyes. He'd never seen her so serious. He wanted to ask another question but stopped himself and, instead, wiped his tears, nodding, "Okay."

Sasha was freaking out, too, but when she saw the fear in Chase's eyes, it reminded her she had to be strong.

"Where the hell are you taking us?" Sasha snapped.

Siren kept walking forward and didn't turn or say a thing.

"Did you hear me? Where the hell are you taking us?" Sasha repeated.

Irritated, Siren turned around and responded, "Are you sure you want to be talking to me like that?" She walked close to Sasha, face-to-face, "Because you're starting to anger me."

"Let us go! We don't even know who you are. Why are you doing this?" Sasha argued.

Siren's face tightened in rage. She closed her fists, and they started glowing bright green. Sasha was scared but able to hold her nerve and look confident. Coerced by Sasha's apparent courage, Siren calmed down. Her hands stopped glowing.

Siren spoke, "Well, look what we have here...another brave human. Okay, I'll play along," she was looking forward to explaining this, "We're here for power. We're here to rule. And we will enslave you all!"

"You and what army?" Chase spoke unexpectedly.

"What did you say, child?" Siren snarled.

"You and what army are going to rule and enslave us? My dad killed them all!" Chase answered, making a valid point.

At first, Siren was quiet; then, she became angry again. After a quick thought, she imposed her energetic power on Aiden's family, forcing them to continue walking. She replied, "Any more mouth out of either of you, and I'll shut you up permanently."

Siren led Sasha and Chase to a super high-end commercial building. It was the tallest building in the city and was a landmark shown in movies and commercials. A jewelry store that owns the largest diamond known to exist is located on the top floor. The bad news for the trio was the building had 84 floors, and the elevator was not working. They began walking up the stairs. Sasha could only assume Siren was heading to the top floor as they climbed each flight. This gave her time to figure out an escape.

"Why the heck are we here? What does she want?" thought Sasha, then she whispered to her son, "When I say go, you run in the direction I tell you. Okay?"

Chase made a confused face at his mom, followed by a nervous nod. Sasha was waiting for a chance to make a run for it, but there hadn't been one yet. Siren was keeping them too close. Sasha had to be patient as they went up and up the stairs. There was nothing she could do right now. It seemed like they had been going up the stairs forever. They were sweating profusely from the stress combined with strenuous exercise. Even though Chase was hanging in there, he had about enough and reeled over in exhaustion.

"We need a break," huffed Sasha.

"No, keep going!" barked Siren.

As if the building was in agreement with Sasha, they came onto a section that forced them to stop. There was a large hole in the wall and debris obstructing the stairs. It was an exterior wall. Beyond the hole was a sheer drop outside of the building.

Siren, Sasha, and Chase stood in the middle of a flight of stairs. The huge gaping hole in the wall was about ten feet in diameter. It was also at the same spot they had to cross the debris. The hole in the wall was broken lower than the stairs themselves, so there was nothing to hold onto when they crossed. They could easily fall out of the building to their death. Sasha peeked out of the hole and saw how high they were.

"Oh...my...God!" Sasha said to herself in complete and utter terror. The trio had gone almost to the top of the building and was literally about 80 floors high.

Siren started to cross unexpectedly, pulling the other two with her.

Sasha yelled, "Wait, hold on!" She lost her balance and almost fell out of the hole.

"You're slowing me down, human," Siren complained.

Sasha grabbed Chase's hand tightly and whispered, "Get ready."

When Sasha lost her balance, she felt Siren's energetic grasp on them slightly weaken as they became further apart. Sasha was now more confident about making her move, and this was a perfect time. Siren started crossing the debris and concrete again while Sasha and Chase followed. All three slowly took steps trying to move forward safely. Chase stepped on loose rubble, and his foot slipped. He started sliding out of the hole.

"No! I got you!" panicked Sasha.

Sasha barely caught hold of Chase's arm. He looked at his Mom with terror in his eyes while half of his body dangled eighty floors up. He tried to grip the wall with his feet, but they kept sliding. Chase's arm began slipping from Sasha's grasp. The boy lifted his leg and found a place to plant his foot. He pushed up with everything he had and fell to his stomach back inside the building.

"Don't ever do that again," Sasha said to her son, exhausted but relieved.

"I promise I won't," Chase replied, breathing heavily.

Sasha looked over at Siren and saw she was pretty far away. She urgently turned to Chase and told him, "Go now! Go!"

Chase looked at his mom for a second. She pushed him the other way, telling him again, "Go!"

The incident had created some extra distance between them and Siren, causing Siren's grasp to weaken. Sasha redirected her attention to Siren and yelled, "Oh no!"

Sasha jerked Siren, acting like she was falling out of the building. She was trying to force her way back to the other side of the debris where they started. Siren was caught by surprise. Sasha felt the momentum, so she drove her legs as hard as possible, trying to make it. The momentum flipped Siren over a chunk of concrete. She rolled out of the hole, pulling Sasha and Chase with her. Chase had widened the gap between him and the evil Druid, but the hold Siren had on him was too strong and pulled him back. Sasha and Chase stopped themselves by grabbing the edge of the broken concrete wall and bracing themselves. Siren dangled out of the hole.

The two humans struggled to hold onto the wall as there was nothing to grab. Their hands continued to slide. Chase wasn't sure what to do next. He looked to his mom for some direction.

"You sly wench!" exclaimed Siren, trying to pull herself up.

The dark sorceress didn't have time to feel embarrassed since she was suddenly in a dire situation. She couldn't pull on her prisoners too hard because it could break the grasp she had on them, sending her falling to her death. At this point, Siren realized she had to let go of the two she held captive. She released her grasp and grabbed the side of the building. Clenching with her fingertips, the evil Druid climbed her way up the cracks in the building. She pulled herself up over the ledge, and Sasha and Chase were gone. Fortunately, she heard the click of the door closing at the bottom of the stairs. Siren's first instinct was to chase after them. She didn't because she heard a buzz. The compass she had was vibrating and pointing up the stairs. Siren thought briefly, aching to chase after them, then shook her head in disgust. She looked down at the door Aiden's family went through and shot it with a small energy blast that melded the door frame and door together. The evil Druid appeared pleased with this. She turned, climbed back over the rest of the debris, and went up the stairs.

Dunagan's Lost Love

Back in the war room, Dunagan asked, "What in the Sam hell was that?" He stared blankly at Aiden, waiting for a response.

Aiden shrugged his shoulders, "I don't know."

"Seriously, Aiden, how did you do that?" Dunagan insisted, "You have powers like these guys? I knew you were a skilled marine, but what the fuck was that? I mean, it was awesome, but wow! You annihilated the entire army!"

Aiden thought for a second, then replied solemnly, "I guess I did, but I didn't save my family."

"They're not dead, Aiden. We're going to go get them," Dunagan reassured again, "Stay here and rest a minute. I'll set up a rescue team."

Dungan left for a few moments and came back. He prompted, "Aiden, we're set to go. You ready?" Aiden held his head down and didn't reply.

Dunagan knew Aiden was feeling depressed. He took a moment to think, then spoke up, "On my first tour in Yemen, I met a gorgeous local girl one night when the guys and I went out. She had the most beautiful eyes, and after that night, we started seeing each other. I would sneak out late to be with her. Sometimes, I would even sneak her onto the base. After only a few months, we had fallen deeply in love, so I planned to leave the military and stay with her. My tour was ending in days when we were attacked. A convoy traveling with the U.S. ambassador came under siege. When we arrived, the convoy had dropped back behind some buildings while protecting the ambassador, so we flanked those assholes. I saw my love kneeling over her father on the street corner during the fight. He had been shot and was dying in her arms. One of those damn terrorists shot him. The same asshole ran out and yanked her off the ground. He was cornered, so he held her at gunpoint, trying to escape. We couldn't take a shot, and the guy ended up getting away with her. I thought she was dead, for sure. It took us months to locate her. Somehow, she got online and sent me a message, setting up a rescue mission. We saved many lives on that mission, but in the end, that beautiful woman gave her life to save others. She was a good person. That's why I loved her."

Dunagan wiped a tear and placed his arm on Aiden's shoulder while continuing to talk, "Even though she died, we wouldn't have saved the others if it wasn't for her. My point is, we can't lose hope. There's a good chance they're still alive, and we can't save them if we don't try. We can't do any good by doing nothing."

Aiden looked up at Dunagan with tears in his eyes. He asked, "What makes you think they're alive? You saw what happened."

The General stared back at him, "They were in that ball forcefield thing, and I don't think Magus was trying to sacrifice one of his leaders. He had her protecting your family for some reason."

After a quick thought, Aiden seemed to agree with Dunagan and gave him a nod. He got up and confidently said, "Let's go kick some ass!"

The Master Aire Gem

There was a sceptre forged in the depths of the mountains on Legends created for the sole purpose of wielding the Master Aire gem. The Prophecy of Weapons describes this scepter as being used for both good and bad. Once combined with this gem, the sceptre will become one of the most powerful weapons a Mystic can use.

Magus had acquired this scepter many years ago and carried it with him. While he traveled to this location, he accumulated more soldiers. When he arrived at his destination...the building Siren was in, he placed a large group of soldiers, including a Gorger, on guard at the building entrance. He then made his way up the stairs. At the top, he ran into Siren.

"Where are the other two?" Magus snarled, demanding to know.

Siren looked disappointed in herself and replied, "They got away. They're a few floors down."

Magus lit his hand up white and held it in front of Siren's face, "You failed me," he said in a grumbling voice.

"We have the Master Aire!" Siren pleaded.

Magus growled, then grabbed her and pulled her close. He instructed, "We will go back for them. Where is the gem?"

Siren reached inside her bag and pulled out the most significant diamond known to exist.

"Aww, yes!" Magus spoke, relishing its beauty.

The Master Aire gem shone brightly when Magus touched it. He pulled the sceptre out and held it near the gem. Immediately, the Master Aire began to float next to the sceptre, then flashed blindingly. It was so bright the evil sorcerer had to close his eyes. When he opened them, he saw the Master Aire had attached itself inside the sceptre, where it fit perfectly.

Pursuing Magus

"We've tracked them to this building, sir," informed Sherri as they rode in a military Hummer. Sherri continued, "It looks like they have a unit waiting by the entrance to ambush us. There's also one of those huge creatures."

"You mean one of those big ogres? Awesome!" Aiden added sarcastically. He looked over to see who was talking and saw it was Sherri. "Hey, there you are! Glad you could make it!" he told her.

"Yeah, me, too! We must save that family of yours! You ready?" Sherri asked confidently.

"Yes, ma'am! And it looks like you are, too. Hoorah!" Aiden replied.

"Hoorah!" everyone in the Hummer replied simultaneously.

There were only twelve in total who came on the mission. The entire team had loaded up in two Humvees. Each Humvee had 50 cal artillery on top and a gunner manning the artillery.

Sherri spoke again, "We're coming up to it. Brace yourselves."

"Ready, boys! Coming in hot!" yelled Dunagan.

The Humvees slid to a stop, sideways, not far from the front of the building. The team sprayed the area with bullets from the 50 cals and their machine guns. Surprisingly, no one, not even the Gorger, was anywhere in sight. The team stopped shooting, and it became tranquil.

Nothing was moving, nor could be heard until Aiden's phone went off. His ringtone was a recording of himself singing, "Bow chicka bow chicka bow chicka bow wow, chicka bow chicka bow chicka bow wow." Everyone in the Humvee looked over at Aiden and laughed.

"It's my wife," Aiden blurted out, "Hellooo? Honey? Are you the...?"

Aiden was cut off by Sasha, "Oh, thank God! We're trapped on the 80th floor of some building. We got away, but Siren did something to the door, and we're stuck."

Aiden was a bit frantic, responding, "Um, that's good! Kind of, I mean. Anyway, we're outside of the building right now! Are you okay? I'm coming to get you!"

"Yes, yes, we're okay!" she replied, "Just come get us! Oh crap, what was that?"

Aiden heard some banging in the background.

"Crap, they're here! Quick, we gotta hide! Over here! I... I love you," she said, then the phone sounded like it hit the ground.

The team heard, "Rraaaahhhhh!" and a THUD, THUD, THUMP. The Humvee was shaking. Aiden looked up and saw the Gorger running full speed at them.

"Oh, shit! Where did that thing come from?" exclaimed Sherri.

The artillerymen swiftly aimed and began firing at the Gorger. The rest of Magus' army showed themselves and started shooting. With bullets ricocheting all around, the Marines aimed through the Humvee windows and returned fire.

The Gorger wore heavy armor, custom-made from metal. Its armor provided good protection, even from the 50 cal bullets, but not total protection. Absorbing many bullet wounds, the Gorger pressed forward. It grabbed Aiden and Dunagan's Humvee and threw it to the side.

The other Humvee began driving away, still shooting at the Gorger. It nailed the beast with a headshot from the 50 cal. The Gorger's head kicked backward, its knees buckled, and it fell to the ground. Taking heavy fire, the Hummer sped off into the distance.

Aiden and Dunagan's Hummer flew through the air. It hit the ground and began flipping. A team member was slung halfway out of the window while the vehicle flipped. The Humvee hit its side and crushed a soldier, flipped a few more times and landed upside down on the roof. It lay upside down, taking heavy fire. Everyone climbed out on the opposite side from where the shots were coming, using the flipped Humvee as cover.

"Shit! Shit! We need that other Humvee!" Dunagan announced. As he did so, the other Hummer made a U-turn and headed back toward them.

CHING, CHING, PEWWW came the sound of bullets bouncing and whizzing by. The military team returned fire. They took out a few Devians as the Humvee pulled up. It was shooting the 50 cal, BAMM, BAMM.

"Keep your heads down!" Captain Dunagan hollered while the 50 cal took out a few more Devians and a Hairy.

"I've got to get in that building!" Aiden yelled to Dunagan over the battle noise.

Dunagan yelled back, "Go ahead! We'll cover! Get ready!" he turned and shouted to the team, "Squad, cover fire ready?"

The team answered, "Yes, sir!"

Dunagan continued, "Good! Readyyyy...fire!" The entire team sprayed bullets at the enemy.

Aiden didn't hesitate. He ran toward the entrance doors. He was almost there when a Devian jumped at him. It swung its sword. Aiden dodged to the left, and it missed. He pulled his Glock 21 and shot the creature in the head. He looked around and didn't see anyone else, then ran a few more steps and entered the building.

Hiding From Evil

Magus looked at Siren and praised her, "Good girl," then kissed her lips. "Now, we have to find and kill that pesky woman and child," he continued, "Lead the way." He held his arm out, prompting Siren to take the lead.

The two villains went down a few floors, climbing over the blockage on the stairs, and made it to the door which Siren had melded together.

"Excuse me," Magus said, nudging Siren out of the way.

Magus readied his stance and stomp-kicked the door. The door barely budged, and he snarled. He lit up his hands, white, to blast the door.

"Allow a lady's touch," Siren said, nudging Magus out of the way.

Siren put her green glowing hands on the melded part of the door and separated it. She turned the doorknob, opened the door, and they went in.

Siren and Magus didn't see anyone. This floor was reasonably large. It had an open layout with many office cubicles and workstations. There were probably a hundred employees working here at any one time. There were also small private offices and a hallway, which separated the large open area from the administrative offices. The exterior wall, facing the direction of the battle down below, had various-sized holes and broken windows.

"Yoohoooo! Come out, come out! Don't be shy. We want to slowly torture you until you tell us about your husband," Siren tormented with a smirk.

Sasha and Chase hid behind a desk in one of the private rooms. Sasha prayed the evil duo wouldn't find them.

Magus and Siren searched the open area, tipping over desks and throwing chairs. Magus shot an energy blast out of the sceptre into one of the private rooms. It annihilated everything inside. "Come out, you two pains in the asses," he scorned, becoming annoyed.

The two villains were getting close to the room where Sasha and Chase were hiding. Sasha pulled her knife. She waited, hoping they would walk past.

Magus destroyed another private room, the one right next to Sasha and Chase. Sasha had no choice. She bolted out from behind the desk and lunged at Siren with the knife. Siren blocked Sasha's attack in the nick of time, stopping the blade right in front of her eye. Siren twisted and threw Sasha over a desk. Sasha rolled, got to her feet, and kicked a trash can at Siren. Magus watched in amusement. Sasha ran at Siren, attacking with the knife again. Siren countered with a back-sweep kick. She tripped Sasha, slamming her onto the carpet-covered concrete floor. The knife flew out of Sasha's hand. Chase popped out from behind the desk and threw his knife. The knife stuck Siren in her back.

"Oowwwwww! You little shit!" Siren retorted. She yanked the knife out from her back. "I've had enough of this!" the Druidess rebuked and stuck Sasha in the quad with Chase's knife. It penetrated to the bone.

"Aaahhhhhh!" Sasha cried in pain.

"Come out here, boy, or she'll make it worse," Magus demanded.

Chase looked at Siren with her hand still on the knife. She began wiggling it back and forth.

"Aaahhhhh! Oowwwww!" Sasha cried again, beginning to hyperventilate.

Chase couldn't watch this anymore. He walked out of the office, allowing Magus to grab him by the back of the shirt.

"Good. Now, where were we? Hmmm, oh yeah. Tell me about that annoying husband of yours," ordered Magus, leering at Sasha while he gripped her son tightly.

Savoring the moment, Siren pressed down hard on the knife. Sasha screamed in pain again.

Aiden ran to the elevator only to find it out of order, then ran to find the stairs and sighed when he saw the sign that said 84 floors, "Are you kidding me!" he said aloud. He ran up the stairs as fast as he could. After 15 minutes, he was exhausted and sweating profusely, but he didn't stop until he was forced to by the debris blocking the stairs. Then he heard a scream from behind him, causing him to look back. He saw the sign next to the door that read "Floor 80." That's the floor Sasha was on.

"Oh no!" he reacted, fearing the worst. He turned and ran through the door.

Explosion

Just as Dunagan thought they were starting to get an edge, another Gorger and a Grandar appeared, jogging toward them from down the block. The Gorger was carrying a missile launcher.

"Grenades! Get the grenades!" Dunagan called out.

One of the soldiers answered, "Got it!"

The soldier ran to the back of the Hummer to find the box of grenades. He looked through the broken window and saw the box tipped over. The grenades were scattered all around. He reached through and grabbed two that were close enough.

THUD, THUD, THUMP, the Gorger, and Grandar were getting closer. The soldier pulled the pins and threw both grenades. The grenades landed in front of the giant creatures and exploded, knocking the Grandar down. The Gorger took a few steps back, dropping the missile launcher, and cried out in pain. The Grandar rolled over and saw something flying through the air, shooting at its comrades. It got to its feet, picked up the missile launcher, aimed, and launched a missile at whatever it was.

The soldier had gone back to grab more grenades. He was about to throw them when he noticed the Grandar launching a missile at a jet. The missile nailed the jet. It exploded, spewing jet fuel, aluminum, steel, and titanium everywhere.

"Take cover!" warned Dunagan.

Aiden's Family

As he walked through the door, Aiden saw his son standing alone, crying.

"Dad! Mom's hurt!" Chase whimpered.

Aiden ran to him in a panic, "What! Where is she? What happened? Are you okay?"

"I'm okay, but I don't know about Mom! She's over there!" Chase answered, pointing in her direction.

At the same time, loud explosions erupted from down below. Aiden looked out the window. Two grenades had gone off next to a Gorger and Grandar, and a jet was shooting at Magus' army. Unfortunately, as soon as he saw the jet, it exploded in mid-air. Weirdly enough, Aiden felt a strong sense of déjà vu, like he had seen this before.

Chase screamed and ran off to another room. Aiden followed, hoping his son was leading him to his wife. He ran around a corner, and there she was. Sasha lay on the floor with her leg wounded.

"Hey, handsome! Thought you'd never make it," Sasha confessed. She looked concerned, yet confident, in her mysterious way.

"Hi, honey! Oh, we both know who the good-looking one is here," Aiden teased and continued, "How do you feel? What happened?"

"Siren stabbed me in the leg. I'm okay, but I can't walk very well," Sasha confided.

Aiden looked at Sasha's injury and saw the bleeding had almost stopped, which meant she didn't have any severed arteries. He told her, "It looks okay. I'm still worried, but I feel better."

Aiden took in a deep breath and let it back out, then wiped the sweat off his brow. He was relieved that his wife didn't appear seriously injured. He ripped a piece of his shirt off and tied it around her wound. After a moment, he urged, "We've got to get you guys out of here! Come on. I'll help you up! Let's go!"

Aiden began helping Sasha to her feet when from behind him, he heard, "Not so fast, Mr. Hero. It looks like you're in a bit of a pickle."

It was Siren speaking as she and Magus stepped out from behind a wall in one of the administrative offices.

"You stabbed my wife! I'm going to kill you! You know that, right?" Aiden replied in controlled anger.

Siren smiled and responded, "Your family is tough. They surprisingly put up a good fight, and your wife wouldn't break. She wouldn't say a word about you. I was not expecting that. I was not expecting humans to be so...," Siren hesitated, "honorable. They are such a fragile species with no abilities. They only have the weapons they create. I must admit some are very powerful, but none more powerful than us," Siren continued speaking in a conniving tone, "Aiden, tell me, where did you come from?" Siren's hands lit up green after she asked this.

"I honestly don't know," Aiden reluctantly answered, "I was a foster child. That's all I know."

"You must know more than that," Siren replied.

Siren threw a green streak of energy across the room. It grabbed Sasha's face and started squeezing. Grimacing in pain, Sasha noticed the green energy smelled like dirt and thought that was strange.

"I'm telling you the truth. That's all I know. Now, let her go!" Aiden yelled, becoming unsettled.

"Pull your pants down and turn around," demanded Siren, ignoring Aiden's threatening nature.

"What!" Aiden retorted, taken back by the odd request.

Siren squeezed harder on Sasha's face, making her groan in pain.

"Okay, okay, here!" Aiden responded.

Aiden pulled down his jeans and turned around. There was a barely audible gasp from Siren. Magus squinted his eyes in his own vexed denial. Aiden had the mark mentioned in the Prophecy of Heroes.

Aiden turned his head slightly and saw the scepter light up. He quickly dropped to the ground avoiding the blast from Magus. The white energy whizzed over Aiden's head, blowing out the exterior wall and leaving a gaping hole. Siren wore a ring. It began shining bright green. Aiden noticed the ring and realized this must be her power supply. Aiden felt power beginning to pulsate through his body. Magus attacked with the sceptre again. Aiden activated a blue energy shield which caused the white blast to ricochet back toward the villains. The explosion nailed the evil sorcerers and sent them crashing through the offices behind them. This released Sasha from Siren's grasp. Sasha lost her balance and fell into a chair. Siren pulled herself out of the desk under which she was buried, smirked at Sasha, then flung an energy dart at her. The dart hit Sasha's chest, pierced through her body, and exited out the backside of the chair. Aiden wasn't sure what happened and looked over at Sasha. She coughed up blood and reeled over.

"Noooooooo!" Aiden shrieked in horror. He ran over to his wife and grabbed her.

Many of the beautiful moments Aiden had with Sasha flashed before his eyes: their first date at Chili's when she didn't realize she had queso all over her face; the first time he looked into her eyes and knew he loved her; the day of their marriage; the birth of Chase; and the day they reconciled after almost getting a divorce. Aiden was speechless as Sasha lay in his arms, gasping for air. "Hon..." coughing blood, "Hon-ey, I-I I luv..." Sasha struggled to talk.

Tearing, Aiden found his voice and spoke softly, "It's okay. I know. I know. I love you, too, so much. You're going to be okay. Honey, you're going to be okay. I'm so sorry this happened."

Quietly crying, Aiden embraced his wife. Chase was sobbing. He was distraught.

Sasha was trying to say something, so Aiden placed his ear close to her mouth, "Take goo...ood care of him. You proommm-isse me. Waaatch after our boy."

"I promise, but we're going to do that together. Okay," Aiden replied confidently, wanting Sasha to will herself to live.

Sasha smiled and placed her hand on Aiden's cheek. She looked back at him and then her son. She told them, "I love you both, and I wiii...." She coughed again. Blood dripped from her mouth. Aiden wiped it with his thumb, and she continued, "And I will always be with you."

After these words, Sasha let out her last breath. Aiden felt her body become limp and lifeless.

"Nooo! God, noooo!" Aiden said under his breath. He knew his wife was gone, and he was devastated.

Magus immediately snatched Aiden up into the air with a streak of lightning. Aiden was convulsing from the electric charge while floating in the air. Magus led Aiden to the gaping hole in the wall. Aiden tried fighting but couldn't. Magus brought Aiden to a stop, right at the hole's edge.

"This is the end for you and your family, Mr. Hero," Magus told his nemesis.

Magus' unused hand lit up in white light. He reared back and punched Aiden in the stomach with incredible strength. Aiden flew out of the building from eighty floors up.

Aiden saw Siren throwing Chase to the ground and then saw nothing but the side of the building. He closed his eyes, hoping this wasn't the end but knew it, inevitably, had to be. Then blacked out. When he opened his eyes, it felt like he was lying on the ground. In the distance, he saw the floor from which he fell explode and a helicopter flying from the roof. Big chunks of concrete and rebar fell straight at him from hundreds of feet above. Aiden closed his eyes again, not sure what to think at this point.

Under the Rubble

"He's somewhere under here! He was right in this area when all this crap came down! I don't know how he could have survived, but I saw that blue light again!" said a muffled voice.

Another replied, "I don't care! I'm not giving up until we find the body!"

The second voice sounded like Dunagan.

"Here! I'm right here!" Aiden shouted. He coughed and surprisingly didn't feel any pain. He kept calling for help, "I'm here, guys!"

"There, you hear that? How in the hell? Aiden, we hear you! We're gonna get you outta there! Can you believe it? He's alive!" the General said ecstatically.

"That's incredible! Um, one problem, sir. How are we gonna move this concrete?" asked the other voice, who Aiden now recognized. It was Sherri.

Aiden tried to concentrate and hoped to move the concrete with his new-found powers, but nothing happened. Wondering why, he thought, "Why can I only use my powers when I'm about to die?"

"Yes, great idea! Get it going!" Dunagan responded to somebody.

After about twenty minutes, Aiden heard heavy machinery. Luckily, there was a crane in the area and a soldier who knew how to operate it. The crane lifted the concrete, one piece at a time, until miraculously, Aiden was free.

Dunagan glanced at the pile of concrete and all the sharp rebar jutting out as Aiden stood up. "Um, well, soooo, would you like to tell me how in the hell you survived falling around 800 feet and being crushed by tons of deadly concrete skewers?" Dunagan asked with an unbelievable look on his face.

Still knocking the concrete dust off his shoulders, Aiden answered, "Um, I, I don't know, Captain. I don't know," Aiden changed the subject to more pressing matters, "Did you guys track that helicopter?"

"What? Helicopter?" Dunagan reacted, surprised.

"Yea, I saw a helicopter fly away when the building exploded," Aiden continued. "My boy," his eyes welled up while he was talking, "I made a promise, but now he's dead, too."

Dunagan stood silent, giving Aiden a moment. Aiden took a breath and tried to collect himself. The last images he saw of his wife and son flashed in front of his eyes; Sasha's head was leaning over, lifeless in his hands, and Siren throwing Chase to the ground.

"Aaaaahhhhhhhh!" Aiden screamed in anger at the top of his lungs, then turned to Dunagan, "I need a helicopter."

Captain Dunagan held up a walkie-talkie and ordered, "Bring over the chopper," then looked over at Aiden and said, "I'm coming with you." Dunagan held up the walkie again, "Did anyone track the chopper that flew from the building?"

The walkie chimed back, "Yes, sir. It's heading to the canyons."

A few minutes later, a helicopter landed by Aiden and Dunagan.

Aiden looked solemnly at the General and spoke, "You don't have to come with me. I don't think I'll be coming back. You shouldn't come."

"Aiden," Dunagan replied, "Don't even try to give me that crap. I thought I saw your certain death and, yet you're here in front of me, breathing, clear as day. I can't explain it, but I know it's something special. There is no way in hell I'm going to watch you get on that chopper and fly away to what might be your second, maybe even third, death of the day. I made that mistake with Danny, and it won't happen again."

Aiden asked, "You saw another soldier die more than once?"

"Huh, no, no, that part's new," Dunagan replied, smiling at the question, "I let the team split up in Yemen and lost the other half. Danny was with them. I'll never make that mistake again."

Aiden thought for a second, then responded, "Okay, Captain! Let's go get 'em!"

Seeking Vengeance

"Dozer, Pecko, Whiz kid, Sherri, you two," Dunagan called out, pointing at two other soldiers, "In the chopper. You're on save the world duty." The group of eight got in the helicopter and flew off toward the location where Magus landed. Pecko was the pilot.

Magus' helicopter landed in an extremely isolated spot in the canyons. There weren't any marked trails for miles around. Whiz Kid, the technology expert, tried to research the area but couldn't find much information. The only data Whiz Kid found was about an archeological site abandoned because of some mysterious deaths back in the 60s. The site was featured in an article describing archeology, aliens, and ancient areas that are potentially stargates.

"Listen up!" the General yelled over the sound of the helicopter, "We're almost there. We will land a few miles away, so they don't hear us. The thermal scan shows about thirty bodies. I've called in an airstrike. We'll be on the ground to clean up the stragglers. Get ready to save the world, boys and girls." He looked over at Aiden and yelled, "Hoorah!"

The whole group hollered, "Hoorah!"

Pecko set the chopper down in a clearing a couple of miles from Magus' location. The group exited the helicopter and hustled toward their target. They were armed with M4 Carbines, M16s, M27s, and Aiden's custom 6.5 Grendel. After traveling a mile or so, Dunagan stopped the team to wait for the airstrike. They all heard jets and looked up. Three F-35s impressively zoomed by and dropped bombs.

The team had reached the top of a canyon where they had a good view of the land. The bombs appeared to hit a small circular valley surrounded by cliffs. Thunderous explosions and fire flew up from the valley. The fleet of jets doubled back and bombed the area one more time. Again, there were numerous fiery explosions, throwing earth everywhere. Landslides and large boulders fell into the gorge. Oddly, the landslides stopped partway down the cliffs. A huge boulder sat in plain view, seeming to float above the valley.

"Do you guys see that?" Dozer asked, bewildered as the dust cleared.

Aiden looked closer and saw a green barrier holding up the boulder and dirt. "Siren," he said aloud to himself, then turned to the others, "I'm afraid the airstrike didn't do a thing."

"Damn it," Dunagan responded, disappointed, "Move forward, soldiers. We've got work to do."

Aiden, Dunagan, and the team found a small path that worked its way down and through the cliffs into the circular valley. They snuck up on Magus and his remaining small army as the foul creatures performed a ritual. The military team took cover to see what was happening. They saw the evil army positioned behind Magus, standing in front of a cliff wall. Siren was standing to the left of Magus, projecting the energy barrier that was holding the boulders and dirt in place overhead. The barrier was preventing thousands of pounds of earth from crushing everyone.

A door shape was cut out of the cliff wall where Magus stood in front. Inside the door shape at waist height was an indention with odd markings. Magus finished chanting the ritual and pulled out a decorative medallion he placed in the indention. He took a step back and blasted the medallion with white energy. The medallion began to glow, and the solid rock doorway started to move and fluctuate. CRACKLE, BUZZ, the door made loud electronic sounds, then flashed brightly. The solid rock wall shifted into a blue transparent screen.

"Whoa, a stargate!" Whiz Kid said, in awe.

There was a silhouette of three creatures on the other side of the screen. The creatures appeared to be close. Amazingly, Regin and two similar-looking giant Grandars emerged through the stargate.

Aiden stood up and tried to run at Magus, but Dunagan grabbed him and held him back.

"Wait," remarked the General, "I have an idea," Dunagan beeped the walkie, "Round two, it's a go for round two."

"Those wretched humans are right behind us. I want you to stay and kill them," Magus told Regin.

"You got it, boss," replied Regin, then asked, "What about the Prophecy?"

"He's dead," Magus sneered.

Immediately after Magus said this, bombs hit the barrier Siren still held. Dunagan saw her grimace as she struggled to maintain it. There was a loud crash as an extra load of dirt and boulders fell on it.

"Again! Again!" commanded Dunagan into the walkie.

More bombs hit the barrier, causing it to flutter and drop dirt and rocks into the valley. Siren screamed in agony as she fell to her knees. Her ring shone brightly, and more bombs exploded. Dirt and rocks were falling in all directions. The barrier fluttered more rapidly. Siren regained control and stood up. The tough fast-thinking Druidess blasted a web of rays up toward the barrier. She maneuvered her blast around the barrier and across all the dirt, rocks, and boulders. At this point, the dirt had accumulated and spread over the entire distance of the valley, from cliff-to-cliff. The dirt and rock melded together. It solidified, creating a dirt/rock ceiling. Siren released the barrier and fell back on her butt, exhausted.

"Son-of-a-bitch! This isn't real!" exclaimed Dunagan.

"What in the hell was that?" Dozer stammered.

"That's impossible!" added Sherri.

Aiden had become numb to these types of crazy events and didn't even react. He simply stood up and unloaded his clip at Magus.

Magus, Regin, and the two Grandars, who must be brothers, were standing in front of the stargate when bullets sprayed in their direction. Magus sensed the shots coming and stopped them in mid-air.

Aiden kept shooting, yelling at the top of his lungs, "Aaaaahhhhh!"

Each bullet stopped inches in front of the targets. Aiden's gun started clicking. It was out of ammo. He dropped the gun and watched as his entire clip of bullets floated in front of the evil creatures. Magus held his hands up in front of him, continuing to hold the bullets in the air. He leered at Aiden in disgust, recognizing he wasn't dead.

"Aiiddeeennnn!" Magus scorned. He brought his hands inward close to his chest.

"Get down!" Aiden warned.

Aiden tackled Whiz Kid, who had been standing out in the open. The rest of the group took cover. Magus threw his hands outward, flinging the bullets back in their direction. Bullets ricocheted every which way off the rocks, dirt, and cliff walls.

Aiden looked at Whiz Kid and asked, "You alright?" She nodded her head.

Aiden glanced over at Dunagan, who was about thirty feet away. The General was doing a silent headcount. He looked grim and signed, "Man down, over there," he pointed over to where Pecko was. Pecko was laid up behind a rock, clutching at his stomach.

"Shit!" Aiden cursed under his breath.

Dunagan signed again, "We need cover fire. On three. One, Two, Three!"

Aiden, Dozer, Sherri, and the other two soldiers sprayed cover fire. At the same time, Magus commanded the creatures to attack.

"Kill them all!" ordered Magus.

The evil army charged. A hail of gunfire mowed down the front row of Devians and Hairies. The remaining creatures quickly changed their strategy and ducked behind some boulders. They returned fire.

Dunagan and Whiz Kid made it to Pecko, who was frantic and gasping for air.

"I'm gonna die! I'm gonna die! Tell my mom I love her! Tell everyone I love them!" he pleaded.

"Hold on, let me see," Dunagan said in a calm voice, "Whizzy here is also a trained nurse."

"Give me your hand. I know it hurts, but you gotta let us see," Whiz Kid spoke empathetically.

"Okay, okay, but if it's bad, shoot me in the head," Pecko responded thoughtfully.

Dunagan and Whizzy looked at each other with concern. Then Whiz Kid raised Pecko's shirt so that they could look at the wound. It was only a scratch, a deep scratch but not life-threatening.

Dunagan smirked, "Son, is this the first time you've been shot?"

"Huh! What? Why?" Pecko frantically asked, looking confused.

Whizzy giggled, then informed, "It barely grazed you. You're going to be fine. It is bleeding a lot, though." She tore Pecko's shirt sleeve and said, "Hold on, this is going to hurt."

"Wait! What? What do you mean?" Pecko reacted, not knowing what was going on. "Rrrrrrrrhhh!" he groaned as Whiz Kid pressed the cloth down on his injury.

"Here, keep pressure on this," Whizzy instructed, ignoring the injured man's anxieties.

Meanwhile, the rest of the team continued in the heated gunfight. Shots were flying back and forth, and bullets were ricocheting everywhere.

"What should we do, boss?" Regin asked Magus arrogantly as if to say, "You want me to take care of this?"

Magus looked over at Siren, who was still winded, then looked up at the dirt/rock ceiling and replied, "Don't waste your energy. I have a plan. Go back through the portal."

Magus turned and pushed something he had hidden in his robe through the portal. Then he grabbed the necklace from Siren and shot a blast of energy into the ceiling. It began shaking and rumbling, dropping bits of sediment and rocks. The two Grandars saw what was happening. They glanced at each other with facial expressions that said, "It's time to go!" then ran through the portal.

Regin calmly motioned for Siren to exit, suggesting, "Ladies first." The evil Druidess accepted the invitation and walked through the portal. Regin followed.

Dunagan and his crew heard rumbling and cracking overhead and looked up. They were terrified by what they saw. Thousands of pounds of earth and rock were coming apart and on the verge of falling and crushing them to certain death.

CRACK, CRACK, BOOM! The ceiling came tumbling down. Magus walked through the portal with a wicked grin. He knew there was no way in hell Aiden would survive this time.

Time slowed down for Aiden. He looked at the two soldiers. He didn't even know their names. Their faces were horrified. They seemed to realize this was the end. He looked over at Dunagan. The General confidently saluted him, giving his respect before the inevitable happened. Aiden returned a heartfelt salute, also thinking he was about to die. While saluting, he noticed his hand was flashing blue. Aiden brought his hand down and realized Dunagan was still saluting him. For some reason, the dirt and rocks hadn't crushed them yet. He looked up and saw the entire ceiling falling at a sluggish pace.

"Time does slow down," Aiden thought and glanced back at his comrades.

Pecko and Whizzy were holding each other as they ducked behind a boulder. Dozer's eyes closed, and he held onto the cross on his neck chain. Sherri was still shooting at the enemies, fighting until her last breath. The two other soldiers had begun to run, trying to get to cover. Dunagan was finally bringing down his salute.

Aiden quickly looked over at Magus and noticed he was only halfway through the stargate. The Necklace of Herana, curiously, was shining brightly in his hand. Aiden set down his 6.5 Grendel, knowing a swinging gun would hinder what he needed to do. Instinctively, he ran at a fantastic speed and grabbed each team member, throwing them out of harm's way onto the path by which they entered. His leg scraped across a boulder and ripped his Glock from him. He turned and saw the portal was on the verge of closing. He bolted as fast as he could. Undetected, Aiden zipped by Magus as the evil sorcerer's foot exited the portal. The stargate closed. Thousands of pounds of dirt and rock crashed to the ground on Earth's side. The villains on Legends cheered in celebration.

Part 3

A New World

Farley and Priya

Aiden kept running. He had no idea where he was. The air smelled rich and refreshing. The sun was warm on his skin. He heard familiar sounds of chirping birds, howling monkeys, squeaking frogs, chattering prairie dogs, the bugle of an elk, and even the roar of a large cat. When he smelled moisture in the air, he stopped running and looked around. He was hovering over a lake. "Crap!" he said to himself and, instantly, fell in the water.

Aiden swam out of the lake and looked around. In his entire life, he'd never seen any place more beautiful. It was amazing how crisp and pure each breath felt. "Wherever this is, there is no air pollution," he muttered.

Aiden could see he was in a forest area. Green trees, bushes, and overgrown grass surrounded the lake. Out of the corner of his eye, he saw movement behind a bush.

"What the..." Aiden said, not sure if he saw anything. Not wanting to alert the potential enemy, he never looked in the direction of the movement and only watched the bush with his peripherals. He saw nothing, so he casually walked the other direction into the trees, acting like he was foraging. As soon as he was sure that whatever was behind the bush couldn't see him, Aiden circled to the other side of it. He couldn't believe what he saw.

"Holy crap!" he whispered to himself, "What in the world is that?"

Hiding behind the bush was a small creature that couldn't have been over three feet tall. The little creature was human-like but covered in red fur. It was wagging its cute red furry little tail in the air as it energetically looked for the human it saw running across the water.

"It looks like a small furry leprechaun," Aiden joked to himself.

The creature was an Evo, short for evolutionary. Evos can absorb energy from this world and replenish gemstones when they run low on power, like charging a battery. The Prophecy of Heroes describes how Evos are responsible for creating the race of Mystics.

"Oh, come on, Farley! Where did he go? How did you lose him, Farley?" the creature mumbled.

It looked as if Aiden wasn't the only one talking to himself. Slightly taken back, Aiden contemplated the believability of this animalish-looking creature talking. He told himself, "Well, I guess animals are talking now, too."

Aiden, obnoxiously, cleared his throat, "Ehhmmm."

Farley jumped in the air, startled, gasping in surprise. He landed and turned with impressive quickness.

"Farley, is it?" Aiden asked.

The furry creature dropped to the ground and covered his head, begging, "No, don't hurt me! I come in peace! I am a peaceful being!" Realizing how weak he appeared, he quickly stood up and lowered his voice, faking confidence, "Or, am I? I have the power to crush you."

Farley pointed at Aiden threateningly, then tried to make a mean face. Instead of a mean face, Farley's face looked more like he was constipated. His hand started to shake.

"You okay there, bud? You eat something you shouldn't have?" Aiden teased.

Farley replied, "No? Not working? Okay, I give up. I will be your slave." Farley submitted and dropped to his knees, bowing.

Aiden held back laughter and decided to mess with the funny little guy. He told Farley, "Your services are accepted. Your first task is to rub my feet."

Aiden walked closer, sat on a stump, pulled his feet out of his boots, and set them in front of Farley. Farley looked at Aiden's sweaty, dirty, stinky feet and gagged a little after catching a whiff of them. Glancing back at Aiden, Farley made a facial expression that said, "Are you serious?" The furry creature searched Aiden's bearing to see if he was serious. Aiden did everything he could to avoid laughing because he knew how bad his feet must smell after everything he had gone through.

Aiden continued sternly, "Well, what's it going to be? Massage my feet or meet the wrath of my blade."

Aiden reached down and grabbed the knife he had on his ankle. Farley immediately grabbed Aiden's feet and massaged them, not wasting a second.

"You got it! Farley's massaging, see? Nice, wonderful massage!" Farley said with a phony grin.

Aiden grabbed a handful of leaves and responded, "Perfect! After this, I need to use the bathroom. You will wipe for me." Still holding in his laughter, Aiden laid down the handful of leaves next to Farley.

Farley realized what Aiden meant and looked disgusted. Aiden's hand never left his knife. He somehow kept a serious look on his face and pulled the blade halfway out of its sheath while peering down at the little creature. Farley made an even more disgusted face. Then, Aiden burst out in thunderous laughter.

"Haha haa haaa! Ah ha hahaha! I haven't laughed this hard in years!" Aiden admitted. His eyes teared up; he was laughing so hard.

"That was a joke? A funny joke?" Farley asked, relieved. "Ahahaaa, that was funny! Hahaha! Disgusting, but funny, hahahahaa! You're a comedian. A funny human, yes?"

Aiden smirked and answered, "Some people call me funny, yes. Soooo, what exactly are you? And, where the heck am I?"

Farley looked a bit perplexed when he responded, "You don't know where you are? And you weren't scared of me? It is my understanding that Earth does not have creatures like me."

Aiden's eyebrows raised, "I'm not on Earth? And no, sorry to say, you aren't very scary," he said matter-of-factly. Aiden paused, then continued, "I mean, we have animals, but they don't...talk." He spoke his last words hesitantly. The Earthling didn't know if calling Farley an animal would hurt his feelings.

Farley was quiet. Then he exclaimed, "Oh, you have so much to see! The world of Legends is magical and full of mythical creatures. So exciting! Exciting times!" He put his hand to his chin and thought out loud, "I wonder if you're the...."

"There you are! I was looking all over for you! And who have we got here?" the voice of an angel spoke.

Aiden looked in the direction of the voice and saw the most beautiful woman he'd ever seen. The woman was a little short, had long flowing brunette hair, pure auburn eyes, slightly tanned skin, a beautiful face with a cute little chin, and an athletically voluptuous body. Aiden was attracted to her. The woman walked up to them and looked at Farley as if waiting for an answer.

"Um, this is..." Farley looked at Aiden and whispered, "What is your name?"

"Aiden," the Earthling whispered back, then he replied to the woman, "Hi, I'm Aiden. Apparently from another world, called Earth, and um, this world is called Legends?"

The woman inhaled sharply and responded, "Earth? You're from Earth? I thought you looked a little different. Welcome to Legends! My name is Priya. I see you've met my little buddy, Farley."

Farley held his head up confidently and bowed when Priya mentioned his name.

"So, how long have you been here, Aiden? And, now that I think of it, how did you get here?" Priya asked, trying to contain her enthusiasm.

"I just got here, and uh, it's a long story," Aiden responded

"You are a good guy, right, Aiden?" the beautiful woman questioned more cautiously now.

"Does a cow go moo?" Aiden replied, "Wait, do you guys have cows?"

"What?" looking a little puzzled, Priya continued speaking, "Yes, we have cows. We have a lot of the same animals as Earth. Most of the animals here are bigger, though, and there are other differences because of the gemstones."

Curiously, Aiden said, "Gemstones, huh? And, big animals, cool," then joked, "Not to mention talking, furry little leprechauns." He motioned toward Farley.

"Huh? I am not a leprechaun or whatever that is," Farley contested. He moved closer to Priya and murmured, "What is a leprechaun?"

"I think leprechauns usually have a pot of gold, Farley, so it's not all that bad," Priya replied, grinning.

"Okay, if not a leprechaun, then maybe a mini-Chewbacca with good English," Aiden added, continuing to tease Farley.

"What? Oh, my goodness! I'm no Chewbacca! That's a weird-sounding creature!" Farley argued, then leaned into Priya again, "You better watch him. He's a funny one."

Priya laughed out loud and said, "I've heard of Chewbacca from a famous Earth movie. Haa ha ha," she changed the subject, "Why don't you come with us to town. You can tell me all about how you got here."

Since it was a reasonably long walk to Heirstone, Aiden had time to tell his new friends the entire story of what happened on Earth: about the magical terrorists who attacked his world; how they stole a magical necklace; how he somehow killed most of the army with an exploding wave of energy and then survived an 800-foot fall including tons of rebar filled concrete falling on him; how his family died, and finally, how he followed Magus, Siren, some other guy, and similar-looking giants to this world through the portal.

Priya and Farley shot worried looks at each other when Aiden said the names, Magus and Siren.

"So they're here? Magus and Siren?" Priya asked, adding, "The other guy was probably Regin."

Aiden saw the panic in Priya's face when she said this and answered, "Yes."

"Oh no, horrible news. The bad guys are back," Farley groaned.

Priya responded, "We must prepare then. Magus disappeared a little while ago. Everyone was hoping he had perished." She stopped walking and looked Aiden in the eyes, "There's a lot we must discuss.

But that is for another time because we are here! Aiden, welcome to Heirstone!"

Heirstone

"Wow!" Aiden said aloud, awestricken. He stopped and took in the exquisite sight. It was as if he was in a medieval movie. He had never seen anything so wonderfully picturesque.

Up until now, Aiden hadn't even noticed the magnificent castle, sitting on an island surrounded by a beautiful clear river. The river flowed down from a mountain and around the castle, creating a natural moat on the backside. The three stopped at the foot of the bridge that crossed the river and led into the castle.

This side of the island had a cliff face that was fifty feet high. The backside of the cliff was a hill that flowed down to water level. Water jutted out from numerous holes in the cliff face creating impressive waterfalls. There were twenty, thirty, and forty-foot waterfalls plummeting thunderously into the water below, stirring up a mist that made a stunning rainbow. The massive radiant white castle with peach rooftops sat on top of the hill. The back of the castle continued down the hill and ended at the bottom in the courtyard. Castle walls surrounded the courtyard.

"Holy crap! This has got to be the coolest place I've ever seen!" Aiden raved, "Sooo, here in this world, we're in like medieval times? That's so awesome!"

Grinning at Aiden, Priya asked, "Would you like to see what's inside?"

"You damned right!" Aiden replied.

Priya led the way across the bridge to the castle gate. It was a rope bridge. It swayed back and forth as they crossed it. Aiden looked down, and although he wasn't afraid of heights, he had to admit he was slightly intimidated. He had never crossed a bridge like this before. To distract himself, he stared at the clear water below him. It looked refreshing. He could not help the huge grin he had on his face.

The trio reached the gate, and it opened. A tough-looking, muscular person with tattoos and piercings greeted them.

"Princess, thank goodness you are back. We were all worried because you left and didn't take your trusted bodyguard with you, meaning me. And...I see you have company," the muscular person looked at Aiden, "And, who might this be?"

"Well, hello, Borak! You know I don't ever listen," Priya responded cheekily, "This is Aiden, and he's from...Earth," she emphasized the word Earth. Continuing, Priya turned toward Aiden, "Aiden, this is Borak, and although he looks very human, he is a Roak. They are known for their strength."

"Very nice to meet you, Earthling," Borak said. He shook Aiden's hand, then looked down at Farley, "And how 'bout you, little guy? What's your name?"

Farley gave Borak a contemptuous stare and replied, "What? You know who I am. Are you a funny guy, too? Why is everyone a funny guy today, and who the heck is Chewbacca?" He ended his sentence crossing his arms in irritation.

"Ha ha, I'm kidding, Farley. How are you today?" Borak asked, trying to lighten the mood.

Instantly becoming happy again, Farley started babbling, "Well, I'm great! I'm glad you asked! We found Aiden, and it's so wonderful! He might be the Hero from Earth, uh, the one who saves us, as told in the Prophecy. I can't wait to find out. That reminds me, Aiden, can you show me your...."

"Hold your horses there, cowboy," Priya jumped in, "Sloooow down, buddy. We'll get to that. First, we have to introduce our guest to the King!"

Aiden had heard what Farley said but decided to be patient and wait to ask about it.

Priya again led the group and went through the open gate into the outer ward. The outer ward was a grassy area between the castle's outer castle wall and inner castle wall. As Aiden followed, he saw massive, secured doors built into the inner castle wall. They were undoubtedly the entrance to the castle. Priya continued to lead the way and walked around to the left, where there was another smaller gate. It was the gate to the courtyard.

Priya told Aiden optimistically, "I will show you the castle later and have a room prepared for you if you wish to stay."

"Sounds great!" Aiden responded.

Priya smiled and opened the gate. Aiden walked through and was dumbfounded. He would have sworn it was a movie set if it was any other day. For a second, he stood with his mouth open, then tried to put what he was feeling into words, "This, I mean, this is huh, wha...., this is friggin awesome!"

There was a large courtyard full of harmonious and intelligent-looking creatures.

"I wasn't sure how you'd react, but um, I think that was good," Priya said, still smiling.

The courtyard was magnificent, with creatures moving about like a typical little town. A path through a grassy field led to a spectacular fountain that propelled water ten feet in the air. Many creatures gathered in this area. It also had a stage, tables, and chairs. Vendors encompassed the fountain and entertainment area. The place was lively, with creature-people shopping, laughing, dancing, and hanging out. Mainly Roaks occupied the courtyard, but some Hairies and Grandars sprinkled in. Catching Aiden's eyes were a few who looked a bit different, not big and scary different or short and hairy different, but illuminatingly different like they had extraordinary magical powers. They were sitting in royalty-type thrones and appeared to shimmer in the daylight. Others around seemed to regard them as if they were celebrities.

"Those four you're looking at are my family. They're Mystics," Priya explained to Aiden, "Um, meaning they're some of the strongest beings in this world. The older two are my mother and father, Carys and Naru, and the other two are my siblings, Sen and Conrad."

"Cool, they look badass! This place is something else," remarked Aiden, very pleased with what he saw.

"Come with me. I want you to meet the King!" the apparent Princess said excitedly. She led Aiden down the path to her family.

"My lovely daughter!" Naru exclaimed as Priya and her friends approached, "How are you? We were worried."

"I'm fine, Dad. I had to get Farley again. The little bugger keeps running off," Priya replied.

Farley hid behind Priya's leg when she spoke.

"Yes, we're going to have to do something about these disappearing acts, aren't we?" Naru scolded, lowering his tone and staring down at Farley while he spoke. Then he turned toward Aiden, "And who might I have the pleasure of meeting? Might he be the explanation for all of Farley's disappearances?"

Farley's eyes opened wide. He energetically jumped out from behind Priya's leg to offer the King an explanation, "Yes, your highness! I have been searching for the one mentioned in the Prophecy. I was trying to follow the signs, and it worked! I found him! It has to be him! He is an Earthling!" Realizing he may have said too much, Farley slid back behind Priya's leg and hid.

Others in the courtyard heard Farley's loud, excited comments, and a crowd began gathering around the group. Naru looked over at Carys, who was listening to the conversation intently, to see if she'd heard what he'd heard. He recognized that she did, then responded, "Hmmm, you say he's an Earthling, do you? How about the mark?"

"Yes, we need to check the mark!" Farley agreed, peeking around Priya's leg.

Deciding it was time, Aiden chimed in, "Okay, everyone, I don't know what all this jibber-jabber is about a Prophecy or a hero, but what kind of mark are we talking about?"

Naru smiled and explained, "The Prophecy says the one who will save the world has a mark on his left butt cheek. It does not describe anything else. It only says there is a mark."

Aiden's eyebrows raised. He was perplexed. He took a moment to think, then said, "Well, there is this." He turned around and pulled his pants down, revealing a gunshot wound on his left butt cheek.

Aiden chuckled inside, thinking about the situation. He was mooning the royal family. There were many audible gasps and even an "Oh, my goodness!" from Carys. Aiden wasn't sure if that was because they liked his butt or because the mark meant he was probably the savior of the world. Either way, it was a positive response. Conrad only sat on his throne, stoically watching what was occurring.

"I mean, it's not like I was born with it. Someone shot me in a gunfight on Earth," Aiden admitted. He pulled his pants back up and turned around.

All at once, several discussions broke out around the gathering. "Hold on! Quiet!" Naru hollered. He was already standing due to the sudden realization of who Aiden might be. Naru walked toward the potential savior of the world and asked, "What is your name, new friend?"

"Aiden. Nice to meet you, King," Aiden answered, holding his hand out a little unsure of how to greet a King. Naru looked at Aiden's hand for a second, then put his hand out and shook it.

"Do not worry. We have many of the same customs here as on Earth," the King reassured. He added, "Your face looks familiar." Naru appeared to have a pleasant thought then put his hands on Aiden's shoulders and said, "You know what? We will continue this Prophecy talk later. This is a joyous occasion! Tonight, we celebrate the arrival of our new friend, the Earthling, um," he looked at Aiden blankly. Aiden whispered his name in Naru's ear.

"Aiden!" the King finished. The crowd cheered in excitement.

Feeling appreciated, Aiden said, "Wow, I never got this type of reception back home. I might stay here awhile!"

Priya smiled, then tapped Aiden's shoulder, "I'd like to show you something. Will you come with me?"

"Um, sure," Aiden answered as he looked around at the crowd, still relishing the cheering.

Priya walked down another path which led to the back of the courtyard. Farley was still by her side. Aiden followed. The three came to a training area where a Roak, two Hairies, and a Grandar were sparring. The training area was a sandpit encircled by a stone wall. There were weapon stands on either side containing wooden swords, bo staffs, and axes. The stands also held dulled metal swords. Next to one of the stands was a Wing Chun dummy.

The Rest of the Gang

"Hyaa! Hewa! Waaa! Hyyaa!" Melia swung a wooden sword at Gil and Cedric while they hopped around, dodging her strikes.

"Haaa, you can't catch us! We're too quick for you!" Cedric teased.

"Focus, Cedric. You remember what happened last time," Gil warned.

The two Hairies jumped in front of Melia, blocking her strikes with their smaller swords. They continued fighting back and forth, block, dodge, parry, strike, block, jump flip, strike, then jumped away in unison. Melia blocked and countered every one of their strikes.

Jack, the Grandar, ran at Melia, hollering, "Ahhhh!" He raised a wooden bo staff and swung it. Melia blocked his strike then jump-kicked him in the gut. As she did so, she did a backflip off his stomach and landed on her feet. Seeing Melia distracted, the Hairies leaped toward her. Jack recovered quickly and rushed her at the same time.

"This is for the King!" shouted Jack, running at Melia.

"This is for the Princess!" yelled Gil in midair.

"And this is for, uh, Farley!" Cedric hesitantly yelled as he came down, awkwardly swinging his sword.

Ignoring all the theatrics, Melia blatantly high-kicked Cedric to his head, sending him flying. She followed with a back-kick, cracking Gil in the chest and throwing him the other way. At this point, she faced away from Jack. Jack swung the staff, and she rolled backward between his legs, dodging his downward swing.

"Wha, noooo!" bellowed Jack.

From behind him, Melia stood up and sliced his back four times in criss-cross patterns. His face turned dire.

Jack fell to his knees, pleading, "Na mate, please don't take me life! I have four boys, three daughters, and two wives. If I die, who will take care of 'em?"

Shaking the cobwebs out of his head, Cedric played along, "Do not worry, my friend. I will take care of your family. Especially the two wives!"

"Wait! I will take care of one wife, and he will take care of the other!" Gil added.

"That is fine, as long as you take care of all the kids, as well," Jack assured.

"Um, I changed my mind! Gil, the kids are all yours!" Cedric joked.

Aiden started cracking up with laughter and told them, "You guys are hilarious!"

Subtly startled, the four in the training circle stopped what they were doing and looked at Aiden, who was standing at the foot of the sandpit with Priya and Farley.

"I am at your service, Cedric. You defended Farley's honor," Farley announced, oddly serious and bowing.

Cedric only smiled awkwardly.

Priya began speaking, "Hey guys! That was good stuff and quite entertaining!" She glanced over at Aiden, "I want you all to meet someone. An Earthling. His name is Aiden."

Cedric contemplated what an Earthling was, then looked over at Gil, Melia, and Jack. Gil, Melia, and Jack appeared quite stunned by this revelation and simply gawked at Aiden for a minute. They had been waiting for the arrival of an Earthling for years.

"Uh, you guys, what's an Earthling?" Cedric asked, interrupting the peculiar situation.

"What! You're joking, Ced? Have you ever even read the Prophecy of Heroes?" Gil responded, annoyed because Cedric always seemed not to pay attention.

Cedric replied, "Well, I know some guy comes from somewhere else, like another planet or something, and he's got crazy cool powers and kicks some serious ass."

Cedric pondered a second. At the same time, Gil stared at him, appearing even more annoyed.

Cedric continued, "And then, um, and then uh, someone dies, and we find out the guy is evil!" Cedric speedily shot an angry look at Aiden, then jumped up from the ground in a defensive posture. He accused, "Ahhaaa! We know what you're up to, Aiden! Give yourself up!"

The Hairy subtly glanced around, trying to appear stoic, and noticed everyone was looking at him like he'd lost his marbles. Cedric ignored them and stood there confidently, ready to fight. Everyone, even Aiden, broke out in laughter.

After a good laugh, Gil spoke up, "Ced, you completely made that last part up. I know you haven't read any of the Prophecies. You only know what I've told you."

"Haha, no, I've read them. I couldn't remember the rest of it," Cedric admitted.

"Man, I went from the town hero to the town zero in no time flat!" Aiden joked as he walked up to Cedric and put his hand out, "Nice to meet you."

A little embarrassed, Cedric shook Aiden's hand and said, "Sorry about that. Uh, soooo you have powers?"

The others had come close and were eager to hear Aiden's response.

Aiden replied, "Um, I mean, I think so. I've been doing some crazy stuff lately. It only started today."

"What started today?" asked Melia.

Aiden told everyone about his adventure earlier in the day, ending with him running through the portal, falling into the pond, and sneaking up behind a bit of a leprechaun.

"I'm not a leprechaun!" Farley snapped.

Aiden reacted by patting him on the back and saying, "I'm kidding, dude. I think you're awesome!"

After hearing this, Farley's cheeks turned red. He smiled and danced in place.

Giggling, Priya commented, "Wow, Farley, I guess you do like him?"

The happy little furry creature hadn't realized he was dancing in front of everyone. He replied, "Oh, uh, he's alright. I had something on my feet. That's all."

Priya giggled again. From a distance, the group heard a bell ringing.

"What's that mean?" asked Aiden.

Remembering about the party, Priya informed, "Oh, I forgot to tell you guys! We're having a celebration! It must be starting. Come on, let's go!"

The group walked up the path toward the fountain and saw the celebration had begun. There were many kegs of ale and wine and massive amounts of food. Lots of people were in line, waiting for refreshments.

"Ahhh, there's the man of the hour!" Naru greeted Aiden as the group walked up, "Here, have a drink!" He handed Aiden a mug.

"That food looks wonderful! I could eat a horse right now," Aiden kidded, his lips watering. He hadn't had anything to eat all day, and it had been a very active day for him.

Naru responded, "We can make that happen!"

The King started waving at servants to get some horse when Aiden stopped him, saying, "No, no! Thank you, but it's an expression. It means I'm famished."

"Ahaahaahaaa, you are funny! Another detail foretold by the Prophecy!"

"Really? I'd love to hear more about this Prophecy. I'm not sure what to think about it," Aiden confessed.

"Yes, tomorrow, my savior. Tomorrow, we shall discuss it all," Naru replied. He called over a servant, and whispered something in her ear, then changed the subject, "I have an idea. Who's up for a game of Coins?" Everyone cheered.

It didn't take Aiden long to realize the game of Coins was exactly like the game of Quarters from Earth. Everyone playing took turns trying to bounce a coin into an ale mug. If a player made it, that player got to choose someone else to drink the mug's contents. Expectedly, only a short time passed before everyone became very intoxicated.

"Dang, you made another one!" Conrad enthused.

"Awww, come on! Yeeer gaaaver me d'last two," Cedric slurred as Naru passed the mug to him. Everyone laughed.

After a few more missed shots around the circle, it was Aiden's turn. He made the shot and passed the mug to Cedric.

Cedric stared at Aiden with a drunken look. He raised his eyebrows and slurred even worse than before, "Arrre yeeoouu frigging serious?" He grabbed the mug and pounded it.

Hours of playing the game went by. Cedric passed out and fell out of his chair. Eventually, the servant to whom Naru whispered earlier returned with a scroll. The servant waved Aiden over and took him to a well-lit room to read it. Aiden opened the scroll and saw what it was. It was the Prophecy to which everyone kept referring...the Prophecy he hoped would tell him everything he needed to know. It was the Prophecy of Heroes.

Reading the Prophecy

In the land of Legends, there are many myths set forth which foretell the coming of days. This is the telling of the Legend of Heroes...

Aiden read the Legend with half-drunken yet curious eyes. Even though he was buzzed, he noticed the bottom piece of the scroll was torn off. When he finished reading, he was in disbelief.

"Holy crap! That's supposed to be me? And hmm, there's, uh, there's no way!" Aiden was talking to himself even though the servant was still standing there, "I mean, I guess, with everything that's been happening, that could be me."

He looked over at the servant. She nodded in agreement as if to say, "Yeah, that sounds about right."

"Wow!" Aiden said again, still getting used to the idea, then asked the obvious question, "What happened to the rest of it?"

The lady Roak only shrugged her shoulders, responding, "I don't know. It has always been that way."

The semi-drunk hero thought it odd that the servant continued standing before him, not saying a word. It seemed like she was waiting for something. She nodded her head again, this time toward the scroll. Aiden realized what she wanted.

"Oh, sorry! Here you go," he apologized and handed the scroll back to her.

Priya walked up as the servant turned and walked away. Seeing the scroll in the servant's hand, she said, "Ah, you saw the Prophecy. What do you think? Can you live up to the hype?"

Caught off guard because he hadn't seen the beautiful Princess coming, Aiden replied, "Huh, oh, uhhh, well, yeah, I think so. I'd be worried about the bad guys. This "Hero" sounds like quite the badass."

Priya giggled, replying, "You are a funny guy, Mr. Hero." She walked closer, so she was face-to-face, staring into his eyes. She flirted, "Handsome, too." She touched Aiden on the nose with her finger and smiled.

Priya was so close; Aiden could smell the wine on her breath and couldn't ignore this chance to admire her magnificent beauty. In the heat of the moment, the two began moving their lips closer together. Before they touched, Aiden pulled away at the thought of his wife. Although he wanted to kiss her, he felt at extreme odds with it. It hadn't even been twenty-four hours since the death of his wife.

"What's wrong? Was it something I said?" Priya asked, concerned.

"No, no, that was...thank you for the compliment. You're amazingly beautiful. I, uh, I lost my wife earlier today, and, um, I haven't even had time to process it." He paused for a second. Tears rolled down his face as he talked, "I, uh, I forgot with all this craziness happening. How could I forget?"

"Oh, my goodness, come here," Priya responded. It had slipped her mind as well. She took Aiden in her arms and consoled him, "It's okay. It's okay. As you said, a lot has happened today." The compassionate princess held Aiden in her arms while he cried, then led him to his room. The two said goodnight, and Priya closed the door. Aiden sat on the bed for the rest of the night, grieving the loss of his wife and son.

Training and Bonding

Days were hard at first, but they got better. Aiden spent the next few weeks depressed, having a difficult time socially, and not leaving his room much. Everyone, especially Priya, was sympathetic toward him, even Conrad. Aiden and Conrad developed a close friendship as they both suffered the loss of a wife and son at the hands of Magus. Over time, Aiden ventured out from his room and participated in events around the castle, such as group dinners, plays in the courtyard, and, most importantly, training in the sandpit. He spent most of his time with Priya, Farley, and Conrad and became friends with Melia, Borak, Gil, Cedric, and Jack. The group was forming a close bond.

"Aiden, are we still on for the play tonight?" Priya asked, standing in Aiden's room.

"You know it!" he replied with a smile, "The last show was hilarious!"

Giggling like she always did, Priya added, "It was! I love the voices! I don't know how he does so many voices."

"Yeah, and what's with Dracula's voice? He sounds like a high-pitched parrot," both laughed after Aiden said this.

The two ended up face-to-face again. They looked at each other for a moment, smiling. Aiden thought about kissing her. Priya might have, too, but Aiden wasn't sure. He still felt weird about being intimate with another woman. The fact that Priya was, as he had already confirmed with himself, the most beautiful woman he had ever seen was encouraging.

The two laughed again, awkwardly, then Aiden spoke, “Um, so I’m going to go train for a while. I’ll meet you down there?”

“Uh, yea, yes. I’ll see you down there later. Don’t hurt yourself like last time, mysterious Aiden. I don’t wanna have to carry you to the play again,” Priya teased but was serious at the same time. She walked out of the room.

Down at the sandpit, Melia and Jack were working combos with wooden swords. Melia swung in a crisscross pattern, then threw a kick, and Jack blocked. Jack followed with a similar sword attack, then a kick and Melia blocked. Back and forth they went.

Aiden walked up to them and said, “Hey, can I get in on this? Can anyone else have a little fun around here?”

Melia laughed and answered, “Hey Aiden! You ready to get your butt kicked again?”

“Yea, bloke. Last time you ran home with ya tail between ya legs,” Jack teased, smiling.

Aiden came back with, “You sure that was me? I could’ve sworn that it was you running home and screaming, ‘ow me ass!’ because I kicked your ass!” All three cracked up.

“I was hoping we could work on activating your powers today. You up for that?” Melia stated in expectation rather than asked.

Ever since Aiden arrived on Legends, he hadn’t been able to use his powers. He figured it was because of his depression.

“Yeah, sure,” Aiden answered, “I’ve been feeling better. Maybe today’s the day!”

“Okay, great!” Melia responded excitedly, “I had an idea. Let’s warm up and then try my idea. I’m not telling you what it is, though.”

Melia pulled a tall table to the center of the sandpit, grabbed a rock, and placed it on the table. Aiden walked ten steps from the table, drew a line in the sand with his foot, and turned around.

Melia gave him a second, then began to speak calmly, “Okay, let’s start with breathing. Breathe in...and breathe out. Empty your mind. Push everything out of your mind while breathing in...and...out, breathe in...and...out. Calm and focused. Keep breathing and open your eyes when you’re ready.”

Aiden continued to breathe for a while longer, then opened his eyes.

“How do you feel?” asked Melia.

“I feel calm. Ready,” Aiden replied.

“Great, then let’s begin. Focus on that rock. Focus on moving that rock. Will it to move. Concentrate,” Melia instructed zenfully.

Aiden had his right hand on his temple while staring at the rock. He squinted his eyes in deep concentration. He knew he could do this. He ran faster than the speed of light, for goodness sake. If he could do that, he could move a stupid rock. After fifteen minutes of staring at the rock, closing his eyes to refocus, and staring at the rock again, Aiden gave up.

"Ahhh, dang it!" Aiden spouted in disgust, "It won't move. I mean, I don't see how I could be any more focused."

"Try this," Melia suggested. She moved the rock and placed something else on the table.

"Whaatt iiisss thaatt?" Aiden questioned, peering intently at the item.

Aiden squinted his eyes to get a better view. The item was small, and it looked like metal. It also appeared broken and had a jagged edge on one end.

"It looooks like a, hmm, a piece of armor?" Aiden guessed.

"Yes, you got it! It is a piece of Magus' armor found in the field after the Epic Battle against Herana," Melia answered.

Aiden's brow furrowed at this new information. He glared at the armor, becoming very serious and angry as he remembered what Magus had done to his family. Then, pleasant memories flooded his mind.

......Sasha's face flashed before his eyes. "Hey, honey! Breakfast?" she asked. It was the morning after their honeymoon, and she brought him breakfast in bed.

Next, he saw Chase. "Dad, catch!" Chase yelled, trying to catch him off guard. It was one of the days they had gone to the park to throw the football.

Then Aiden remembered the three of them sitting in their living room during the Christmas after Sasha, and he reconciled. Sasha assured their son, "Of course. We will always be together. Your Dad and I love each other." ......

The last memory angered Aiden again. Instantly, he pulsated blue energy and threw his arms forward. A powerful blue wave zipped outward toward the table. It hit the table, and the table flipped backward through the air. Ten feet away in the wave's path, a tree ripped out of the ground and began falling over.

"Ahhh, watch out!" a Roak by the tree screamed. He ran and dove out of the way.

"Whoa! Ya alright, mate?" Jack shouted at the Roak, who was lying on the ground.

"I'm fine," the Roak yelled back, "Glad no one else was there."

"Alright! I knew that would work!" Melia hollered, unable to hold her enthusiasm any longer.

"Ya blew the hell outta that table, ya sneaky bugga," Jack added.

"Good call, Melia!" Aiden complimented. He put his hand up for a high five.

Melia gave Aiden a funny look.

"Oh, it's a high five. Um, you give me five like this," Aiden explained. He grabbed her hand, then high-fived it.

"Why is that five?" Melia asked, smiling.

"It's five fingers, see, one, two, three, four, five," Aiden answered, giving another high-five.

"Oh, I see," Melia responded, then changed the subject, "Um, so we now know it's an emotional trigger. Somehow you have to tap into your emotions to trigger your powers."

"Yeah, I guess so. Maybe we need to find more items that can help me with that," Aiden said.

The three practiced until the sun was setting, then went up the hill to get refreshments and wait for the play to start. Every day at dusk, there was different entertainment, but everyone's favorite was the play. It was a puppet play. Nobody knew who did the voices. The premise was usually some funny skit, and the voices were hilariously not good.

"Are you guys ready for the play tonight?" came a brusk voice. Aiden, Melia, and Jack looked over to see Borak standing on the side of them, having an ale. "I hope he uses Dracula again," Borak continued, "He always cracks me up. He sounds like a parrot."

Aiden chuckled, "That's what I said. Whoever heard of Dracula squawking like a parrot? Like, does that mean he turns into a colorful parrot instead of a bat when he changes form, and does he suck blood, or does he want a cracker?"

The Puppet Show

The group laughed and was followed by an announcement, "Hear ye, everyone in the courtyard. The play will start in ten minutes!"

"Yaaaarr! Woohoo! Yeeaaa!" a bunch of voices shouted, accompanied by whistling and clapping.

The stage had a stone foundation. On it was a horse carriage with a sign on top that said Spinners. The carriage was sitting sideways with its large window facing the seating area. Hanging off of the window was a smaller make-shift stage. A blue curtain was drawn closed on the stage. Farley was already seated, holding seats for the rest of them. The group walked over and sat next to him. The last to sit was Aiden.

"Hey, I grabbed some drinks for us!" Aiden said, holding out a mug of ale for the Princess.

"Oh, why thank you, Mr. Aiden, but I don't drink," Priya replied with a serious tone.

Aiden was confused for a second because Priya was drinking with him the day prior.

Priya laughed and grabbed the drink saying, "Kidding! That's exactly what I was hoping you would bring me!"

Aiden smiled and laughed under his breath, then replied, "You're a goofball."

Priya smiled back, then asked, "Has anyone seen Gil and Ced? They always miss the play. Oh well, never mind. I think it's starting."

The group saw the torches flicker brighter and heard another announcement begin. They turned their attention to watch the show.

"Ladies and Gentlemen! Welcome to another play! One of Heirstone's finest entertainments! We have all been talking about these quirky puppets. I know I have questions about Dracula. For instance, if Dracula is a parrot, then what in the heck is a parrot doing in Transylvania?"

The crowd laughed.

The announcer continued, "And don't forget about Elvira. Man, she's got some big ol' bazoongas, but why in the heck does she sound like she's eighty?"

The crowd laughed again.

The announcer proceeded, "Alright, folks. Well, that's enough of my shenanigans, so without further ado, ladies and gentlemen, welcome the Spinners featuring Dracula and Elviraaaaa!"

The crowd cheered as the announcer stepped away. Everything became quiet with all attention on the window stage.

The curtain opened after a moment of silence to reveal a puppet-sized Count Dracula. Dracula was purple, had a pointy nose and ears, big bushy eyebrows, two large fangs hanging from his mouth, and was wearing a black suit with a cape. Specifically, he looked very similar to the Count from the Earth puppet show. Not only was his appearance similar, but he also sounded the same, except for an odd parrot noise sometimes at the end of his sentences.

The Dracula puppet spoke, "Hello again, gooood people of Heirstone, squuaaaawwkk! And welcome to the stories of Dracula and his stubborn wife. Everybody remembers my wife, Elvira, squuaaaawwkk!"

Elvira came parading out from the right side of the make-shift stage with her chest pushed forward, showing off her amazingly exaggerated bosoms. The crowd roared. Elvira had a green tint to her puppet skin, long black hair, long eyelashes, pink blush on her cheeks, pink eyeshadow, and red lipstick. She was wearing a black, elegant dress that was very revealing, barely covering her ginormous boobs. Elvira began talking to the crowd. She sounded like a very old lady.

"Hello, everyone! Very nice to see everybody! Do you know what that idiot over there said to me? He said, 'Babe, why must your breasts always be hanging out?' And you know what I said? I said, 'Because if I don't let them breathe, they'll suffocate me!'"

The crowd laughed.

Elvira continued, "And also, these things are a gift. I need to share my gift with the world!" Elvira flipped her hair back, holding her head to the side pompously, while she posed with her hands on her hips.

The guys in the crowd cheered loudly. Most of the women in the audience didn't react much, except surprisingly for Priya. She cheered with the guys. Aiden noticed this and thought, "She is a cool chic."

Looking at his wife, Dracula interrupted, "Babe, enough with the boobs, please," he turned back toward the crowd, "I present to you the story of the missing wedding ring, squuaaaawwkk!"

The crowd laughed again because of Dracula's ridiculous parrot noise. A couch, a door, and a tv slid onto the stage. Both Dracula and Elvira sat down on the couch. While they sat, Dracula took off his wedding ring and showed it to the crowd to signify he didn't have it on, then put it in his pocket.

Dracula began the skit, saying, "Wow, did you see that? That ref made a horrible call, squuaawwkk!"

Elvira looked down at her phone when she responded, "Yes, honey, horrible call."

Continuing, Dracula raised his voice, "See! Look at that replay! Oh, my goodness! That was a catch! How could he call him out of bounds, squuaawwkk!"

The entire crowd was laughing, especially Aiden. He had to admit; the show was oddly funny.

Still looking at her phone, Elvira replied calmly, "Yes, honey, such a horrible call."

Dracula glanced over at Elvira and protested, "You're not even paying attention! I can't believe you! Look, look, here's the replay, squuuuaaaaaawwkk!"

The purple puppet let out a long parrot noise this time and pointed at the tv. Elvira put her phone down to look at the tv, but first, out of habit, she peeked at Dracula's hand and was shocked by what she saw. Her mouth dropped open in horror because her husband wasn't wearing his wedding ring. The crowd chuckled again when Elvira's mouth dropped open.

"What the hell!" Elvira screamed, staring at Dracula's hand.

Dracula responded while still watching the tv, "I know! Can you believe it! That was the worst call I ever saw! I'm about to..."

SLAM! Dracula was interrupted by the door slamming shut.

Dracula looked over at the crowd and said, "What was that? What did I do?"

The purple puppet got up and walked over to the door, trying to figure out what the problem was. He glanced at the crowd again and shrugged his shoulders.

Very lightly, Dracula tapped on the door, "Babe, are you ok, squaawk?" He let out a tiny parrot sound.

"Would you stop with the stupid squawking!" came a voice from behind the door.

Again, Dracula looked at the crowd, then back at the door and questioned, "What do you mean squawking, squaawk?" He let out another tiny parrot sound.

The audience laughed.

After a moment, Elvira decided to admit what the real problem was, "Oh geez, you're not wearing your ring again!"

Dracula peeked at his ring finger and saw no ring. "Dang it!" he said under his breath.

"Are you trying to flirt with the girls at work again? Is that it, you cheater!" Elvira accused from behind the door with her old raspy voice.

The crowd laughed.

"Um, what? I don't work, babe. I hardly leave the house. You know that, squaawk!" Dracula responded.

"Well, you're trying to flirt with the maid again, you backstabber!" Elvira was talking louder from behind the door.

"Oh, boy. Our maid is like eighty years old," he replied and lowered his voice to say something to himself, "But she does have a beautiful voice, squaawk!" This time the squawk was barely audible.

"What was that? I heard you squawk again!" Elvira bickered. It was silent for a second, then she continued, "Well, you're flirting with the neighbors again, you bastard!"

Looking irritated, Dracula explained, "Honey, our neighbors are gay. You already know that, and I haven't been there in over a year, squuaawwkk. I must have taken my ring off to cook the chicken."

"I don't care what you say! You're a liar! You're sleeping on the couch tonight!" said the voice from behind the door in a very serious tone.

Dracula put his head down.

The crowd let out an "Awwwww" in unison.

Dracula walked over to the couch with his head still down, acted like he turned off the tv, and laid down. As the crowd thought the act was over, Dracula rolled over and farted loudly.

"Take that! Squuaawwkk!" he said in retaliation.

The crowd erupted in laughter.

The torches dimmed, the curtain shut, and the announcer said, "The End."

The crowd stood up and gave a standing ovation, hollering, clapping, and cheering, "Yaaaa! Woohooo! Hilarious! That was great!"

The curtain opened again, revealing the two puppets. They both bowed. Dracula jumped from side to side, holding his hands up in celebration, while the crowd threw coins at them. A coin landed on the make-shift stage. Elvira picked it up and put it between her bodacious bosoms.

Dracula jumped around more rambunctiously and began slipping off the puppeteer's hand. The puppeteer felt its puppet falling, but it was too late. The puppet slipped entirely off, revealing a little hairy hand. The puppeteer leaped forward in a last chance effort to try and catch the purple puppet but missed. Instead, Dracula fell to the floor, and the puppeteer's head broke through the make-shift stage. It was Cedric. The crowd became silent, then laughed hysterically. Cedric, at first, looked embarrassed, then threw up his hands and laughed. It was even funnier knowing that Cedric was the one behind Dracula.

Cedric and Gil came out from behind the carriage to take a bow. The duo continued to do entertaining flips and dances for a few minutes, then left the stage. They each grabbed an ale and a wine mug on their way to Priya and the group.

"Oh, my gosh! It was you guys the whole time?" asked Priya excitedly as she grabbed a wine mug from Gil.

"Yea! We figured you would eventually catch on because we were always gone during the play," responded Gil.

"Well, heck, you guys are comedians! Cheers!" the Princess complimented. The whole group raised their mugs in cheers.

"One question, though," asked Aiden, "What is the deal with the parrot squawking? Seriously, it's funny, but why does Dracula sound like a parrot?"

"Um, isn't Dracula a parrot?" Cedric replied, looking around for help. He realized he had made a mistake when everyone started cracking up. "Oh, haha, I thought he was a parrot!" he remarked. He was a little embarrassed while everyone continued to laugh.

"He's a bat, ya doofus!" Jack barely got out between breaths of laughter.

"Yes, he turns into a bat. Why in the world would you think he was a parrot?" asked Borak, smiling.

"Well, um, I saw something about a Dracula Parrot in Earth's readings. I figured that was Dracula," Cedric answered honestly. The group stopped laughing for a second, then erupted in laughter again.

"You don't read, Cedric!" Gil maintained, still not believing him.

Merv's Demise

The night continued with more mugs of ale and wine, stories, jokes, and laughter. The group was becoming even closer. At one point in the evening, Borak placed an apple on top of Cedric's head to throw a knife at it. Although Cedric would let him, Melia stepped in, saying, "No! Here!" She grabbed the knife and switched it out with a carrot. It was a good thing, too, because when Borak threw the carrot, it hit Cedric smack dab in the forehead.

Melia and Borak arm-wrestled at another point in the night while Jack commentated, "The crowd is watching as they go back and forth. Borak will never hear the end of it if he gets beat by a gal. Oh no, Melia has the advantage! Can Borak come back? And it, it, oh, Borak is down for the count!"

"Ohhhhhh!" rang out loud by the spectators.

"I can't beat you anymore, Sis," Borak admitted.

"Maybe next time, Bro," Melia replied, patting his shoulder.

Later that night, Conrad joined the fun, although he looked sad. Aiden was concerned, so he asked, "What's wrong, my man?"

"Aw, it's nothing. I'm trying to keep my mind off things," Conrad responded, not looking Aiden in the eye. He could feel Aiden still looking at him, so he continued talking, "I, uh, it's hard losing a child. Yeah, today was his birthday."

Conrad looked up from the ground and saw Aiden was staring at him intently. He choked up a little, and tears rolled down his cheeks.

Aiden embraced him, empathizing, "It's the hardest thing I've ever done." He kept holding Conrad tightly for a moment before letting him go. "Is there anything I can do?" he solemnly asked.

"No. I mean, I don't think so. I don't know what there is to do," Conrad responded sadly. He glanced over in the distance beyond the castle wall.

"What is it? What's out there?" Aiden asked again, searching for a way to help.

Conrad revealed, "That's where he is. I buried him where he died."

The two decided to travel outside the gates and visit Conrad's son's grave. Conrad stopped to pick flowers along the way and placed them on top of the rock headstone when they arrived. It was a lovely site marked by one tree standing alone surrounded by colorful flower bushes in a grass field. A few large rocks were sitting in front of the tree. The one in the middle had an etching on it that said "MERV" in big letters and smaller letters saying, "You will not die in vain."

The royal warrior immediately put his head down and began tearing up again. Aiden put his hand on Conrad's shoulder to comfort him.

"I'm sorry, man," Aiden consoled, putting his head down also.

They stood in silence for a few minutes while Conrad cried until he eventually built up enough strength to tell the story about the horrendous event.

"We never knew it was coming. We had no idea Magus was who he was until it happened. He was our Commander-in-Chief, for crying out loud. Can you believe that?" Conrad said, looking at Aiden but not asking, "The army bombarded the walls and the gates. They weren't as reinforced as they are now, plus Magus must have left them unlocked. It was mass murder. Magus came into the Great Hall, zapping people with Mystic power. That necklace he stole must have initiated enlightenment because we had the same amount of power one second, and the next, he was much more powerful. He killed everyone there except Sen, Mom, Dad, and me. We managed to fight him off and chase the army, but it was too late. After the fight was over, I realized Merv was missing. Magus grabbed him when he fled from the city. I found him lying in this tree, already, you know, he was gone."

Conrad broke down, fully crying. Due to the overwhelmingly similar circumstance, Aiden also succumbed to his emotions. The two cried together with bonding compassion.

Training with Mystics

A few more weeks passed, and Aiden became more serious about training. After initially using Magus' piece of armor to access his powers, it wouldn't work anymore. He tried using other items that reminded him of Magus numerous times, but nothing worked. He spent a lot of time in the sandpit.

On this day, while Aiden was sparring with Melia, Borak, and Jack, they received a pleasant surprise. They heard someone say, "You guys got room for two more?" The four looked over to see Conrad and Sen standing at the entrance of the sandpit.

"Hell, ya!" Aiden replied, "I've been waiting for you guys to show up!"

A few days after meeting the royal family, Aiden found out that Sen was mute. She wasn't born mute but hadn't talked since the day Magus attacked them and killed her nephew, Merv. Sen hadn't spent much time with Aiden, but she watched him with curious eyes.

The weirdest thing happened while Conrad and Sen were walking into the sandpit. Aiden heard an unfamiliar female voice say, "You ready to get your ass kicked?" He was looking right at Sen when he heard the voice and saw her mouth didn't move.

"What? Who? Did you say something?" Aiden questioned, studying Sen's mouth.

"Yes, I did. So, what's your answer? You ready?" the voice spoke again. Still, Sen's mouth didn't move.

Aiden replied. "Wait, I'm confu..."

WACK, Sen jabbed Aiden in the face before finishing his sentence. Aiden blocked the following three punches and a roundhouse kick.

"Not bad! Not bad at all!" came the voice again, while Sen nodded her head in agreement.

"Okay, stop! What the hell is going on?" Aiden assertively asked. His seriousness demanded a response.

Sen laughed, and Conrad answered, "Sen can speak telepathically."

"Huh? Bull crap!" Aiden remarked, glancing around, searching for someone to tell him this was a joke, "This isn't a movie, for crying out loud! You're shittin' me! She can speak inside my brain?"

Everyone replied, "Yes."

"My God. There isn't anything else I won't believe about this world. Next, you're going to tell me she can read my thoughts," Aiden continued, glancing around again to make sure the answer wasn't yes.

"Actually, yes, I can read your thoughts, Aiden," answered Sen in his head, "Right now, you're thinking, 'I hope she can't read my thoughts.'"

Aiden made a weird face, then laughed under his breath. Sen also laughed.

"No, she can't read your thoughts, Aiden. She can only project her voice into your head. She started doing this ever since she stopped talking," Conrad explained, smiling, knowing his sister was probably messing with him.

"Okay, so let's do this!" called out Melia. She ran at Conrad and jump-kicked.

Conrad put a glowing blue hand forward and stopped Melia in mid-air. He gave Melia a look that said, "Did you think that would work?" Then, he released her.

Melia dropped to the ground with a thud. This move didn't shock Aiden since he had seen Magus do it, but he was a little surprised to see Conrad do it. Borak and Jack followed Melia, attacking with punches and kicks. Borak was quick, throwing a left, right, wheel kick, and sweep kick. Jack was slower but more powerful, throwing a left, right, and front kick. Conrad dodged and blocked Borak's strikes, lifting his leg to avoid the sweep kick while simultaneously blocking Jack's strikes. Countering, Conrad threw a quick one, two to Borak's face and spun back-kicking Jack in his stomach followed with a left-cross. Jack spit out blood as his head spun around from the blow.

Aiden took the other's sparring as his cue to attack, so he lunged at Sen with a superman punch. Sen dodged the strike and countered by grabbing Aiden's arm and using his momentum to throw him over the block wall around the sandpit.

Aiden got back to his feet. He nodded, saying, "Okay, okay," then ran at the royal Mystic. The two exploded into a flurry of punches and kicks. They both dodged and blocked almost every strike, only allowing a few to land. Aiden ducked under one of Sen's punches and landed a body blow. He followed with an uppercut and spun away.

Wiping blood from her lip, Sen acknowledged, "You have some skills, Aiden, but can you handle this?" She pulled her hands into her stomach, charging blue energy, and pushed her hands forward, throwing an energy burst. An energy shield appeared in front of Aiden. The energy burst deflected off it.

Sen was caught off guard and asked, "How did you do that? Are you a Mystic? But how can an Earthling be a Mystic?" Aiden ignored her surprise and jump-attacked. They resumed throwing punches and kicks.

Melia rose to her feet, picked up a wooden bo staff, and swung it at Conrad's head. Conrad blocked the attack, grabbed the bo before it hit his face, and whipped it around like a baseball bat. Melia held onto the bo and was whisked off the ground. Her grip slipped, sending her soaring twenty feet through the air. Borak and Jack pushed forward, throwing more strikes. Although Conrad was backing up, he was yet to be hit, still blocking and dodging every assault. Borak and Jack threw punches at the same time. Conrad blocked them both, or so he thought. Borak had thrown a double-punch and nailed Conrad's abdomen with the second punch. Conrad was stunned. Jack swiftly swung a wooden ax. He hit the top of Conrad's head, dropping him to a knee.

Conrad pulsated blue light and threw his hands at the two who had surprisingly hurt him. A small energy wave left Conrad's hands, knocking Borak and Jack off their feet. Conrad heard a commotion occurring in the fight next to him, so he looked over. He couldn't believe his eyes.

Borak and Jack got to their feet, ready to attack again but saw Conrad watching Sen and Aiden. When they saw what was happening, they understood what had caught Comrad's attention.

Aiden and Sen were punching and kicking so fast it could barely be seen. It was a blue blur of punches and kicks. Now and then, the spectators could tell when one of them got hit because there was an audible, "Ugghhh or awwhhh!" They worked around the sandpit trading blows, parry, punch, block, punch, kick, punch.

Sen accidentally stepped on a bo staff and lost her balance. In the heat of the battle, Aiden punched her savagely in the chest, knocking her backward on the ground. Before Aiden could think if he accidentally hurt her, Sen blasted a beam of energy at him. Aiden reactively blocked the ray with a beam of his own. The two ended up in an energy beam battle of will.

The rest of the group could see where the two beams met and how they went back and forth as the beam wielders gained or lost an advantage. Sen seemed to have the edge while her beam slowly worked closer to Aiden. Aiden fought back. His beam now headed toward her. Sen gave it everything she had. Aiden heard her scream in his head, "Aahhhhhhhhhhhhh!" In an instant, her beam demolished Aiden's, hitting him like a ton of bricks. The impact shot him back into one side of a dwelling and out the other. He landed in a haystack. Aiden was smoking from the ordeal, and the haystack caught fire.

Aiden's friends ran over to help. A woman came out of the house through which Aiden had flown. Melia yelled to her, "Water! Quick, grab some water!" The woman looked over at Aiden, lying in a burning haystack, and briskly ran inside to fetch some water.

Priya happened to hear of the epic battle occurring down at the sandpit and thought she would join. On her way, she heard a strange buzzing noise followed by a couple of loud crashes. The alarmed Princess scanned the area and saw Aiden lying in a fire out in the field. Instinctively, she waved her glaive and thrust forward a watery blast of energy. The wet energy zipped across the courtyard, across the field, and splashed over Aiden. The fire was put out.

"Oh, no! Aiden!" Priya said dreadfully and ran toward him.

Since they were closer, the other five made it to Aiden before Priya. When she arrived, Melia already had Aiden's head in her arms.

Melia lightly slapped his face, pleading, "Aiden, wake up! Aiden!"

Priya reached down and shook him, imploring, "Aiden, snap out of it!"

Nothing seemed to work. Aiden was lifeless. The situation grew direr with each passing second.

......"Aiden, wake up! Aiden, your son needs you! You can't quit now. I know you can do it. GET UP!" said a voice.

It was Sasha. Aiden could hear her. But where was she? For that matter, where was he? Wherever it was, it was completely white, and there was nothing around. It was like a big white room of nothingness.

"GET UP!" Sasha said again.

Wait, maybe that wasn't Sasha. He wasn't sure, but the voice was trying to help him.

"You don't have much time! You need to breathe!" the angelic voice told him....

Seemingly out of nowhere, the oxygen-deprived hero heard a loud CLAP and felt a jolting awakening. His eyes opened. He gasped for air, followed by wild coughing. His chest hurt every time he coughed, but he couldn't stop.

"I'm sorry. Are you okay?" Aiden heard over the others because it was in his head. It was Sen. Aiden glanced over at Sen and saw the concern on her face.

Still coughing, Aiden sat up and was able to say, "I'm okay. I'm okay, I think."

"Ya scared the crap outta us, mate!" Jack admitted, "I thought we was gonna have ta say sayonara."

Conrad reached over and offered Aiden his hand to help him up. Aiden took the offer and got to his feet. He snuck a look over at Priya and saw her smiling. She was glad he was alright.

Feeling better, Aiden praised Sen, "Nice one!" He gave her shoulder a whack, then winked and teased, "Next time, that won't happen!"

As the group headed up the hill to the courtyard, a servant caught Aiden's attention, "Excuse me, Aiden, the King has summoned your presence."

Aiden replied, "Well, I guess I'm going to go see the King then." He glanced at the others and joked, "You guys, it's been fun. Hopefully, I'm not in trouble. If you don't see me again, you know where I went."

The group laughed, and Aiden threw a shaka as he walked off with the servant.

The King Reveals His Secret

"Ah, there's the man of the century!" Naru greeted, while Aiden walked up to him in the throne room. Naru motioned for everyone else to leave the room, then began speaking, "Aiden, I want to apologize for not calling for you sooner. I've been so busy, you know, with King's business, but that's an excuse. I've been putting off this conversation because it involves something significant. I spent these past months debating whether I should tell you which was wrong of me. I need to tell you, no matter the consequence."

Listening intently now, Aiden gave the King his full attention.

Naru was pacing back and forth and paused to think for a second. He spoke again, "You remember that piece of the scroll that was missing when you read the Prophecy of the Heroes? That piece was missing for a reason. I tore that piece off the scroll because it describes the "Hero" as my son, a half-Earthling, half-Mystic who arrives here in time to thwart evil's plan.

"Son? You said, son? My father died a few years back. Are you saying he wasn't my Dad?" Aiden remarked, having mixed feelings.

The King responded, "We used to have access to Earth before Magus stole the medallion. I traveled there a few times. That's where I met your mother. I brought her here once. She even met Carys. Of course, it was a secret, our affair. I loved your mother even though it could not be. I had to be here. The Prophecy mentioned you as my son, and I did not know what to do, so I ripped off the piece and kept you in secrecy. But no more, Aiden. The truth must be told. I must deal with the pain I've caused. Here, take it."

Naru handed Aiden the piece of the scroll he had ripped off so many years ago. Aiden took the torn piece of paper and read it.

It must be told that the Leader of Heroes is the King's son. Half-Earthling and half-Mystic, this hero's psyche will have been hardened by Earthen experiences yet have the genetic adeptness to become the strongest Mystic in existence. When the Leader of Heroes is present, evil will have strengthened formidably. The Heroes of Legends can only succeed if they all find each other. This includes summoning a Mystic, once thought lost, back from the Spirit World. May the Heroes of Legends prevail and save two worlds.

Aiden continued staring at the scroll, taking a minute to think about what he had read. Breaking the silence, he asked, "What is my mother's name?"

Naru paced a little more, then seemed to decide something with a nod.

Naru began speaking, "We had been trying to figure that medallion out for years. We finally came across another scroll in a cave to the west, which described how to use it. I think the cave was in the direction you came when you arrived here. You must have come through the portal outside the cave."

Naru's Journey to Earth

......Naru told his most trusted servant, "Quick, give me the medallion! It says to put it here."

The servant pulled the medallion out of his pocket and gave it to Naru.

Naru placed the medallion in an indention located inside a makeshift doorway in the middle of a cliff wall. The indention expanded and grabbed the medallion, sucking it in. It fit perfectly. Naru then chanted some words that sounded Latin and blasted the medallion with blue energy. The cliff wall crackled and turned into a portal.

"Whoa!" the servant said in awe.

The King was impressed. He started to walk into the stargate, but the servant grabbed his arm.

"Wait! Are you sure this is a good idea?" the servant asked.

Naru replied, "I have no choice. The scroll says I must take this journey. If I do not return, tell my family I love them dearly." Naru seized hold of the servant's collar, "You hear me? Tell them!"

The servant earnestly responded, "I will! I will not let you down!"

Naru took a deep breath and added, "Farewell, my friend," then turned and walked through the portal.

Naru appeared in a desert landscape surrounded by cliffs. He looked around to assess his situation quickly. It seemed he was alone and in the middle of nowhere. It took hours for him to hike out of the cliff-ridden desolate location. He finally made it to a road. At the time, he did not know it was a road and called it a path with a hard black surface. A car passed him, which he had also never seen before, and honked, probably because of his crazy attire. He had on greenish quilted leather armor. Even more odd was the white robe he was wearing over his armor. Yet, most bizarrely, he had a large, immaculate sword with a dazzling diamond embedded in its gold handle on his waist.

Naru continued his journey without knowing what he was looking for or where he was going. All he knew was he was foretold to be here. A couple more cars passed him in the next few hours. Luckily, the last one stopped and backed up. Naru wasn't sure what to expect, so he grabbed hold of his sword handle.

A woman popped her head out of the window and bluntly asked, "What the heck are you doing walking out here?"

"Um, I'm not sure. I'm a little lost," Naru answered.

The woman spoke again, "And what are you wearing? You one of those cosplay guys that act like you're in medieval times or something?"

The woman seemed a bit quirky and energetic. She talked fast and was very observant. She had glasses on a cute face with minimal makeup and short, blond hair.

Naru was unsure what this meant but did his best to reply, "Uh, cosplay? No, I just um, I've been traveling awhile and could use some water. Maybe some wine?"

"Haha, what do I look like? An alcoholic? I don't typically drive around with wine in my car?" the energetic girl joked, then asked, "You're not a murderer, are you?" She stared at him intently.

"No, absolutely not! I am no murderer! I am a very respectful being. There is no threat of harm from me. If you help me, I will protect you," Naru answered confidently, giving a stern nod after his last sentence.

Giggling, the cute woman remarked, "Well, now we're talking. I could use a bodyguard. There's a lot of riff-raff around the city."

Naru smiled. The perky woman stared at him as if she was expecting something.

When he only stood in place, she finally urged, "Well, you gonna get in or what?"

Naru was grateful for the ride. He was indeed very thirsty. He hadn't thought things through, forgetting to bring water with him. However, he hadn't expected to find the scroll, use the medallion, and be teleported across space to Earth either. The fact is, Naru should have told his servant to grab his water for him before he walked through the portal.

"Oh, well," he thought to himself.

Naru was here where he needed to be. The problem was he was running out of time. Herana was going to attack soon. He could feel it.

Missy started introductions as she began driving, "Sooo, my name is Missy. Some people call me Mystery because I'm always up to something. Aaand, what's your name?"

"Naru, I am the leader of...uh, well, my name is Naru," he replied.

Missy frowned, sensing some dishonesty. "Sooo, where are you from, Naru?" she continued in a more investigatory tone.

"I'm, uh, okay, look, I don't want to lie to you, but this has caught me a little off-guard. I'm worried you won't believe what I'm about to tell you," Naru responded. He sensed Missy anticipating what he was going to say next, so he kept talking, "Okay, I am the leader of the rebellion from another world called Legends. I arrived here a few hours ago through a portal and am unsure what to do. That about sums it up."

Missy's eyes opened wide. Naru wasn't sure what she was going to do. Then, out of nowhere, she laughed hysterically. She laughed so hard she swerved a little.

"Oh, I'm sorry. I got it," Missy reacted, holding in her remaining laughter. She regained control of the car and kept talking, "I knew you were one of those cosplayers. That's a new story, though. From another world, huh? Called Legends? Ooooh, I like the name!"

Missy drove for another half-hour and continued asking questions and talking a lot. She spoke so much, and she now sensed a good feeling about Naru even though he seemed a bit delusional.

Naru was patient, as he was with Carys, and answered all of Missy's questions. He was happy and comforted to have a good conversation because he knew nothing about this new place called Earth. Although Missy asked many questions, she elaborated on her questions, giving Naru answers.

By now, they reached the outskirts of town, and Missy realized Naru hadn't told her where he was going.

Missy felt a little foolish but asked anyway, "I can't believe I didn't ask this earlier. Where am I taking you, Mr. Naru?"

"Uh, well, that's honestly a great question. I don't know. Only fate will show me," Naru replied, looking very serious and confident. Missy couldn't help but innocently laugh again.

"I'm sorry," she apologized, "I don't mean to laugh at you, but you are serious about this cosplay stuff, aren't you? Okay, I'll play along. You look famished, and I have a huge dog who will protect me if you're some deranged psychopath," Missy watched Naru intently to see how he reacted. Naru only smiled back at her, listening. She continued, "And, uh, so I guess we can go to my place and get you something to drink and, maybe, eat?"

"That sounds great, my lady!" Naru responded.

The two drove another ten minutes to Missy's house. When walking inside, Missy's dog ran up to greet her but stopped in its tracks when it saw Naru. It wasn't actually a "huge" dog. It was a small pug. The dog bared its teeth and ran straight for Naru. He scooped it up, saying, "Aw, what a cute little guy!" At first, the dog tried to nip at Naru, so he put his hand in the dog's face, allowing it to bite if it wanted to. It chose not to. Instead, it turned its head sideways with a weird look on its face. Naru continued to hold the dog and pet it, and the dog, rather quickly, warmed up to him.

"Wow, he doesn't like anybody! How did you do that? I'm impressed!" Missy exclaimed, then walked toward the kitchen. "What's your poison?" she asked.

Naru gave her a funny look and replied, "Did you say poison?"

Giggling, Missy teased, "You've never heard that term before? It's our Earthlings way of saying, what would you like to drink? Like, what alcohol?"

"Aww, I see. Wine, please!" Naru answered with a grin.

They hit it off and kept talking nonstop. Missy showed Naru how to use a stovetop, and they made dinner together. Throughout the night, the conversation flowed continuously about everything from types of food, food preparation, types of clothes, energy, magic, creatures, cars, and even airplanes.

"Whhaattt! It flies through the air? How the heck does that work?" Naru remarked, completely astonished. He had never heard of such a thing.

"Yes, it has engines and propellers that create lift to hold the plane up. Tell me more about the magic and creatures where you're from, would you?" Missy asked. Although the alcohol had made his story more believable, she wondered how far Naru would go with his fantasy.

"Well, how 'bout I show you?" Naru suggested and stood up. He drew his sword from its sheath.

"Oh, my God!" Missy blurted. She was startled, seeing the sword was real. She quickly jumped up defensively from the couch.

"No, no! Look, it's beautiful," Naru reassured.

Calmingly and gently, Naru held his sword on the palms of his hands, showing Missy the diamond or Aire gem inside the handle. The diamond shimmered iridescently, grabbing her attention. It appeared pure and powerful, as if it was highly concentrated with an element. She thought she heard something, so she put her ear close to the sword. The gem gave off a faint humming sound.

"Wow!" was the only word Missy could muster as she stared at the diamond.

Naru held the sword's handle with one hand and Missy's hand with the other. He put his head down, summoning power. The gem in the sword illuminated in a deep blue color. The blue light then traveled into both of their bodies.

Missy waited for something to happen. Everything seemed the same. She looked around, unsure of what to expect. She noticed that although her dog was sitting on the couch, disgustingly cleaning his under region like he usually did, he was doing it very slowly. She glanced over at the tv and saw the newscaster on the screen speaking at a prolonged rate. Missy's jaw dropped, recognizing what this meant.

"Did you slow down time?" She managed to ask.

"I thought I would show you some magic," Naru explained, trying to comfort Missy. He knew this was a lot for her. He explained, "The Aire gem in my sword is from my world and contains energy which allows me to do this."

"Sss...ssooo, sooo, it's...all real? What you've been saying is all real?" Missy stammered in shock.

Missy paused a minute in deep thought, then walked away. She disappeared into her room. Naru didn't see her again until the next day. He woke up on the couch to Missy apologizing for leaving him the way she had. She had many more questions and now completely believed his answers.

Naru ended up staying at Missy's house. Over the next couple of weeks, Missy and Naru became very close. They spent a lot of time together. Missy's dog loved the otherworldly being and always waited at the door for him when he went somewhere, making Missy a little jealous. Naru ventured out daily in search of his purpose. He also wanted to learn more about Earth. Legends had some reading material about Earth, but it was different in person. Plus, Earth seemed to have changed compared to what he had read.

One day, Naru came back from a trip to the library to see Missy had prepared a steak dinner. This time though, the setting was different. There were roses on the table, wine glasses filled with red wine, the light was dim with candles burning, and sensual music played.

Naru spoke nervously as soon as he saw Missy, "Uh, hey, smells good! Wha...what's all this?"

Missy replied, "Hi! Huh, what's all what? Oh, just making dinner!"

It was apparent Missy had arranged a romantic dinner. Although Naru had a wife back home, Carys had tolerated his indiscretions before. The public did not frown upon him for sleeping with other women because of his stature. It was also difficult for him to ignore the deep connection he already had with Missy and how much he liked her.

Naru grabbed the wine glasses and walked close to Missy. He handed a glass to her and looked deep into her eyes.

Naru spoke, "I think you are lovely. I can feel our meeting was destiny. I told you I didn't want to lie to you when we first met, and I meant it. I do not know how to tell you this. Um, I..."

Missy kissed him before he could finish telling her he had a wife......

"That night with your mother was amazing," Naru told Aiden, "And I don't mean that part." Naru rolled his eyes, smiling, not wanting Aiden to get the wrong idea, then continued, "What I mean is, we spent all night together and didn't even have to talk. We truly enjoyed simply being next to each other. We didn't leave each other's side after that. I kept waiting for something to happen, like an attack or catastrophe, but nothing did. I was always looking over my shoulder and a little jumpy at night. One time, I took the trash out and thought I heard something. When I looked behind the trash can, a raccoon leaped out and scared the crap out of me. I almost sliced it in half," Naru rubbed his chin, "The thing is, I was waiting for something to happen when it already had. The moment I met your mother, fate had already taken place. I was sent to Earth to meet your mother to create you. I spent a couple more months there until I found a ripped scroll page. It told me I must return. Yes, I found it on Earth. Our two worlds are more connected than you realize."

Naru paused from talking for a moment while he paced. It appeared he was trying to gather his thoughts.

Naru continued, "I was on one of my trips, searching for any sort of sign. I walked into a museum, coincidentally called, The Museum of Legends. The name was what drew me to it. It was a museum of theories that held historical artifacts of unknown origin. A section in the museum told a story very similar to the Prophecy of Heroes. The area contained artifacts similar to ones I had seen previously on Legends and had statues that looked eerily similar to Herana, myself, and even you. I didn't know who the other statue was until I saw you. It is definitely you. At the foot of my statue was a locked chest with a keyhole. I inserted my sword into the keyhole, and the chest opened. Inside was a torn scroll page. It read..."

After the Hero has been conceived, the King must return on the next full moon, for Herana will attack. It is only he who can save Legends at this time.

..."Conceived? King?" Naru thought. He spent much time thinking about these two words.

It was already the afternoon. Naru remembered it would be a full moon that night and hurriedly rushed to Missy's house. He didn't know how to explain the situation but knew he did not have a choice. He had to leave. If he didn't, everyone on Legends would perish. They were counting on him.

Missy arrived a little before sunset. Naru was anxiously waiting for her. She took one look at him and asked, "Okay, what's wrong? I've never seen that look on your face."

"My love, I have to go. I think you should read this. It will explain," Naru replied. Woefully, he handed the scroll page to Missy.

Missy finished reading and responded, "What is this?"

Naru answered, "It is part of a prophecy from my world. I must do what it says, or all will be lost. The full moon is tonight."

Tears ran down Missy's face. She whimpered, "I knew it was too good to be true. I also knew this day would come, but I was hoping we would have more time together." Wiping her tears, she looked into the eyes of the man she now loved and said, "I understand, and I guess I don't need to tell you. I'm pregnant." She smiled a sad smile.

A few tears escaped the eyes of the usually stoic Mystic. Naru put his hands out and told her, "Come here, my love." Missy stepped into his arms, and they embraced. He continued sorrowfully talking, "I'm so sorry it happened like this. It was fate. I swear I will find a way back to you."

Naru and Missy kissed, long and passionately. More tears ran down both of their cheeks. He pulled away and stared into her eyes. He kissed her again on the forehead, then, without hesitation, turned and left. It wasn't easy, but he knew he had to focus on saving his world. He had gotten a little Moped to get around on. He rode fast and hard, trying not to think of what he was leaving behind. He had never done anything like this; leave a person he loved who was pregnant with his child. He had no choice. It was fate and foretold in the Prophecy. He could not change fate.

Naru tried to remember exactly where he walked out of the cliffs. After riding for a while, he stopped at a spot that looked familiar. He got off the Moped and left it on the side of the road. He searched for the same trail he had taken before and couldn't find it. Oddly, he began feeling a slight pull on him as he walked. The further Naru walked, the stronger the invisible tug felt on his body, so he went with it. The pulling force led him to the trail. He followed the trail through the canyons to the circular valley between the cliffs. He saw the doorway portal. Above him, the full moon shone brightly in the dark desert.

Naru approached the makeshift doorway and wondered what he should do since the portal wasn't activated. He had left his medallion on the Legend side when he came through. Naru stared up at the full moon, hoping it would give him some sort of answer. He decided to take a closer look at the doorway and pushed on it. Nothing happened, but he noticed the indention where the medallion went was slightly illuminated. He pressed on the indention, and it moved. A flash of light spread across the entire doorway, converting solid rock into a stargate.

Knowing this was it, Naru looked back and said one last goodbye to Earth. He stood there for a second, thinking about leaving Missy and his unborn child. He didn't know when he would see them again, if ever. He pushed his emotions away, took a deep breath, and went through the portal.

As soon as Naru stepped through the portal, he saw an explosion off to his right. The wind from the blast knocked him over onto his hands and knees. The leader of the rebellion looked up and saw the medallion was in the indention on this side of the portal, glowing. He figured that was why the portal opened. Someone must have put the medallion there, but who?

Unexpectedly, Naru felt a hand on his shoulder. It was Carys, his wonderful wife. She helped him to his feet.

"You made it back, my love!" Carys said, speaking intently while staring at him.

Naru stared back into her eyes, half-smiling. His eyes welled up with mixed feelings. Before he could say anything, another explosion rang out. They quickly ran to cover. The Epic Battle against Herana was beginning......

Naru's eyes were closed while he daydreamed. He opened them and glanced over at Aiden. Aiden's eyes were watery. He had been tearing up by the end of the story. Aiden stood there thinking, trying to grasp the situation.

"I can't believe Mom never told me. After all these years," Aiden said to himself, then turned his attention to Naru, "Okay, so you're my dad. What do we do now?"

"We must fulfill the Prophecy!" Naru stated, matter of factly, "We must continue to prepare you for when the time comes!" He walked up to Aiden face-to-face and told him in complete seriousness, "Son, our worlds need you!"

Battle of Good vs. Evil

Almost as if planned, they heard an explosion in the distance. The ground rumbled.

A guard ran into the room and informed, "Your Highness, we are under attack! We need your help!"

Naru quickly looked over at Aiden, "It looks like the time may have already come. Are you ready?"

Aiden nodded, and they rushed to the door.

Aiden and his newfound father ran outside to see an enormous white ball of energy falling from the sky. It was heading straight for the castle. Naru started to pulsate blue light as a blue blast of energy was shot from the courtyard. The blue blast hit the giant white energy ball and diverted it into the field. The white ball of energy hit the ground, exploding into fire. Two more enormous balls of energy flew into the air from the hillside, giving away the enemy's location. In the shimmer of light, the King and Aiden saw the outline of an army in the field and a prominent figure standing behind the army at the top of the hill. They both knew the figure could only be Magus.

Magus ' army charged as the massive balls of light peaked in the air and began their descent toward the castle. Everyone could hear a faint war cry steadily becoming louder, "Rraaaaaaaahhhhhhhhh!"

Aiden and Naru ran toward the courtyard and saw two more defensive blue blasts shoot out at the two massive energy balls in the sky. Aiden noticed the defensive blasts were coming from Conrad and Sen, who were standing in the courtyard. A third blast came from the castle tower. The defensive blasts hit their targets, but they did not change the energy balls' courses. The white energy balls continued their descent upon the castle. Unless someone did something immediately, this would be the end of Heirstone.

The King took a second to charge up and flashed an intensely bright blue light. He raised his arms and yelled in exertion, "Yaaaaaaaahhh!"

Amazingly, Naru created a magical shield covering the entire courtyard and most of the castle. The energy balls hit the protective shield with a thunderous crash, throwing sparks and fire everywhere. They bounced off the shield and flew into the field, hitting the ground and exploding.

"Nice, Pops!" Aiden told the King. They then heard crashes on the castle wall.

The first wave of Magus' army had reached the moat in front of the castle wall and could go no further. Siren was with them. She was shooting green blasts at the wall, knocking chunks out of it. The wall trembled after each blow and started to crack in spots.

Sen acted fast. She shot a reinforcing burst of energy into the wall, binding it back together. She could not release it, though. She was stuck holding the binding charge to keep the wall up. Naru and Conrad both jumped on top of the wall and shot bolts of lightning at the army. After numerous evil Devians fell, Siren encircled the army with an energized shield. The shield blocked any more bolts of lightning from hitting them.

Seeing the situation from her vantage point in the tower window, Carys shot an arrow with a rope attached. She was known as a great archer who wielded the sacred Bow of Myrial. The arrow stuck into one of the wall towers where the army was bombarding. She yanked hard on the rope, stretching it tight across the courtyard, then tied it to an anchor inside the tower. Carys pulled off her dagger with the sheath still on it, placed it on top of the rope, grabbed hold of it with both hands, and jumped out of the window. She ziplined over Aiden's head and landed on top of the wall next to Naru and Conrad. All three began blasting the army, which was still protected by Siren's energy shield.

Priya ran out of the castle, flustered, trying to catch a grip on what was happening. The last thing she was expecting was for Magus to attack, but sure enough, here he was. Looking in the courtyard, Priya could see Sen beginning to struggle as she used all her strength to hold the wall together. Priya also saw Aiden running back and forth, trying to figure out what to do. Two more colossal energy balls released into the air by Magus seized her attention. A moment later, she watched Magus build up a charge, then saw his scepter come forward and unleash a lightning bolt. It headed straight for the Royal Mystics on top of the wall.

Magus yelled, “All forces attack! Move-in!” The remainder of the army rushed forward aggressively.

The first wave of the army next to the wall shot arrows at Naru, Carys, and Conrad. A few Devians tried to cross the moat but were swept away by the tremendous current which flowed through it. Siren weakened, losing energy from holding the protective shield over the army. Carys noticed this, so she let loose a barrage of arrows at the evil Druidess. Siren shielded herself with the energy she still had. She blocked all but one arrow, which snuck through the shield and struck her in the shoulder, knocking her to the ground. The energy shield protecting the evil army disappeared. The army was now open for attack.

Seeing the army vulnerable, Naru and Carys desperately wanted to inflict their fury upon them but couldn’t because more enormous energy balls were falling from the sky. Instead, in unison, they summoned all their power, hollering from the exertion of energy, “Rrrrraaaaaahh!”

This time, the two created an even larger magical shield that covered the entire castle and courtyard. Distracted by the massive energy balls, Naru and Carys did not see the incoming lightning bolt Magus had shot at them, but fortunately, it slammed harmlessly into the shield. The energy balls then crashed into the shield; WHAM, BAMM! They ricocheted into the field and blew up in a fiery inferno, leaving huge craters in the ground.

It was too draining for the King and Queen to maintain the immense shield, so they released it. When they did, they immediately felt their energy loss.

Siren saw the King and Queen’s shield disappear and strained to build up energy for another attack. She charged up enough and let loose a blast at the King and Queen. Naru saw it at the last second. He quickly blocked the attack with his magic. The blast deflected in another direction. The impact from Siren’s blast knocked Naru and Carys backward off the wall into the courtyard. The deflected blast flew over the courtyard and accidentally nailed Priya directly in the chest. Priya fell to the ground, where she remained motionless.

Conrad, the only Mystic left on the wall, was hit in his leg by an arrow. An explosion next to him knocked him on his butt. He snapped the arrow in half and got back to his feet. He saw the shield which Siren had held over the evil army had disappeared. He jumped off the wall, over the moat, into the middle of the army, and slammed on the ground. The slam generated a shock wave that obliterated the Devians in the vicinity. Siren was able to shield herself from most of the impact of the wave, minimizing any damage. That same shock wave destroyed part of the castle wall and blew a portion of the embankment into the moat, forming a dirt bridge. A gaping hole was left in the wall, giving Magus' army easy access to the castle.

Another evil Druid came barreling down the hill, riding a gigantic wolf at full speed. Another wolf followed.

"It's Regin and the Nywolves!" Conrad alerted his comrades.

Regin zoned in on Conrad, shooting fiery energy blasts. Conrad deflected the blasts, then turned and ran through the busted wall into the courtyard to regroup with his family.

As Regin and the Nywolves came within reach, Siren swooped on top of the vacant Nywolf. Both Druids rushed forward atop the Nywolves.

Naru and Carys had gotten to their feet. They were deeply concerned about Priya. They saw Aiden running over to her.

Conrad joined the King and Queen and asked, "Is she okay?"

Carys replied, "We don't know, my son, but we need to protect her and our home.

Regin and Siren unleashed a fiery fury of blasts through the hole in the wall. The Mystic trio deflected the attacks. The two Nywolves, on which the evil Druids rode, ran at full speed seconds from breaching the wall. Naru summoned power, placing an energetic barrier within the extensive hole in the wall blocking their entry.

Regin saw the barricade and commanded, "Up!"

The Mystic family saw figures coming into view out of the dark sky. Two prominent figures soared through the air, and two smaller figures leaped from them. After a second, it was apparent the Nywolves had leaped over the wall. Regin and Siren had jumped from them and flew directly toward the Mystics.

Priya's Dying

Aiden ran over to Priya, yelling, "Nooooooo! Priya! Priya!" He kneeled over the motionless Princess and pleaded, "Priya! Please wake up! I need you to wake up!"

Priya showed no signs of consciousness, and it didn't look like she was breathing. Aiden tried to find a pulse and couldn't find one.

"Oh, my God! Nooo!" Aiden cried out.

Aiden knew he didn't have time to perform CPR. He could hear the on-coming army. He put his head down on Priya's stomach.

Aiden's eyes welled up, and he shouted, "Why does this always happen? Everyone I care about always dies!"

Instinctively, Aiden lifted his head and placed his hands on Priya's chest. He closed his eyes and took a deep breath doing his best to block out all sounds.

Aiden took another breath and told himself confidently, "I will not lose her."

Blue energy flashed through Aiden's body, traveled down his arms, and flowed into the beautiful lifeless Princess. The energy collected around Priya's heart and shocked her. Her chest rose in the air and back to the ground.

"Priya! Can you hear me? Wake up!" Aiden implored. She still did not respond.

Aiden heard the army bearing down on them. He knew this was his last chance. He hit the Princess with another shock. Her chest jutted forward again. Priya's eyes opened, and she sucked in much-needed air.

"Oh, my God! I thought you were gone!" Aiden stressed as he lightly hugged her. He cupped Priya's head in his hands and asked, "Are you okay?"

Their faces were almost touching. Aiden looked deep into her blue eyes. Priya didn't say a word. It was hazy for her. She was still catching her breath and trying to get her bearings. She stared back into his hazel eyes, moving her eyes back and forth from one of his eyes to the other, trying to figure out which one to trust. She realized who it was and decided to trust them both. Nothing had to be said. Aiden saw her demeanor change from concern to loving, joyous understanding. They both went in for a kiss at the same time.

The kiss was passionate, soft, and sensual. Their lips hugged each other as if they had been searching for one another their entire lives. They lost track of reality, totally forgetting they were in a heated battle.

"Wow, she's amazing!" Aiden thought, mesmerized by the way he felt.

Battle cries of an army right behind them and explosions interrupted what was the most passionate kiss either of them had ever experienced. Aiden lifted Priya in the air, rose to his feet, and ran to the castle.

Unpleasant Reunion

Regin and Siren let loose a barrage of energy blasts as they flew through the air. The Royal Mystics deflected them with ease and returned fire. The two evil sorcerers blocked the attacks as well. They landed in front of the Mystics and slid forward in a brazen attack.

Carys jumped over the foolhardy enemies. She aimed to defend against the Nywolves, who landed on top of some dwellings in the courtyard. Freki and Geri began tearing up the courtyard, ravishing anything in their way. Dwellings, tent setups, vendor establishments, and any other type of structure in the vicinity were demolished. A couple of families ran for their lives. One was a mother carrying her young child.

Acting quickly, Carys released zaps of lightning bolts. The bolts hit both Nywolves and grabbed their attention. They huffed and dashed straight for Carys. She shot out a couple more blasts of energy which the Nywolves dodged. As Freki and Geri closed the distance, she ran at the ugly beasts. She threw her hands out in front of her, slowing time. The Nywolves' heads bared down on her slowly, displaying their vicious teeth. Carys dove between the animals, dodging their bites. She twisted in the air and initiated an energetic grasp on both Nywolves. As she landed behind the humongous animals, she resumed time and used their momentum to fling them up and over her. The Nywolves whipped through the air, still being held by Carys' grasp. The animals were slung back down with tremendous force and slammed into the ground. They yelped as they bounced off the ground and rolled to a stop by the castle wall. Neither of them moved.

Before Carys could feel a sense of accomplishment, she saw the hole in the castle wall was unprotected again. Naru, who was fighting Regin, had to release the barrier since his hands were full. The evil army was flooding into the courtyard.

Naru flipped in the air and spun 180 degrees. He shot a blast at Regin while Regin slid under him. The Druid absorbed the blast with a grimace, slid to a stop, and bounced up to his feet.

Conrad ran and jump-kicked Siren in the chest, stopping her slide and knocking her backward. Siren landed on her back and rolled to her feet. The four squared off in a ten-foot radius.

Regin began taunting with his overbearing tone, "That all you got, old man? I figured you had a bigger bite than that."

"That was only a nibble. Do not forget who you're talking to," Naru replied.

Regin laughed, "Haha, still as arrogant as I remember. I always did everything you asked, and you still treated me like shit. You always acted like you were better than me. Like I was never good enough."

Naru remarked, "I was teaching a lesson that was too big for you. You weren't strong enough then, and you aren't strong enough now."

Siren paced, flirtatiously, teasing, "Ah, the mighty Conrad! Yummy! What do you say we take a time-out and go find an empty room, prrrrrrrr!"

"Be quiet! You're a disgrace to all Druids. You were there when my son died. You watched and did nothing!" Conrad spouted.

"It wasn't my job to save him, cutie-pie. I must say, it was a bit sad to watch," Siren thought for a millisecond, then continued, "How did you know? You weren't there."

Visibly angry, Conrad answered, "When I found him lying on that rock, I held him, crying, and I saw a vision. I saw you watching, wanting to stop Magus, and then I saw him plunge the dagger into my son's chest. Your face dropped. You looked at Magus and couldn't believe how heartless he was, but you left with him anyway. You didn't do anything. You're his puppet!"

Becoming annoyed, Siren snapped, "You're not so cute anymore. I've had enough talking."

Where Have You Guys Been?

Aiden entered the castle and ran into Melia, Borak, and Jack.

"Where have you guys been? We're fighting for our lives!" Aiden exclaimed.

The three looked at Priya in Aiden's arms, and Melia shrieked, "Oh, no!"

Priya nudged herself out of Aiden's arms to stand and remarked, "It's okay! I'm fine! Aiden saved me." She looked back at Aiden comfortingly after she said this.

"Oh, thank goodness!" Melia responded, "We came as soon as we heard. We were up at the feast in the Great Hall. You know how loud it gets in there. We heard some bangs and rumbling but thought Naru was setting off fireworks again. It wasn't until we heard a servant scream that we realized something was wrong."

Priya nodded reassuringly, "It's okay," then asked, "Where are those darn Hairies? Don't tell me they're drunk?"

Melia looked over at the other two, and Jack replied, "Yea, bloke, those two are pretty fried. So, what in the heck is going on?"

Priya answered, "Magus and his army are attacking. The King, Queen, and Conrad are fighting them." After saying this, Priya paused, realizing she didn't know where Sen was. The Princess exclaimed, "What happened to Sen?"

They looked at each other, and everyone shrugged their shoulders. The muffled sound of fighting from outside rose to a roar.

Priya became anxious, “We’ve got to get out there and help!”

Borak was first to respond, “Well, what are we waiting for?” He headed for the door.

The rest of the group followed, except Aiden. He grabbed Priya’s arms, asking, “Are you sure you’re okay?”

Priya smiled and pulled him into her, planting another passionate kiss on him. The two embraced again, kissing as if it might be their last.

When they came apart, Aiden hesitantly spoke, “Um, there’s something I need to tell you.”

Priya covered his mouth, insisting, “Tell me after.” She turned around and ran out the door.

Once outside, the scene was insane: Magus’ army was pouring in from the breach in the castle wall; Carys was shooting a beam of energy, trying to mow down the oncoming army; two Nywolves were lying unconscious on the far end of a smashed-up courtyard, and Naru and Conrad were in a heated battle with Regin and Siren. They glanced at each other and already knew what they needed to do. They rushed to help Carys with the quickly multiplying number of Devians bombarding their home.

“Let’s get ‘em, boys!” Jack hollered.

Naru and Conrad vs. The Evil Druids

The two conversations ended abruptly. The King, Conrad, Regin, and Siren bolted at each other. Regin lunged at Naru with a punch. Naru countered, smacking Regin's arm down and punching him in the face. Regin took a step backward, blocking Naru's successive two punches, then threw a headbutt to Naru's cheek. Regin followed with a jab, right cross, and roundhouse, but Naru blocked all. Naru caught Regin's kick and spun 360 degrees, throwing the evil Druid twenty feet. Regin hit the ground and rolled. He rose back to his feet, summoned energy, and hurled red-orange flames at Naru. The King invoked his blue energy and spun like a small tornado into the flame. The spinning force attracted the flame, causing it to encircle but not touch Naru while he spun. Naru punched Regin in the face with such force that he flew across the courtyard and landed next to his Nywolves.

Conrad stomp-kicked Siren in the stomach and knocked her back on the ground. She speedily threw her legs in the air and flipped back to her feet. Siren sneered and jumped at Conrad with a flying punch. Conrad dodged the punch and grabbed her arm, using her momentum to slam her to the ground. Softening the impact with her magic, Siren hit the ground and sweep kicked Conrad's feet. He fell to the ground. Both parties pushed themselves back to their feet and continued to throw a barrage of strikes: punch, block, kick, punch, dodge, punch, punch, kick, counter. Conrad threw a high kick. Siren caught his foot. Her other hand flashed green. She thrust it toward the ground, causing the ground to open and close over Conrad's other foot. He ripped his foot out of Siren's grasp and tried to yank his other foot out of the ground. It wouldn't move. It was stuck.

Siren knew she had him. Reveling at the opportunity, her fists began glowing bright green. She threw numerous lefts and rights until they were too much for Conrad to handle. Her fists connected with his face. WHAM, CRACK, Siren nailed him one, two, three, four times. She ended her barrage of blows with a powerful punch to his chest. The Mystic dropped to one knee with his foot still stuck in the ground and took some deep breaths. He winced in pain. Knowing he was running out of time, he closed his eyes and concentrated. Conrad's arms flashed blue. He thrust them forward, yelling in exertion, "Yyyaaaaaahhh!" As Siren threw a roundhouse to Conrad's head, he hurled a shock wave forward with tremendous propulsion. It annihilated her, launching her backward like a toy doll. She landed next to the Nywolves and Regin.

Help Has Arrived

Priya and crew arrived by Carys' side. Carys was shooting glowing arrows at the oncoming army. She was flinging arrows at a fantastic speed, so fast the act of her shooting the arrows was barely visible to the naked eye. What gave it away were the glowing streaks splicing through the air, and more telling, the Devians flying backward as the tremendous force of the energetic arrows hit them. Although Carys had killed many, it was merely a dent in the overwhelming numbers attacking.

Priya reached Carys first and sliced through a Devian with her glaive as it was swinging its sword at Carys. She cut through two more and teased, "Thought you could use some help!"

"Very thoughtful of you, daughter! You got here just in time! I could use a breather!" Carys shouted over the battle noise, not bothering to look at Priya while she continued shooting arrows. Priya noticed the sweat dripping off Carys' forehead.

In the distance, up on the hill, Aiden saw what looked like a firefight between two people. Flaming bluish fireballs and white blasts shot back and forth. He wondered who could be up there fighting. WHAM, SMACK, THUD! A horde of enemies interrupted his concentration, slamming into the group of heroes. An arduous battle of hand-to-hand combat began.

Aiden lifted his arm, blocking the edge of an ax head. It stuck in his armguard. Looking over the ax head, he saw the Devian sneering at him. It was trying to pull its ax out of his armor. Aiden pulled a dagger out from his waistband and shoved it up through the ugly creature's chin.

Borak front kicked a Devian before him, dropping it to the ground. He followed with a downward sword plunge. Jack close-lined two Devians and hammer-fisted both when they hit the ground. Their heads were smashed under his brute strength. Melia threw her boomerang blade, then spun and chopped off the heads of two Devians with her sword.

Carys quickly activated an energy shield between the good guys and the evil army. Priya and the rest of the gang began stabbing through the shield in what seemed like a futile effort to reduce the looming number of hideous Devians, evil Hairies, and sporadic, angry Grandars. They saw two evil Hairies leap over the shield with their swords drawn. They were in line to come down right on top of Carys. No one was close enough to stop them, but Melia knew her boomerang was on its way back. She caught a glimpse of it returning in its flight. Since the boomerang blade returned to her hand, Melia dove to the side, trying to aim its return path so it would hit the Hairies as they descended. The boomerang hit one Hairie and knocked it sideways. It flailed off-course to the ground. The other Hairie was about to land on Carys.

Suddenly, Cedric appeared, flying in from the darkness. He yelled, sounding a little woozy, "Na'rt this time yer hairy bastert!" The evil Hairie in the air looked shocked as Cedric's dagger plunged into its neck. Both fell to the ground beside Carys.

Gil flew in, headfirst, behind Cedric. He landed on the other evil Hairie, and both tumbled. Gil ended up on top and began pummeling the Hairie under him with a barrage of punches. Even though Gil didn't appear to need his help, Cedric got up to one knee and threw his dagger at the evil Hairie being pummeled.

The dagger missed its mark and stuck into Gil's calf. He shouted in annoying pain, "Aaaahhhh! You IDIOT!"

Gil pulled the dagger out of his calf and nonchalantly sunk it into the evil Hairie's forehead.

Using all her power and with no time to spare, Carys brought her hands inward, then thrust them outward, transferring the shield into an energetic blast. The blast knocked the entire army to the ground. Carys was propelled backward with such force she slid on her feet to Naru and Conrad, who were almost a hundred yards behind her. She came to a stop, staggered, and fell to the ground.

Conrad reached for Carys' arm and missed, "Mother!" he cried out.

"I'm okay. I'm okay. I need a moment," Carys responded, breathing heavily.

There was an explosion on the hill where the other firefight was taking place, followed by falling trees. They heard more fighting, then a loud bang, and finally, a bright light. The bright light shone for a few seconds, then went out.

The King, Conrad, and Carys saw a white streak coming from the hill. It jumped in the air over the castle wall and landed with a momentous thud next to them. It was a man. He paused in a crouched position, holding a gloriously glowing scepter. He looked up, and everyone saw his face. It was Magus.

Magus stood up, grinning arrogantly. "The King! It's the King!" he mocked, throwing his hands up emphatically, "It's been a while, Naru. How have you been? Hopefully, you've been a little nicer to that one." He motioned with his chin toward Carys.

"Magus, you son-of-a-bitch! What the hell are you talking about?" He continued before Magus could answer, "I've been waiting too long for the chance to kill you! Ever since you stole the necklace and the medallion and killed my grandson!" Naru was seething with anger.

"Ah, yes, your grandson. Merv, was that his name?" Magus replied emotionlessly, rubbing his chin, "A special little boy, that one. He had a lot of power in him. It's a shame I had to consume it. He died, crying, begging for his father!" Magus glared at Conrad.

Overwhelmed

Priya, Aiden, and the rest of the group watched what was unfolding between the Royal Mystics and Magus. While they were distracted, some of Magus' army creatures began rising to their feet.

Jack nudged Priya, saying, "Um, we may have a problem here, mate," as more of the creatures regained their stance.

"No problem we can't handle!" Priya replied confidently. Raising her glaive in the air, she ran at the enemies in front of her. Aiden and the rest of the group were right behind her.

Priya swung her glowing weapon in a sweeping motion, slicing every Devian standing before her. She swung again, chopping more enemies in half.

Aiden jumped in the air, swung his sword downward, and split open the chest of a Grandar. He turned, blocked a sword strike, punched the Devian in the face, sliced another Devian, and stabbed the first Devian in the stomach.

Borak ran and flipped, broke a Devian's sword with his, and sliced the vile creature across the face. The martial artist quickly side-kicked another Devian in the throat. He turned, swiped his sword across a third Devian's neck, then spun, blocked an attack, spotted the weak spot in a fourth creature's armor, and jammed his sword into it.

Melia threw her boomerang blade and mowed down any Devians in its path. She jump-kicked another Devian; spun backward, jamming her dagger into a Hairie's temple; pulled the dagger out, and punched another Devian in the face.

Jack picked up a large log and whipped it back and forth. He smashed the chests and heads of many Devians, killing them instantly.

The smaller, speedier, yet still drunken Hairys, Cedric and Gil, used teamwork and distraction in their attacks.

"That all ye're got, ya ugly mongrels?" egged on Gil, messing with the Devians.

"Yaaa, you move as fast as Gil's, uh........" he hiccuped, "Grandma!" chimed in Cedric.

Gil glanced briskly at his partner and gave a "What the heck is wrong with you" look, then retorted, "Why would ye're say that? She's always feeding you!"

Cedric reassured, "Oh, ya, I love uh," he hiccuped again, "Her food," then teased, "You got'er admit though, she's perty slow!"

"That's uh, that's uh, you should be nicer!" Gil replied, almost losing his train of thought.

"Yaa, I guess so," Cedric admitted. Zoning in on another Devian, he told it, "You smell as bad as Gil's grandpa!"

The Devian stopped in its tracks, turned its head sideways, lifted its arm, and smelled itself. Cedric jumped forward and slit the Devian's throat. It fell to the ground, dead.

Gil stood for a second, staring at Cedric. He almost said something but stopped himself. He simply chuckled and stabbed another Devian.

Although they were killing the evil creatures in staggering numbers, the heroes became encircled by the recovered army. Bodies were piling up, tripping some of the villains as they attacked but not slowing them down enough to keep up with the pace. The circle inched smaller. It was becoming apparent the good guys were running out of time.

Borak and Melia were fighting side-by-side. They were keeping an eye on one another as they flipped around, slicing and dicing Devians and Hairies. A Grandar rushed ahead, knocking Devians out of its way in a bold, rash attempt to kill them.

Borak yelled, "Go up!"

Borak immediately grabbed Melia's hand, whirled around, and slung her up in the air. She flipped over the Grandar's head, cut through its neck from behind, and landed on her feet. The Devians watched as the Grandar's head slid off its body and fell to the ground. After seeing this, the Devians hesitated and looked at each other. They were all waiting for one another to attack, but none wanted to go first.

Priya and Aiden were fighting ferociously on the other side of the circle. They sensed the circle shrinking but ignored it as they continued to fight.

Jack was next to them. He ditched the log he used as a bat and substituted it with an unconscious Devian. He swung the limp Devian, hitting evil creatures and knocking them back into the crowd.

"You, too, aye, ya bloke? I'd think twice about that! Ah, another one! Come on, ya pissheads!" Jack provoked enthusiastically, appearing to be having the time of his life. He teased the angry creatures while they rushed at him. "You guys should try this! It works great!" he shouted to Priya and Aiden.

"Uh, I'll leave that on for you, Jack!" Aiden replied, grinning at the comical sight.

The Devian Jack was swinging looked like a large, ugly, red bat whipping around in the giant's hands.

Priya heard what the two said and managed a giggle. She was exhausted and worried she might not have much energy left. The beautiful Princess crippled two Devians with energy blasts and swung her glaive around, slicing another's chest but lost her footing while doing so and fell to the ground. A group of Devians ran at Priya while she was down. One made it within striking distance and slung its sword through the air, aiming for her neck. Just before the excited Devian's sword decapitated her, Aiden stuck his sword in the way and blocked the attack.

"Uh uh," Aiden said, smirking at the Devian.

Aiden spun, whipping his sword around and cutting the Devian's throat. The Devian clutched at its throat, piecing together what happened, and fell over. It lay on the ground bleeding out. Aiden tried to pick Priya up, but they were immediately overwhelmed by more Devians.

A dog-pile of villains began forming on top of Aiden and Priya. They heard, "Catch, ya ugly buggers!" It was Jack. He threw his Devian bat at the group of Devians over them, knocking the creatures down like bowling pins.

Cedric and Gil weren't talking as much now that they were running out of energy. Their arms and legs were burning, and their weapons were heavy. The circle was breaking down, but they weren't giving up.

Cedric wanted to say something to his friend, just in case they didn't make it. "Gil, remember when you told me you love me?" he asked while still fighting.

"Yea," responded Gil.

"I love you, too!" Cedric admitted genuinely, "Your family was always good to me. I want you to know that."

The circle of enemies collapsed. Many creatures flooded in. Even though there were piles of bodies and more than half of the army had been killed, it wasn't enough. Cedric and Gil went down, swinging and stabbing more Devians. Gil felt a sharp pain as a dagger pierced his shoulder.

Jack ran and dove on more Devians piling on top of Aiden. He was stabbed in his thigh and sliced across his back in doing so. Aiden felt a numbness in his stomach as a sword entered his body and exited his back.

Priya looked around and couldn't believe her eyes as the creatures closed in. She could hardly see Cedric and Gil buried under a pile of Devians. Jack was bloody and trying to get to Aiden under another pile of creatures. Aiden had disappeared entirely. Borak and Melia kept a small window around her, preventing the army from swarming her. The martial arts duo used incredible skills to take out as many Devians as possible.

Priya closed her eyes and searched for an answer. While her eyes were closed, she remembered something her father told her during the ritual of completion. After he inserted the Watre gem into her chest, Naru had said, "Remember, you are now one with the world. You can not only wield your weapon's power, but you can summon the world's energy through you."

Priya opened her eyes dramatically wide. She raised her glaive and yelled, "GOOD...WILL...PREVAIL!!!"

Priya's glaive lit up gloriously. She jammed her weapon into the ground. The glaive seemed to gather energy from the ground, and at the same time, the sky darkened, thunder clouds formed, and lightning darted in all directions across the heavens.

The Royal Mystics vs. Magus

Conrad erupted in a fury. Time slowed as he charged Magus, determined to impose his revenge. Conrad pulled out a miniature halberd as he rushed forward. Magus saw Conrad's shoulder drop to the right and knew Conrad would lunge using that arm. Moving in a Matrix-type motion, Magus stepped to his left and leaned backward. The halberd skimmed by his cheek, shaving off pieces of hair. The dark sorcerer grabbed Conrad's left arm and whipped Conrad over his shoulder with a judo throw. Conrad slammed hard to the ground.

Carys gave Naru a nod to encourage him to help their son. The King's attention quickly adjusted to Magus, and he pulled the sacred sword from its sheath. The legendary sword glistened, radiating blue color. Naru held the sword up by his face, readying himself in an attack stance.

Magus saw the King draw his weapon. Magus pulled a concealing cover off the bottom of his sceptre, revealing a blade. The sceptre was also a naginata. Magus twirled the sceptre, displaying his weaponry skill. He flipped it end-over-end until he finished in a ninja stance, ready for battle.

"Get ready to die, Magus!" Naru promised.

"I'm afraid I won't be the one dying, King," Magus calmly declared.

Two of the most powerful beings in the land rushed at each other. Carys was still on the ground and forced herself to stand. Magus whipped the blade end of his sceptre around. Naru leaned back, slid under the strike, felt the breeze from the passing blade, and stopped behind Magus. Naru turned and sliced with his sword. Magus blocked the strike with the scepter, then flipped around and swung the sceptre again. Naru blocked the attack with his arm guard. The two continued fighting, striking and blocking with their weapons. Sparks were flying from the ruthless strength of the assaults. Carys dove into the mix, slicing with her sword. Magus blocked her strike while dodging another blow from Naru and side-kicked Carys with such power that white energy flashed at the end of his foot. The Queen flew backward and hit the ground. She tried to suck in air but couldn't because the breath was knocked out of her. Naru and Magus continued to fight.

The powerful Mystics went back and forth...block, punch, punch, dodge, kick, counter, punch, block, kick. Magus dodged a strike and rushed Naru. He tackled the King to the ground. Naru used the momentum and rolled backward, reversing the take-down. He ended up on top of the warlock. Magus kicked him off. Naru landed five feet away from Magus.

The King held the sacred sword in the air and commanded, "World of Legends, give me strength!"

The sword lit up in a vibrant blue color. Naru whirled the sword around, again displaying his extraordinary weaponry skills. He ended the dazzling show in an intimidating stance, ready to deliver the killing blow. At this time, Conrad gained consciousness and realized he had been knocked out when he was slammed. He noticed his father had summoned the world for more power and knew it was his turn.

Conrad held his halberd in the air and shouted, "World of Legends, give me strength!"

The Royal Mystics weapons now radiated with extra power. Naru and Conrad attacked at the same time.

Naru ran at Magus so fast; he skipped through the air as if teleported. The King instantly went from ten steps away to directly in front of Magus. Naru swung his sword and cracked the evil sorcerer's chest, obliterating his armor. Conrad followed, swinging his halberd, and cut Magus' arm at the shoulder. Magus' arm fell from his body. Magus fell to the ground from the impact. Completely astonished, he looked over at his arm. He never thought these royal bastards would ever get the best of him.

"You have anything to say before you die, you murdering son-of-a-bitch?" Naru threatened. He had been waiting a long time for this moment.

Magus ignored Naru and crawled toward his arm. He was thinking about the sceptre in his arm's hand.

Naru followed Magus. He confidently whipped his sword around, preparing to kill the man who represented the end of the world. He stepped on Magus' severed arm before Magus reached it and held his sword to the dark wizard's throat.

"What's wrong? Now, you have nothing to say?" Naru badgered as he glared into the evil sorcerer's eyes. He waited, giving Magus one last chance to say something.

Eyes narrowing in growing frustration, Magus scolded, "You imbecile! What? You think you've won?" He paused to see Naru's reaction, looking annoyed as if he thought Naru should know better. He continued, "I've barely begun, King. It is you who has lost!"

Magus swiftly grabbed Naru's foot and pulled it out from under him. As Naru fell, Magus lunged for his severed arm and caught a piece of the sleeve. With a wicked smile on his face, the dark wizard dragged his arm to him. Conrad saw what Magus was doing and dove to stop him. Magus pulled the sceptre out of his detached hand and raised it in the air. It instantly activated, sparked, and built power.

The fight returned to slow-motion as all three Royal Mystics attacked at once: Carys used all her will to run at Magus full speed and was only a few steps away from him; Naru rose to one foot, slicing at the villain's neck with the sacred sword; Conrad was diving through the air, his halberd only inches away from the wicked sorcerer's face.

Magus yelled triumphantly, "The King is dead!" He jammed the sceptre into the ground.

Lightning in the sky came together, forming one colossal bolt. It raced from the depths of the dark clouds and hit Magus' sceptre with a thunderous bang. This activated an electromagnetic field that halted the royal Mystics in place. The lightning bolt continued electrifying the sceptre, creating one constant terrifying bolt from the sceptre to the sky. Electric arcs shot out from the sceptre and began shocking the Mystic heroes.

Rain-Flooded Tornado

The thunderous bang was jolting. It caused the heroes and the evil army to stop fighting and look at what was happening over by the Royal Mystics.

Priya's glaive continued to glow. A torrential downpour began, and a tornado vortex formed in the clouds above her. The vortex dropped down and connected to the top of her shimmering weapon. The rain swirled in the tornado. The evil army of creatures was distracted by Magus' massive lightning bolt. They felt the whirl of wind and water trying to pick them up and looked back to see what they had missed. Fear overtook their faces as the vortex sucked them upward, lifting them off the ground. The wicked creatures' victorious demeanor evaporated.

Aiden couldn't feel anything. He coughed up blood. He looked at his stomach and saw a sword handle sticking out of it. He knew what this meant. It meant he didn't imagine being impaled by it. He reached behind him and felt a sword blade sticking out of his back.

The savior of the worlds thought, "How can this be? I can't die now. How can I save the worlds if I die?"

Aiden looked around and saw Jack lying next to him on his back, bloody with multiple stab wounds and clutching his leg. Cedric was freaking out while putting pressure on Gil's shoulder. Melia and Borak, wounded and exhausted, were kneeling and staring up in the air. Priya, holding her glaive, was exerting a massive amount of energy. Above the glaive was the most violently beautiful sight he had ever seen. The entire evil army was spinning around in a giant rain-flooded tornado. As he stared at this miraculous event, lightning struck the tornado, lit it up, and zapped everything inside with thousands of volts of electricity. Aiden then noticed another enormous lightning bolt electrifying Magus' sceptre. He saw the three Royal Mystics lifted into the air while being electrocuted. It appeared they were being burned from the inside out.

Saying Goodbye

Naru looked at his wife, who had her teeth clenched while she convulsed in pain. Carys held her hand out, reaching for her husband, the King, who had done so well protecting this world. She wanted to touch him one last time. Naru grabbed his wife's hand, then shifted his gaze over to his son, who had a solemn look on his face. Conrad acknowledged the circumstance, doing his best to ignore the immense pain. He gave his father a dignified nod as if to say, "I'm proud of the life you gave me."

Naru nodded back to his dying son. He confided, "I'm proud of you... my son," then looked back over at Carys endearingly and told her, "And I love you dearly, my wife." He turned his head slightly to address both his wife and son. He smiled optimistically and said, "Now, let's go say hi to my grandson."

The clouds seemed to recharge and released one last blast of energy. Another tumultuous boom and the remainder of the momentous lightning bolt was sent into the sceptre. The sceptre flashed brightly, and the electric arcs electrocuting the Royal Mystics intensified. The extra force blew Naru's sword from him like a shot from a cannon. The sacred sword soared high in the sky and dropped as it came to the river. It flew by the waterfalls below the castle and disappeared into the depths of the water. The electric arcs electrocuting the Royal Mystics returned to the Aire gemstone on top of the sceptre. Held within those arcs remained the Mystics souls. Their bodies dropped to the ground. The King, Queen, and Prince of Heirstone were dead.

Magus stood up. His entire body and his sceptre were glowing extravagantly. He placed his severed arm on his shoulder, and it melded to his body like it was metal. He turned to where his army was fighting and saw them electrocuted by a whirling vortex. He also saw the rest of the heroes gathering themselves up.

Magus smirked arrogantly, saying to himself, "Everyone will die!"

With Naru dead, Magus was now the most powerful being in the land. He lifted his sceptre high in the air and slammed it back to the ground. The ground erupted in a vast explosion, producing a massive tidal wave of dirt. The gigantic dirt wave barreled straight for her.

Hurry Up

Aiden managed to push himself to his feet. He felt as if something even worse was going to happen. He had gotten the attention of Borak and Melia and motioned for them to help him drag Jack close to Priya. Priya was still stuck holding her glaive and powering the vortex.

Once they drug Jack close enough to Priya, Aiden's body gave out on him, and he collapsed. He told Melia and Borak to get the two Hairies, so they did. No one questioned why Aiden wanted them all close together. Aiden had an unfamiliar "all-knowing" look in his eyes, so they did as he asked. It was as if he knew what to do even though he had never done it before.

Aiden peered over at the Royal Mystics and witnessed the disappearance of the ginormous lightning bolt. There was an ear-splitting crack, and the three Mystics fell to the ground, lifeless. Then Aiden saw Magus stand to his feet, beaming with power, reattach his arm, and turn toward him.

"Let's go, let's go, let's goooo!" Aiden yelled.

Melia and Borak semi-carried and dragged Gil and Cedric as fast as they could to Aiden and the others. They felt the urgency even without fully understanding the reason for what they were doing. They just knew this was what they needed to do.

Aiden glanced over at Priya and saw she was still entirely consumed by her glaive. He looked at Magus and saw the warlock lift his sceptre in the air and slam it back down. KAABOOOOM!!! He heard the sound first and then saw the extensive explosion. For some reason, it sounded muffled. He immediately felt the wind blow past his face. A monstrous wave of dirt followed and rushed at them. A familiar surge of power activated Aiden's body, and a blue illumination encircled him. Before he could do anything, a bright light flashed in front of his eyes and, strangely, he heard that familiar voice again.

Vision

......" Wake up, honey! Honey, wake up!" the voice said. "Hellooooo! I thought we were going on a date?"

Again, that voice. Aiden knew that voice. Aiden opened his eyes to see Sasha standing before him, continuing to talk, "Don't worry, just a friendly date. I know you see that..." She paused a second, tapping her chin, "Priya girl. She's a pretty one. Good pick! Although, moving on kind of fast, huh?" Sasha stopped talking to look into Aiden's eyes.

Shocked, he was looking at his dead wife; Aiden responded the best he could, "Um, uh, I didn't mean...um, where are we? Are you here?" He grabbed Sasha's hand.

Sasha pulled her hand back, elaborating, "And aren't you guys, like... family or something?" Aiden began to answer, but she cut him off, "Anyway, come on, let's go! We're going to miss the sunset!"

Before Sasha could walk away from him, Aiden grabbed her hand again, turned her around, and hugged her tightly.

Aiden genuinely told her, "I missed you soooooo much!"

They pulled off the highway and parked at a spot overlooking a cliff and the ocean. The sun was setting into the sea.

"Remember when you brought me here? It was our first date. This place is where our family began," Sasha said, staring off into the ocean. For some reason, she didn't seem like herself.

Aiden's eyes became watery, and he asked, "Hon, why did we come here?" After Sasha didn't answer, Aiden spoke again, "I remember that day. It was a wonderful day and a great memory, but now it's a memory that hurts."

It was quiet for a minute. A tear rolled down Aiden's cheek.

"Did you keep your promise?" Sasha finally questioned. She said it as matter-of-factly as he had ever heard her.

"I'm sorry, promise?" Aiden replied, trying to remember.

"You said you would watch over him. You promised!"

Abruptly, there was a cry coming from below the cliff. Aiden quickly got out of the car and scanned the rocky cliff bottom. His heart sank when he saw what or rather who was crying. It was Chase. He was lying on a large rock, bloody and injured.

"Oh, my God, Aiden! You promised! What happened to our son? Why didn't you protect him?" Sasha screamed lividly.

Aiden did his best to explain, "I, uh, I tried! They blew up the building!"

"Dad, help me! Why did you leave me here?" Chase shouted. He had stopped crying and was staring directly at his father.

Aiden was becoming frantic. He yelled down to his son, "Buddy, hold on! I'm coming to get you!"

Then, chillingly, Chase hollered, "I'm going to die!"

Aiden didn't know what to think and told Sasha, "Honey, stay here. I'm going to get him. Everything will be fine!"

"Stay here!" Sasha argued as if what her husband said was unheard of, "This happened because I trusted you! I'm not staying here! I'm going to save our son!"

Having her mind already made up, Sasha turned and jumped off the cliff.

"Noooo, wait!" Aiden shouted as he grasped at her shirt and felt it slip through his fingers, "What? Honey!" He watched his wife fall to her death.

Aiden barely kept from falling himself, although, at the moment, he didn't care. He fell to his knees, tears pouring from his eyes. He held his hands over his eyes while he cried. He realized he hadn't heard anything for a few minutes, so he dropped his hands and looked back down at the cliff bottom. To Aiden's astonishment, no one was there, not even his wife's body.

Oddly, he heard another voice. This one sounded like it was coming from the sky. It was familiar, as well.

"Hey, it is him! Aiden! Hey Aiden!" BANG! CRACK! WHAM! "Come on! Get up, you lazy bum! I've been looking for you for weeks!"

Aiden's surroundings became fuzzy. He continued to hear loud bangs and thuds until he heard something shatter. Suddenly, the scene in front of him vanished, and everything became white. He felt like he was sleeping and being shaken awake.

"Is he alive?" said the voice, and the same voice replied, "I think so. Wakey, wakey, lazy bum!" "Be careful! Don't hurt him!" warned the same voice again.

Confused, Aiden shook his head, trying to figure out what was happening...

Part 4

The Journey

The Fate of the Royal Mystics

It was extremely bright, but Aiden forced his eyes open. After a moment, he recognized the body in front of him was Farley.

"Farley? What the heck? What happened?" Aiden mumbled, still disoriented.

"Yes, it is me! No worries! Farley is here to save you! I'll have you back on your feet in no time! A little bit of training should do the trick! A little bit of this, and a little bit of that!" Farley remarked, excitedly flexing his biceps, hidden under his fur. He began throwing combos of punches and kicks in the air.

Wow, you sure we have time for all that?" Aiden asked jokingly.

Farley ignored Aiden. He was trying to do a handstand pushup. "And can't...mmph...forget...rrrr...this!" the little furry Evo said and fell over half-way through the pushup.

Aiden enjoyed a moment of laughter before reeling over in pain. "Owwww! Oh, my goodness. Don't make me laugh. It hurts," he informed.

Remembering a sword had impaled him, Aiden felt his stomach and lifted his shirt to see a scar where he had been stabbed. He felt his back and found another scar.

"How am I okay? I mean, what the heck could have happened?" Aiden wondered out loud, hoping Farley would answer.

Farley wasn't paying much attention. He was entertaining himself by shooting colorful energy from his hands. Then, he realized Aiden was waiting for him to say something.

"He's looking at you, Farley," the Evo said to himself, then answered, "Um, sorry, you wondered how you are okay? Uh, well, you created healing shields before the tidal wave of dirt hit you guys." He started playing with his magic again, casually.

Aiden persisted, "Healing shields?" He raised his eyebrows prompting Farley to explain.

Farley continued, "Aww, yes, it is an orb that protects any entities within it and heals them over time. It also charges them up to full power. You must have reacted when you saw the others injured and put healing shields around them before it was too late. Haha, almost squashed into a pancake! Good job, hero Aiden! Farley would have been sad."

The little Evo stopped after he said this and stared at Aiden with an awkward smile. At this point, it occurred to Aiden that Evos sometimes have difficulty portraying emotion.

"Is that your sad face?" teased Aiden before resuming the topic of conversation, "So, elaborate, please. You said it heals over time, and my wounds are healed. How long have I been here?"

"Hmm, well," Farley responded, "The shields speed up healing time, but I've been looking for you for a few weeks; sooo, I'm not sure. I'd guess a few weeks. I'm so glad I found you! Everyone thought you were dead! They will be so happy! Come on, let's go! We have to find the others!"

The impact of the healing shield crashing to the ground created the crater. The animated furry character waved for Aiden to follow him and, enthusiastically, hopped out of the crater.

Not moving as spry as usual, Aiden caught up to Farley, asking, "So am I the first you found?"

"You are the first," Farley replied.

"Do you think the rest of the gang is still alive?" Aiden asked another question.

"Alive, yes, I hope so, boss man!" Farley answered, skipping around.

"Yeah, me, too. I'm still trying to wrap my head around everything. I had the craziest dream. It felt so real," Aiden continued.

"Hmmm, dream. You mean vision! You will have visions from the healing shields," Farley explained.

"Vision?" repeated Aiden, "That would mean there's something real about it. Wouldn't it?" He turned his head to the side and said out loud to himself, "But what?"

With a sly look on his face, Farley added, "That is the question, Master Aiden. That is the question."

Suddenly, a realization hit Aiden like a ton of bricks, and he exclaimed,

"Shit, what happened to the King? My father, half-brother, and step-mother?" The last he remembered was them being electrocuted and falling to the ground like lifeless puppets. Aiden exclaimed desperately, "Farley! What happened to them?"

The Evo put his head down, accurately representing his emotion this time. Farley was regretting having to tell this story. It was the worst story he was ever going to tell. He knew he had to tell Aiden, though.

Woefully, the small furry creature inhaled a deep breath, then began talking, "Farley was low on energy, so I left on my usual travels to find more power. It is odd, though. I have had to wander further than normal ever since Magus returned. He is absorbing much of our world's energy. Anyhow, I was way further out than I wanted to be, but I was on to a good spot. I could smell the energy as I got closer, and when I found it, Farley was so happy! But then, I saw the clouds change, and lightning consumed the sky. It looked like a huge lightning bolt was frying the land in the castle's direction. I could only assume the worst."

......"Holy Moly!" reacted Farley, "What in the heck is that?" he asked himself.

"Whatever it is, it is not good," he responded to himself.

"I better get back! Am I full?" he asked himself again.

Farley took a second to assess himself, then answered, "Yes, I'm good. I should hurry! They probably need my help!"

For some reason, many Evos talked to themselves, especially when they were alone. Nobody knew why and learned to ignore it.

The concerned Evo hauled butt toward the castle, uncharacteristically, running past every peculiar-looking geological formation. He wished he hadn't had to travel so far, but it was the only place he could find. Farley ran and ran, sprinting without regard for his well-being. He became more worried by the minute. As he was racing to save his friends, he saw the enormous lightning bolt disappear and heard a loud boom. Exhausted, Farley stopped. After a moment, he heard another thunderous bang then saw four healing shields soaring through the air in different directions. He was relieved by this sight. Those who were in the shields were most likely okay. Not wasting any more time, the little Evo sprinted off again.

When Farley reached Heirstone, it was a disaster. He could only think of one person who could have caused this much destruction, Magus. The entire community was in ruins. The only thing left was a tattered castle. The tidal wave of dirt and rock had wiped out everything in its path. It looked like a massive earthquake tore up the land and left it ravaged and desolate. The partially dirt-filled moat was flooding. Thankfully, residents were starting to show themselves and search for other survivors. Farley made his way into the courtyard and couldn't believe his eyes. He saw what he was dreading most.

The King, Queen, and Conrad were lying dead in front of him. A few residents had gathered the bodies of the Royal Mystics and laid them together in a respectful manner. Farley knelt in front of them, weeping. It could not be true! There was no way! This horrible turn of events dumbfounded Farley, and he continued to cry.

In his agony, the Evo realized, "Wait, Priya is not here! Or Aiden! Or Sen! Or the rest of them! They must have been in the healing shields!" But sadness overtook him again, and he fell face forward, crying. "Nooo! Whyyyy!" he wailed......

Farley continued, "After I felt better, I vowed to find you guys. I knew I had to find the healing shields and reunite us. The King would want that. The worlds depend on it. Farley's so sad. I'm sorry, Master Aiden."

Aiden wiped the tears from his face. It was the news he had feared. He didn't think there was any way the Royal Mystics could have survived, but he still had hope.

The little Evo cheered up, saying, "But, at least, I found you! And there's more to find!"

Aiden forced a smile and replied, "That's right. We have to keep our heads on straight so that we can save the rest of us." His shoulders slouched, and he said under his breath, "But I can't believe they're gone."

Master Aiden

The two pushed forward. Farley led the way to a peak on a small mountain, giving them a good view of the land. Looking around, they took in its beauty. A large, lush valley extended into another mountain ahead of them. Various colorful trees and bushes ranging from greens, oranges, reds, and blues to purples covered the valley. One tree had pear-sized lavender fruit on it that looked delicious. Aiden walked toward it.

Farley stopped him, warning, "I wouldn't do that if I were you, Master Aiden. Those are desires fruits. They trick you with hallucinations of your most wanted desires, and you usually end up dead!"

Aiden was still processing the deaths of his newly discovered family, so the fruit of the desires tree didn't sound like a half-bad option. Of course, he didn't want to die, but he'd love to see his father again.

Aiden looked at Farley curiously for a second, then spoke lightheartedly, "Thanks for telling me. That sounds both good and horrible at the same time!" Aiden chuckled, followed by a pause, then spoke again, "Why have you been calling me Master? I would have thought Priya was your Master."

"Priya is my friend, so I replenish her magic, but she is not a Mystic like you, Master Aiden. I served the Royal Family, who are gone now, and who we loved so much, but their deaths left me without a master," Farley answered.

The small creature put his head down, mourning, then looked back at Aiden with his weird half-smile. He optimistically said, "You are the

Legendary Hero of Worlds, and you fight for good, like the Royal Family. You possess more power than you realize, which means the Legend is true; that you will be the most powerful Mystic in the land and overcome all evil. Because of this, it would be my honor to serve you and help you on your journey!"

Farley bowed and released a stream of yellow energy. It floated up in the air, bouncing back and forth like a feather, and found its way to Aiden's chest. Aiden's body absorbed the energy, and he felt an instant connection with the little Evo.

"Holy crap! What was that?" Aiden exclaimed, taking a step back in surprise.

Aiden shook his head and realized not only could he sense a connection with Farley, but he also felt more aware of his surroundings. It was as if he was more in tune with nature.

"What did you do? I feel..." Aiden held his chest, looking around while he talked, "I feel amazing!"

"We are connected now," explained Farley, "Once I choose a master, we become bonded, and you feel as I do...one with the world."

Aiden nodded and excitedly responded, "Sweet! So, this is how you feel? I, uh, I can feel the plants, and, and the animals!" He pointed down the mountain, "Over there! You see that? There's a rock deer!"

Aiden pointed at a group of rocks that he could see through a thicket of brush and trees. Oddly enough, one of the rocks had what looked like branches sticking out of it. As Aiden and Farley stared at the rocks, the one with branches moved and, sure enough, revealed it was a short, stubby, sandy beige, camouflaged deer with antlers.

"And there's a fohawk! Over there in that... oh... that death tree!" Aiden continued, recognizing he was pointing at the desires tree.

While they looked at the fohawk, it flew off with a desires fruit in its claw. The bird was colorful like a Macaw parrot but had the body structure of a predatory hawk. Uniquely, the bird's feathers on its head made a faux hawk.

Farley only watched with a smile, amused at Aiden's reaction to his newfound senses.

"Wow, that's a gorgeous bird!" Aiden complimented.

As Aiden watched the bird fly away, he noticed something or felt something through the trees. It was the presence of other beings, hidden deep in the side of the mountain ahead.

"I see something else! Over there! It's... wait... it's a few human-like creatures! It's... uh... two... no wait... there are two smaller ones over there, and they're not moving! I sense four bodies, I think! There, and there," Aiden spoke, exhilarated.

Aiden was pointing at two spots near to each other on the side of the mountain in front of them. On further investigation, they could see circular areas of the tree canopy missing, which suggested something big had crashed there.

Grinning even wider, Farley remarked, "You are a quick learner, Master Aiden. It seems you have found our next destination!

Training with Farley

After traveling several miles, Aiden and Farley arrived at one of the spots in the forest where the canopy had a sizable circular hole in it. It was impossible to miss the massive crater in the ground, angulated into the side of the mountain. They peered into the crater and saw it opened into a vast cavern that dropped about one hundred feet. The cavern traveled northward toward where Aiden sensed the location of the bigger bodies. Remarkably, when they scanned the bottom of the crater, they saw a blue circular orb with two small figures in it.

"Do you see that?" Aiden asked, "I think it's Cedric and Gil. I hope they're okay."

"Yes, me, too. How should we proceed, Master Ai...." Farley said but was cut off.

"Stop, please!" Farley's new master directed, "No more of this master stuff. It feels weird. Just call me Aiden, okay?" Farley nodded, and Aiden continued talking, "Um, that's a super far drop. I'm not sure how we're going to get down there." Aiden put his thinking cap on, trying to figure out what to do.

Farley spoke up, "Might I suggest something, Aiden? Why don't you use your powers? Your magic?"

"Well, that's a great idea, but the problem is I don't know how to control it. It seems no matter how much I practice, I can't figure it out," Aiden answered, shrugging his shoulders. He glanced down into the deep cavern, continuing to think.

There was a moment of silence. Then Farley's excited voice, "Let's try something! Can we? Farley will help!"

Aiden had his hand on his chin in thought. He turned toward Farley and shrugged his shoulders again, replying, "Okay, what should I do?"

The small Evo couldn't contain himself and hopped around in excitement. He realized Aiden was watching and stopped. He looked at Aiden with that awkward smile again.

Farley began speaking, "Perfect! Great! Okay, first we close our eyes..." He waited for Aiden to participate and continued, "And then, we take a deep breath in and let it out. Try to relax your body and breathe in again, and then out. Now, keep breathing and relax. Let your body feel the world around you and all the wonderful energy it has. Let your body take over and absorb the energy. Then think of what you want to do with that energy, and your body will react."

The magical creature began glowing and pulsating with power when he finished speaking. Aiden sensed Farley's energy building up and opened his eyes to see what was happening. He saw Farley flashing with immense power, appearing to be on the verge of performing something spectacular. The small furry Evo raised his arms, and...at first nothing...then...he grunted and Aiden heard a long, high-pitched fart that sounded, at first, like a trumpet, then sputtered into a whoopie-cushion noise.

Initially grinning from ear-to-ear, Aiden reeled over, laughing the hardest he'd laughed in quite a while. "Oh, my God! Haha. Oh, my God! Hahaha. Was that supposed to happen?" he asked between laughter.

"Uh, well," Farley was embarrassed and replied, "No, no, that was an accident. I had another accident."

Aiden tried his best to suppress his laughter as he didn't want to hurt Farley's feelings, but it was so funny he couldn't help but show he was holding it back.

"No worries, dude! It's happened to the best of us!" Aiden finally said, still holding back laughter.

Farley, feeling a little better, added, "You never know what might happen when you're that relaxed. I hope you don't mind. Sometimes I have gas when I concentrate. It's always been a problem for me."

Aiden placed his hands on his knees, not able to hold back his laughter any longer, and exclaimed, "What! You're a magical little creature who farts a lot? Hahaha, I've heard it all now. Of course, it's fine. It's friggin' great! Ha ha ha ha ha! What I'd like to know is where all that came from!" Aiden motioned, alluding to Farley's small stature.

Once Aiden regained his composure, they tried again. When they arrived at the part where Farley was glowing and flashing, Aiden smiled and peeked through one eye to see if Farley was going to fart again. This time he didn't. Farley made it past the moment and walked toward the edge of the hole, still glowing. He didn't stop at the edge. Instead, he planted his front foot and jumped, disappearing into the crater. Aiden quickly ran to the edge, fearing the worst. Instead, he saw Farley calmly free-falling, or floating, to the ground and landing on his feet.

Half-expecting to hear a crowd applaud with satisfaction as if this was an entertaining planned stunt, Aiden hollered into the hundred-foot-deep cavern at the magical Evo, "That was awesome!"

"Yes, Aiden! Awesome! Now, it is your turn!" Farley replied, grinning. He threw a thumbs up.

Aiden let out a fake laugh. He responded, "Right...um, you gotta be kidding me!" He gave another fake laugh and asked, "You're joking, right?"

Aiden's face changed from a sarcastic grin into a profound understanding of what Farley expected of him. It was absurd. Farley wanted Aiden to launch himself into a hundred-foot hole and float to the ground as if he was Superman. He took a minute to think about it.

Aiden replied, knowing it had to be done, "I, uh, I guess, I'll try." He took a few steps back and began pacing back and forth, talking to himself, "Well, I guess this is it! The end of my life! No...he did it. I mean, come on, Aiden. You fell like eighty floors from a building, and then the building fell on you. Not to mention, you practically stopped time and ran faster than the speed of light through a friggin' stargate. This is possible! Okay, what did Farley do?" Aiden thought for a second, then told himself, "Breathe. I have to breathe."

The practicing Mystic took a few deep breaths, trying to gather himself and mimic what Farley had done. After a few breaths, Aiden felt better and continued directing himself, "Okay, Aiden, now focus. Breathe and focus." He stood there for a minute, meditating.

A tiny spark appeared in his feet, followed by more sparks traveling up his legs. The sparks turned into a wave of energy fluctuating through his body, and he lit up even brighter than Farley. In the cavern, Farley sensed what was happening and smiled proudly. At this point, Aiden didn't even think about potentially dying. He walked to the edge of the enormous hole and jumped.

Electrified, Aiden looked magnificent but fell like a rock. "Ahhhhhhhh!" he yelled as he realized he wasn't in control. He smashed into the ground, creating an eight-foot pit.

Farley scurried over to the pit, not worried, and complemented, "Very impressive! You energized to full capacity! You weren't able to slow yourself in the air, but you'll get it! It took Conrad many efforts to master this. And I sense more strength within you, an ability to harness more energy than I have ever felt!"

In the pit, Aiden was lying flat on his back, moaning, "Ohhhhh! Ugghhhh! I'm sorry? You said that was impressive?" He rubbed his head while he talked, "I felt like flying concrete; thought I was a goner." Seeing Farley's lack of concern, Aiden commented sarcastically, "Um, don't worry about me, though. I do that all the time!"

Farley laughed before replying, "I don't think you understand. No one reaches full capacity, even after years of practice. You are unparalleled. Above all others!"

Aiden stared at Farley, wondering how this could be true when he honestly felt like a failure. Studying Farley's unrelentless, calm seriousness, which somehow displayed the truth and reality of what he said, Aiden decided to believe the magical creature. After all, Farley was the one who knew about this stuff. It was also fantastic for Aiden to realize how powerful he was. Aiden arrogantly yet jokingly remarked, "You damn right! Now, help me out of here, would you?"

Once out of the pit, Aiden's attention redirected toward the extensive depth of the cavern. He noticed how the light from the broken ceiling, where the orb went through, gleamed off the sparkling gray walls.

"Why do the walls sparkle like that?" Aiden questioned out loud to himself.

Farley overheard and answered, "It's the magic, Mas...I mean, Aiden. The energy is everywhere!"

Cedric and Gil

Aiden looked over at what appeared to be his two buddies stuck inside the weird blue orb, or healing shield, as Farley called it. Aiden and Farley ran over to the orb to look inside. When they arrived, they could tell the two creatures were alive and were, without a doubt, Gil and Cedric. Both Hairies had gotten to their feet and were arguing and fighting over something.

"Get your hands off me! They smell horrid! Like you were picking butt. Oh no! You didn't, did you?" Cedric, very seriously, inquired.

"Shut up and give me my shoe!" replied Gil, completely ignoring Cedric's shenanigans.

Gil's hand slipped off Cedric while the two were tussling and flung a slippery substance.

"Ewww, what was that? You're a sicko! Get away from me!" Cedric pleaded and backed up to the other side of the orb.

Gil decided he'd had enough and pulled his other shoe off. He began chasing Cedric around the orb, protesting, "Quit messin' around and give me my damn shoe, for cryin' out loud! You always have to be a funny guy! My name's Cedric, and I'm hilarious, hahaha!"

Cedric continued, "Ewww! Somebody help me! Find me some sanitizer!"

Aiden decided it was time to let their presence be known and spoke up, "I'm sorry. I don't mean to interrupt this heartfelt, obviously, significant bro quarrel, but how did you guys wake up?"

Upon hearing Aiden's voice, Cedric stopped in the front of the orb. Gil, not hearing Aiden, continued running and whacked Cedric on top of the head with his shoe.

"Owww! Quit it! Look!" Cedric said, pointing at Aiden, then jubilated, "Aiden! You're alive! And Farley, too! Glad you're here! Where the heck were you two?"

Gil chimed in, "Oh, wow! I'm so happy to see you guys!" He glanced around, "Where is everyone else? Are they okay?"

"We think so!" replied Farley gleefully, jumping in excitement since the Hairies were happy to see him, too. He continued, "So happy! We are so happy! Hold on, guys! I'll get you out!"

Cedric banged on the side of the healing shield, thinking out loud, "What the heck is this thing?"

Still noticeably excited, Farley cracked the orb with a ninja strike and broke open a hole. The Hairies peeked out of the hole, examining the orb.

Farley informed, "It's a healing shield. It protected you from the dirt tidal wave, and it restored your wounds."

"Dirt tidal wave?" Cedric repeated as memories returned to both Hairies.

"Restored our wounds?" stammered Gil.

The Hairies looked themselves over. Cedric turned Gil toward him to examine his shoulder and found it healed. Gil also inspected Cedric to see if he was injured. He wasn't. The Hairie buddies jumped for joy, hugging each other.

The two exclaimed, "Hurray, we're both okay! Hurray, we're both okay!"

Initially, Aiden laughed but stopped to ask his question again, "I'm thrilled you're both okay, but I'm curious, how did you guys wake up? I was stuck in a confusing vision when Farley woke me up. I was under the impression we'd have to do the same for you."

The Hairie creatures looked at each other, and Gil spoke first, "I remember hearing a loud bang like something crashed." He tapped his chin in thought, "Or maybe, that was in my dream? Anyway, I jolted awake, throwing my shoe off. My shoe flew over and hit Cedric in the head, but he didn't wake up. Instead, he grabbed my shoe tightly and kissed it. He was talking in his sleep, saying, 'I'm sorry, baby. I won't do it again.' I tried to pull my shoe from him, but then he woke up and wouldn't let go. I think you guys saw what happened next."

"Ha," Cedric chimed in, "Ha, that's not what happened! I was kissing the beautiful Hairie princess from our homeland, who, now that I think of it, smelled like sweaty feet, and then you were trying to steal her from me with your disgusting dirty hands!"

It was quiet for a second. Cedric looked confused.

Gil was staring back at him with an expression that could only say one thing, "You're an idiot!"

Cedric looked away and started talking to himself, "Wait, I kissed the princess, then Gil came at me with his nasty butt juice hands, then I had the shoe...hmmm."

While Cedric pondered what happened, Aiden replied, "Well, that was interesting, but um...I guess that answered my question."

Cedric then smacked himself in the forehead and said, "Oh, my gosh, duh! The princess left me her shoe and ran away from Gil!"

Aiden chuckled and changed the subject, "Let's go this way, guys. There's another orb somewhere over here."

"Alright! Let's go!" Cedric agreed and told Gil, "You owe the Hairie princess an apology!"

"She's not here! That was a vision!" Gil replied, irritated, then asked Aiden, "Who do you think is in it?"

"I don't know. Maybe Melia and Borak," Aiden replied, "I saw two bodies."

The team made their way further into the cave, talking minimally and ignoring Cedric's banter about the Hairie princess. As they walked, they began seeing carvings and drawings on the walls, signifying others had been there before.

Farley said something interesting, "Farley feels deja vu. There's something familiar about this place."

Cedric agreed, "You're right! It does feel familiar! It seems like I've heard about this place before!"

"Yea, I'm sure you've heard all kinds of stuff," Gil teased.

Ignoring Gil's joke, Cedric finished his thought, "No, you know what, I've read about this place!"

Gil rolled his eyes, replying, "Ya, right!"

The Weapons Prophecy

The massive cavern dwindled into a smaller dark cave. Unlit torches were hanging on the walls. Aiden handed a torch to Farley, and he lit it with his hands like an incredible magic trick. The group continued through the narrowing cave. They searched the area, looking for another orb and more interesting markings on the walls. Gil noticed something written on the cave wall.

Gil announced, “Look! You guys see that? What does that say?”

A spider web concealed part of the writing, so Farley used the torch to burn it away. The heroes couldn’t believe what they saw. It said, “A weapon lies ahead. Do not proceed if you are not a hero. All others risk death for naught.”

“That’s it!” Cedric blurted out, “The Weapons Prophecy! It’s the Weapons Prophecy! That’s where I read it! This message is leading us to a trial!”

“Ah, yes, I believe so!” Farley exclaimed, moving his arms up and down in eagerness, “So much excitement! Such exciting times!”

The heroes from this world knew the backstory of the Weapons Prophecy. Although Aiden was amused, he was utterly lost.

Aiden asked, “Alright, sooo can someone fill me in?”

Cedric explained, “It’s my favorite prophecy! It describes mystical weapons hidden around the world. Each weapon was created for one of the heroes. Only that hero can wield the weapon’s true potential. Also, each weapon has a trial that only the hero for whom it was made can complete without dying. In other words, this weapon has been made for one of us! Well, hopefully, not Priya or Jack because they're not here."

Aiden raised his eyebrows at the prospect of the Weapons Prophecy. Then the group noticed something moving beside them. They looked over and saw Farley twerking by himself. Farley glanced up to see the group staring at him weirdly and froze in place.

Aiden broke the silence, questioning, "Where did you even learn that?"

Farley stood embarrassed, still bent over, and didn't know what to say.

Borak and Melia

The four comrades continued on their quest, although now they were looking for two things: their friends and the weapon trial. After traveling a bit further, the cave opened into another vast cavern. Yet again, the ceiling had an opening where the orb busted through. Sun rays, beaming through the hole, were warming. As soon as they walked into the cavern, they saw the orb sitting about twenty feet off the ground, dug into the wall where it crashed. No one could see inside the healing shield because of how high it was. Since they now had light, they threw aside their torches and darted toward the orb.

The cave wall was slick and steep. There was some kind of goo on it that prevented any type of grip for climbing. Cedric was first to the wall, and even with his ninja-like wall-climbing skills, he only slid down the wall when he jumped on it.

"Eww, the walls are slimy! I can't get up there!" Cedric complained.

"What the heck is that stuff?" Gil asked.

Before anyone could reply, Farley was already floating up toward the orb. Farley's floating threw Aiden off because he was watching Farley fly. However, the initial shock wore off quickly. Farley's feet and hands emitted energy specs as he floated upward and landed on the ledge. The magical Evo looked inside the healing shield and saw Borak and Melia.

"Farley, seriously? You couldn't tell me that you could fly? I mean, I saw you float down into the cavern, but I didn't think you could actually fly,"

Aiden expressed in his sarcastic manner. He reverted to the matter at hand, "Is it them? Are they okay?"

Aiden, Cedric, and Gil stood motionless, waiting for an answer. Not a moment later, they heard the orb shatter, then WHAM, THUMP! Farley flew backward over the ledge. This time, though, he wasn't flying. He fell twenty feet, landed on his back, and tumbled. Instantaneously, Borak and Melia jumped from the ledge, ready for battle.

"Whoa, guys! It's us!" Aiden reacted, putting his hands up defensively.

Borak locked eyes with Aiden, prepared to swing his sword. He was waiting to counter. Something felt off. Why hadn't the enemy attacked yet? Borak's grip on his weapon loosened as he recognized his friend.

"Aiden!" Borak shouted and put his arms out for a hug. Aiden embraced Borak, patting him on the back. They were happy to see each other alive.

Melia, half-confused but putting the pieces together, sheathed her sword. The two Hairies pounced on her, acting as if she had been gone for years, and finally came home.

Farley rose to his feet and enjoyed watching the true friendship they had developed for one another on full display. The group formed a circle. Aiden turned to Melia and caught her eyes. He gave her a compassionate hug.

Aiden thankfully told Melia, "I'm so happy you two are okay!"

"Me too, but what happened?" Melia responded in a severe tone, "How are we here? How are we all...alive? The last thing I remember was fighting the army and knowing we were gonna die. And then I woke up here, being attacked, or so I thought." She turned to Farley, "Sorry 'bout that, little guy," then asked another question, "And...and all of us are okay?" She glanced around and realized not everyone was there, so she corrected herself, "Or, almost all of us. Where's Priya... and Jack?"

"They're next on the agenda. Hopefully, they made it, too, but first, we have to find them," Aiden answered.

Finding a Weapon Trial

As the others caught Melia and Borak up to speed, something shiny at the far end of the cavern caught Farley's eye. This cavern was about half the size of the first one but looked very similar. It also had grayish zig-zagging walls that sparkled in the sunlight. The cavern continued for another fifty feet to the right of where the healing shield landed. Close to the end was something flickering on and off, almost as if it were a small blinking light.

"Look at that, guys!" Farley interrupted the conversation, pointing at the apparent blinking light. He immediately walked toward it.

"Wow...what is that?" added Cedric, sharing Farley's curiosity.

Farley and Cedric hurried over to the blinking light. They made a rare discovery. A small piece of the wall had been cut out and replaced with a shiny rock that pulsated energy. These rocks are called shiners and are very uncommon. They are natural lights the cavepeople used before they went extinct. Cave fungi grew partly over the shiny rock and on the wall above it.

"Something is blinking a little higher! Can you see that?" Farley called out, again being the one to notice.

"Yea, I see it! It looks like another shiner!" Cedric answered, "We gotta get this fungus off here! We need..."

Before Cedric could finish his sentence, Borak slid his sword across the wall a few times, clearing the fungi. Under the white slimy fungi, there was another shiner rock and more writing. Cedric and Farley looked at each other with huge grins.

The writing said, "Enter to find a weapon for a ninja. He has trained his entire life with his sister. This is a test meant for one."

Everyone in the group looked at Borak.

"Brother," Melia said, locking eyes with Borak, "It's your trial!"

Borak wasn't expecting this. He knew the trial could be his but didn't think it would be. The ninja was unsure of what to say.

All the children of this world dreamed about these trials. They learned of them through fairy tales and stories passed down for generations by their parents. Finding a trial explicitly designated for you meant you were, without a doubt, one of the Heroes of Legends. During their childhoods, Borak and Melia role-played being heroes and finding their designated weapons. They never imagined it would come true.

Soaking in this realization, Borak composed himself and said, "Yes, this is it. This time it's for real." He took a deep breath, attempting to stay calm, "We need to find the way in."

Melia was concerned for her brother to confront this destined yet life-threatening task, but she was also thrilled. The entire group of heroes gained an invigorating boost of energy. They put their heads together, trying to find the entrance.

After searching for a while, Aiden found an odd-looking crack. "There it is! That's the door!" he proclaimed. The crack ran up and around the wall in the shape of a rectangular door. "How the heck do we open it?" he added.

"I remember something in the prophecy about this. It says to look up," Cedric said and began thinking out loud, "Looking up is the key to the beginning. Loookkiinngg uuupp..." He looked up while saying this, "...is the keeeyyy to the beginning."

When Cedric finished his sentence, he saw it. There was a vine hanging from a short rigid bar camouflaged by a covering of fungi. The end of the vine hung about ten feet under and to the bar's right. About fifteen feet below the end of the vine was a ledge, presumably from where someone was supposed to jump to reach the vine. The ledge was five or six feet off the ground and had a small rock stairway leading to it.

Cedric didn't say a word and took off running. He ran up the rock stairway, jumped off the ledge, ran three steps up the wall, and leaped again for the vine. Stretching as high as he could, he hooked the vine with his fingertips and managed to pull the vine down a smidge to get his whole hand around it. He held on tight to the vine and swung to the other side of the wall. The impulsive Hairie swung back and forth until he came to a stop.

Gil looked up at Cedric while Cedric hung on the vine and teased lightheartedly, "What the heck did you do now?"

Everyone was looking at Cedric. He replied, "I... uh... I..." He tugged on the vine, and nothing happened, "This was supposed to open the door!" Cedric started bouncing up and down on the vine.

While he was bouncing, Gil teased more, "Now, you're making a fool of yourself!"

Cedric continued to bounce, and the bar moved down slightly. Everyone saw the movement and flinched enthusiastically.

Borak shouted, "Keep doing that!"

Realizing his buddy was onto something, Gil jumped into action. He sprinted toward the ledge and lunged through the air. He didn't make it as high as Cedric but caught hold of his buddy's legs. From the impact of Gil's weight, the bar moved further and continued lowering as they swung back and forth. Unfortunately, by the time they stopped swinging, it had only moved halfway. Now, Cedric was stuck holding onto the vine with Gil grasping onto his pants.

"What the heck are you trying to do to me? You're pulling down my pants!" Cedric shouted as he grabbed his waistband with one hand to stop his pants from sliding down,

Gil was more worried about not completing the task at hand. He knew he had to do something, so he whipped his body back and forth, trying to build momentum.

Cedric struggled to hold his pants up and felt them sliding further down. "Hey, quit it! You're doing that on purpose," he accused with an odd look on his face.

Gil placed his feet on the wall and ran, giving them a good push. They swung back and forth twice, then Gil flung himself high in the air, did a flip, and grabbed the vine where Cedric was holding.

As gravity pulled Gil down, the lever yanked entirely into its downward position. The Hairies hung there, waiting for something to happen, but for some reason, something felt off. Cedric felt a breeze in an odd area and glanced down to see his pants were at his ankles. Gil saw Cedric's reaction and looked down to see the precarious situation in which they found themselves. They awkwardly looked up at each other.

"Stop staring at me, weirdo!" Cedric complained.

"I'm not! I, um, shut up! Why are your pants down?" Gil replied.

"Oh, right! Why are my pants down! Are you serious?" Cedric fumed.

"I didn't...I wasn't trying...I was just..." Gil couldn't help but laugh and told his half-naked friend, "Hahaha, would you pull your pants up!"

Cedric stared at Gil, super annoyed, and said, "You son-of-a-bitch."

Thankfully, the two Hairies heard a loud clunk that sounded like a mechanical door unlocking. They looked down at the others and saw them laughing. The other heroes heard the clunk as well but were having trouble focusing.

Borak's Bo-Blade

Cedric and Gil jumped down from the vine.

Cedric pulled his pants up and grumbled, "That was not funny!"

Borak chuckled, then looked at the makeshift door. He pushed on it. The wall budged slightly backward. Anxiously, Borak pushed harder, and the door creaked open, revealing a low-lit cave hallway. The ninja Roak glanced at his sister. She gave him a quick approving nod. Not missing a beat, he turned and disappeared through the door.

The cave hallway was a claustrophobic six-foot in diameter tunnel that led the way forward about fifty feet. More shining rocks lit up the tunnel. Borak could see an opening at the end of the tunnel and headed for it.

At the end of the tunnel was more writing. It said, "Use agility to cross, then float on the trees." Borak was bewildered by what this meant.

The tunnel opened into a broad cave that dropped over a hundred feet into a clear bubbling liquid. At the other end of the cave was another tunnel entrance with a platform. There were bits and pieces of a bridge that jutted up every five to ten feet from the depths of what appeared to be death water. The parts of the bridge which existed were only big enough to place one foot and weren't in a straight line. They zig-zagged from left to right. Borak concluded the only way to cross was to jump from one tiny piece of bridge to the other.

Looking at the liquid below, Borak noticed an acidic smell and knew it was not something to mess with. He also saw suspicious holes in the walls, mostly placed at chest height. He decided to find out what they were before moving forward.

Borak picked up a rock and threw it. He aimed to hit one of the pieces of the bridge on which he hoped to jump. The rock hit and bounced off, falling into the depths below. It landed in the liquid and fizzled as if the liquid was breaking it down. Not satisfied, Borak took a dagger and threw it across the middle of the cave. The dagger flipped end-over-end.

A spear flew out of the first hole proving his intuition right. The spear nailed the dagger, ricocheting it off into the distance. Now that Borak knew what he was dealing with, he took a moment to think. He not only had to leap from one small piece of bridge to the next, which could crumble under his feet, he also had to dodge incredibly fast flying spears at the same time. Borak quickly decided what he would do. He wasn't sure if he could pull it off but knew he had to go for it. He pulled out his sword and dagger, inhaled deeply, lowered his head, and closed his eyes. When he exhaled, he entered a meditative trance. The ninja hero inhaled and exhaled a few more times, focusing.

"This is it!" Borak told himself, trying to pump himself up.

Finding his weapon and saving the world was what he had been working for his entire life. Borak knew this would be one of the most significant tests of his life.

Borak opened his eyes and declared, "It's now!"

Borak burst into a sprint. He was moving surprisingly fast, only taking a few steps, and leaped toward the first small piece of the bridge. Just as his foot touched the dirt, a spear shot out from one of the holes. Anticipating this spear coming, he jumped, flipping sideways to the left, and blocked it with his sword. The spear deflected in another direction. He landed with his left foot on the next piece, and another spear shot at him. Borak bounced off his left foot, jumping forward. He spun in the air and sliced the spear in half before it hit him. Then landed with his right foot on the next piece and jumped again as soon as he landed. Somersaulting end-over-end, he blocked another spear and landed on the last piece. Still using his momentum, he flipped forward, flattened out in the air, and squeezed between two more spears. Amazingly, the spears barely grazed him on each side, tearing bits of cloth off his shirt. He landed in a crouched position on the other side of the cave, safe and sound.

At first, Borak didn't move. Then, he confidently raised his head and looked at the tunnel ahead. He wasn't one to show his emotions, but he felt terrific. He headed into the tunnel and saw it looked exactly like the first one, then continued into another cave. This cave-room was huge and even more perplexing than the first. Borak thought he was seeing things, or rather seeing nothing, because, at first glance, there was no floor. He blinked his eyes and shook his head, hoping he was mistaken, but when he looked again, the view in front of him hadn't changed. There was no floor!

Borak's weapon was glistening in all its glory at the far end of the room. It was an immaculate bo staff with a shining blade at each end. It was floating upright above an island of dirt. Borak had no idea how he was going to reach it. Again, the walls had spear-flinging holes, except there were many more this time. They spanned across the entire cave. While he stared at the spear holes, he noticed they were much larger than the last ones. He took a minute to contemplate what this might mean.

Borak rubbed his chin and spoke out loud, "There's no floor....aaannd a bunch of large impending death spears waiting to impale me..." He looked down, "Nnooo floooor...," and glanced back at the wall, "Large death spears, hmmm. That's interesting."

Borak thought back to the script he saw at the end of the first tunnel, "Then float on the trees." His thoughts continued, "Maybe that's what it meant. There's no way!" Suddenly it came to him. Although it was an insane idea, this high-flying martial artist knew what he had to do.

Borak took a deep breath, lowered his head, and entered his meditative routine again. What he was about to attempt was unheard of. "Am I really going to do this?" he said to himself. Of course, he was. He already knew that. He responded to himself, "I must be crazy." He nervously laughed.

Once Borak was ready, he moved into a crouched stance, pulled a dagger out, and twirled it in his hand elegantly, preparing to throw it. He inhaled deeply and bolted toward the edge of the cliff. He hurled the dagger as he ran. The dagger flipped end-over-end and began crossing the paths of the holes. He launched himself off the cliff as the spears were triggered. Borak timed it perfectly. An abundance of log-like spears streaked under him at the perfect tempo, forming a floating bridge. He ran across the floating bridge, placing each foot on the spears right as they crossed under him. Borak knew he had to run lightly, or he would push the spears too far down and lose altitude. Now fully committed, he noticed the dagger gaining distance on him and the spear-path beginning to move ahead of him. He gave it everything he had, and then the dagger dropped. He knew no more spears would be triggered. Borak figured he was about three-quarters of the way across the room. With hope and a prayer, he launched himself off the last spear and soared through the air, stretching to reach the island of dirt...stretching... reaching...

"Ahhhhh!" he yelled.

Borak sensed he was coming up short. He was right. He missed the island and disappeared.

Everything was quiet and still except some loose dirt hitting the liquid below and fizzing as it dissolved. Many seconds passed, and nothing.

Borak's hand appeared on the side of the dirt island. He had managed to grab hold of a vine in the nick of time. With adrenaline racing through his veins, he pulled himself up to safety. Relieved he was alive, Borak crawled away from the ledge and stopped to kiss the dirt. Distracted by his gratitude, he briefly forgot what stood before him.

The bo-blade, Borak's destined weapon, was magically floating three feet from his face. Hearing the hum of the weapon, he peered up. The glow made it challenging to see, but after his eyes adjusted, he saw it. The weapon was immaculate. He bathed in its beauty. He could sense its power. Now that he was close, he could see the detail in the wooden staff. It had intricate lines and patterns which mimicked tribal designs. These designs traveled across the staff from end-to-end and connected to a shimmering Fierna gemstone at its center. Feeling unworthy, Borak humbly bowed to the weapon to show it respect, then stood up and placed his hand around it.

Immediately, the bo-blade activated. The power from the weapon surged through his body. Borak stood there, soaking in its energy, and a red light flashed brightly. Red energy exited the gemstone, transferring from his new weapon into his body. This completed the bond. Borak lifted the bo in the air, twirled it around extravagantly, and, with authority, stuck the blade in the ground. The dirt island shook dramatically.

A door opened in the wall behind him. Borak turned to see the open doorway, pulled his bo-blade out of the ground, jumped from the island to the ledge on which the door was located, and went through the door. He found himself outside. At this point, he had no idea where he was or how he would find the others.

As Borak was about to start his search, he heard someone yell, "Hey! Hey, there you are! Oh, thank goodness, you're still alive!" Melia ran up and gave her brother a tight hug. She asked, "Soooo, did you do it?" She hadn't noticed the bo he stuck in the ground when she ran up. He reached over and grabbed it.

"You tell me!" Borak smirked and handed her the bo-blade.

Melia's mouth dropped open and stayed open while she examined the stunning artistic weapon.

"Holy crap! This weapon is amazing! The detail is soooo impressive! It's your favorite weapon, too! You love the bo staff! Wow! It's beautiful!" Melia exclaimed. She took a step back, then twisted and whirled the bo with impressive skill. She stopped in a poised stance. "Very nice!" she complimented and threw the bo back to her brother.

Everyone was happy that Borak was still alive. They all made sure to acknowledge his accomplishment. The two Hairies persisted on hearing what happened, so Borak told them.

Traveling to the Druid Tree

It was time to continue their journey. Aiden instinctively walked toward the top of the mountain. After a short distance, he noticed no one was following him.

"This way! I feel something pulling me as if nature wants us to go this way!" Aiden shared, pointing up the mountain.

Farley saw the others look at each other oddly, so he explained, "He has become one with nature. He can feel the world like I do. We should listen to him." The group simply shrugged their shoulders and followed Aiden.

During their trek up the mountain, Borak had a curious thought. He asked the two Hairies walking beside him, "How did you guys get out of the cave? You couldn't have gone the way I did, and the hole in the ceiling was about a hundred feet up."

"Oh yea, there was another door. We found it after you went in. It led us around a corridor and outside," Gil replied.

"Ah, another door. I should have known," Borak responded, "I'm glad you guys made it out."

At the top of the mountain, Aiden stopped in a clearing to survey the land again. He scanned the valley below, searching for any signs of destruction where an orb might have hit.

Aiden saw more extraordinary animals. Jumping around in a few trees was a band of monkeys with tails that appeared to have third hands. Not too far away in another tree, he sensed a large puma sleeping among the branches. The puma didn't seem different, but then again, it was asleep and not moving. As if the puma wasn't unnerving enough, Aiden also caught a glimpse of a large bear, or at least he thought it was a bear. At first, he didn't believe his senses because the bear was sitting upright with its legs crossed and looked like it was reading a book. Directly behind the bear was a humongous tree that stood three times higher than the forest canopy.

Aiden glanced back at his fellow heroes. They were all waiting for him with anticipation. He pointed at the huge tree and said, "I think we should go that way!"

"That's the Druid tree! Is that where you're pointing?" asked Farley in an excited voice.

"Yea, that tree over there. We need to go there. A weird bear is sitting out front of it. It's, um, reading a, a book," Aiden responded, saying his last sentence a bit hesitantly.

"You're talking about Cornelius! He protects the Druid tree," Cedric added.

"A bear protects a tree?" Aiden questioned.

Proudly, Cedric gave more information, "The Weapons Prophecy says Cornelius protects the Druid entrance at the sacred tree, and the heroes must defeat him by answering three questions correctly. If the heroes succeed, the Druid Master will give them the key to cross."

"Greeeaat, we're going to Druidia. I always heard how hospitable it is," Melia chimed in sarcastically.

Aiden replied, "It's not hospitable?"

Melia answered, "Well, not exactly. It's not like Cornelius meets strangers with open arms. Aaaannd, I've heard stories of many being exiled. Siren was exiled from there. I heard she slept with the Druid King, and the Queen banished her for it. Priya is from there also, and she was exiled, too. She says it was her destiny to leave. That's how she ended up at Heirstone. Farley found her wandering around the woods frightened when she was a young girl. He brought her to Heirstone, and my father took her in when he was King. Anyway, I don't know about you, but from what I've heard, Druidia is not a nice place."

"Wow! No kidding?" Aiden replied, "So, Priya wasn't born in Heirstone? She's not related to...um..." He put his head down, "May he rest in peace, Naru?"

Melia shook her head from side to side and answered, "No, she was adopted as part of the family. Why do you ask?"

Aiden had thought a lot about his relation to Priya ever since Naru told him the truth about being his father. He had been feeling weird about kissing her.

Aiden responded, "Oh, no reason. I was curious, that's all." He changed the subject, "We're gonna have to be careful when we go to Druidia and keep our wits about us."

Melia stood in front of Aiden, squinting her eyes with suspicion and a half-smile on her face.

The team of world-savers made their way down into the valley within a few miles of their destination. To help pass the time, Cedric and Gil began light-heartedly teasing Farley.

"Wow, Farley! Did you shrink?" Cedric began.

"Yeah, I swear you were taller. I feel like a Grandar next to you," Gil added, chuckling.

"Of course, I didn't shrink," Farley replied, perplexed, innocently being sucked into the joke, "How could I shrink? And I'm quite tall for my species."

"Haha, sure you are. You're so short; I bet you constantly get over... looked," Cedric joked.

"Yeah, you're the literal definition of down...to...earth," Gil teased.

Cedric looked at Gil and said, "Can you believe I asked him for five coins yesterday, and he said he was a little short." Both Hairies cracked up.

Gil came back with another joke, "Do you know what Farley and his mom have in common? Very little! Haha!"

It was amusing watching the short-sized Hairies making fun of someone else's height. Aiden, Borak, and Melia couldn't help but laugh. By this time, Farley had figured out they were joking and became entertained by it. He was becoming used to their silly antics.

Cedric told another joke, "Do you know why Farley laughs when he plays soccer? Because the grass tickles his balls! Haha!"

The whole group laughed hysterically. While he was laughing, Cedric tripped over a stick.

"Um, guys," Cedric said in a tone that exemplified fear.

Everyone saw what was in front of him and instantly stopped laughing. It was a rattling serpent coiled up a foot from Cedric's face.

"What do I do?" Cedric asked, frozen in fear.

"Don't.... move...." Aiden instructed while he figured out what to do.

"You don't have to worry about that," Cedric admitted.

Aiden had never seen a snake like this before. It had bright multi-colored pink, blue, and black bands, a cobra hood, and a rattle. There was something weird about its eyes, too. They shimmered, first dimly, but became brighter with each second.

"Don't look the snake in the eyes! It will put you in a trance!" warned Farley.

"What! Okay," Cedric replied. He closed his eyes which made the situation even scarier as now he couldn't tell if the snake was coming at him or not. "You guys, I'm freaking out!" he said. As Cedric held his eyes closed, he was second-guessing Aiden's advice of not moving. He was about to bolt.

Borak raised his dagger, but Aiden stopped him. Aiden picked up a stick. He took a moment to aim, then launched the stick. It flipped end-over-end and hit the snake's body, knocking it back a few feet. The snake was a bit stunned but didn't waste any time disappearing into the grass.

Cedric heard a noise and flinched. "Whoa! What was that?" he desperately asked.

Aiden answered, "Shoot, I missed! Run, Cedric! Get out of there!"

Cedric bounced to his feet without missing a beat and ran backward so fast he probably could have won a race against a horse. He tripped again, this time over a tree root, and flipped into a bush.

Farley was enjoying this joke and gave Aiden a high five. Gil had a good laugh, too. After a minute, Cedric appeared from behind the bush with leaves, grass, and dirt stuck in his thick hair. He inspected the area to make sure the snake was gone.

"Watch out! There's another one!" Farley shouted, pointing at nothing.

Cedric jumped in the air, hollering, "Ahh, where? No, there's not! Damn it, Farley!" Everyone laughed again.

The group walked for another half hour and stopped when they saw Cornelius. They hid behind a large bush and watched the bear as he sat beside a large opening in the tree. The opening looked like some type of entrance.

"I can't believe it's a bear, sitting cross-legged, reading a book. And he's been doing this for hours. You would think he'd get bored or something," Aiden thought out loud, in disbelief.

Right after Aiden said this, the bear stood up and stretched. He mumbled something to himself, then walked toward the nearby bushes.

"Are you serious? He can walk upright and speak, too? Of course, he can. What was I thinking?" Aiden added sarcastically.

The bear was much larger than bears on Earth. Cornelius stood about twelve feet tall on his hind legs. He was also gray instead of black or brown.

As Cornelious made his way toward the bushes, the heroes saw his long fangs protruding from his mouth and resting on the sides of his jaw. The intimidating bear walked behind some high shrubs and hunkered down out of sight. They quickly realized that he was using the bathroom.

"Everybody see that? Look over there!" Melia exclaimed, pointing to the shrubbery on the other side of the tree. There was another orb, broken in half and empty. It had to be the one Priya and Jack were in.

Cornelius' Test

"We found them! We found them!" Farley quietly exclaimed.

"Nice!" Aiden added.

"Now's our chance. We should go for the entrance," Melia suggested.

"I agree. What do you guys think?" Aiden asked the others.

The rest of the group nodded, and of course, Melia ran off first. Following suit, all the heroes made a beeline for the tree entrance. They were surprisingly quiet and moved like a team of ninjas infiltrating enemy territory.

Melia was the first to the entrance. Although it looked open, she slammed into an invisible barrier and fell back on her butt. They all grouped around her, and Borak helped her up. They quickly ducked behind the tree on the opposite side of where Cornelius was, but it was too late. Cornelius was already peering over the bushes.

"Who are you?" Cornelius bellowed.

Aiden looked in the direction of the bear and saw Cornelius staring directly at him. Unluckily, he was the only one the tree didn't entirely hide. Aiden froze, trying to figure out what to do, but was distracted because the bear was moving weirdly. That's when Aiden realized the bear hadn't finished cleaning himself. Cornelius quickly wiped and stood up, doing his best to pretend he wasn't wiping his butt.

Cornelious spoke in a stern voice, "Why do you think you can enter the land of magic? Why do you think you're worthy?"

Aiden wasn't sure what to say, especially after seeing the bear wipe himself, but before he could think of an answer, the colossal gray bear charged through the bushes.

Aiden jumped out in the open, drew his sword, and pointed it directly at Cornelius. Borak and Melia jumped out as well with their swords drawn.

Cornelius slid to a stop. Aiden's sword tip lightly pressed against his body. The bear roared, baring his massive fangs. Drool dripped from his mouth. Cornelius' jaws were only a foot from Aiden's face, and he licked his lips with his enormous tongue, insinuating he was hungry.

The three were ready to fight. Borak braced himself, prepared to perform an aerial strike. Oddly enough, before anyone attacked, Cornelius' mood changed. He dropped his menacing glare and sat back on his haunches.

The bear studied the trio for a moment, then spoke, "You must answer three questions correctly to enter."

"Wait, what?" Aiden responded, confused by the sudden change of events.

The three looked at each other, silently asking one another if they believed the bear and if they should stand down.

"It is true," Cornelius began speaking again, "You have demonstrated your braveness. Now you must demonstrate your true intentions. Why have you come here?"

Seeing the situation calm down, Gil, Cedric, and Farley revealed themselves. Cornelius flinched when he saw Farley.

"Oh my!" said the bear, "You have an Evo with you. Oh, my goodness, gracious! That is tremendous news!"

"Now you show up! Let us do all the dirty work, huh guys?" Melia teased, talking to the three who came out of hiding.

"Aw, we knew you could handle it," Cedric kidded back, "Farley was ready to make a run for it!"

"I was not! I was about to make a move!" Farley defended himself.

"Yea, what, a dance move? Or maybe a run-away-from-the-bear move?" Cedric continued.

"You don't have dance moves!" Farley replied.

Cedric became quiet. Farley was right. Cedric couldn't dance.

The short creatures bickering amused Cornelious. He resumed the test and asked again, "Why have you come here?"

"We have come in search of our friends. The ones who came in those orbs," Aiden replied. He pointed at the empty healing shields.

The huge bear's eyes squinted as soon as Aiden said this. He asked the second question, "Where did you come from?"

Aiden answered honestly, "We came from Heirstone. We fought Magus and almost defeated him. The city is in ruins, and the Royal Family has been killed. Our friends who were in that orb are the last of our group...who, we hope, survived."

Cornelius' eyes opened wider as he began to believe Aiden and understand who was standing in front of him. The bear asked the last question, "What do you plan to do?"

Unsure of how to answer, Aiden looked at the others. They hadn't talked about this yet. They had focused solely on recovering all their companions and hadn't planned for after that.

Borak took the initiative to answer for everyone, "We will get revenge, and we will save the world."

There was a slight hum, and the mirror-like barrier at the entrance in the tree rippled and revealed a portal.

"Oh, wow!" Gil reacted in awe.

"You have proven yourselves worthy and may enter the Druid Kingdom! Inside, your friends await you," Cornelius said, then bowed and stepped out of the way so the others could pass.

Aiden was ecstatic at the prospect of seeing Priya again, alive and well. When they were fighting Magus' army, he thought they would all die. He thought that would be the last day he saw her. Now, somehow, he was going to see her again. Of course, Aiden was excited to see Jack too, but the feeling wasn't quite the same.

Gil asked the bear excitedly, "So, they're alive! Our friends are alive? Priya? Jack?"

Cornelius didn't answer. He only stood there, bowing. The group looked at each other awkwardly.

Cedric shrugged his shoulders and said, "Only one way to find out!" He walked through the portal, and the rest of the group followed.

Druidia

The crew of heroes appeared in the middle of an extraordinary and eccentric village. It had the same feel as the courtyard at Heirstone. Creatures were socializing and loitering around vendors...mostly Roaks but also Grandars and Hairies meddling around in the mix. The main difference between this village and Heirstone was the type of vendors. As they looked around, they saw vendors selling small gems, crystals, magical items, many kinds of weapons, smoking potions, and odd things in jars. Aiden thought it looked like stores for witches. There were also vendors selling colorful foods, including some strange live food items.

With a slightly disgusted yet intrigued interest, Aiden watched as a local slurped down a slimy live squid that was pulsating with orangish light.

On the outside of one of the merchant's cabins was a poster that read, "Tonight's entertainment, The One! The Only! The Invisible Comedian!" The visual aspect of the sign insinuated the entertainer was invisible.

Unexpectedly, Aiden's view became obstructed by a beautiful middle-aged brunette wearing platinum decorated armor and a crown on her head. She had a magical-looking ax hanging on her side. A band of Druid soldiers followed behind her. They appeared to be her guards as they were all dressed in similar armor but not as extravagant. They had their swords drawn. This very impressionable threat managed to grab everyone's attention, except for one.

Cedric was mesmerized by another lovely Druid woman, wearing extremely skimpy clothes and dancing on one of the tables in a more adult-friendly establishment. She stared into Cedric's eyes, held her finger up, and beckoned him to come to her. Cedric took a step toward her. Seeing what was going on, Melia whacked the back of his head, knocking him out of his daze.

"Hey, what the heck!" Cedric remarked, irritated, "Did you see that? She likes me!"

Melia acted like she would slap his head again, and he flinched. Melia then scoffed, "Will you pay attention!" She motioned her head in the direction of the Druid Queen, who was staring at them.

"Well, hello there," spoke the Druid Queen, loud and clear.

Everyone in the village stopped to watch what was happening. The Druid Queen pulled the ax from her waist and pointed it at them while she walked toward them.

The Queen continued, "And how pray tell, did you get past Cornelius?"

"We killed him! We killed the bear!" Cedric hollered with dishonest conviction.

The entire gathering gasped. The Druid Queen quickly reacted. She flipped her ax back and launched it directly at Aiden, who seemed to be the group leader.

The ax flipped end-over-end straight at Aiden's head with such speed, he didn't have time to duck. Aiden shut his eyes and threw his hands in the air, defensively, in a last-ditch effort to catch it.

The ax stopped right before it plunged into his forehead. Aiden re-opened his eyes, surprised to see his hands flat across each side of the ax head. Although it appeared he had skillfully caught the ax between his hands, he knew that's not what happened. He didn't feel an impact from catching the weapon. He must have stopped the ax telekinetically, and his hands landed on it.

Understanding what really happened, Borak slapped Aiden on the back and exclaimed, "Nice catch!" then winked.

You could hear the astonished crowd inhale. Some of the villagers let out, "Ooohs," and, "Whooaas," and even a, "Did you see that?" After witnessing their potential adversary's skills, the guards quickly shifted into fighting positions and prepared to attack.

"Hold on! No one killed Cornelius! He's right outside the door or portal or whatever that is!" Aiden proclaimed, motioning to the portal by which they entered.

The guards didn't look convinced and inched their way closer to the heroes.

As the guards crept toward them, Aiden implored, "Can't we call him in here or something? I'm telling you he's right outside, by the tree."

"Who's right outside by the tree?" a familiar gruff voice questioned.

Aiden looked over and saw it was Cornelius.

"We never thought we'd be so happy to see you!" joked Gil.

The bear looked confused. The Druid Queen screamed at him, "What in the heck is going on, Cornelius? How did they get in here? Who are they?"

Cornelius responded quickly, "Respectfully, your Highness, I am sorry for the confusion, but they passed the test. They did not run. They prepared to fight, and they answered all the questions correctly. They must be the ones for whom we've been waiting! The Heroes of Legends!"

It was quiet. All eyes were on the Queen, who had her eyebrows raised. She addressed Aiden, "Is this true? Are you all the Heroes from the prophecy? Do you know the Druid Princess?"

Aiden thought and replied, "Druid Princess?"

The Druid Queen stepped forward and asked again, "Well, what do you say?"

Aiden started to answer, "Um..."

Melia jumped in, "Yes, we know her!"

Finally, Aiden found his voice and asked, "Do you mean Priya?"

The crowd gasped at hearing the name.

Aiden kept going, "Where is she? We've been traveling for miles looking for her and Jack. We saw the orb outside, and the bear told us they're here."

"Aiden! Aiden!" a familiar female voice called out from a distance.

"Ay, ya blokes! What took ya buggas so long?" another familiar voice called out.

Aiden and the rest of the gang knew exactly who was talking even before seeing Priya and Jack running in their direction. They came from one of the cabins up on the hill. The tension in the air immediately evaporated as everyone watched what was unfolding. Jack reached the group first. He grabbed Aiden, Borak, and Melia, at the same time and picked them up in a giant bear hug.

Jack spun them around and exclaimed, "I knew y'all would make it! I wasn't worried one bit!" The two Hairies jumped on Jack's back. Jack let go of the other three to greet his little buddies, "Hey, fellas!"

"Dang it, Jack! You big ope!" Gil teased.

"Yeah, we thought the bear ate you!" Cedric joked.

"Ah, no worries, mates!" Jack replied, "Who, Cornelius? He's a big teddy bear!"

The three glanced over at Cornelius. He was standing next to them with an innocent and rather large comical smile on his face.

After Jack put him down, Aiden turned around and saw Priya directly in front of him. She had been about to touch his shoulder before he turned around. As she reached for him, he turned and ended up face-to-face with her.

Priya stared into Aiden's eyes and saw them begin to well up. He smiled with his impeccably authentic smile. At that point, she knew he had missed her as much as she missed him.

Aiden took in Priya's beauty and wondered what he would have done had he lost her. He placed his hand on the alluring Princess' cheek and gently brought his lips to hers.

The kiss was passionate, and although lustful, their caring for each other was evident. No one had ever before seen the Princess and Aiden kiss. Even though the mutual consensus among the heroic friends was that they had a thing for each other, no one had ever witnessed anything. Aiden and Priya were unsure of what was happening between them, but this kiss solidified their feelings and removed any doubt.

"Well, well, well, Casanova!" Cedric teased, elbowing Aiden in the gut.

Aiden ignored Cedric as he focused on Priya. He told her, "I am soooo friggin' happy to see you! Are you okay? Everything's okay?"

Priya elaborated, "Yes, yes, they're great here. I grew up here before they sent me on my voyage. That is my mother, my true mother, and that's her ax in your hand. How did you get her ax?"

"Uh," Aiden suddenly remembered he was holding it and replied, "Well, that's uh, let's say, we didn't hit it off at first."

"You didn't tell me that you were seeing this friend of yours," said a voice from behind.

Priya looked over and saw it was her mother. She had walked up to them.

Many low murmurs were coming from the audience of Druid villagers. They saw the kiss transpire and were gossiping on the subject.

Smiling, Priya confidently replied, "Well, you know now, Mother. Aiden, this is my mother, Hyra. Mother, Aiden."

"Very nice to meet you," Aiden greeted with a bow of his head and remarked, "Here is your ax back. Maybe next time, we can simply sit down and talk things out, instead of you trying to split my head in half."

Taking the ax, Hyra apologized, smirking, "Sorry about that. You can never be too careful these days. Sooo..." She turned and spoke to her daughter, "These are your friends, huh? The ones who are here to save the world?"

Priya answered, "Yes, Mother. It's all true. We are here."

Hyra spoke again, "It's all true, hmmm." She spun around to the crowd and yelled, "It's all true, and they are here!"

The crowd roared, "Yaaaa! Raaaaa!"

Speaking for all to hear, Hyra continued, "We have been waiting for this day for a long time! So long, I almost lost hope. I sent my daughter from here fourteen long years ago. I thought I might have made a mistake until she fell from the sky in a flying shield with a giant by her side! And now, the rest of the heroes have arrived! My friends and family, I give you the Heroes of Legends!"

The crowd went nuts, screaming and hollering even louder this time. This called for a celebration. Unbelievably, in all the commotion, no one had noticed Farley, the little Evo who could replenish magic and was now in the most magical place in the world. Farley hid behind Borak and stuck his head out from behind Borak's leg.

Hyra saw Farley and expressed her delight, "Oh, my goodness! You guys have an Evo with you? Ours is sick, and the other disappeared years ago. Because of this, our magic is depleted. We could use his help if you allow it."

Hyra was looking at Borak since Farley was behind his leg. No one said anything at first.

Farley looked nervous, so Priya jumped into the conversation, "We will talk of this later. Right now, let's celebrate!"

After a short pause, Hyra agreed, "Yes, you are right! Let us celebrate!" The two walked away together.

Cedric's Dagger

The celebration had begun. Aiden and the gang started settling in now that everyone in this hidden magical community was catching a buzz. They were treated like celebrities, especially Aiden since he was Priya's special someone.

The heroes were sitting at a group of tables and different locals, most of whom were Druids in training, came to them offering gifts. One villager brought a purple crystal and explained how the crystal helped her focus. She added she couldn't wait until she became a full Druid and bonded with a gem. She offered the crystal to Aiden.

Another villager brought a smoking potion to the table. He also offered it to Aiden. Aiden wasn't sure what to think of it, but he gracefully accepted the gift after a brief description of the item. The local explained that the potion activates a pathway to communicate with the spirits who reside within the Spirit World.

Aiden asked what that meant exactly. The villager answered, "You will know when the time comes."

A third local with a strong presence walked up to the tables and stood there, confidently, without speaking. He was wearing luxurious armor, which looked like Hyra's. It seemed odd that a few other locals snuck away as soon as they noticed him. It became apparent that he was someone important, most likely an accomplished Druid; possibly, one of seniority. From a distance, Hyra looked on with curiosity as she knew this villager well.

"Caaaan we help you?" Aiden asked.

The villager stood there, silently. He did not respond.

Borak placed his hand on his bo-blade, preparing to defend, if necessary.

The villager spoke, "There is no need for violence, Borak. I am simply here to find out who is the owner of this." He pulled out a dull-looking dagger. It was iron and had a small green Dirte gem in its walnut handle. It appeared to be extremely old and ragged.

"I'm sorry. What was your name?" Aiden asked. The villager only stared at him silently. Aiden continued, "Okay, look, I'm sorry, my man, but that's not ours."

The intimidating villager replied, sounding a bit angry, "Are you sure about that?" He slammed the dagger flat on the table.

Borak and Melia jumped to their feet and drew their weapons. Hearing the commotion, Jack, Cedric, Gil, and Farley stopped playing their game of coins to see what was going on.

The dagger began glowing on the table and started to spin. At first, the dagger turned slowly but picked up speed and whipped around in circles, exceptionally fast.

Abruptly, the dagger stopped and pointed in the direction of the four heroes in the back. They looked on, confused. WWHHOOOSSHH!!! The rugged iron dagger flew off the table in their direction, barely missing Jack, Gil, and Farley. Cautiously, they leaned out of the way and revealed that Cedric had caught it, although he didn't appear to have meant to catch it. He was still covering himself defensively, and the dagger was in his hand.

Cedric boasted, "Ha! Bet you couldn't do that!" He was talking to Gil.

The dagger lit up in green light. It fluctuated with power, radiating more brightly as it fluctuated. Cedric stared at the dagger, not sure what was happening. Green energy left the gem, floated in the air, and then flowed into his chest, solidifying the bond. Cedric sat there, for once, speechless.

Impressed, Aiden turned to the villager and said, "Well, I guess it's Cedric's!" Then, he realized he was talking to nobody. The villager had swiftly and silently disappeared. "That was weird! What do you guys make of that?" he asked Melia and Borak.

"Agreed. Very weird!" Melia answered.

Borak added, "Weird, but important. The dagger bonded with Cedric. I think that means he's a Druid now."

Aiden reacted surprised and added, "Wow! I bet that dagger will come in handy on our journey." He thought for a second, then added, "Cedric, who would have guessed? Wait, does that mean you're a Druid? Because your bo-blade bonded with you, right?"

Borak contemplated, then simply stated, "Something like that."

Leaving Farley

Priya spent time with her mother at a table a short distance away. They saw what happened with the dagger and decided to join the others.

Jack was teasing Cedric as they walked up, "That ragged thing's befitting of ya! We shoulda known it was yours, haha!"

"Hi, stranger!" Aiden joked, looking at Priya, "You two missed the spinning dagger show!"

They all glanced over at Cedric and saw him enamored with his ugly dagger.

"We saw!" the Princess remarked, "It's awesome Cedric bonded with his weapon! Pretty soon, you'll all have one! At least, that is what the prophecy foretells."

"It does, does it? Does it say what our weapons will be?" asked Aiden, intrigued.

Priya answered, "Yes, but I'm not telling."

In the background, Gil, Jack, and Farley continued teasing Cedric about his new drab-looking weapon.

"What is that? An ancient butter knife?" Gil cracked. They all laughed.

"Yea, it looks like ya pulled it out of a wizard's butt!" Jack added, still laughing.

"Haha, that oddly made sense!" Gil muttered in between laughter.

"You, uh, pulled it out of a wizard's butt and used it for your butter, haha!" Farley attempted to be humorous.

The Grandar and Hairie stopped laughing and stared perplexedly at Farley as if he said something dumb. Then they cracked up again, ecstatically, and fell from their chairs. Gil rolled over, balled up, and was crying from laughing so hard. Suddenly, he stopped laughing, as if he was trying to prevent hurting Cedric's feelings.

Making an earnest face, Gil asked, "Seriously though, Ced. Are you gonna use that for your butter?" The three burst out in laughter again.

Everyone in the area who heard the conversation was laughing, as well. The dagger was crappy-looking. It looked as if it wouldn't hold up in a fight. Priya and Hyra also giggled at the entertaining heroes.

Priya wanted to tell the rest of the group about the plan she and her mother had made. She stood up and raised her voice barely loud enough to be heard over the banter, "Hey guys! Listen! That was fun and all, but there's something we need to talk about." No one was paying attention, so she raised her voice even louder, "Listen up, there's something important I have to tell you guys!"

Most still weren't paying attention, so Priya yelled, "Farley's going to stay here! They need his help. In return, the Druid warriors will fight with us!"

The place instantly became quiet. It became so quiet they heard a rat scurry from under the table into the grass.

Priya was looking intently at Farley, not knowing how he would take the news. Her main concern was him feeling betrayed, but the situation was more significant than his feelings. This situation was a matter of gaining allies and saving the world. Plus, she was not only the Princess in Heirstone; she was also the Princess here and the daughter of the Druid Queen. She needed to make good decisions for all her people, even though she hadn't seen the people of Druidia for over a decade.

Farley locked eyes with Priya, then looked down, visibly going through mixed emotions. She saw this and walked over to him.

Priya asked, "Are you okay? I was going to talk to you alone, but we don't have much time. We're leaving tomorrow, soooo..."

Farley was still looking down. Priya prompted him to look at her by placing her hand on his head before continuing. She told him, "Hey Farley, come on! You're still my little guy, and we won't be gone for long."

The little Evo looked up and saw her cute, worried puppy eyes. He asked, "I'll always be your little guy?"

"Oh, of course!" the Princess replied, giving Farley a shocked look, "I thought you knew that already! You're my little dude, through thick and thin!"

Farley's gaze was locked. He stared intently, wanting her to say more.

Priya noticed this and had an idea. She kept talking, "Let me tell you something, okay? I remember when we first met. Do you?"

Farley responded quickly, "Yes, of course! Farley remembers well!"

Priya carried on, "Well, good. I want to tell the story again. We were children, and I was walking through the woods all alone, crying..."

......After being sent away from her home in Druidia, the land of the Druids, Priya walked through the woods for days. She didn't fully understand why they sent her away. While traveling, she had crying spells. At times, she recovered control of herself and was completely lost at other times. She hadn't eaten the entire time and was lucky to have stumbled across a small pond of water.

Priya was so thirsty, her crying reduced to a small whimper because of the lack of moisture in her throat and the pain it caused. She knelt at the edge of the pond to take a drink and saw movement in the water. She thought back to stories her mother told when she warned about places like this. The stories warned about hideous creatures lurking in the woods and of one who lived in isolated water. Again, the water rippled in front of her.

Priya heard another sound coming from the tree to her left. She hastily looked up into the tree and saw a puma crouched, ready to attack.

Instantly, the water erupted, whooshing back and forth. A large object jetted through the water like a torpedo heading straight for her.

Priya didn't know there was another set of eyes watching from the bushes. It was a set of young, curious, and concerned eyes that had been watching the crying girl wandering around the forest for a couple of days. The eyes belonged to nine-year-old Farley, and it was time for him to take the first heroic action of his young life.

Before Priya could react, Farley hurled magical energy toward her. The energy seized her and yanked her to him. She tumbled into Farley, and they rolled over each other, flipping out from behind a bush.

A large odd-looking animal shot out from the lake's surface and slid up on the bank where Priya had been. It looked like a cross between an alligator and a monitor lizard; only its body and head were more rounded than a typical alligator. It also had long fangs, a long monitor-like tongue, and longer legs, causing it to walk higher off the ground like a monitor. This eerie animal was black and made a strange sound, similar to a raptor. It searched around the bank for its prey. The puma leaped from the tree with perfect timing. It somehow charged up energy while in the air. It landed on the "monigator's" back, driving its claws deep into the water beast. The puma began electrocuting its catch, completely paralyzing it until its heart ceased to beat. The big cat looked back at Priya and Farley, who were, dumbfoundedly, watching this extraordinary event. It gave them a slight nod before turning around and feasting on its meal.

In a state of shock and fright, Priya switched her gaze to the small, cute, furry little Evo. She sat there trying to decide if he was a threat.

Farley saw her concern, but all he could muster up was, "Wow!" The future Princess continued to stare at Farley. She was not sure what to think. Farley kept talking, "I, I'm Farley. We should get out of here!"

Priya looked back over at the puma, ravaging the monigator, and replied, "Yeah!" ......

Priya continued, "You saved my life! After that, you led me to Heirstone and have always been there for me. You're my best friend, Farley. I will always remember what you have done for me. We must do this to save the world. It's best you help the Druid community replenish their powers, so they can help us defeat Magus. You guys will catch up to us later, okay?"

The furry Evo smiled from ear-to-ear, acting as if he only heard one thing. He responded, "I'm your best friend?" The Princess returned the smile and hugged him.

The other heroes watched the entire interaction between Priya and Farley. There wasn't anything left to say. They understood the plan.

The Invisible Comedian

"The show is starting! The show is starting!" announced one of the villagers. Those who heard became excited and rushed over to the staging area, where there was plenty of seating. Posted on a horse carriage next to the stage was another poster advertising, "The Invisible Comedian!"

Priya grabbed Aiden's hand and urged him, "Come on! Let's go watch the show!"

The crew found an area with enough seating for all of them. Aiden and Priya sat next to each other.

Priya remembered something she had been thinking earlier, so she asked, "Hey Aiden, remember when you said there was something you wanted to talk about? What was it?"

At first, Aiden was caught off guard and was unsure what she meant. Then it came to him. It was when he first found out he was Naru's son. He wasn't sure if that meant he and Priya were related. That was when he said he wanted to talk. If they were related, it would've made things very strange. Since then, Aiden found out there was more to the story. Naru and Carys were her adopted parents, and the Druid King and Hyra were Priya's blood parents. Therefore, they were not related.

Priya was focused intently on Aiden, waiting for his answer.

Not knowing what else to say and wanting to be honest with her, Aiden replied, "I'm Naru's son."

Priya choked on her drink, spitting out half of it. She was barely able to blurt out, "What?"

"Yeah, he told me right before the attack," Aiden confided, "At first, it made me feel weird about us because I thought we might be related; so I wanted to tell you."

After a quick pause, Priya concurred, "That would have been weird!" She smiled at Aiden, and they both laughed.

Priya started thinking out loud, "Wow, the Royal King's son, huh? Wait, doesn't that mean you're the next heir in line?" The beautiful Princess looked at Aiden with big eyes and proclaimed, "Aiden, you're the King of Heirstone!" Her statement resonated within him, and he realized she was right.

Introductory music interrupted their conversation. The show began, "Daaaaaaa Da Da Dunt Dun Dunt Daaaaa, Da Da Dunt Dun Dunt Daaaaaaaaa!"

A voice rang out, "Ladies and gentlemen, I hope everyone's having a great night!"

The crowd cheered, "Raaaaa! Yaaaaa! Where's my beer?"

The voice continued, "Awesome! Boy, do we have a treat for you! Our act tonight has been all over the globe, making every creature imaginable laugh, and yes, that includes a Gorger. Tonight, he is here to work his comedic magic on you. So, without further ado, here he is, the one, the only, the Invisible Comedian!"

The crowd cheered with enthusiasm. Not many outsiders come to the village, especially an entertainer of this caliber. The cheers were short-lived. No one walked out onto the stage. The crowd waited patiently for the jokester to show himself.

There was an awkward silence, and the crowd began to mumble as the stage appeared to remain empty.

A sarcastic voice broke the tension, "Well, jeez, as soon as I walked out here, the applause stopped. Usually, it's the other way around. I figured you guys would be happy to unsee me."

There was a little laughter but mostly confusion from the audience.

The comedian continued, "Are you kidding me? No one here thought my name might mean I'm actually invisible? Maybe I ought to change my name to, 'I'm-really-fucking-invisible-so-when-you-watch-my-show-you-won't-see-me comedian,' or, 'You-can't-fucking-see-me-so-don't-be-surprised-when-you-can't-fucking-see-me comedian.'"

More laughter came from the audience. Out of thin air, the comedian appeared in the middle of the stage.

He jested, "Just kidding, guys! How is everyone doing tonight? Are we getting plastered yet?"

The crowd cheered eagerly, finally seeing the comedian, and laughed a little more.

The funny man continued, "Just to let you all know; I do invisibly perform my act, so don't be alarmed." The comedian disappeared.

There were some gasps of surprise from the audience, but mostly the crowd seemed impressed and excited.

Again, they heard the voice, "Has anyone ever felt, you know, like, no one ever pays attention to you? Well, that's how I feel ALL the time. Every time I walk into a room, everyone acts like I'm not there. Even when I say something, people think someone else in the room is playing a joke on them. Usually, I'm like, 'Helloooo everyone. I'm heeerrrre!' And they're like, 'Haha, real funny, stop messing around.' And I'm like, 'No, for real, I'm right here! Why doesn't anyone ever pay attention to me?' And they say, 'Because you're annoying, Billy,' or whoever they think is playing a trick on them. And I say, 'Actually, I'm the Invisible Comedian,' and their response is, 'Riiight, and I'm fuckin' Superman. Now, would you quit messing around!' So, I always give up and leave."

There was modest laughter from the audience.

The jokester continued, "Being invisible is horrible for a relationship, also. When we first got together, I tried to make a move on my girlfriend, and she called 911. Now, I always make sure to wake her up first."

The comedian continued, "Another time, I put my arm around her in bed, and she elbowed me right in the face. She acted like she didn't know I was there. She told me, 'Oh, I'm so sorry,' and, you know, I believed her, so I told her, 'It's okay. Don't worry about it.' But now, every time she's mad at me, for some reason, I get decked in the face. She gets mad and knows exactly where I am, and then WHAM, I get hit in the face, and she's like, 'Oh, I'm so sorry. I didn't see you.'"

The crowd was letting out a steady roar of laughter now.

Carrying on with his act, "It's not all bad, though. It's easy to play pranks on people. One time, I beat the crap out of a mime for the hell of it, and he made a killing! He made soooo much money, he thanked me later and gave me some of the tips. We worked together for a while after that.

The funnyman continued, "Another time, there was a couple having sex on the beach, and I appeared right next to them and told 'em, 'Good form!' They got up and ran away."

The audience was laughing, louder now.

Aiden glanced at Priya and saw how much fun she was having. She noticed him looking at her, laid her head on his chest, and giggled. It seemed odd for him to be developing such strong feelings for her already. He thought it would have taken him a lot longer as it was only a matter of months since his wife died in his arms. After all, they'd only been on a few "dates." Technically, you could say they had been seeing each other for a month or so. He figured this whole savior-of-worlds-and-teleporting-to-a-new-world thing contributed to his feelings. It didn't hurt that Priya was the most beautiful woman in the galaxy.

"He is pretty funny!" Aiden said, cracking up.

"Yeah, I like him! I like his sarcasm!" Priya said back, still giggling.

Lust-stricken, Aiden vowed to always keep Priya safe, at all costs. After this thought, he bent his head down and kissed the top of her head. Realizing he was missing the rest of the show, he blocked out any more thoughts and paid attention to what the comedian said.

"I need a volunteer! Who'd like to come up! You, sir? You, sir? How about you, sir?" the funnyman said.

Everyone was roaring in laughter because they couldn't see where the invisible jokester was pointing.

"Oh, I'm sorry, guys! How could I forget?" the comedian teased. He reappeared, pointing at Jack.

"What! Me?" Jack replied. He was taken aback and turned bright red while he talked, "Na, na, mate! He'd be a betta choice." He pointed at Cedric, "Go on, Ced! Get on up there!"

Cedric quickly redirected the attention back to Jack, "Nope! I'm afraid this is your calling, Jack! I wouldn't wanna steal your time to shine!" He began chanting Jack's name, and the audience followed suit, "Jack, Jack, Jack, Jack!"

"Alright, alright!" Jack responded. He stood up, and everyone cheered. He began to walk to the stage and joked, "Somebody owes me a beer!"

Someone in the background teased, "You're gonna need more than that!" The audience and even the comedian laughed.

Jack walked onto the stage.

The funny man said to him, "Well, thanks for coming up. Jack, is it?"

Jack was about to answer when the comedian cut him off, "Ah, it doesn't matter anyway. No one's gonna care when this is over. I didn't think you were gonna come up. Thought you peed a little because of how red you turned."

The invisible entertainer was still visible at this point and held the microphone up to Jack for an answer.

"I, uh, I," and again, as Jack began speaking, he pulled the mic away.

"I'm just messin' with ya! A big ole guy like you wouldn't pee his pants, would he?" the comedian kept razzing the Grandar.

Jack only looked at the jokester, not sure if he should answer.

The entertainer turned to the crowd and continued to talk, "Wait, or would he? What do you guys think?"

The overwhelming consensus from the audience was, "No, na," but there was that same voice who teased earlier, which said, "Yep, he would pee his pants!"

The crowd erupted in laughter.

Jack scanned the audience looking for who said that. He saw it was Cedric and mumbled to himself, "That bloody bugga!"

"Okay, we're all kidding here!" the comedian began again, "I haven't even gotten to the reason why I brought you up here!" The funny man disappeared and continued talking to Jack in a loud whisper as if he didn't want the crowd to hear, "Hey, I'm sorry about all the teasing. It's part of the show. Don't beat me up, okay?"

Jack nodded like it was okay.

"Oh, that's great!" the jokester responded in a loud whisper, then began speaking normally, "Alright, Mr. Jack, if you will hold this real quick, please."

The Grandar was unsure of where to grab since the object was invisible. He reached out with his hand and moved it slowly from left to right.

"No, no, right there. Yes, ope, you almost had it!" said the comedian, "There you go, perfect! If you will leave your hand right there. Hold on one second. Yes, yes, nice, hold that for a bit."

The jokester had Jack reaching over and holding something at waist height. Jack made a weird face like what he was holding was strange, or even like there was no way he was holding what he thought he was holding.

The comedian continued, "Now, if you would ever-so-slightly shake what's in your hand around a little."

Jack looked in the direction of the entertainer and shook his head, protesting, "I don't think so."

The funny man persisted, "Go ahead. You have nothing to worry about. Go ahead and give it a little shake."

Not wanting to ruin the show, Jack shook whatever he was holding.

"Okay, great!" the comedian kept going, "Now, as the object hardens, you're gonna want to move your hand faster."

Repulsed, Jack let go of whatever was in his hand and retorted, "You sick son of a...." Everyone broke out in tremendous laughter.

The Invisible Comedian reappeared smiling and holding a sausage, "Relax, relax; it was just a sausage! Not really what you thought it was!"

Jack angrily balled his fists up and approached the funny man, whose smile immediately faded. He grabbed the comedian by his shirt and lifted him into the air.

The crowd became quiet, expecting Jack to cold cock the comedian in the face. The entertainer was extremely scared and closed his eyes, crossing his arms over his head in defense.

Instead of hitting the funny man, Jack grabbed the sausage out of his hand and took a bite of it. He admitted, “That was a good one, mate! I thought it was your willy!”

Jack glanced over at the audience and gave them a wink. They all began laughing and cheering again. The Grandar released the jokester, who was relieved Jack was a good sport.

With a revived grin on his face, the Invisible Comedian boasted, “Give him a round of applause! Great job!”

Jack bowed a couple of times, then grabbed the comedian’s hand and raised it, gesturing for the crowd to applaud for him, too. The crowd applauded even louder. The funny man bowed and thanked everyone.

“That was great! The whole sausage thing was ridiculous!” Priya said and giggled. She stood up and tugged on Aiden’s shirt for him to follow her.

“Yea, it was hilarious! I can’t imagine what Jack was thinking!” Aiden responded, laughing.

Priya laughed, too, and led Aiden to the wine kegs to get a couple of refills. “What do you want to do now?” she asked, flirtatiously stepping in closer.

Every Color of the Rainbow

Aiden knew it was the perfect time for them to get away. It seemed Priya, like himself, wanted them to be alone. Now was probably the only chance they were going to get. He noticed a cool-looking, possibly romantic, place earlier and wanted to take her to it.

Aiden told Priya, "Come with me. I want to show you something!"

Earlier, when Hyra was interrogating him, Aiden saw colorful flashes in the forest area behind her. The flashes were bright and fluctuated through the colors of the rainbow. At one point, he thought he saw something that looked like a giant hummingbird fly out from behind a tree and back into the forest. He could have sworn the hummingbird had more of a humanlike body, though.

Priya and Aiden ran down a path past all the vendors and cabin-dwellings and away from the drunken gathering. They ran up a small hill, then left into the woods. Aiden couldn't wait to show Priya what he saw, but the forest was dark, and they could see nothing.

"What are we doing out here?" Priya wondered out loud.

"This, uh, there was, there were bright colors. It looked like something special, and, and there was a big hummingbird or maybe a fairy or something," Aiden replied. He was doing his best to find the place.

Fairly buzzed, Priya thought she heard Aiden say a word that brought back memories and asked, "Did you say fairy? You know, there used to be fairies here. A long time ago. When I was a child, I saw them, but my mother never believed me."

As Priya talked, Aiden continued searching. It was so dark; he could barely see his hands in front of him.

Priya continued, "I saw three fairies flying around me. It was sooooo beautiful. I swear I saw colors I had never seen before. Come to think of it; I was somewhere...out here."

Aiden took one more step, and the entire place lit up with every color of the rainbow. They were stunned by what they saw. This place had to be the most fantastic, stupefying, breathtaking, perplexing, and extraordinary place they had ever been. It quickly became evident the colors were coming from an assortment of fireflies, continuously flying in a circular pattern above them. Thousands of fireflies swirled, radiating brilliant colors. They began dripping these colors from their bodies in some sort of liquid solution. Picturesquely, the solution fell from the illuminated bugs, creating a multi-colored rain effect. They stood and soaked in this breathtaking enigmatic scene.

They were in a hidden pocket in the woods, encircled by thick trees that seemed to be curiously staring at them. Aiden noticed there was an energetic barrier protecting this magical place. They must have unknowingly crossed it to get in.

"This is the place!" Priya joyously shouted and spun with her hands outstretched, "I can't believe it! You found it! I have dreamed of coming back here and never thought I would ever get the chance!"

The happy princess walked over to Aiden and placed her lips on his. They became intertwined in sexual desire as the multi-colored rain poured on them. They slowly spun while Aiden cupped the back of her head and french-kissed her. The colorful rain-like solution dampened their hair and flowed down their faces, gradually soaking their clothes. The lovebirds separated from their kiss. Aiden stared into her eyes, moving some of her hair from her face and caressing her cheek. As Aiden looked in her eyes, Priya gave him a subtle nod, permitting him. Aiden reached down with one hand and firmly squeezed her buttocks while he gently set his lips back upon hers. He then laid Priya across a soft, moss-covered nook in a tree, and they lost themselves in a rush of passion.

Aiden woke up alone, covered in a dried multi-colored solution. He saw a hummingbird appear. It had flown out from a large hole in a tree. Or wait, it was bigger than a hummingbird. "A fairy," he said out loud.

Two more fairies flew out from other holes in trees. The three fairies hovered over Aiden, observing him until the one in the middle decided to speak, "Savior of worlds, it is a great pleasure to meet you."

The three fairies bowed in the air.

"Did you have a pleasant evening?" teased the fairy on the left, knowing precisely what happened.

The fairy in the middle looked over at the fairy next to him with a sly smile, then turned back toward Aiden and spoke again, "We have something for you. It is of great importance. You will need the King's Sword when you fight Magus and Herana. As Naru's gem was destroyed during the last battle, we offer you another one...a greater gem that will bond you to Naru's sword. You will then become the wielder of one of the most powerful weapons in the land. When you need the sword, use your powers to call it."

After the fairy spoke, a large Aire gemstone appeared on top of a tree stump in front of Aiden. It had been there the whole time, but no one could see it. He was amazed by the gem's beauty. It glowed in white light and hummed from the immense amount of energy stored inside. When Aiden turned back to thank the fairies, they had disappeared. He quickly put the gemstone away and got up to find Priya.

Thora's Intervention

As soon as Aiden stood up, he heard a succession of loud explosions.

"What the heck!" he said to himself.

Aiden ran out of the woods and back toward the village. While he ran, he heard swords clanging and more explosions, but he couldn't see what was happening because of the hill in front of him. When he reached the top, he saw a scene of horror. It was Magus and his minions attacking the village. Aiden could see Devians pouring in through the portal, going after anyone in sight. On one side of the battle, Aiden saw the rest of the gang fighting Devians. They were trying to get to the other side, where he saw Priya with her mother. Hyra's guards had assembled a circular blockade surrounding Hyra and Priya. They all were blowing back swarms of Devians with energy blasts.

Magus saw his troops having trouble. He raised his sceptre, charging it up. The evil sorcerer whipped his sceptre around and unleashed a devastating wave of energy. The attack hit everything in its way, including the Druid warriors who were protecting Hyra and Priya. It was so powerful, it sent everyone flying. Aiden watched this happen and began glowing bright blue in anger.

Before Aiden could release his fury, gray smoke encircled him and yanked him inside a nearby cabin. Inside was an old lady. The lady had long white hair and was hunched over, leaning on a cane. She wore old, raggedy clothes and reminded him of a homeless person. Surprisingly, this woman did not look like a Roak or any other being from this world. She looked like an old human lady.

"What are you doing? I was about to save them! I need to save them!" Aiden snapped angrily.

"You will have plenty of time for that, boy, but now is not the time," the woman spoke in an all-knowing voice, "You are not ready yet. If you attack now, you will die."

Squinting his eyes, Aiden protested, "What the hell do you know? They're going to die if I don't do something! Who the hell are you?"

Aiden tried with all his might but couldn't break the grasp of the magical gray smoke.

"My name is Thora. I'm the one who brought you here," the old lady divulged.

The name sounded familiar, but Aiden couldn't remember from where. His emotions took over, and he responded, "No kidding! You smothered me with this hocus-pocus crap and yanked me in here before I could save my friends!"

Smirking, Thora explained, "I am the one who foretold that you would save the worlds." She watched Aiden intently, waiting for a reaction, but he still looked confused, so she added, "I am the writer of the prophecies. I can see the future."

There was a loud bang outside. Aiden tried breaking free of the smoke again but couldn't budge.

"Damn it!" he yelled.

Thora ignored the noise outside and kept talking, "Your people are fine. Well, everyone except Priya."

Aiden felt his body fill with anxiety, and he replied, "What?"

The witch-like lady moved faster than the speed of light, ending up face-to-face with him.

Thora talked with urgency, "Listen, there is not much time left. Take heed of your decisions. Only with your help can Priya be saved. You will be tested, and you must prevail!"

The lady disappeared as fast as she appeared. The smoke vanished as well. Aiden sat in shock for a moment, then got up and ran to the door. He broke through the door, dreading what might lie behind it. He couldn't fathom what he would do if any of his friends were dead, especially Priya. There wasn't time to think about it. All he could do was face the outcome of what Magus had done since that stupid witch stopped him from helping.

Once outside, Aiden saw Magus, and his minions were gone. There were many Druid soldiers on the ground. Some were being treated for their injuries. Only a few were dead. Their magic had protected most of them.

"Aiden!" Jack shouted from down below the hill. The rest of the heroes sat around him, recuperating.

Aiden sprinted to them. When he arrived, he noticed how solemn they all looked.

"Ah, mate, I was worried about ya!" Jack admitted.

Aiden acknowledged Jack, then looked around and asked, "What's wrong, guys? Where's Priya?" Everyone looked down toward the ground or away from Aiden except Melia.

Melia spoke in an endearing voice, "She's...she's gone, Aiden."

Melia stood up and walked to him. She put her hand out, aiming for an affectionate touch that might be calming for him. As she placed her hand on Aiden's arm, he dropped his head and fell to one knee in disbelief. The witch had hinted this would happen, but now it was real.

Desperate for answers, Aiden asked, "What happened? She's alive, right?"

Melia proceeded to tell Aiden what had happened, "Magus appeared with his Devians through the portal. We gave them a good fight. The Druid soldiers defended Hyra and Priya, but Magus' power was too much for them. Magus hit them with an energy wave and knocked them all down, blinding the rest of us. Magus grabbed Priya and jumped back through the portal by the time we could see. Before he went through, he turned and shot a huge energy ball at us. Luckily, Hyra blocked it with an energetic shield."

Aiden nodded in understanding. He was quiet at first. then questioned, "So, she was okay when Magus took her?"

He stared at Melia, who tentatively answered, "Yes, I think she was okay."

Aiden felt relief. He stood up and confidently stated, "And we will save her. We need to hurry."

The remaining team consisted of Aiden, Jack, Borak, Melia, Cedric, and Gil, since Farley was staying behind to replenish the Druid community's magic. After saying their goodbyes to Farley, they ran into Hyra at the portal during their exit.

Hyra placed her hand on Aiden's chest and said, "I sense great power in you! Here, take this." She handed him a potion and continued to talk, "This will help you heal if you become badly injured. Now go! Go save my daughter!"

Aiden took the potion, stared boldly into Hyra's eyes, and promised her, "I will. You have my word." He turned and walked through the portal.

Cornelius' Last Breath

On the other side of the portal, Aiden saw everyone huddled over something lying on the ground. He ran over to see what was wrong. It was Cornelius. He was bloody and cut up. He also had a big chunk blown out of his side.

Melia was holding the bear's hand while he was trying to talk, "I, I, I tried. There were too...there were too many."

"It's okay. Do not worry. It's okay," Melia replied, trying to calm him.

"I, I," Cornelius gasped for air and coughed, "I heard them say...they're... uh, they're going to..." The bear's head fell to the side. He looked as though he had died.

"Where?" Melia urged, "Where are they going?"

Cornelius' eyes struggled to open. He fought the feeling of faintness and answered, "To the Outer Divide. They're going..." He took a breath, "Southeast." The bludgeoned bear grabbed Aiden's sleeve and gravely spoke, "Go...get...that...bastard!"

Aiden confidently replied, "You got it!"

Cornelius nodded and smiled. The bear wavered, then exhaled for the last time. His head fell back into Melia's hands. Cornelius was gone. Everyone bowed their heads in respect. The group performed a speedy ceremony, then continued on their journey.

"Looks like we're traveling outside the realms. But I think we knew that" Aiden began as they walked. He looked over at Borak and Melia and asked,

"Am I right? Did we already know that?"

Borak answered, "We had a suspicion that's where he was. There are rumors he has a castle out there and a deep network of tunnels and caves. It was an older lady, a witch, who told us. She came through the town many years ago and claimed Magus held her prisoner at his castle. She also claimed she escaped. The lady disappeared the next day. We never found out exactly where the castle was. We know now, thanks to Cornelius."

Aiden agreed, "Yes, now we know, and we have no time to waste. Who knows what Magus plans to do with Priya."

The team traveled all day. As they walked, they heard a noise in the bushes. A puma jumped in their path. Borak pulled his bo staff, but Jack stopped him. At first, the puma was hesitant, as was everyone else. Aiden cautiously walked near it and knelt with his hand out. The puma initially took a step back, but once Aiden knelt, it came forward and sniffed his hand. Gil and Cedric threw the cat some food, which it ate, but when they tried to pet it, it darted back into the trees.

The group continued on their journey. As they traveled, they sensed the puma following them. They couldn't be sure whether it had good or bad intentions but figured they would simply keep an eye out for it and see what happened.

They decided to rest for the night before they entered the Outer Divide. It was better to have a full day of light to explore and keep their wits about them. No one knew anything about this part of the land. They had heard a few old stories passed down for generations, but these stories were considered folk tales rather than real stories. The stories were scary. Many parents used the stories to frighten their children and keep them from wandering into the Outer Divide. For the most part, these stories kept children and even adults at bay. Of course, many were curious whether there was any truth to them. It looked like Aiden, and his friends were going to find out.

The heroes built a fire and found themselves with a bit of downtime. The two Hairies began talking about folk tales. Aiden overheard and became very interested. Everyone quickly joined the conversation.

The Tale of Theda, the Scorpula

Melia asked, "So, you guys remember the one about Theda, the Scorpula? That one always scared the crap out of me!"

Jack nodded, remarking, "Of course, mate! The giant half tarantula, half scorpion. How could anyone forget it? That one's freaky. Tell it to us, aye!"

"Well," Melia began, *"There was a young boy who lived on a farm on the border of the Outer Divide. The Outer Divide began on the other side of the fence at the back end of his parent's property. This is also where the mountains began. In these mountains were caves that claimed many lives over the years. The young boy's mother constantly warned him to stay away from the caves because of Theda, the giant scorpula, who lived in these caves. Theda enjoyed trapping children in her web and sucking their guts out."*

Cedric interrupted, "I hate this story! I will not go into a cave because of it!"

"Eehhmmm," Melia cleared her throat, insinuating Cedric should be quiet. She stared at him, with her eyebrows raised as if to say, "Are you finished?" Cedric motioned like he was zipping his mouth closed, and she continued, *"One day, the boy decided he was going to search for his friend, who had disappeared a couple of days earlier. His friend always wanted to explore the mountains and caves, but the boy was always the voice of reason and usually prevented them from going. One time, the boy gave in, and they snuck off to explore the mountain. That day they found a cave. They heard noises coming from inside, but the boy stopped his friend from going in.*

They went home after that. A couple of days later, the boy heard his friend was missing. He had a horrible feeling something bad had happened. That night, the boy snuck out to the pasture, past the horses, and hopped over the fence. He headed up to the cave.'This has to be where he is!' the boy thought."

Melia continued, "Once the boy made it up the mountain to the cave entrance, he could tell his friend had been there. He could also tell there was something wrong. A child's footprints led up to the cave and turned into a scatter of mixed footprints by the cave's mouth. Mixed in with what appeared to be his friend's footprints were the footprints of a large creature with pointy feet. It was apparent a fight had taken place. Closer to the cave's entrance, it looked like something fell and was dragged into the cave. The boy didn't want to jump to conclusions, but, so far, it didn't look good."

Melia glanced around to see everyone listening intently. Hence, she resumed the story, *"The boy was starting to panic and seriously thought about running away but overcame his fears because he didn't want to leave his friend. Despite what his body urged him to do, the boy walked into the cave.*

...The boy followed the drag marks and continued deep into the cave. At first, it seemed like an ordinary cave. As he went further, he began to see areas with spider webbing. Initially, there was only a bit of webbing, but eventually, all the walls were covered. He saw very large spiders dart back into the shadows. He traveled deeper into the cave and found a shoe. He was confident it belonged to his friend. Eventually, the boy came upon a fork in the cave. The drag marks continued left, following a path coated with webbing. He made a left turn and followed the drag marks. At the end of the path was an opening. The opening led to a room overflowing with thick webbing. The only way to get into the room was to walk directly into the web.

Not thinking as much about the danger as saving his friend, he moved some webbing out of the way to peek inside the room. What he saw was shocking. He cringed at the horrifying sight. His friend was wrapped in spider webbing, hanging in the middle of the room. He could barely make out his friend's face. The boy then saw hairy legs lying motionless on the right side of the room and cringed in fear. These legs were undoubtedly Theda's.

The boy desperately wanted to save his friend and began to panic. He put his hand over his mouth to silence his hyperventilation and, quietly, took some deep breaths. After a couple of minutes, the scared boy managed to calm himself and take another peek inside the room. At second glance, he thought he saw his friend move. Wait! He did! His friend moved his head and nose a little, although he still looked unconscious. Unfortunately, as a glimmer of hope appeared, Theda started to get up.

The humongous scorpula's legs curled in, moving into position to brace themselves for her to stand up. The boy wasn't sure what to do but knew whatever it was; he had to do it fast. He almost bolted into the web-ridden room to grab his friend but rethought his options and stopped himself. Instead, he picked up a large rock, ran about fifteen steps back to the fork in the path, and launched the rock down the right side. Quickly, the boy hid behind a boulder near him. The rock bounced off the cave wall and skipped around until it landed on the floor and came to a stop. He was disappointed because it had not made as much noise as he wanted.

By this time, Theda had made her way out of the room and was suspiciously searching the area. She crept down the path and gradually edged her way to the boulder the boy was hiding behind. Slowly, the scorpula began to peek around it.

The boy was trying to figure out what to do next. He was oblivious of the lurking giant boy-eating tarantula/scorpion about to catch a whiff of him and pounce. He heard a fluttering sound. Theda also heard the sound and stopped. It was a colony of bats awakened by the thrown rock. They were angrily flying out of the cave.

The scorpula turned, salivating at the thought of eating a tasty bat morsel before she sucked down more of the live dinner she had hanging in her web. The bats saw Theda and shrieked. They knew meeting the massive scorpula could be their demise, but there were so many, they couldn't stop their momentum. It was like a bat tornado. It took the scorpula off her feet, sending her tumbling down the cave. Theda landed on her back and flipped over a few times. She eventually landed on her feet and chased the bats the other way while shooting her webbing. Meanwhile, the boy couldn't have asked for a better distraction.

Ecstatically, the boy ran down the trail and into the room. He waved his arms in the air, hoping to clear a pathway through the webbing. The web smothered his body and face, stopping him in his tracks. It was strong. He tried to wipe the webbing away, but it only smothered him worse. The boy frantically pushed forward, pulling off one thick strand of webbing after the other. He became even more entangled. He could see his friend now, and surprisingly, his friend's eyes were open.

"Jamis! Jamis! Hey, are you okay?" the boy yelled to his friend.

Jamis shivered a little and seemed out of sorts. He was trying to catch his bearings. Then Jamis saw his friend, Fields, trapped in the spider web in front of him.

Jamis warned in a low whisper, "You have to get out of here! It's going to eat you, too!"

"Hold on! I'm going to save you!" Fields responded, ignoring what his friend said.

Fields heard something behind him. Theda was zoning in on a lone bat struggling to catch up with its colony. Fields realized it was now or never. He thrashed around with all of his strength, trying to break the web's grasp to no avail. The ravening scorpula had caught the bat and finished its web-wrapping duties. Fields gave it everything he had one last time with nothing to lose. He tried to rip his hands from the web but only managed to loosen the grasp it held on his left hand. At this point, he imagined the worst.

Theda heard Fields scuffling and saw him stuck in her sticky mesh. The scorpula completely forgot about the newly wrapped bat and rushed over to secure her fresh catch.

The grotesque blood-sucking creature crept up behind Fields. She delicately ran one of her legs up against his body and over his shoulder, relishing the moment. Fields was paralyzed by fear. He could smell old rotting vomit-mixed blood on the giant scorpula's fangs as she brought them close. Her fangs hovered an inch above his neck. He felt clumps of blood drip on his neck. She seemed to be struggling with whether she wanted to taste him now or later.

Somehow, through this dreadful situation, Fields remembered he had a few matches in the front left pocket of his pants. He created a little room on this side when he was trying to break free from the web. He reached in his pocket and grabbed a match with the tips of his fingers. He wasn't sure how much time he had, but he wasn't giving up.

Fields pulled out the match. It was a strike-anywhere match. He needed to strike it on the cave wall, but he wasn't sure if he could reach that far. Desperately, he forced his hand over as far as he could, straining against the webbing, and was able to brace the match on the wall. The boy half-smirked, realizing Theda had no idea what was about to happen.

Praying it would light, Fields swiped the match across the cave wall. It lit up impressively. The webbing surrounding him inflamed in an instant. A wave of fire surged through the room, transformed into a fireball because of the dense webbing, and exploded out of the room. The two boys and the scorpula were shot out of the room. Theda had caught on fire. She rolled to her feet and ran off, screaming in a high pitch.

Fields rose to one knee, smothered out any lingering fire on their clothing, and hollered, "Get up! We must go! Get up!"

It wasn't until now that Fields realized how badly his friend was injured. Jamis had several puncture wounds on his neck where the scorpula had been feeding on him. The wounds were leaking thick, gooey blood.

Jamis tried to lift himself but couldn't. Fields helped his friend to his feet, laid him over his shoulder, and picked him up. Fields ran for the cave's exit. He didn't know he could even carry Jamis, let alone while running. As he got closer to the exit, he could see the light growing larger and brighter. The muscles in his shoulder ached from carrying Jamis, but he didn't let the pain stop him. He continued driving his legs forward, not giving up on both of their lives. Fields had snot dripping down his lip and felt a twinge of pain shoot down his spine. He was so close; he could smell the air outside.

"Only a few more steps," Fields said aloud.

Unbelievably, another scorpula dropped from the wall above the cave's exit and blocked them from leaving. The stunned boy turned around and saw Theda creeping up behind them. Her body was still smoking and missing most of its hair, but she didn't appear weak.

Fields fell to his knees and set Jamis on the ground. He looked at his friend, visibly distraught, and told him, "I'm sorry! I tried!"

The boys, who would have been the only children ever to confront Theda and live, began crying. Fields lowered his head in submission. The scorpulas didn't waste any time and pounced on their meals...

"Oh, my goodness! That was incredibly vivid!" Aiden complimented with a blank look on his face, still processing the story.

"Yeah, Melia! Well done!" Gil agreed, "I always wished the boys would have made it. It's so sad, and I promise you, as a kid, I never went into a cave!"

Gil glanced over at Cedric, half-expecting him to add a sarcastic comment, but instead, he was only sitting with his mouth wide open, not moving, and staring straight ahead.

Gil whacked his buddy on the arm and remarked, "Ceed, what's wrong?"

Cedric replied in a monotone voice, "I hate that story."

The Tale of Tyrock the Dragon

Everyone laughed at Cedric.

Melia realized she was in the mood to tell another story, so she asked the group, "Have you all heard the one about the dragon?"

Cedric instantly became animated, "Oh, I love that one!" he exclaimed.

"Yeah!" Gil agreed, "I could never tell if he was good or bad."

"Who?" Aiden asked.

"The dragon! At first, he seems evil, but then he saves the boy," replied Gil.

"Don't tell him, dummy! And I don't think he saved the boy!" Cedric interjected and turned to Melia, "Go ahead, tell the story!"

"Well," began Melia, *"The city of Hogglestein was a magical place. It was one of the first settlements in this world, and yes, it was located in the Outer Divide; but nobody knows, for sure, if it ever existed. It was a renowned destination for many, which is why the city had grown so large. The city was a hub for merchants and trading. Many traveled across the globe to enjoy entertainment like theater, dance, comedy, and more high-end events such as the gladiator ring, poker, and the Devian games. Others would come to spend their coin at the infamous bars, brothels, and underground clubs. An assortment of rare items such as the youth fruit, dragon scales, and healing potions could be found there as well. There was one itsy, bitsy problem which caused many to think twice about going there. There was a murderous dragon who lived in the hills above the lake."*

Aiden glanced over at Borak, saying, "Murderous dragon? Interesting."

Borak only raised his eyebrows and sat stoically like always.

Melia resumed the story, *"One day, while many families were enjoying the lake, a group of children played together. The children, absentmindedly, wandered off to the side of the lake where they weren't supposed to be. The forest grew thick on that side of the lake, so people normally stayed away from it unless they were hunting. There were also local stories of hunters seeing a dragon further in that part of the forest, but no one paid any attention until this day. The children were playing hide and seek, and one of the kids found a cozy hiding spot in the middle of some trees. It was so cozy that after some time, the child snuggled up in some of the hay-like material in which he was sitting and fell asleep."*

"Uh oh! Don't tell me another boy dies? Sheesh, with these stories, I bet kids here never even leave home!" Aiden teased.

Melia grinned at him, pausing for a moment to remember her train of thought, then began again, *"This boy's name was Ernie, and he was never again seen alive. There are a couple of different versions of what happened next. Basically, in one version, a Reever showed up, startling the boy. Then the dragon came out of nowhere, killed the Reever, and ate Ernie.*

Melia continued, "In a much less believed and less told version, the dragon saved the boy by killing the Reever and ate one of its freshly hatched babies. In this version, the dragon flew off, holding Ernie in its claw. No one knows for sure what happened."

"What is a Reever?" interrupted Aiden.

Melia replied, *"It's a huge, ancient, land-dwelling bird. They are the dragon's favorite food. Anyhow, what we know happened was the kids heard a commotion, and when they ran over to see what was going on, they saw the dragon killing the Reever."*

...The children watched in horror as the dragon chomped down on the huge Reever. The Reever shrieked in pain. The kids heard a loud crunch, and the Reever fell dead from the dragon's mouth. The parents arrived and couldn't believe what they saw. Even more horrifying, next to the Reever body was another small dirt-covered body lying in the "nest." It was partially eaten, and its organs were hanging out. This body looked like a child's. Some Roak men had their bows in hand and immediately unleashed a barrage of arrows. The arrows were no match for the beast. They didn't do any damage... simply bounced off the dragon's armored scales. Oddly, the dragon ignored its attackers and lowered its head, looking for something. It was as if the dragon was distracted by something else. It, then, picked up the partially eaten dirt-covered body and swallowed it. Ernie's mother shrieked in terror at what she saw. The dragon looked inquisitively at her, then turned

and grabbed the eggs from the nest. He chomped those down, as well, making more crunching sounds. Unfathomably, the savage beast flipped around toward the families, and everyone froze. Instead of the dragon attacking, it only huffed a fiery breath from its nose and fled the scene, uncharacteristically, leaving the dead Reever's body.

While all the families were panicking, Ernie's sister walked up to the giant bird body because she thought she saw something no one else had noticed. It was a foot, but peculiarly, it was a small foot. She picked it up. The girl examined the foot and was relieved it wasn't her brother's. It appeared to be a baby Reever's foot, which made absolutely no sense since no baby Reever was spotted. What boggled her mind even more was she thought she had seen her brother hiding behind the dragon while it was chowing down on the eggs. The girl's mother, distraught from witnessing what appeared to be a dragon devouring her son, saw her daughter standing by the Reever's body with a bloody foot in her hand and ran over to her. The mother knocked the horrid foot out of the little girl's hand and dragged her away...

Melia continued, *"After a short time, the Tale of Tyrock the dragon emerged. The tale described how the dragon killed and ate Ernie, and because Tyrock ate the dirt-covered body, no one thought any different. No one else had seen the foot since no one went back to the lake for almost a year. Only Ernie's sister had seen it and, after that, it disappeared. Although the children were terrified by the incident, Ernie's sister believed her brother was still alive and Tyrock had saved him. However, the little girl's protests didn't stop the many hunters who tried tracking the dragon down in the hope of riches and fame. All who tried must have paid with their lives as none on the hunt for Tyrock ever returned. He showed up one time in the city and burned a grain storage building down but didn't kill anybody. People took it as a warning. Because of this, the city retracted Tyrock's bounty and prayed he would stay away. He did. Years later, the threat of Herana arrived."*

"Oh, that's right! Herana attacked the city!" Cedric blurted excitedly.

"Wow! I forgot how good this story was!" Gil added.

"Either that or Melia's an amazing storyteller! I swear to you guys, if I see a dang dragon here, I don't know what I'm going to do," Aiden joked.

Smiling, Melia moved forward with the story, "That's right, Ceed! It had been about seven years. The Legend of Tyrock became more of a myth, and life had moved on."

...Tyrock stayed away from the city and only killed when threatened. With nothing better to do now, the dragon hunters became drunks, passing their time going to the bars and brothels.

Herrana's wrath was spreading through the land. The residents of Hogglestein received word she was near. Not too long after, Herrana attacked, bringing havoc upon the city. She had powers the world had never seen and almost leveled the entire city. She captured the King's son and placed him in an energetic grasp. The Dark Queen squeezed the Prince's face, forcing the King to give up.

As the King proceeded to offer himself in place of his son, Tyrock showed up and saved them both. The dragon flew down from the sky, blowing fire. He incinerated most of Herrana's army and landed next to her. She had no choice but to release the King's son so that she could fight Tyrock. The Prince and King fled to safety, followed by the remainder of his guards...

"It's a heck of a story! That's for sure!" spoke Jack in a louder than normal voice.

"One of my favorites, definitely!" Cedric agreed.

"Soooo, does this city really exist?" Aiden asked, intrigued.

"It does. I've been there. And the dragon exists, too," the stoic ninja Borak spoke up.

"W...wh...what?" Melia stammered, surprised, "When? I never knew that!"

"It is a long story," her brother answered, "Maybe I'll tell it another time, but the city is real. Even though it is in ruins, it is still magnificent."

The entire group wanted to hear about Borak's adventure to Hogglestein, but they could tell he wasn't up for it. Aiden interrupted the silence with more questions, "Whatever happened to Tyrock and the creatures or people? I don't know what to call them, um, the city's locals? The King and Prince? What happened to them?"

Melia was still stunned by her brother's admission but shook it off and looked at Aiden to answer his questions, *"People is fine, and some say Herana killed Tyrock after an epic battle. Others say Tyrock got the better of Herana and escaped. I'll leave those stories for another time, but that was the end of Hogglestein. All the people fled. The King and Prince never returned. I have heard the city is still there but in ruins, even now from my brother. There are also whispers that Tyrock still lives in the forest behind the lake, but no one knows for sure. As you know, we haven't been to the Outer Divide for many years. That will change tomorrow."*

"Well, bravo! Great story!" Aiden acknowledged, "A dragon! Wow, so we might run into a dragon! Noted."

The group continued with some small talk, then fell asleep. They were exhausted. Although the healing shields had healed them, the protection didn't provide nutrients. The heroes were still regaining their strength. Their rations weren't very sustainable and were almost gone. If these world-savers were going to be in optimal physical condition to take on Magus and his army, they would need a healthy portion of protein before pursuing their attack. It looked like they would be on the hunt for the next day or so.

Hunting for Dinner

Cedric could hear something very clumsily rummaging in his bag. "What is that?" he thought. For some reason, he couldn't see his bag or anything else. Everything was dark. "What the heck is going on?" he thought again, "Oh crap, I'm dreaming!" He woke up to see the puma was staring directly in his face. The puma growled.

"Ahhhhh!" Cedric yelled. He leaped into the air and disappeared into some thorn bushes twenty feet away.

Gil heard the commotion and hopped to his feet. He had his sword in hand, ready to strike.

The puma sat down, half-grinning.

"Hey, guys! Do you see this? I think it's smiling!" Gil concluded as Aiden and Borak crept over, still overcoming grogginess.

"Well, would you look at that? It is smiling!" Aiden agreed.

Aiden tried calling the puma over. He knelt, made kissy sounds, and patted his knee, urging the puma to come to him. The puma only stared at him. Strangely, it appeared to laugh, turned, and sped off into the shrubbery.

"Ceed, you okay?" asked Gil, only slightly concerned.

"Oooowwwwwww!" came a noise from inside the thorn bushes, "Man down! Man down! I can't move!"

Aiden, Borak, Jack, and Gil chuckled, knowing Cedric must be stuck by hundreds of thorns. Melia didn't think it was funny.

"Quit playin' around and get out of there!" Gil jokingly urged.

The thorn bushes started moving ever so slightly, followed by a disgruntled, "Ow, oooo, ow, arghh, ouch!" from the Hairie working his way out of them. Cedric could hear them laughing at him. He poked his head out of the bushes and calmly yet angrily suggested, "I could use some help, guys. Or, are you gonna stand there and laugh at me?"

The thorn-ridden Hairie had a piece of thorn bush stuck in the side of his cheek. He looked so mad; it made the situation even more comical. Everyone, even Melia, began to laugh. By this time, Melia had admitted it was a little funny. They all enjoyed a good laugh. Even Cedric let a chuckle slip out, then stopped himself.

"Sorry, Ceed, you gotta admit, it's kinda funny!" Aiden said, trying to ease Cedric's irritation. Aiden picked up a log and threw it at the thorn bush.

"Oooowwww!" Cedric hollered again after the log landed on the thorn bush and pushed it down.

Thorns tore the Hairie's flesh. Initially, Cedric didn't know why Aiden would do that but saw the path the log created for him to get out. He felt like a pin cushion forcing his way out of the bush and grunted in pain, "Ahh, owww, rrrrr!"

Cedric made it out of the thorn bush, yanked the piece of it from his face, and remarked, "THAT was NOT funny!"

Everyone cracked up again.

"That'll wake you up, huh, Ceed?" Gil kept teasing.

"Whatever, Gil. That puma thinks he's funny. I'll get him back next time," Cedric promised, looking forward to the chance.

"How do you know it was a male?" Gil asked curiously.

"I could smell the musk on him. It was a male. And he thinks he's funny!" Cedric repeated.

Aiden interrupted, pointing at something to get everyone's attention, "Hey, you guys see that?"

It was a group of rock deer crouched down by some bushes.

"That would be some good eating!" added Aiden.

"Yes, it would!" agreed Borak.

The two didn't say a word. They looked at each other and gave slight head gestures indicating, "You go that way, and I'll go this way."

The rock deer were about half a mile away. Borak and Aiden closed the distance on them quickly, flanking around on either side. Luckily, the wind was blowing the opposite way so that the deer couldn't smell them. As they moved closer, they saw a sign that said, "You have now entered the Outer Divide."

Aiden thought out loud, "We're not in Kansas anymore."

They made it within a hundred yards of the rock deer. Aiden pondered,

"This would be much easier with a bow or a rifle," and then he wondered, "How in the heck are we gonna do this?" All Aiden had was his sword and a dagger. Borak carried only his bo-blade and a dagger, but he seemed to have a plan.

Borak moved steadily forward, flanking the left side of the deer while Aiden moved around to the right. They were within a hundred feet now, and Aiden stopped to let Borak make his move. The Roak moved impressively stealthy. He lowered down to all fours and crept forward. Somehow, to Aiden's disbelief, the ninja-like stalker managed to get within thirty feet of the deer. Only once did a deer lift its nose to smell the wind. Borak lined up a clear shot and raised his dagger, ready to throw it. As Borak braced to unleash the dagger, Aiden accidentally stepped on a twig. It cracked. Borak heard the twig snap and quickly threw the dagger. The deer had already flinched. The dagger missed the critical zone and hit the deer in the stomach.

"Wow!" Aiden thought to himself, "That was still a nice throw!"

The rock deer bolted into a cave right next to where they were lying. Borak shot Aiden a disappointed look which implied, "What the heck, man!" Aiden shrugged his shoulders in response, insinuating, "Sorry."

The two met at the mouth of the cave to figure out what they would do.

"Well, what do you think?" Aiden inquired, gesturing toward the cave with his chin.

Borak looked at the cave for a second, then calmly gave his opinion, "Looks like we're going in."

"That's what I figured," Aiden responded, tightening his lips in apprehension after last night's story. Borak armed himself with his bo staff and headed into the cave. Aiden dropped his head and sighed, "Right behind you, bud!"

Aiden hadn't even taken two steps before they heard the trample of hooves coming in their direction. The rock deer were screaming in a high-pitched tone as they made their way back to the cave entrance. Aiden and Borak reacted quickly, jumping to the side as the deer erupted from the depths of the cave. One deer dashed out, flying at top speed, and another tumbled, flipping over and over on its side. It landed halfway on its feet in a way that allowed it to prop up on all fours and continue wobbling away. A second later, a third deer, the one Borak hit with the dagger, was tripped by a hairy black leg as it exited the cave. The deer hit the ground and rolled to a stop. A scorpula pounced on the deer and began wrapping it in webbing.

Aiden and Borak were stupefied. They couldn't believe that in front of them was a scorpula, like Theda from Melia's story. Although Borak had seen Hogglestein from the Tale of Tyrock, this was the first time he saw a giant spider/scorpion.

"Holy crap!" Borak quietly revealed his thoughts. Both hunters prepared to fight.

The giant scorpula wrapped the rock deer tightly and securely. It then realized other eyes were on it. It quickly jumped, landing in front of the deer, and raised its front four legs like a tarantula ready for battle. The hairy spider made a hissing sound, warning its competition to stay away.

Right when Aiden was about to make a move, another monstrous scorpula showed itself from the darkness of the cave.

"This one's mine!" Borak yelled, already honed in on his target. He was staring at the first giant tarantula creature.

Aiden moved around to the right, trying to sneak up on the other scorpula. It was creeping out of the cave, distracted by what was happening with the first giant scorpula and Borak.

Borak ran and launched himself, lifting his bo-blade high in the air. He sliced downward, thinking he would cut through the scorpula, but unbelievably, the hideous creature began glowing purple and blocked the strike. Borak's blade clanked off the scorpula's arms like they were metal. Aiden saw what happened and stopped before he lunged at the other scorpula.

"How in the heck?" Aiden said.

Borak did a backflip away from the scorpula. Aiden also backed away from the other one.

"What should we do?" Aiden asked. He noticed something happening to one of the scorpulas and spoke up, "Do you see that? Its head and its body are smoking!"

Borak looked and saw it. The creature's entire body was beginning to smoke, and it backed out of the sun into the shade.

"It's the sun!" Borak yelled, "Quick, grab the deer!"

Aiden raised his eyebrows and repeated to himself, "Grab the deer?"

Aiden realized he was within ten feet of the rock deer. It occurred to him that after the scorpulas so rudely revealed their existence, he had forgotten about the meat. Aiden could see the first scorpula was still attached to the deer by its webbing, and it could take off at any moment back into the cave. The other giant tarantula/scorpion was edging forward toward him. Without thinking any further, Aiden took two steps and dove at the rock deer. He slashed the web line connected to the first scorpula. Both giant tarantulas flinched backward, then raised to attack.

Borak threw his bo like a spear and hit his target. This time the weapon pierced through the side of the first scorpula's head. The ugly creature slumped over, dead. Aiden saw the other scorpula moving its mouth strangely. It then shot a purple fluid directly at him. Aiden put his arms up in defense. An energetic shield formed around him and the deer, blocking the venom. With surprising force, the venom spewed in long thick strands, hitting the shield and sizzling down its sides. Borak ran and yanked the bo-blade from the head of the dead scorpula, flinging brain matter. He hurled his weapon at the other scorpula. The giant creature saw the bo in the air, stopped shooting venom, and ducked in time to dodge the death blade. Disappointed that he missed, Borak realized he was now weaponless.

Aiden saw his chance and immediately jumped to his feet. He began to drag the rock deer to a nearby bush. The scorpula saw its buddy on the ground, dead with blood pouring out of its head. It screeched and lunged at Borak. Borak dove to the side and rolled out of the angry scorpula's strike zone, but the hideous creature chased him. Borak dove again, this time flipping on his hands and feet, looking like a gymnast. He flipped around doing cartwheels and backflips, manipulating the scorpula back and forth. The giant tarantula/scorpion began smoking profusely, continuing to chase and barely missing Borak several times. Aiden finished hiding the deer and ran to help but was having trouble. The fight was moving so fast, it was hard to follow. It was amazing to see Borak flip around so fluently. As he was flipping, he landed on a rock. Borak stumbled, lost his balance, and flailed onto his back.

Aiden saw his friend in trouble and called out to him, "Here!"

Aiden had retrieved Borak's weapon. He threw it to Borak, but it appeared it might be too late. The scorpula was already on top of him, preparing to plunge its fangs into his neck. Borak grabbed the bo and stabbed upward. The scorpula glowed purple and blocked the strike. It spread its fangs. The ugly creature lowered down to bite. Borak closed his eyes, making peace with his life, ready to die. A sound interrupted all others, "Whoo, whoo, whoo," and then a splatter as Melia's boomerang cut into one side of the scorpula and out the other. The grotesque arachnid raised and screeched in pain. Borak stabbed upward again and cut into the hairy monster's abdomen. He sliced across its body cavity, ripping it open. Blood and guts fell atop Borak, followed by the creature's body.

"Bout time you showed up, sis!" Borak yelled, sounding muffled from under the dead scorpula's body.

"Whew! That was too friggin' close!" Aiden admitted. He ran to his friend's aid and helped him get out from under the carcass.

"You're telling me! I thought I was toast!" Borak added while covered in scorpula guts.

"Hey, guys!" Melia shouted from fifty feet back, "Well, I didn't see that coming! I guess the creatures in the old stories are real! Maybe you two should wait for us next time?"

Aiden and Borak looked at each other a little embarrassed, and in defense,

Aiden remarked, "Hey, at least we got food!"

Aiden walked over to where he hid the deer in the bush, and as he approached, he heard the brush shaking. Aiden stopped, and the brush stopped.

"That's weird," he said to himself.

Aiden started walking again, and the brush began shaking again. Quickly, he drew his sword, darted toward the bush, and jumped to the other side of it. He saw the puma trying to steal the deer, but something was wrong. It was caught in the webbing. The puma must have gotten tangled up while performing its thievery. Aiden crept up to the trapped cat and noticed the deer was dead. After their previous encounter, he didn't think the puma was a threat to him. For some reason, he felt safe with the large feline. The puma didn't even try to run. It was exhausted, and knew it was stuck. Aiden put his hand out, and the puma stared at him. He placed his hand on the puma's head and felt its fur. It was surprisingly soft. As he caressed the creature's head, it began to purr.

"Hold on, buddy," Aiden told the remarkable animal, "I'll get you outta here."

Aiden carefully cut the strands of webbing holding the puma. It bounced up and ran a short distance, then stopped, looked briefly back at him, and disappeared into the brush. The rest of the crew didn't see the puma. Aiden decided not to say anything.

It was easiest to process the meat right there, so they burnt off the scorpula's webbing, then cut up and packed the meat. They were salivating at the thought of eating it. They hadn't eaten a proper meal in days and were anxious to sit down by a fire and devour some delicious deer kabobs mixed with local vegetables they found during their journey. After traveling an acceptable distance, they finally settled down to have their meal and camp for the night.

The Tale of Momma Snake

"I think we're getting close, don't you?" Cedric asked Jack.

"I reckon, mate," Jack responded, "You see that there?" Jack pointed ahead of them down into another valley, "That there is Snake River. And yeah, it's full of those awful snakes like the one we ran in ta before. I heard the big Momma Snake lives in there!"

"Big Momma Snake?" Cedric's eyes widened, "How big is this big Momma Snake?"

Jack leaned in close to Cedric, "Word is she's so big, she stretches from one end of the river to the other. You should ask Melia to tell the story."

Cedric shook his head, visibly shaken, and whispered, "I do not want to see another snake!"

"Wow, this deer is delicious!" Aiden complimented, "I don't think there's any deer this good on Earth."

"Yep, don't know 'bout the Earth thing, but this is good!" Jack agreed and changed the subject, "Hey Melia, Cedric wants to hear the story 'bout big Momma Snake! You know, since we're 'bout to cross Snake River 'n all."

"Ah, yes, that's a great idea!" Melia perked up, "I've been thinking about it. Now that we know the stories are real, it will help us prepare."

"Now that we know they're real!" Cedric interrupted, looking unsure of himself. He rambled, "You know what? Maybe it's better I don't hear it. You know, I'm good. I think I'll hit the hay, fellars!" Cedric fake yawned and rolled on his side.

No one had ever seen Cedric so anxious. Amusingly, he started peeking over his shoulder in a paranoid manner. Aiden motioned to the others while Cedric looked into the distance, telling them, "Watch this!" He grabbed a stick and threw it, so it landed next to Cedric's foot.

Aiden yelled, "It's a snake! Run!"

Cedric jumped almost ten feet in the air, hollering, "Nooooo! Oh noooooo!" The little snake-fearing Hairie landed on his feet, and everyone exploded into laughter. After realizing it was a joke, Cedric pouted, "Thanks, guys. That was nice of you!"

"Aw, come on, mate! Don't worry, Ceed. We're here to protect ya," Jack teased, "Melia, tell us that story, would ya?"

Melia took a drink of water to moisten her mouth. She began telling one of her favorite stories, *"Okay, soooo, the valley below us is cut in half by the Snake River. It gained its name because the area is riddled with snakes. There was an incredible battle many years ago down in this valley. The battle was the first between Naru and Herana and came after Herana had decimated Hogglestein. Hogglestein was Herana's first large-scale attack. It was also when she enlightened the world, including Naru, of how strong and powerful she was. After the destruction of Hogglestein, Naru knew he had to stop her. This battle was the beginning of the Great War between the two.*

Many snakes appeared on the battlefield and caused hysteria and turmoil, which strangely may have been what saved Naru's life. These snakes affected people in different ways. When they looked into the eyes, sometimes, the snakes caused euphoria and hallucinations, and other times the snakes caused paranoia or even arousal.

Melia pointed out, "I imagine you guys can understand the implications this might have on a battlefield." The skilled storyteller glanced around the group of heroes huddled by the campfire and saw everyone listening intently, so she proceeded, *"...So, both armies had no idea what they were about to face.*

Naru and his army emerged from the mountains above the valley. They saw Herana and her band of cronies waiting for them on the other side of the river below. Herana didn't have a large battalion, but Naru knew how dangerous she was. He wanted to show strength, so he sent half of his troops bull-rushing straight ahead. Oddly, Herana and her minions didn't move. They watched as if they knew something Naru didn't. Sure enough, as soon as Naru's army came close to the river, hundreds of snakes appeared out of the bushes and attacked, but not in a usual way. The snakes all sat, curled in a poised position, seeking to lock eyes with anyone who dared. All hell broke loose...

Melia paused for a second. Cedric became impatient, urging, "Sooo, what happened next?"

"I thought you didn't want to hear the story?" Melia teased. Cedric only looked back in anticipation.

"Ok, where was I? Oh, yea," the storyteller began again, *"Naru watched as his once unyielding militia transformed into a massive congregation of emotion and confusion."*

Most of Naru's troops began crying, singing, laughing, and even kissing each other. Madly, the rest of the soldiers succumbed to paranoia and fled in different directions. They even jumped into the river, trying to swim across to where Herana and her army stood. Naru was beside himself. He watched the insanity unfold, not knowing what to think or what was happening. Then, the unimaginable happened again—large ripples formed in the river. At first, they were small but rapidly turned into waves. While the waves rustled around, a figure appeared between them. It was something monumental in size and ran the length of the river. As Naru struggled to make sense of it, Momma Snake showed herself. Her ginormous head broke the water's surface. She raised fifty feet in the air. Tons of water flowed down her face and body, splashing back into the river and onto the ground.

Naru had entered a state of disbelief. "There is no way this is real!" he said to himself.

Naru watched as Momma Snake attacked his troops. She lowered her head and devoured some of the crazed soldiers who were swimming across the river. All the troops he had sent on the attack were psychologically disoriented and wholly incapacitated by this time. Some had fallen to their knees, wailing in sadness; others were roaming around cackling in delight; and still, others found someone they suddenly adored and were caressing each other in some love spell. They were oblivious to what was happening.

Herana glanced around the battlefield and smirked, savoring the scene. She had planned this perfectly. Now, it was time to attack.

The evil Queen raised her arm and shouted, "Readyyyy! Firrre!" She dropped her arm as she said fire.

Herana's army sent a barrage of arrows into the sky. The arrows partially blocked the sun creating a cloudy overcast effect. The sun reappeared, and deadly piercing shafts rained down over Naru's distracted army.

The arrows devastated the oblivious soldiers, tearing through their bodies. It was literally like shooting fish in a barrel, and even when hit, the hypnotized warriors did not wake up to reality.

Herana ordered her minions to attack. At first, they hesitated, watching the enormous Momma Snake chomp on Naru's mesmerized fighters like bite-sized snacks. She shot a vicious glare at them, and they immediately charged, knowing they had a better chance against the giant snake.

As the evil army approached the riverbank, snakes appeared and stared them down. Herana's Devians, evil Grandars, and foul Hairies became crazed as well.

Herana ordered her army, "Kill them! What are you doing? Kill them, or I'll kill you!"

After no response from her lackeys, the evil Queen whipped her hand around and released a beam of energy, cutting many of them in half...

"Now, hold on!" Gil spoke up, "You're telling me she killed her own fighters?"

"Yes!" responded Melia, "That's how the story goes."

"Why would she do that? She was crazy," Gil vented, imagining if that happened to him.

"I agree. I mean, what do you expect from the worst villain our world has ever had?" Melia commented, then added, "Soooo, you done interrupting?"

Gil shut his mouth and sat quietly.

Melia carried on with the story, *"Herana killed many of her troops and dashed toward the river. She threw energy blasts at any snakes who dared show themselves.*

Naru commanded the other half of his soldiers to charge. This time, he led his comrades, throwing fireballs and burning any snakes in his path.

Momma Snake saw Naru and his band of warriors coming and sneered, displaying her mouth full of vicious fang-like teeth. She braced herself, then lunged at the oncoming threat, trying to crush Naru in her jaws. Naru shot the humongous snake with an energy blast, barely phasing her, and dove to the left, dodging the serpent's attack. While Momma Snake munched on some soldiers, Naru got up and ran straight for Herana. Naru and the wicked Queen sprinted at each other, unleashing a bombardment of energy blasts and fireballs. The adversaries easily deflected each attack. Herana reached the river and jumped high in the air, attempting to jump over it. Momma Snake realized what was happening and swung her head around like a baseball bat. The massive snake smashed Herana with a direct hit. Herana protected herself at impact with an energy shield but was knocked hundreds of feet backward. The dark Queen hit the ground and tumbled to a stop. She shook her head, stood up, looked at the aftermath, and assessed the situation. All her goons were dead, and although more than half of Naru's soldiers had been killed, he still had some in the fight. Momma Snake was staring at her. Herana didn't feel any hypnotism from the staredown of the giant snake but knew it was a warning. She took a step forward, contemplating an attack, and realized she was injured internally. The evil Queen glared at the monstrous serpent while struggling within herself as to what to do. Ultimately, with little alternative, she chose wisely and fled.

Momma Snake saw Herana flee and turned to Naru. At first, Naru prepared to defend himself, but the mammoth serpent only sat poised and vigilant. She watched as almost all of Naru's army remained in an unthreatening trance. A soldier who wasn't affected was about to kill a little snake.

Naru stopped the soldier, commanding, "Hoooold!"

The giant snake lowered her head to Naru's level and squinted her eyes at him. After a moment, Momma Snake grunted, and all the little snakes disappeared.

The colossal serpent spoke, "You have disturbed my children! Leave at once and never return!"

Naru nodded in agreement.

Momma Snake turned away from him, lowered herself into the water, and vanished. She was gone as quickly as she arrived. Nothing but silence ensued. Herana was gone, and her warriors were dead. The remainder of Naru's army, who weren't under the snake's spell, stared at him and awaited his orders.

Naru needed a minute to focus his thoughts. While doing so, something caught his attention. He saw a flicker by the edge of the water. He walked closer and identified it as a post with a keyhole in it. The inside of the keyhole flashed light, then faded. There was writing on top of the post, but he couldn't make out what it said.

"That's odd," Naru commented to himself and didn't think any more of it. He turned to his comrades and shouted in victory, "Yeeaahhhhhh!"

They triumphantly responded, "Raaahhhhhhh!"

Naru gathered all his soldiers and led them away from the river. Once all had recovered from the spell, they traveled home to bring word of their success...

"Yep, it's official! I'm not going with you guys!" Cedric blurted out.

Everyone laughed.

Gil added, "Me neither! Screw that!"

Borak was smiling with a hint of concern, "I hope you guys are joking. We need everyone if we're going to do this!"

Jack spoke up, "Ya mate! I ain't gonna lie. That snake sounds scary as hell, but I'm not backin' down!"

The two Hairies didn't reply. They sat there as if they were still contemplating whether they were going.

"We need to make a plan!" Aiden suggested, "And what about that keyhole in the post? It sounds like we might need a key."

They didn't think too long about the keyhole since they didn't have a key but did devise a plan before they rested for the night. It was a plan about which Cedric wasn't too happy.

Crossing Snake River

They got an early start and advanced toward the river. As the group traveled closer, Cedric and Gil both became visibly anxious. It was very apparent they did not want to go near the river.

"This is probably a good spot to stop, guys!" Gil said.

"Ow, my ankle. We better stop!" deceived Cedric.

"Will you two quit!" snapped Borak, "You both need to focus! We're almost there!"

As they traveled, they looked over the terrain. The river was directly ahead. It was beautiful and, at present, seemed tranquil, but the team knew different. It was going to be a hell of an ordeal, and it was going to happen very soon.

Cedric thought about the plan they had made. To his dismay, they decided that he would walk up to the river's edge with his eyes covered. While he was walking, the others would kill the snakes attempting to hypnotize him. If Momma Snake showed herself, they would defend and run. It sounded simple enough.

They made it to some bushes about 100 feet from the river. The rest of the way to the water was an open rocky area. It was quiet as the team waited for Cedric to proceed with the plan.

Cedric stared back at the others, annoyed. He grumbled, "I can't believe I'm doing this! I'm the one who's scared of these dang snakes, remember?"

Melia replied, "That is why you're doing it. So you can overcome your fear.

"Yeah, right!" Cedric muttered. He covered his eyes and began hesitantly walking forward.

Only a few snakes slithered out into the open. They stared at Cedric, waiting to make eye contact, but he kept his eyes covered. It was perplexing to see only a few snakes. It was as if they knew something was up.

Since Cedric couldn't see, Borak directed him, "Go further! Straight ahead!"

Cedric threw one hand in the air, mumbling, "Oh, you want me to go further? I shouldn't even be doing this! But nooooo, Melia said it's for my own good! So I can overcome my fear! What a crock!"

Cedric persevered despite his bickering, stumbling his way forward over rocks with his hand still over his eyes. He slowly moved closer to the riverbank.

Having second thoughts, Cedric stammered, "Guys, um, uh, guys! I don't, uh, think this is safe!"

Curiously, the snakes eyed him, wondering to whom he was speaking.

The rest of the heroes watched from a short distance away, ready to pounce as soon as the snakes showed themselves in full force. There were still only a few out in view.

After scanning the area more closely, Borak tapped his sister on her shoulder and pointed to hidden spots in crevices and under rocks. Melia saw hundreds of snakes staring at them, camouflaged by the natural surroundings. The sly serpents could barely be seen and were waiting to ambush them. It was time to figure out a new strategy.

"Maybe we should have thought this through a little better," Melia admitted, "What do you wanna do?"

Borak pulled out a couple of potions he purchased in the Druid community. The red and fiery-looking potions appeared unstable. The liquid inside bubbled and gurgled.

"They're magma bombs. We should use these," proposed Borak.

Melia glanced at the potions, then back at Borak, and agreed, "Damn right!"

Cedric walked dangerously close to the water's edge. The water began to stir. At the same time, he felt a vibration on his thigh and wondered what it could be. He uncovered his eyes to see what was buzzing on his leg. It was the dagger brought to him by the Druid King. It was lit up green and pulled him as if it was attracted to something. The intrigued Hairie looked in the direction it was pulling him and saw a light flashing from a keyhole in a post.

"It must be the key," Cedric murmured, "But, what is it for?"

The bewildered Hairie walked over to the post, inserted the dagger, and turned it. The light dimmed. Sitting behind the post was a snake, staring him dead in his eyes.

Borak was about to throw the potions when the entire group heard crackling and popping sounds. To their astonishment, a transparent tunnel-type bridge appeared over the river.

"Wow! Look at that!" exclaimed Gil.

"Get ready!" Borak instructed, holding up a potion.

No one said a word. The others looked at the potion Borak held in the air and could tell it meant business. They readied themselves to run.

Borak threw one potion to the left and the other to the right. The potions hit the rocks and exploded into burning liquid magma. Two ponds of fiery liquid began forming and continued to spread. A flood of flames flowed over the rocks and crevices where the snakes were hiding. The magma engulfed the terrain on either side, sweeping over the area like hot lava. It burned anything and everything in its way. Burning snakes fled the area. A path was left between the magma ponds, leading to Cedric and the bridge. The team ran down the path. While they ran, they heard the snakes screaming in horrific pain.

They made it through the flames and came upon Cedric, sitting down in an awkward position. It became apparent he was making out with the post.

"What the heck are you doing?" shouted Gil.

Aiden added, "Quit having sex with the post! We have to get out of here!"

Right then, Momma Snake broke the water's surface and showed herself.

"Oh, my! Big Momma is real, fellas!" Jack informed the obvious, "We need to go now!"

Momma Snake sat high out of the water, baring her mouth full of sharp fangs. She spoke, "I sense relation to the other one! No one was to return! Now, you die!"

Jack threw Cedric over his shoulder and bolted toward the bridge. The rest of the group followed. Momma Snake struck viciously at them. Gil was directly in her strike path, about to become a snake snack. Aiden grabbed him and flung him into the tunnel bridge. The giant serpent's mouth crashed on the ground as it finished its attack.

"Noooo!" Gil screamed as he watched Aiden disappear into the huge snake's mouth.

Hearing Gil, Melia looked back over her shoulder and didn't see Aiden. She saw only Gil, sitting on the edge of the bridge with an outstretched hand. He was reaching in the direction of the giant snake. She put two and two together and was in disbelief for a second. She couldn't understand how Aiden could die since that's not what the prophecy foretold. Then she snapped back into action.

Melia ran to Gil and urged, "We have to go!" She helped get him to his feet, and they both ran as fast as they could.

The rest of the group was almost halfway across the bridge when Momma Snake caught up to them. She could see them through the bridge's transparency. She struck again, aiming at the most prominent target, Jack. SMASH! Her face crashed into the top of the tunnel.

"She can't get through the bridge!" Borak shouted.

Momma Snake struck again with the same result.

Jack saw something and hollered, "What in tarnation was that? There's something in her mouth!"

Still hanging over Jack's shoulder, Cedric stared intently at the colossal snake. Momma Snake opened her mouth, and he saw Aiden inside, grasping his sword.

Aiden had managed to pull his sword when Momma Snake seemingly ate him and stuck it in the side of her throat before being swallowed.

"Hi, Aiden! What are you doing up there?" Cedric said casually, still out of it.

"What in the heck are you talkin' bout, boy?" Jack remarked as the massive serpent struck the tunnel again. He shot a glance back at the giant snake. This strike caused the bridge to shake and sputter as if it would disengage. Aiden flew out of Momma Snake's mouth, sword in hand, and landed on top of the tunnel.

"It is Aiden!" Jack rejoiced, "Crap, he's in trouble!"

By this time, Melia and Gil had almost caught up to the others, and they, too, saw Aiden.

"He's alive!" Gil exclaimed.

"Yeah! Hope he stays that way!" added Melia.

Aiden got to his feet and sprinted down the top of the tunnel bridge. At first, the giant snake was confused. She thought she had eaten him but dismissed that thought and repositioned herself to do the job right. Momma Snake lashed out an angry attack. Aiden sprung himself high in the air, performing a gainer. The snake's viscous teeth bounced off the tunnel, throwing sparks, and her head slid under Aiden while he backflipped. The bridge shook again from the impact and, when he landed, knocked Aiden off his feet. He began sliding and tried jabbing his sword into the bridge to stop. The sword wouldn't catch, and he continued to slide. He dropped his sword, pulled his dagger, and tried again. The dagger worked. It stuck into the bridge, somehow penetrating through the odd material made from energy. Aiden came to a stop and hung, dangling off the side of the tunnel bridge.

The evil snake saw her chance. She didn't strike again, though. This time electricity began coursing through her face as if charging up. Aiden heard a buzz and looked over his shoulder to see what was happening.

"Oh crap!" he reacted. The snake's head was overloaded with power.

Aiden swung himself forward and backward, building up momentum. Momma Snake unleashed a massive beam of electricity. He yanked himself up as hard as he could, flipped, and landed on top of the tunnel bridge.

The others were almost to the bridge's exit when they saw hundreds of snakes in a poised position waiting for them. The snakes were staring them down.

Borak and Melia looked at each other, and Borak insisted, "Remember our training!"

Melia nodded, responding, "When we were blindfolded!"

"Yes, now is the time!" Borak replied in an all-knowing voice.

The two closed their eyes while running, focusing on the enemy. The gems in their weapons began glowing. They ran a little further, drew their weapons, and started a spinning attack. Melia, with her boomerang and Borak with his bo-blade, spun side-by-side as they exited the bridge and decapitated numerous snakes. The snakes tried striking, but the sibling's spin attacks were impenetrable. They chopped all snakes within range in half. The rest of the group was amazed by what they saw. A pathway of snake carcasses trailed behind the spinning duo. The remaining heroes drew their weapons, closed their eyes, and followed the path. They sliced on either side as they ran.

Aiden had dodged the beam, but Momma Snake followed him with it. He ran and jumped over the beam, dodging it again. The snake whipped the beam back in his direction. Magnificently, he blocked the attack with an energy beam of his own. Momma Snake and Aiden engaged in a battle of wills, fighting to overcome each other. At first, the serpent had the upper hand. Initially, her beam almost hit him. Aiden pushed back, forcing Momma Snake's beam away until the two beams met in the middle. They struggled, gaining and losing ground, continuing with tenacity in an energy beam wrestling match. Aiden was giving it his all but felt his energy-draining and was worried he might not outlast his adversary. Once again, the giant snake's beam began edging its way toward him. As it encroached on him, he saw flashes of his loved ones.

... "Save our son! You better save him!" Sasha told Aiden as she lay on the ground, dying.

"But I, I can't," Aiden replied, "He's already gone!"

"You idiot!" Aiden's dying wife sassed, "No, he's not! Go save our damn son!"

Aiden's mind immediately jumped to another dreamlike scenario.

"Dad! Dad! Come back!" Chase shouted as Aiden fell from the building back on Earth.

"Nooooooooooooo!" Aiden yelled, "I won't leave yooouuuuuu!"

Then he heard, "They're going to kill me!" He recognized this voice. It was Priya. She spoke again, "Aiden, hurry up! They're going to sacrifice me!"

Aiden felt a sudden surge of power and belted in a mighty voice, "THEY... WILL...NOOOTTT!"...

Aiden snapped out of his daze and blasted Momma Snake's energy beam with a newfound strength. His energy beam turned from pale blue into a vivid, bright blue and gained ground toward the serpent.

Aiden shouted at the top of his lungs, "Aaaaahhhhhhhh! YOOOUUU... WOOOONN'TT...WIIIIIINN!!!"

Aiden's body lit up the same shade of blue as his beam. His beam began fluctuating radiantly, then gained in width. A loud hum overtook the land. Aiden's beam tore through Momma Snake's beam, disintegrating it, and exploded in her face. A massive shockwave threw Aiden off the tunnel toward the rest of his comrades. The others had made their way through the field of snakes and were waiting. Aiden, reactively, created an energy shield before he hit the ground and slammed off the grass. He rolled to a stop in front of Jack. Cedric was still over Jack's shoulder.

"Ah, there you are! Come here and plant one on me!" Cedric said, still hypnotized. He puckered his lips.

Ignoring the overly friendly Hairie, Aiden looked back at the giant snake. She was missing her bottom jaw. Blood and other biological goo gushed from her broken face as she slid down into a watery grave.

"That was amazing, mate!" Jack retorted, "You'll have to teach me that one!"

Aiden nodded, replying, "No prob!"

Melia ran up, exclaiming, "Aiden! You're okay! You are one lucky son-of-a-gun!"

Borak held out his hand to help Aiden up. "Good job!" he said with a smile.

Back on his feet, Aiden surveyed the aftermath in the field and saw hundreds of snakes lying dead on the ground. Death consumed the land. A scarce few snakes scurried back into hiding.

Aiden remarked, "Looks like you guys did pretty damn good yourselves.

The Passageway to Magus' Castle

The heroes turned their attention to what was ahead. A barren forest funneled upward and into an opening between two small mountains. It appeared this was the only forward path.

"It looks like we're going that way," Aiden said.

"Yep, I guess you're right," Melia agreed, "That looks exactly like what the tale describes. It says once you cross Snake River, you will travel through the twin peaks. There's a guarded passageway between the mountains that leads to Magus' castle."

Aiden made a slightly amused face, "Guarded? It's guarded?"

"Yes," replied Melia, "The story says the mountains protect the castle, and the passageway is the only way through. So, Magus keeps guards there."

"How many guards are we talking about?" Aiden inquired, becoming less amused.

"I'm not sure," Melia hesitated, "I guess we'll find out."

They made their way through the bare forest, not seeing even a hint of wildlife, and stopped short of the passageway. There was a gate blocking access and not a guard in sight. They hunched down behind some bushes to formulate a plan.

"What ya guys think?" questioned Jack, "It looks like no one's home."

"Where are we?" came a hungover voice, "I feel like I was on something."

Everyone looked to see Cedric sitting on the ground, dumbfounded.

"Well, good mornin', sunshine!" Jack teased, "Bout time you joined us, mate!"

After further investigation, it seemed this gate was unguarded. Gil began to walk toward it when Aiden stopped him.

"Hold on!" Aiden whispered, "I think Borak found something."

Borak was on his knees, looking at something low to the ground. He raised his head and continued to peer around. He pointed at something and warned, "It's a trap. Look."

They all looked closely and saw them. At first, a few and then many. Countless trip lines made from cordage ran across several areas at different levels, leading up to the gate. Some lines also ran in a diagonal direction. A final low line ran in front of the barred gate. All the cordage was disguised with vegetation.

"We're going to need to pull a mission impossible," Aiden joked, then added, "You see the one in front of the gate? How are we going to open it? It will hit the line."

They scrutinized the situation, but no one had any ideas.

Borak spoke up, "I'll go. I can make it to the gate, but I don't know what to do from there."

Aiden examined the area and saw part of the mountain jutted out on the left side of the trip lines. He also noticed many small holes in that part of the mountain.

Aiden had a thought and said it out loud, "What if someone holds the other side of the line?" He paused for a reaction. The rest of the team stared at him silently, waiting for him to explain. Aiden continued, "Um, soooo the killer projectiles are shooting from there..." He pointed at the holes in the mountain, "Which means the lines function from that side. Someone could sneak around to that side and hold the line while Borak cuts it. Then Borak can drive his sword into the ground and tie the line to it to hold the line in place." He turned his attention toward Borak, "The only problem is, you have to tie the line with the same amount of tension on it, or, uh, I'm sure a flying death arrow or something will shoot out and impale you."

The crew had unsure looks on their faces. Melia looked at Aiden as if to say, "That's your bright idea?"

"Look, I'm winging it here, guys. That's all I've got," Aiden remarked, "I mean, what do you think?"

"I like it!" admitted Borak, "Hold the line while I cut it, then tie it to my sword. Makes sense, but who's gonna hold the line?"

"Me, me, me!" came a disguised voice that sounded like Gil.

They could tell it was Cedric. Cedric was hiding behind Gil and raising Gil's arm, making it look like Gil was speaking.

"What are you doing?" Gil asked his mischievous little buddy.

Cedric let go of Gil's arm and hesitantly replied, "Um, I was letting them know you want to do it."

Gil only stared at Cedric, irritated. Then he revealed, "Actually, I was going to volunteer myself, but now that I think about it, I think you should do it. What do you say, Ceed?"

"Well, uh, nope. It would be better if you do it," Cedric argued as he wobbled. He was still exhibiting signs of being hungover.

"No! No! No! As your best friend, I think it is the best choice for you to stop being a coward and do it yourself," Gil maintained. He slapped Cedric on his back and pushed him forward.

"All right, you two. That's enough!" Melia interrupted, "I'm gonna do it. We need someone with strength, anyway," she teased.

The Hairies glanced at each other sheepishly, as if they were in trouble, but didn't complain about Melia taking charge of the task.

Borak and Melia were confident they could pull this off. Borak made his move through the maze of cordage. He stepped over the first line and ducked under the next, then slid between crisscrossing diagonal lines and stepped over another one. He ducked under another, worked his way through a few more diagonal lines, and stopped because he saw something out of the corner of his eye. Luckily, sunlight peeking through the forest canopy flickered off a line he hadn't even noticed. Borak peered closely and saw numerous lines running laterally from the ground up in a parallel fashion. They were less than an inch in front of him. There was barely enough space in between the lines to fit his body. He sucked in his diaphragm and tried to squeeze through. One of the lines grazed across his buttocks, so he delicately lowered his pelvis and went for it. He made it. Borak was at the gate. He started to stand up, and another line snagged tight across his forehead. He stopped immediately. Borak heard the sound of the line stretching, on the verge of snapping. He closed his eyes, hoping it wouldn't. The line held. Borak slowly backed off, easing the tension off the death trigger.

Melia worked her way through the cordage lines to the other side. It was an easier route, so she reached her position quicker. While waiting, she watched her brother and held her breath a couple of times. He nearly set off one of the lateral lines and then almost triggered another line with his forehead.

"Whew!" Melia whispered when he made it.

Borak lifted a leg over the last trip line in front of the gate and looked at his sister. She saw he was ready, so she took a step over the line and braced herself.

"You ready, sis?" Borak asked her.

"Ready when you are, bro," she replied.

Borak cut the line.

Melia felt the line pull on her hands with extreme force. Everyone held their breath as she grunted from the amount of strength she exerted, but to their relief, she was able to hold it. Borak briskly stabbed his sword deep into the ground, sideways and at an angle for more leverage, and grabbed the end of the line. He pulled it tight and tied it securely to his sword handle. Melia watched him as he did this, while she struggled to hold the line.

Melia asked through clenched teeth, “Are...you...ready?”

Borak made eye contact with her and counted out loud, “One, two, three!” She released the line, and they both dropped to the ground on their stomachs.

The team tensed up, fearing the worst, but nothing happened. The line was intact. No traps were triggered.

“Holy crap!” Cedric let out, “I can’t believe that worked!”

“Shut up,” Gil said, still annoyed at his buddy, “Maybe next time you’ll do it instead of making love to the trees.”

“I was making love to trees?” Cedric replied, taken back.

“Well, a post, and you tried to kiss Aiden, too!” Gil added.

“Yeah, right!” Cedric replied, laughing. He looked at everyone else, expecting agreement but got none.

Borak opened the gate. They heard a clunk, which seemed to disengage all the traps. He entered cautiously. Everyone followed, working their way around the lines of cordage.

On the other side of the gate was a long, gloomy, outdoor corridor between two mountain cliff walls. A thick tree canopy had grown overhead, allowing only a tiny amount of sunlight to peek through. The trees forming the canopy grew from the walls. Although it was a bit morbid inside, the top was beautiful, with shades of blue, red, yellow, and even purple. They stopped to evaluate the area for any danger. The only movement detected was from birds and monkeys hopping around overhead. Not discovering any guards, they moved forward. They took a few more steps, and Cedric stepped on a stone that lowered and clicked. Everyone stopped in their tracks, knowing it was a trap.

“Get down!” Aiden yelled, tackling Cedric.

The others dove to the ground. A handful of arrows shot across the passageway at waist height. No one was hit. There was a rumbling, and the bottom section of the cliff walls, which were about 15 feet tall, began closing in.

Another arrow shot out from a different direction and hit Jack in the shoulder.

Jack yelled in pain, “Ahhhh, damn it!”

Wondering where the single arrow came from, Gil looked ahead and saw Devian guards firing arrows at them. “They’re up ahead!” he warned.

They all jumped to their feet and ran as fast as they could toward the Devians. They weaved back and forth, dodging the arrows while the walls crept closer and closer. Jack broke off the arrow in his shoulder and knocked another arrow out of the air with his sword. The walls were slightly inclined, allowing Borak and Melia to run up them, using the small natural footholds created by the rocky surface. Borak sprinted up the wall, then leaped into the air. From this vantage point, he could see five Devians. In mid-flight, he slung his bo-blade. The weapon cut through the air like a bullet. The bo nailed its target in the chest and killed the Devian.

Simultaneously, Melia ran up the other wall, drew her boomerang blade, and flung it at the enemies. Her weapon curved through the air undetected and decapitated a Devian. The remainder of the guards ducked, not sure what happened. The boomerang flipped around for its return trip. A Devian stood up and aimed to shoot another arrow. The boomerang barely missed the Devian and flew back to Melia. She caught her weapon and waited. The two remaining Devians watched as their fellow combatant's head slid off its neck while it was still aiming. The guard's decapitated body fell backward and released the arrow straight up in the air. Terrified, the last two guards ran the opposite way.

They weren't out of the woods yet. The walls were still closing in on them, and they were only halfway down the corridor. Although Melia, Borak, and the two Hairies could run above the enclosing walls, Jack and Aiden could not. They ran as fast as they could as the walls inched closer to their doom. The exit gate wasn't far ahead now. Warm light shone through, teasing them with its feeling of safety. Almost there, but they were out of time. Jack stopped about twenty feet short of the exit and held the walls.

"Aaahhhhh!" Jack yelled. He gave it his all to keep the walls open.

Everyone made it through because of Jack. Unfortunately, he was now stuck. The walls cracked and split as they squeezed tighter upon his hands. He looked helplessly at his friends. He didn't want to die. Then he gained a sense of accomplishment, knowing he had saved them.

Jack bravely told the others, "Go on now! Go save the world!"

Jack's friends looked on. They weren't ready to give up, but there didn't seem to be any way to save him.

"Hold on, Jack!" Aiden hollered, "We're not leaving you!"

Aiden and Borak glanced up at the canopy, trying to figure out what to do. It gave them both the same idea. Borak ran up the wall, jumped, and lunged upward with his bo-blade. He sliced a thick branch in half. The broken branch fell at Jack's feet. Jack maneuvered the branch, so the ends were facing each wall. It barely fit. The walls closed in on the branch causing it to bend and crack. Somehow, the branch held, and the walls stopped.

"Good job! Now, come on! You got this!" Aiden shouted again.

Jack closed his eyes, took a deep breath, and let go of the walls as he bolted toward the gate. The branch cracked and popped while the walls compromised its rigidity. Jack was only a few feet away. He dove as the branch gave way, and the walls slammed shut, throwing a bunch of dust in the air. When the dust cleared, everyone saw Jack lying on the ground, unscathed.

The Grandar rolled over, sat up on his butt, quickly scanned his body to see if everything was still intact, then joked, "Well, ya can't say I'm not a team playa!"

The group laughed and smiled, overjoyed they hadn't lost their odd-accented buddy.

"You're definitely a team player," Aiden complimented. He helped Jack to his feet, adding, "What do you say we call it a day? I'm beat."

Exhausted, they found a little nook on the edge of the mountain where they could take refuge for the night. The nook was hidden, but they could still see the land in front of them. They began setting up camp.

"Can you believe those other Devians ran?" Cedric snickered, "Where do you think they were going?"

"There," replied Aiden. He pointed ahead, "They were going there."

Everyone looked where Aiden was pointing and saw Magus' lustrous castle sitting in plain sight not too far ahead of them. They were so tired that no one had paid any attention.

"Wow, we made it!" Cedric acknowledged.

"Yep!" added Gil.

The rest of the gang silently looked on, knowing what that meant. They were on the verge of another crazy battle; possibly, the battle of their lives.

Part 5

Magus' Castle

Melia's Boomerang-Blade

Their encampment was hidden well enough to conceal a fire. They cooked the rest of the deer and attempted to enjoy the night together, not sure of what the future had in store for them. Up to this point, there wasn't much conversation.

Cedric broke the silence, "Why are you so quiet, Gilly?"

Gil didn't reply. Instead, he took a bite of his deer steak and burped.

Aiden chuckled, then proposed, "Why don't we take our minds off things with another story? Melia, do you know any more stories?"

Melia sat thinking for a minute and couldn't come up with anything. She shrugged her shoulders.

"How 'bout the one 'bout ya blade?" Jack recommended, "That's always a good one, aye!"

"Hmmm, yes! Good idea, Jack! I haven't told that one in a while!" Melia remarked excitedly, "Okay, so ummm, hmm, where to begin...*It was quite a few years ago, not too long after Magus stole the necklace."*

Melia was angry and saddened ever since Magus had deceived her. He not only deceived her but also the entire community of Heirstone. It was personal to her. She had grown quite fond of him in the years he was there. She thought they had developed a close bond.

After Magus pulled his atrocious stunt, Melia vowed to avenge herself and the people who lost their lives during his attack. She was angry with herself because she allowed a heartless bastard to dupe her. In addition to her anger, Melia also went through bouts of depression and lost interest in her training. One day, she decided to do something different and go on a trip. She hoped this trip would do something to reignite her drive.

"Hey, little dude. You want some company?" Melia inquired, figuring Farley would because he loved the attention.

"Ha! Would I? You bet your twinkle toes I would!" the little Evo excitedly replied. Then he said, "You hear that? I'm gonna have company!"

"Farley, stop talking to yourself. You gonna do that the whole time? It gets kinda weird." Melia teased, knowing him for so long.

"Uh, haha. No worries. I won't. You know we'll be gone a few days, right?" Farley asked.

"Yeah, I know. I need to get away from this place anyhow," Farley's new travel companion remarked, "I need to do something."

Happily, the furry Evo did a little dance and shouted, "Onward and upward!" The two of them left the castle on their journey.

The traveling duo made their way through the forest, searching for a hot spot, as Farley called it. They weaved one way and then the other, following Farley's senses. After some time, Farley hadn't found anything worthwhile. At one point, Melia saw a fohawk sitting in a desires tree.

Melia asked, "Have you ever had one of those fruits?"

Farley glanced at the desires tree and looked bewildered. He answered, "Why would I do that?"

Melia didn't reply. They kept walking. Eventually, they came upon the lake...the same lake where Aiden met Farley. Sensing a solid energetic pull, Farley stopped.

"You know, I always feel something here, but I can never find anything. It feels like something's in the lake," the Evo told Melia, delighted to be able to share this experience with someone, "I can never figure it out. One time, I even swam the lake in search of it but found nothing."

"Really?" Melia responded, "Where exactly? Show me."

Farley pointed to a spot not too far out in the lake.

"Hmmm, interesting," the curious Roak pondered.

"Yes, it feels like it's around there but under the lake somehow," Farley mentioned. He saw Melia's growing interest and became slightly concerned.

Farley knew Melia too well and started to worry he may have opened a bag of worms. If Melia made her mind up to do something, there was no stopping her, and finding this hidden pocket of energy could be dangerous.

"You know what? It's nothing. Let's go find another spot," the Evo encouraged.

Melia searched the area Farley had mentioned with her superior eyesight. As Farley was walking away while trying to redirect her attention, she saw something.

"Wait! What is that?" Melia lightly shrieked in excitement.

The puzzled Evo scanned the area at which Melia was pointing. Inexplicably, he saw something, too. Farley saw a light flash under the water. There'd only be one reason why that would happen. His suspicions must be correct. Hidden in a secret underwater cave was an active gold mine. At this point, the ordinarily lone traveling magic replenisher wasn't sure whether he regretted Melia coming with him or if he felt lucky she did.

Melia, being Melia, darted at the flashing light. She dove down into the water. It wasn't too deep. When she arrived at the light, she saw an overgrowth of underwater lake weeds covering it. The weeds looked like typical aquatic plants, except for the purple flowers attached to them. There were numerous flowers. They somehow resembled decay as if the flowers were rotting. Melia noticed an algae-covered handle by the light, so she reached for it. The flowers moved in the direction of her hand and opened a little. She pulled her arm back.

"That was weird," Melia thought to herself and swam back to the surface.

Farley saw Melia come to the surface and yelled at her, "What happened?"

"I found it! Hold on," Melia hollered back. She took a minute to think, "Why were those flowers opening? It must be some sort of protection, but what can a few little flowers do?"

"What's wrong?" Farley called out, knowing something was up for her to be thinking the way she was.

"It's nothing," Melia replied, "Give me a minute."

Not wasting any more time, she confidently drew her sword and plunged herself like a torpedo toward the weeds.

The flowers looked revitalized and seemed to know Melia's intent. They completely opened, anticipating her attack, and some shot forward. Melia twisted in the water and swiped her sword in front of her while she submerged. She sliced many of the flowers off their stems. Suddenly, the remaining flowers sprang at her. The spry water ninja scored those with ease. The flowers reclosed and floated independently in the water. They surrounded her. Melia curiously gazed closely at one near her face and wondered how a flower could be so aggressive. The flower opened and squirted her face with a solution that burned like fire.

The rest of the floating flowers opened and showered everything in front of them with a poisonous substance. Unfortunately, most of the flowers pointed toward Melia, and the burning chemical splattered all over her body.

"Aaaahhhhhhh!" Melia screamed in pain and thrashed around under the water.

She was in searing agony. It was like a box jellyfish had wrapped itself around her entire body. The pain intensified. Melia whirled around, minimizing the pain and pushing away any lingering flowers. Her biggest fear was how long she would have to endure this excruciating pain.

Melia had been under the water for some time. It was time for her to resurface. Farley waited another ten seconds. A grouping of bubbles floated to the surface and popped into the air. He couldn't take it anymore. He ran and dove into the water, streamlining through the lake with dolphin kicks until he saw Melia. She was still spinning in circles and clutching at her face. Evidently, she needed help, but Farley wasn't sure what to do. Then, he saw the flowers floating around and knew what had happened. The magical Evo immediately zapped any blooms in the vicinity and swam up to Melia. She was twisting in crippling pain.

Farley grabbed Melia to stop her spinning. He positioned her flat in the water and placed his hands on her stomach. Her hands were still covering her face. The pressure seemed to help with the pain. She was not able to cry out any longer since she had used all her breath. The magical Evo's hands began to glow. An icy sensation worked its way outward from Melia's stomach, calming her. The fiery pain slowly diminished.

That soothing feeling soon evaporated when Melia realized that she was about to drown. She ditched the horizontal position and swam as fast as she could toward the sunlight until she broke the surface of the water. She took in a much-needed deep breath of air.

"Are you okay?" Melia heard from behind her.

She turned and saw Farley wading in the water. He was exceedingly concerned.

Melia responded, "I, uh, whew! That was a close one! You saved me! Thank you." She took a second to recover and splashed her face in an attempt to dull the lingering, throbbing pain. She continued, "I've never been in so much pain in my entire life. What the heck are those things?"

"Those are burn blooms," Farley answered, "I have heard their poison stings the worst of anything on this planet. There is a story about a warrior who cut off his arm because he couldn't deal with the pain."

"Yeah, they hurt bad, but whatever you did helped a lot. It doesn't hurt near as much now," Melia added.

"I'm glad I was here. That would not have been good, otherwise," the Evo replied, then changed the subject, "Did you see anything while you were down there?"

"Uh, yeah, I did! There's a handle down there. It must open something," Melia informed. Before Farley could respond, she dove into the water again.

Now that all the burn blooms were gone, Melia sliced some of the lake weeds out of the way. Under some muck, she saw part of something written.

She cleared the muck off the writing and waited for the silt to settle to regain visibility. Once she could see clearly, she read the script. It said, "Enter to find a weapon for a ninja. She has trained her entire life with her brother. This is a test meant for one."

"Wow!" Melia thought, "It sounds like a weapon trial! My weapon trial!"

Eagerly, Melia grabbed the lever, but she felt a small hand on her arm before she yanked on it. It was Farley. He shook his head not to do it. The problem was, Melia had been waiting her whole life to find her weapon. Nothing was going to stop her. She nodded and motioned for Farley to go back to the surface. She gripped the lever tightly and pulled it.

The ground started rumbling. Farley hurried to the surface and swam rapidly to the shore. Melia watched as a door in the bottom of the lake slid open. It came to a stop, leaving a relatively large hole. A plethora of bubbles blew out, escaping from whatever depths the opened door had unsealed. Melia braced herself, half-expecting a whirlpool to suck her into the hole, but that didn't happen. She quickly swam to the surface to take a breath, then dove back down, anticipating what was inside.

When she arrived back at the hole, she curiously stuck her head in it. There was another flashing light and more writing at the bottom of what appeared to be the beginning of a small underwater cave. The script said, "You must trust the way. Swim fast to find a breath and beware of the weapons' protectors."

She contemplated what that might mean, "Swim fast to find a breath, hmm. And I may have to fight these...protectors."

Melia knew this was a dicey situation, and if she didn't get it right, it would be the last thing she ever did. She returned to the surface for another breath, then dove into the mysterious water cave.

Melia glided swiftly into the cave and took a sharp left, pumping her legs as fast as she could. The writing warned her to swim fast, so she did, praying she would find the place to take a breath. It was incredibly dark. The only light Melia could see was quite a distance ahead of her. It was a thin sliver of light similar to a dull night light. She dolphin-kicked and thrust her arms as if her life depended on it, which it did. The light didn't seem to be moving any closer. She felt as if she had been swimming forever. Her lungs began to strain, burning from oxygen deprivation. Fully committed at this point, she persevered and continued to propel herself forward.

Melia was out of breath. She knew she only had a few more kicks in her. She fought the urge to breathe because that meant sucking in water and initiating the start of her death. At once, the dim light was right above her. Desperately, Melia reached for it, still grappling against the urge to inhale.

Her hand felt air. On the verge of fainting, she drove her arms backward and surged upward. She broke the water's surface and took a deep breath.

She made it. The place was dead silent. She was light-headed and seeing spots. It took a minute for her to regain full consciousness. Melia looked around and realized her head was in a small air pocket, so she knew she had limited oxygen. The light came from a stone placed in the ceiling of this air pocket. Melia got her wind back and peeked under the water. She could see she made it to the end of a straightaway, and the cave made a right turn into a vast opening. It appeared to be a sizable underwater room with no obvious way to find more air. She thought to herself, "This is nuts!" Remembering the sign said to trust the way, she ignored her inhibitions, took a few more deep breaths, and swam into the room.

A gate behind Melia closed. Some small doors on the walls slid open. Many unhappy-looking fish appeared from the chambers concealed by the doors. There were about thirty small piranha-type fish that had huge fangs protruding from their mouths. Melia knew of these fish but had never seen them until now and preferred to keep it that way. She was trapped in this underwater room full of flesh-eating fish with no way to breathe. She drew her sword and prepared for battle.

The fish surrounded Melia and stared at her maliciously, displaying their impressively long and horridly sharp teeth. They seemed to move in unison as if they were communicating somehow. They turned sideways together like synchronized swimmers. Ready for the predatory fish to attack, Melia gripped her sword tightly in anticipation. Out of the corner of her eye, she saw a fish dart at her with surprising speed. It opened its mouth wide. Melia whipped herself sideways and skewered the fish right through its open mouth. It looked like she was holding a fish kabob. The rest of the fish stared her down for a second, then one-by-one, they attacked. She sliced left, right, spun around, slicing again, then turned left, carving downward, and cut in half every fish that attacked. The fish took another second, appearing to brainstorm. Then, they all charged her at once. Instinctively, Melia spun rapidly, slashing through the water with superior quickness. As the fish entered Melia's strike zone, her blade cut through them effortlessly. Gobs of fish chunks floated to the ground. The last fish made it past her defense and bit her on the side. She halted her spin and ripped it off her. Melia held the fish close to her face, stared at the hideous creature, and crushed it in disgust. Urgently, she realized she was out of breath again.

Having no idea where she might find air, she frantically looked above her for the water's surface or at least for another air pocket. She felt an overwhelming sensation of hopelessness. There was nothing but water.

Bubbles blew out from the small door openings where the fish had been, and the water level rapidly dropped about a foot. Melia quickly thrust her arms, propelling herself upward. She made it to the water's surface with no time to spare.

Melia sucked in air, and even though feeling lightheaded, breathing never felt so satisfying. At this point, she hoped the weapon trial was almost over. From below, there was a loud clunk. She looked in the water and saw a gate had opened on the side opposite where she entered. "Oh boy. Another room," she presumed.

Melia's body couldn't take much more, but there was no turning back. The gate through which she entered was now closed. There was only one way out, and that was to go forward. The recently turned aquatic ninja hyperventilated to help hold her breath longer, then dove into the depths of another room that, once again, didn't promise a way to breathe.

Melia swam into the room, and like the last room, a gate closed behind her. This time, four large doors opened. Four long, fat, grotesque, serpent-like eels casually slipped into the water-filled room and surrounded her. The eels looked extremely evil, as most eels do, and were the longest eels Melia had ever seen. They were about eight feet long, brownish-black, and had teeth like barracuda. Oddly, they flickered with energy from time to time. Every time they blinked, Melia could feel a slight charge in the water. The eels turned sideways, as did the fish, and she prepared to defend herself.

The eel in front of Melia flipped its tail in her direction, throwing a charge of energy at her. She whipped herself to the side with high-speed reflexes, and the charge whizzed by her. The rest of the eels followed suit. They unleashed a barrage of electrified blasts. She twisted around and flipped upward, dodging the attacks.

As she was about to retaliate, an eel thrust a late blast from behind her. The charge nailed her in the back. Melia convulsed from the shock, floated motionlessly, and slowly sank to the bottom. The eels grouped, watching. One of the eels came close to her, checking if she was still alive. She didn't move. The eel smiled sinisterly and opened its mouth to take a bite. Melia stealthily jerked her sword around and chopped its head off. She pushed off the floor and streaked toward the other eels. They saw her coming, but it was too late. The aquatic ninja sliced left and then right, cutting off the heads of two more eels. The final eel, the furthest back, had time to charge up and sling another blast. Melia dodged it again by flipping forward. The eel attacked head-on, diving straight for her. She avoided the attack and caught the eel behind its head. It shocked her. She dropped her sword. She fought through the electricity and pulled her dagger. Melia delicately stuck the dagger in the eel's head and killed it. The electrocution stopped, and the eel's body went limp.

Melia had survived the overpowering electric eels, but she was still in a fight for her life. She was out of breath again and had been out for a while. She felt an overbearing faintness come over her. Her lungs burned worse than ever. There was nothing she could do but give in to what her body urged her to do. In desperation, she inhaled, but instead of air, she sucked in only water. Melia convulsed as if trying to regurgitate the water, then ceased to move at all.

A plethora of bubbles blew out from the walls and some floor openings. All of the water in the room quickly drained out. Melia lay on the floor, still not moving. A weapon rose from the floor next to her. It shone impressively while it hovered over a stone. The weapon was Melia's boomerang blade...

"Wait, that's how you're going to end the story?" Cedric exclaimed, "We know you didn't die, but how? How did you not die?"

Melia smiled, enjoying Cedric's enthusiasm, and replied, "Well, I know what Farley told me, but it's hard to believe. All I know for sure is I woke up coughing up water, and Farley was kneeling over me. I was happy to be alive, but, at first, I didn't know where I was. The whole place looked different because the room was filled with water when I almost died. When I woke up, there was a glorious, luminescent boomerang with blades on it floating next to me. Farley knew what it was and looked upon me proudly. He motioned toward the weapon, telling me to get it, so I made my way to my feet and walked up to it. As soon as I took hold of it, the boomerang flashed brilliantly and bonded with me. I, instantly, felt connected with it."

"That's amazing! But, it still doesn't tell me how you didn't die!" Cedric reiterated, "So, what happened?"

Melia grinned again and answered, "Maybe Farley will tell you another time. We should all probably rest up now. We've got a big day tomorrow."

Cedric sighed in disappointment and remarked, "Are you kidding me?"

Gil laughed at his buddy but didn't reply. It became quiet again, and everyone turned in for the night...everyone except Cedric. He couldn't stop thinking about how Melia didn't die.

Farley and the Fairies

Meanwhile, back at the Druid Kingdom, Farley had replenished not only all Hyra's and her guards' magic but the entire community's. It was a simple process. All Farley had to do was place his hand on the gem in a weapon or item. Rarely, the Evo would put his hand on the chest of a being who had gone through the sacred ritual and had an internal gem that needed charging. The rest organically happened. Farley's hand and the gem would fluctuate light, and a transfer of energy would occur. When the charge was complete, the gem that Farley was energizing would glow brightly. Having to execute each charge individually was the only complication with the process.

The essential Evo had never performed such a big job in his life. It drained all his energy. Farley was exhausted, but he couldn't rest too long. He had to replenish his own magic. Fortunately, he sensed a hot spot very near, up the little hill past the last cabin in the forest. The day prior, he felt a much greater power in the area, but it had oddly vanished since then. After resting a few hours, the furry hero managed to summon up enough energy to stand up and, weakly, make his way to the forest. He knew the future of two worlds was at stake.

Once he made it into the forest, Farley couldn't believe how concentrated with power the area felt. A little further up, trees surrounded a circular clearing. He walked to the clearing. It felt like he was in the right place, but nothing was there. The perplexed Evo searched around. All he found were sticks, rocks, and some fairy poop.

"Hold on!" Farley told himself, "Fairy poop! Holy moly! There are fairies here! We found the Holy Grail!"

The ecstatic magic bearer did another one of his goofy dances, believing he had found a stronghold of energy. He spun around and threw his hands in the air to end the celebration. He hoped the fairies had shown themselves by now, but instead, nothing changed. There was only silence. Farley stood in the woods and realized how dorky he must have looked, dancing around alone in the middle of nowhere.

The little Evo walked around trying to absorb magic to no avail. He found a log and sat on it, disappointed with the situation.

"Farley made a mistake," he said aloud, "But what about the fairy poop?"

Farley picked up a rock and threw it, not watching where it went. Oddly, there was no sound of the rock hitting anything. Inquisitively, he picked up another rock and threw it, this time watching where it went. The rock stopped midair as if something caught it, and a fairy appeared.

"If you want to hurt me, I'll leave!" the fairy barked.

Farley was stunned at first and then super excited. He responded apologetically, "Oh no, no! Not me! I would never do that! I forgot you guys could disappear! Holy moly! It's a fairy! You're really a fairy!"

The jovial Evo almost started dancing again, but the fairy stopped him, teasing, "Please, don't do that again. And yes, I am really a fairy." There was an awkward silence, then the fairy asked, "Sooo, why have you come here, Farley?"

"Um, well, I need to replenish my energy. I sense a great power source here," the Evo replied. His face turned solemn, and he questioned, "Can you help me? Can you help me save the world?"

The fairy smiled, and two more fairies appeared beside him. The original fairy replied, "Yes, Farley, we can help."

The three fairies waved their hands in a horizontal motion. Countless gemstones appeared, covering the entire floor of the clearing. Farley soaked in the sight of the gems and turned to thank the fairies, but, as with Aiden, they had disappeared into thin air.

The little Evo bowed anyway to show his gratitude and said, "Thank you, your eminences."

The Catapult

Aiden and Borak woke up first. In the daylight, they could see the lay of the land. The mountainside was gray and steep. It was covered with many varieties of shrubs, trees, and grass. Past the mountain cliffs was a small collection of trees. Once through the trees, the land opened up to a grassy field. Yellowish-green grass grew at different lengths, from a couple of feet to over five feet tall. A big creek ran across the field, not far from Magus' castle. It was a beautiful and majestic sight.

The two decided to investigate the area. After a half-hour, they returned with exciting news and attempted to wake the others.

"Hey, you guys, wake up!" Aiden said, shaking the two Hairies.

"I barely fell asleep, damn it!" Cedric complained, "I need my beauty sleep!"

Gil laughed groggily, teasing, "Haha, you mean less ugly sleep."

Cedric remarked, annoyed, "Shut up! Thanks to you guys, I didn't sleep a wink. Someone's gotta tell me how Melia is still alive."

Gil laughed again at his friend, then looked over at Aiden, "What is it, Aiden?"

Grinning at the two funny Hairies, Aiden replied, "We found a catapult! It's perfect for a distraction!"

In the meantime, Borak woke Melia and Jack to tell them the good news.

When everyone was ready, they all headed to the catapult.

"We were doing some recon, and I ran smack dab into it!" Aiden explained, "I was walking and looking at the castle and, WHAM! I hit my face on it! Vegetation is covering it, so I didn't see it. I hope it still works!"

Aiden and Borak led the group a short distance to the tree line. Beyond the tree line was the large grassy field.

"You see! You can barely see it!" Aiden insisted.

At first, no one saw anything until Jack spoke up. "Ahhh, yeah, mate! There it is!" he said, pointing at the camouflaged catapult.

The catapult was gigantic. It sat a little inside the tree line. It was peculiar how well hidden it was, provoking curiosity of whether someone purposefully hid it. An arbor of trees had grown around and over it. Vines and moss had grown all around it, as well. The catapult had a greenish tint to it. There were some spots on the contraption that showed signs of rot. After examining it further, it was very questionable whether it worked.

Jack walked up to the catapult and smacked the side of it. It made a cracking sound. "Ooops! That wasn't supposed to happen!" he reacted, seeing his hand had gone into it.

"Be careful!" Melia cautioned, "We need that thing! If it still works, that is." She approached the catapult and slid her hand across it, accidentally scraping off some of the moss. "Eeewww!" she said, then nudged it, "I don't know. It looks like it might roll. Who knows if it will throw anything?"

Aiden walked to the back of the questionable contraption, doing an inspection. He added, "Well, there's only one way to find out!"

Aiden placed his hands on the catapult and stared at the rest of the gang, waiting for them to help him. The others looked at each other, realized what Aiden wanted, and ran over to help push.

It was a struggle, mainly because one of the wooden wheels had a flat spot on it, but they managed to push the catapult to an area right at the tree line.

"I'd say this is good. What do you guys think?" Aiden asked.

Borak replied, "Agreed. It's still hidden from view and will give us easy access to use it."

Jack had a notion that nobody had brought up yet. He was hesitant but said it anyway, "Um, so does anyone know how ta use this thang?"

Borak and Melia glanced at each other, eyebrows raised. Then, they glanced at Aiden, who only shrugged his shoulders.

"I do!" Cedric adamantly informed his friends.

Gil looked at his buddy suspiciously and told him, "I hope you're not full of it because this is serious. Where in the heck would you learn that anyway?"

Cedric answered, "I read it in one of the old Earth books. I told you I read, but you never believe me." He strolled arrogantly over to the catapult and continued talking, "Look. You see this handle? You have to crank it until the arm comes aaaalll the waaaay baaack." He cranked the handle until the arm was fully cocked back, "Then you yank on this rope...Aaaah crap!"

Cedric didn't realize there was slack in the rope and pulled over-enthusiastically. The momentum caused him to lose balance, trip over a tree root, and fall face-first into some mud. He held onto the rope as he fell, pulled the slack out, and yanked the hook free, holding the arm in position. SLAM! The catapult arm whipped forward and cracked the frame.

Everyone ducked down, worried the noise might have alerted the enemy of their presence. After a moment, it seemed it hadn't.

"Whoa, mate! Whatcha tryin' ta do? Kill yourself?" Jack commented.

"It's not time for a mud bath, Ced?" Aiden teased. Everybody lightheartedly laughed.

Cedric lifted his head out of the mud, "You pull the rope, pteww!" He spit out some mud and finished his sentence, "And it shoots the boulder."

"Well, I guess it works!" Gil added, "Good work, pal!"

They stopped joking around and used this instant to gander at their destination, directly in front of them. Magus' castle was impressive but in a different light than Heirstone. It was another massive-sized castle with a large courtyard but had a darker, gloomy appearance. The castle was gray instead of white and surrounded by statues of wicked creatures. Many of these statues were Devians. There were also statues of a Gorger, Magus, and Herana.

The castle's most remarkable component wasn't the castle itself but the intricacy of its underground dungeon network. These dungeons housed thousands of Devians and other evil creatures, as well as many caged prisoners. The castle didn't have a moat, but it had a high reinforced wall.

"Okay, so now that we have a functioning catapult, should we use it as a distraction?" Aiden asked the group.

Everyone, except Gil, replied, "Yes."

"I don't know. Are you sure we shouldn't all go in together?" Gil replied.

Borak responded, "I think we have a better chance if we attack from inside and outside at the same time. Misdirection is an art of war."

"Okay, that makes sense!" Gil agreed.

"Alright, good! We agree, then. You guys wait here while Melia and I find and sneak in through the secret tunnel that's supposed to be there. Why is this tunnel there again?"

Melia answered, "There's another story of a Devian who was good. Without getting into it, he and his group dug the tunnel to escape. I'll have to tell the story another time, but it must be true since everything else has been."

"I hope so," Aiden continued, "Give us some time to find the tunnel.

We'll light a fire to signal you guys when we find it. As soon as you see the smoke, shoot the catapult."

"Where should we shoot it?" Cedric questioned.

"At the wall, bloke! We're gonna obliterate that wall!" Jack answered.

Aiden resumed, "That'll work! So, we find Priya and kill Magus, or we keep killing those bastards until we do. If there's any trouble, let's regroup on the inside." Aiden had one last thing to say, "You guys, we can do this! We have overcome so much already! I want to sit down and watch another comedy show with each and every one of you after we kick Magus' ass, alright?"

Jack was the only one who replied, "You got it, chap!"

They all understood what Aiden meant and placed their arms around each other in a tight huddle. This huddle signified the deep bond they had made.

Aiden looked at Melia and said, "Let's do this!"

Melia nodded. They left the others and rushed toward the castle, keeping low to escape detection.

Breaching Magus' Castle

Melia led the way as she was the one who knew where the tunnel was supposed to be. Aiden hastily followed. They came upon the creek in the field and heard voices. They paused, listening to decipher from where the voices were coming.

"It's a small band of Devians, right over there," Aiden whispered, pointing about a hundred yards up the creek.

Melia and Aiden traveled further down the creek, away from their enemies, to escape detection. The two crossed the creek and made it to the castle wall but ran into a slight dilemma. They couldn't find a tunnel or a door for a tunnel anywhere. Nor was there much cover in which to hide, so they needed to hurry.

They knelt in the open field in semi-tall grass that partially covered them. The castle wall was directly in front of them, with nothing obstructing their view of anything that might lead to a tunnel.

Melia sat down, disappointed, and said, "The story implied it's supposed to be right here. How could there possibly be a tunnel? There's nothing here but a wall."

Aiden looked down the wall both ways. He didn't see anything either, at first. But then, he saw one spot that looked a little off.

"Hold on! What is that? Do you see that?" Aiden asked, trying to hold back unwarranted excitement if he was wrong.

Melia quickly answered, "What? Where?"

Aiden responded, "I don't know, but it looks like something is there. Let's go over to it."

Melia didn't see anything, but she followed him. All she could do was hope for the best. Aiden stopped in front of a section of the wall. For some reason, he had a big grin on his face. There was nothing there, and from Melia's perspective, he looked like a smiling idiot staring at the wall.

"Come over here," Aiden told her.

Melia walked next to him. She saw what he saw. This part of the wall was an illusion. When you stood precisely in front of it, you could see the tunnel plain as day. Aiden immediately lit the signal fire, and they disappeared into the tunnel.

Patiently Waiting

"What's taking them so long?" Cedric complained.

"Would you be patient for once in your life!" Gil remarked, annoyed, "We have to wait. Jack and Borak haven't even loaded the catapult yet!"

"Oh, yea," Cedric replied as the apparent laborers emerged, rolling a large boulder.

Jack halted for a breather and razzed the two Hairies, "You know, we could use an extra hand over here, fellas!"

"Um," Cedric came up with an excuse, "We have to watch for the signal."

Jack inquired sarcastically, "It takes two of ya to do that?"

Jack and Borak finished moving the boulders, three in total, and loaded one onto the catapult. The foursome was ready to fulfill their part of the plan.

"You guys seen anything yet?" Borak asked, walking up to the Hairies position.

"Nope, we're castle watching at this point. I hope nothing happened," Cedric answered, a bit worried.

Borak offered some advice, trying to keep Cedric focused, "We cannot change what cannot be changed. Patience is a key virtue."

Cedric glanced at Gil and gave him a "What the heck is he talking about?" look before responding, "Whatever you say, Confucius!"

"Look!" Gil interrupted, "Smoke! That's the signal!"

The four jumped into action. They ran behind the catapult and pushed it forward as best they could. The heavy, clumsy contraption edged ahead until it was out in the open. They aimed it at the spot they wanted to hit. Gil ran over and tugged on the rope. The rope wouldn't budge, and nothing happened. Cedric ran behind his buddy and grabbed onto the rope. They both yanked hard. WHAM! The catapult sprang forward, launching the boulder toward the castle. The boulder lifted high in the air. They watched as the boulder soared, hoping their aim was on target. In its descent, the massive rock gained speed and dropped down with vicious intent. The boulder crashed, short and left of the castle wall. On a positive note, the aerial assault did cause a tumultuous noise that should warrant some attention.

"Crap! That was way off!" Cedric groaned, "Hurry, let's adjust it."

The group started moving the heavy catapult up and to the right as rapidly as possible. Now, it didn't matter if the enemy could see them or the catapult. They had already made their presence known. Grunting and huffing, Jack, Gil, Cedric, and Borak pushed the catapult to a good spot.

"There, that should work!" Borak said, then he warned, "Uh oh, we have incoming!"

Magus' Army Attacks

A group of fifteen Devians, who were out at the creek, ran at them, screaming for blood.

The four reacted with a swiftness born out of instinct, bravely rushing the evil unit. Borak reached the Devians first, jumped high in the air, performed a double full, and stabbed a Devian through its heart with his bo-blade. He pushed the Devian off his blade, and it fell dead. The other Devians stopped for a second, slightly amazed, then pursued their attack. Jack ran through the ugly creatures, close lining one after the other, while Cedric and Gil hopped back and forth like agile mongooses attacking with their swords. Borak became entangled in a swordfight with three Devians: sword swing, block, left sidekick, block, block, right punch, back kick, spin, sword swing. He cut a leg off one of the Devians. It fell to the ground in agony. The other two swung their swords downward at Borak. He jumped to the side, dodging the attacks, threw his dagger, and stuck one in the neck. The remaining Devian was hit in the back by a different flailing Devian before striking again. It was Jack's doing. The two Devians fell to the ground. Jack followed behind the Devian, jumped in the air, and stabbed both Devians while they were on the ground.

"Bet he didn't see that comin'! Ha! Ha!" Jack boasted.

The two Hairies loved fighting together and purposely allowed four Devians to surround them. The Devians thought they had the Hairies right where they wanted them.

Gil hollered, "Roundabout, right?"

"You got it!" Cedric replied, "Ready! Right...now!"

Cedric jumped in the air. Gil grabbed his legs in a spinning motion and whipped Cedric around like a merry-go-round. Cedric repeatedly slashed with his sword as he spun. Gil flipped Cedric up in the air. The flying Hairie landed on the last Devian and stuck it in the head. The other three Devians lay on the ground, dead.

Six Devians remained. They were staring at Borak and Jack, raging with anger because they couldn't get the upper hand over them. They all charged at once. Jack struck one in the face with a hard right cross, killing it instantly. Its body flipped backward. Another Devian sliced Jack's arm. Unphased, Jack seized that Devian by its head and used its body as a shield against another Devian's assault. The Devian he was holding was slashed twice across its chest. Jack threw it aside to face the attacking Devian. Borak looked like a gymnast. He did a front aerial over a sword attack, landed, and jabbed his weapon into the Devian's stomach. Borak followed with a full twist over another sword slash and cut that Devian's head off.

Gil and Cedric snuck behind the last two surviving Devians, who anxiously ran back and forth, concerned for their lives. Both Devians stopped, seeming to gain control of themselves, and hollered wildly, "Raaaahhhhh!" They were ready to go out fighting. Ironically, they didn't get the chance, as the two Hairys stabbed them from behind.

"That was a good warm-up, mates!" shouted Jack in his enthusiastic tone.

"Yeah, good job, guys!" Borak praised, "We need to reshoot the catapult. There's no telling what Melia and Aiden are dealing with!"

"I'm on it!" Jack called out. He headed to the catapult.

While Jack was trying to load the enormous contraption, the rest of the heroes caught up and helped him. Cedric and Gil took turns rewinding the arm. Borak assisted in lifting the rock. As soon as the catapult was ready, they double-checked their aim and set it off, flinging another boulder in the air. The boulder sailed high, this time appearing more on target. The massive stone plummeted downward. CRASH! It was a direct hit. The giant rock destroyed a section of the castle wall and left a gaping breach.

The four cheered with excitement, "Yeeaahh! Yaaahhh! Raaahhh!" They gave each other their version of high fives, hitting their forearms together and bumping chests.

After their celebration, it became oddly quiet for minutes. Nothing stirred over by the wall. They expected a strong retaliation, but the only thing they saw was dust settling.

Cedric broke the silence, "Where are they? What now? What do we do now?"

"Um, we attack! Right?" Borak answered, not sure himself, "I can't believe that didn't get their attention."

As if they heard the heroes' conversation, a swarm of enemies finally appeared.

"Uhhh, guys! You might wanna look again!" Gil pointed out.

The other two looked ahead and saw what they initially expected to see. It was an army of Devians. Unexpectedly, there was a gigantic Gorger who stood in front. They also saw two giants.

"It looks like there's a couple of Grandars, too," Borak warned.

"Yep, I see 'em, mate!" Jack returned, "I'll take care of 'em"

"Well, enough talk! Let's go get 'em, boys!" Cedric urged, ready to take on the world after whooping those other Devians.

"You don't have to tell me twice!" Gil added.

Borak had an idea, "Wait, we have one more boulder. What do you say we give that Gorger one hell of an introduction?"

The Hairies smiled broadly.

Jack replied, "I knew you was a smart feller!"

Borak and Jack loaded the last boulder onto the catapult. They made a minor adjustment and set it free. The boulder soared smoothly through the sky. Unbelievably, it clobbered the monumental ogre in its chest. It luckily was wearing metal armor. The Gorger was knocked backward but somehow didn't fall. It roared in pain. The heroes confidently rushed ahead.

The enemies charged as well, all except the Gorger. He stayed to guard the breach in the castle wall. There were three times as many Devians as in the first group they fought, but that didn't discourage the heroes one bit. The two opposing parties met at the creek in the field and stopped. They scowled at each other from either side.

"Let them come to us!" Borak told his teammates. He knew whoever crossed the water had the disadvantage.

Both sides stood there on pins and needles, anxious for blood. The Devians more so since they had evil coursing through their veins.

Borak's bo-blade began glowing. This had never happened before, so he wasn't sure what to do.

"Use it!" Gil said. Borak looked uncertain, so the Hairie said it differently, "Use your magic!"

Borak's eyebrows raised. He looked at the vile creatures. They appeared to be on the verge of rushing through the creek. He held his weapon up while it shined radiantly red, then whipped it around with ninjutsu skills. He ended his proficient display with a final sideways slice toward his enemies. A horizontal line of fiery energy slung out of Borak's bo-blade and hit the front rows of evil creatures, knocking them down.

"Beginner's luck, aye!" Jack teased while keeping an eye on his adversaries.

"Wow! Nice!" exclaimed Gil.

"That was sick! Do it again!" urged Cedric.

"I, uh, I'm still getting used to this," Borak humbly replied.

On the other side of the creek, the Devians were steaming with anger. Many of the fallen were dead, and the wicked army had enough. The enemies bellowed a loud war cry and charged the four warriors head-on. The Devians fought their way through the shoulder-high water. Seeing their opportunity, Borak, Jack, and the two Hairies positioned themselves in the creek, ideally, so they could pick off their combatants one by one.

The four hacked and slashed the creatures before catching their bearings. As each villain tried lunging out of the water, many lost their balance, and some tripped and fell. The resistance from the water was tough to overcome while in the middle of hand-to-hand combat. At one point, a barrage of enemies rushed up the middle, and a few made it to the other side. Borak took them out with three swipes of his bo-blade, turned around, and continued defending against the onslaught. Eventually, after half the enemy army was killed, the creatures ceased their attack and took a moment to regroup. The Devians dropped back behind the two Grandars and awaited Borak and his companions to make their move.

"Looks like it's on us now, fellas," Jack pointed out the obvious.

"Yes, it would seem so," Borak replied, then thought out loud, "I wonder how Aiden and Melia are doing? Maybe we should check on them?"

"We'll go!" Gil offered for Cedric and himself.

"Wait, I didn't agree to that!" Cedric argued, but no one paid attention, "What? I don't have any say in this?"

Borak nodded back at Gil and added, "What do you say you put a few out of their misery on your way!"

"You got it, boss! " Gil answered, happy to be helpful. He looked over at Cedric, who was staring blankly at him in disbelief.

Cedric remarked in a smart-ass tone, "Thanks, pal! Sure, I'll come with you! Good to know I have you around to make my decisions for me!"

Gil chuckled, responding, "No prob! You know I've always got your back!"

Assuredly, all four turned to face the scowling creatures ahead and crossed the creek. They waded into the creek, keeping their wits about them in case the Devian army was playing a trick. The evil villains didn't budge and allowed them to cross. Once they worked their way up the small bank, the Devians assailed them with authority.

Fake-Out

The two Hairies made their move. They ran to the right where the tunnel was supposed to be. They hoped some of the Devians would follow them. None of them did. Instead, a group of Devians only stared ignorantly, thinking the hairy combatants were running away. The group roared triumphantly. Cedric and Gil stopped in their tracks. The Hairies looked at each other. Almost as if they read each other's minds, the two pulled their pants down and mooned the unsuspecting villains while they were in the middle of their premature celebration. The Devians were offended and chased after the quick-witted Hairies.

Cedric and Gil pulled their britches up and bolted toward the castle wall with six Devians pursuing them. Gil saw a tree ahead and ran in that direction. Cedric saw where Gil was headed and followed.

As Cedric changed directions, a spear whizzed by his head, shaving off a chunk of hair. "Whoa, that was close!" he remarked. He rubbed his head, then shouted at Gil, "What's your plan?"

"Fake out! Let's do a fake-out!" Gil shouted back and disappeared up the tree.

Cedric followed Gil up the tree. The two Hairies hid, but the Devians saw them. They soon arrived at the tree, as well.

One domineering Devian provoked, "Awww, are you scared? Don't worry. We won't hurt you. I promise!"

All the Devians laughed as if the lie was an intelligent joke.

Another Devian tried to keep the joke going by adding, "Yeah, we only want to talk to you, and, um, and, uh, and see if uh..." He looked at the first Devian for help.

The first Devian whacked him on the head and scolded, "You idiot!" Then he threatened the Hairies, "Come down, and we'll kill you fast. Make us come get you, and I'll make sure you wished you were dead."

Initially, there was silence. Then a voice came from above, "You sure you're in the position to make threats?" It was Cedric, poking his head out from the tree.

The Devians all looked at each other and laughed, "Ahh ha ha ha ha!"

A yell erupted from behind the Devians, "Aaaaahhhhhh!" It was Gil on the attack. He stabbed and sliced three Devians before they could even turn around.

Cedric yelled out now, "Raaaahhhhhh!" He leaped out of the tree and landed on a Devian, piercing its back with his sword.

The Devian bucked like a bull. Cedric held on for dear life. He pulled his sword out and sliced another Devian's head off. The Devian on which Cedric was riding fell to the ground, dying.

In the blink of an eye, only the domineering Devian who first spoke remained. He glanced around and realized he was the only Devian left.

The Devian put his hands up, pleading, "Nooo, don't kill me! I, uh, I was kidding!"

Cedric spoke to Gil in a condescending tone, "I don't know. What do you think?"

Gil replied, "I thought he said he'd kill us fast. So how 'bout it? Go ahead! Kill us fast."

"Oh, no, no, no! Like I said, I was only kidding. I would never do that!" the Devian replied. The hideous creature hesitated for a second, still holding its hands in the air and gripping its sword.

Knowing time was up, the Devian struck viciously. Gil quickly ducked under the sword attack and sliced the villain across its belly. Cedric reacted, stabbing the Devian in its neck. The foul brute coughed up blood, then fell to the ground, dead. The Hairies double-checked how Borak and Jack were doing and saw they were engaged in a heated battle. Reluctantly, since they already had a plan, they pressed on in search of the tunnel.

Borak and Jack Attack

Borak and Jack sprung into action, racing ahead toward their threat. While Borak focused on the Devians, Jack veered toward the giants. As Borak ran, two Devians flipped high out of the hostile crowd like ninjas. The Devians dropped from the sky, slicing violently with their swords. Borak deflected both strikes with snakelike quickness. He side kicked the Devian on the right, knocking it to the ground, and engaged in a sword fight with the other. Clang, Clank, Ching, the swords rang out as they connected. Borak timed his assailant's next strike, spun under it, grabbed the Devian's arm, and flipped it over his shoulder. The Devian hit the ground, and Borak mortally stabbed it. He quickly threw a jump spin kick at the other, who had gotten up and was rushing him. This skilled Devian caught Borak's foot in the air and jabbed his thigh with a dagger. Borak winced in pain but did not hesitate and dodged more dagger strikes while the Devian held his leg. He jump-kicked off the leg on which he was standing and nailed the Devian in its head, knocking it out cold.

Meanwhile, Jack bull-rushed the two wicked Grandars and dove at them. One of the evil Grandars swung its sword. Jack dodged the blow mid-dive and cracked them with his shoulders. The Grandars were knocked backward and tumbled on the ground. Jack fell to a knee, lifted himself, and charged again. Unrelentingly, he bombarded his enemies with kicks and punches while they tried to get back to their feet. Jack swept the legs out from under one of the Grandars and kicked the other one in the face. The first Grandar managed to rise to all fours. Jack soccer kicked it to the stomach and hammer-fisted it back to the ground. He continued beating the same Grandar with a barrage of punches. The other Grandar, still on the ground, grabbed Jack's foot and yanked it out from under him. Jack fell to the ground. Both sinister Grandars quickly got to their feet before Jack did.

Cedric and Gil to the Rescue

Cedric and Gil had trouble finding the tunnel, but eventually, they found it. They ran through the tunnel and headed down a trail, searching for Aiden and Melia.

"Which way?" Cedric loudly whispered.

"How should I know?" Gil replied, whispering in the same fashion. He put his arm out to stop his buddy, "Hold on! Let's think about this. What do you think happened?"

Cedric pondered for a second before he gave his opinion, "Well, I mean, I don't know. Maybe they got caught."

"Right, that's what I was thinking," Gil quickly responded, "And if so, where the heck would they be?"

The two Hairies hunched down next to some small cabins extending out from the main castle. As they scanned their surroundings, two Devians, Dagon and Kroni, walked out from one of the cabins talking to each other.

"Juggy's such an idiot!" said Kroni.

"Haha, yeah! He thinks he's special cuz' he has the keys, but all it means is that he's the one responsible for the prisoners!" responded Dagon.

Kroni stopped and anxiously replied, "Wait, nothing's gonna happen, right?"

Dagon remarked angrily, "It better not, or we'll feed him horse crap!" The Devian thought for a second, "Now that I think of it, maybe I should get the keys back."

They both heard a thump from inside the cabin. The two Devians stared at each other suspiciously.

Kroni lightheartedly interjected, "Na, those two are chained up good. He must have bumped into something. You know how he gets. There's no way they could get loose unless...Juggy got so drunk he unlocked them, ha!"

Dagon replied, "And why would he do that?"

"Um," Kroni answered the best he could, "Because...they promised him more wine or something?"

Dagon looked angry again, then suddenly smiled and started laughing, "Hahaha, he would do that, too! Juggy's a lush! Haha!" The Devians' laughter quickly subsided when they heard a loud bang and a roar. "What the hell was that?" Dagon sneered.

Kroni responded, "They're attacking! Drakkar got hit!"

Dagon scowled, becoming irritated, "Where is Juggy? Juggy quit drinking and get out here! Drakkar needs help!"

They listened and heard no response.

Dagon gave Kroni a sly look and told him, "Why didn't he answer?" Swiftly, the leader Devian bolted back into the cabin, followed by Kroni.

Fortunately, Cedric and Gil had listened to the entire conversation and now had a good idea where their friends were.

"Well, there you go! They're in the cabin! That wasn't hard!" Cedric excitedly whispered.

"We got lucky!" Gil barked, "Don't jinx us."

"So, what do you wanna do? Should we go get them?" Cedric seriously asked.

"No, let's sit here and do nothing," Gil answered in a smart-ass tone, "What the heck did we come here for, goof! Yes, let's go get them!"

The Hairies briskly took off and ran into the cabin. On the way in, Gil snatched a couple of pots hanging outside.

Borak and Jack Continue the Fight

Borak turned to face the oncoming Devians. He continuously slashed with his bo-blade to keep them at bay. The Devians stopped. Borak's smooth strokes cut back and forth with high-speed fluency and made it extremely difficult for the Devians to advance. One Devian lunged. Borak sliced across its stomach, disemboweling it. The rest of the army hesitated. None wanted to move forward. As Borak's weapon relentlessly whipped through the air, it began to glow bright red again. The blades on each end became molten hot and burst into flames.

Instinctively, Borak thrust his bo-blade forward, unleashing a flame-thrower-type attack at a Devian. The evil creature was engulfed in flames. It caught on fire. Borak thrust his weapon again, immersing two more Devians in a fiery inferno. He paused for a moment and saw Drakkar roaring in rage. Borak focused on his weapon. He tightened his grip, not knowing what to expect. His weapon charged up, then flared brightly. The warrior slung his bo around and whipped it in the direction of the Gorger, releasing an enlarged fiery charge. Drakkar saw the attack coming and blocked the blazing blast, but it hurt him. He howled in pain.

The skilled Devian that Borak had knocked out a minute ago regained consciousness. It snuck next to Borak while he was distracted. The sneaky Devian kicked the bo-blade out of Borak's hands and followed with a blistering punch to his face. The only thing Borak saw was a bright flash of light.

Borak was knocked half unconscious. The Devian wanted Borak all to himself. It directed the remaining army to flank to the other side of Borak. This put Borak between the army and Drakkar. The skilled Devian was very confident now. Although weakened, Borak stood to his feet, trying to catch his bearings. Bravely, he prepared to fight, then realized he didn't have his weapon.

The skilled Devian smirked and threw three knives at lightning-fast speed. Borak intuitively sensed the knives coming and leaned back parallel to the ground. Time seemed to slow as the blades whizzed by his stomach, cutting a slit in his gambeson. Borak returned to his upright position and immediately charged with an acrobatic attack. The Devian continued a relentless bombardment of sharp blades streaking through the air. Borak flipped left, flipped right, then ran forward, did a cartwheel to back handspring, and launched himself high in the air. The Devian continued to throw knives, barely missing Borak with every shot. It threw its last two knives, and they looked to be on target. Borak twisted in the air, holding his arms in a blocking posture. The knives ricocheted off his arm guards. He landed on the Devian and walloped the creature with a right cross to the face. The Devian hit the ground with such force, it sank into the dirt, never to move again.

While Jack was on the ground, the two giant Grandars tried to stab him with their swords. He deflected one of the swords, but the other stuck him in his side.

"Aaahhhh!" Jack yelled in pain as he simultaneously dug his dagger into the shin of that Grandar.

Jack rolled over, got onto all fours, and side-kicked the other giant in the stomach. It stepped backward, giving Jack room to stand up. Back on his feet, Jack ran and jump-kicked the same Grandar with tremendous force and sent it flailing backward. The Grandar that Jack stabbed pulled the dagger out of its shin and charged. Jack side-stepped it and deflected the enemy's sword strike. The two went toe-to-toe, testing each others' blade-wielding skills. Their blades clashed. The Grandar swung a powerful strike, knocking the sword out of Jack's hands. The creature jumped at Jack with a down-swing. Jack caught its blade between his hands. Jack quickly front-kicked the Grandar in the stomach and yanked the sword from it. Before the horrible Grandar completely processed what happened, Jack speedily flipped the sword around and chopped down on the giant. The evil Grandar tried to block the attack, and Jack's sword caught its elbow. The enormous creature watched as half of its arm fell to the ground.

Jack stabbed the one-armed Grandar in the stomach. It went down. Hearing footsteps behind him, Jack turned to defend. The other evil giant tackled him halfway into the turn. Jack's weapon flew from his hand again. Both Grandars tumbled. Jack kicked the enemy off him. The Grandar landed next to the injured one. Side-by-side, Borak could tell the evil Grandars were brothers. The uninjured Grandar looked over at its brother and saw he was bleeding to death. It wailed in agony and pounded the ground.

The distraught Grandar ignored Jack and spoke to the other, "Brother, you are a warrior. I will kill him! Know that I will kill him!"

Jack used the distraction to move closer to Borak. The angry giant rose back to its feet, determined to exact revenge. Jack saw the irate Grandar coming at him. He glanced over his shoulder to see how far he was from the overbearing massive-sized Gorger, who was making a commotion behind him. Drakkar was only yards behind the two of them. The Devian army was closing in on them and hollered for help. A few injured Devians, who could still fight, stood up and rejoined the army. Solemnly, Borak and Jack looked briefly at each other and prepared to make a stand.

Seconds from being swarmed by Devians, Borak, and Jack heard Drakkar yell in pain. It sounded like he turned around. Borak looked to see what was happening and was astonished to see all his friends on the other side of Drakkar. They were sprinting at the beast to fight him.

Borak shouted, expressing more emotion than usual, "There they are! Jack! They're alright! They're coming to help us!"

Jack was unsure at first, but when he saw his friends, he answered with overjoyed sarcasm, "Hell ya, mate! I mean, it's about damn time!" Jack and Borak found weapons on the ground and, feeling a second wind, blitzed their enemies.

Part 6

Saving Priya

A Turn of Events

Having been stripped of their armor, Dagon, Kroni, and Juggy ran into the cavern in their drawers.

Dagon shouted, "They're here! The intruders have escaped!"

Magus looked down at the broken piece of latch on the ground and shot a glare into the crowd. He locked eyes with Aiden.

The wicked warlock yelled at Siren, "Now! Do it now!"

Siren was waiting for the planned command. She started running to Priya to insert the last gemstone into the necklace. Once all the gemstones were attached, Magus could zap the necklace and activate it to finalize the ritual. This would resurrect Herana. It would also send Priya to the Spirit World in place of Herana.

Priya focused all her energy on using her magic to break the necklace. She strained with everything she had. She could feel the necklace dampening her powers but could also feel some energy escaping its magical hold and penetrating the necklace's metal. The Princess slowly felt more and more power surging. Moisture began developing around the necklace, and it started vibrating.

Magus saw what Priya was doing and scorned, "Nooo!" The warlock's hands flared with power as the tremendous lightning bolt continued charging him.

Siren made it to Priya and tried to press the gem into its original spot. Priya fought with her. Somehow Siren achieved her goal and snapped the gemstone into place. Magus saw Siren complete her task. He raised one of his hands and thrust it toward Priya. Electricity shot at the Princess.

Aiden was quite a distance away, but that didn't keep him from trying to stop Magus. A couple of Devians grabbed his arms. He managed to break free from his enemies and rushed the warlock. A brilliant light flashed as Magus unleashed his attack upon the Princess. It blinded everyone within the vicinity. The only thing Aiden could do, at this point, was dive. He did so, slashing with his sword.

There was a SNAP as the latch on the necklace completely broke. The necklace popped off the Princess and flipped toward an unsuspecting Siren. The voltage from Magus redirected. Instead of hitting Priya, it was attracted to the necklace. When Siren realized what had happened, the necklace landed around her neck and was powered by the voltage. Siren convulsed, spasmodically, as the electricity shocked her. After a moment, the electricity disappeared. The once overly confident evil Druidess fell to her knees in disbelief, not knowing what was about to happen. At first, her hands became transparent. She looked at Magus. Her face turned pale from fear. The transparency gradually spread from her hands to her arms until it overtook her entire body. Siren's soul was ripped from her body. It hovered above her. The necklace flashed white light, and her soul was sucked into it. Siren's body fell lifeless to the ground, smoking. The cavern became dead silent.

Magus peered over at Harana's body to see if he succeeded in raising the dark queen. Nothing happened. Her body continued to lay in the coffin, and the fighting commenced.

Unfriendly Surprise

Dagon, Kroni, and Juggy were about to attack when they felt a presence behind them. At first, they felt as if something was watching them, then they heard a sniffing sound. The three Devian henchmen turned around, and what they saw would have scared the pants off them if they had on pants. Xena stood behind them, growling and showing her intimidatingly sharp teeth.

"Uhhhhh, I think we should go," Juggy commented, frozen in fear and only moving his mouth.

"I would agree with you for once, but I'm already gone," Dagon replied and sprinted away into the crowd.

Kroni didn't say a word and followed Dagon, leaving Juggy there to fend for himself.

"Um, uh, hey now. Let's all be calm and not, uh, jump to conclusions," Juggy stalled, "For all you know, I'm on your side, right?"

Xena turned her head sideways at the almost naked and very evil Devian, responding with a smirk that implied, "Are you serious?"

Juggy understood and continued, "Well, okay. I get your point, but, uh, I've been thinking about changing sides. It's come to my attention that I may be working with the bad guys."

Xena swiped at the dishonest Devian as he finished his sentence, knocked him into the cave wall, and chased after the other two.

Dagon and Kroni didn't skip a beat, knowing they had no chance in a brawl against the sister of Freki and Geri. It was no secret that Xena had whooped her two brothers on several occasions. Everyone knew she was the toughest Nywolf. Dagon and Kroni tried to disappear into the crowd, but Xena's eyes locked on them. It wasn't difficult to see them because they were running in the opposite direction of the evil army and were practically naked. Struggling against the flow of the one-track-minded army, Dagon and Kroni managed to force their way through to the back side of the cave and stepped into the open. Exhausted, they leaned over, placing their hands on their knees. As they began to feel relief, they heard the pant and smelled the stink of an annoyed Nywolf. Dagon reluctantly peeked up from his hunched-over position and saw Xena standing before him, staring at them.

Xena bit down aggressively, snatching Kroni in her jaws. She shook him back and forth.

"No, you damn beast!" Dagon hollered and chucked a dagger at her.

Xena yelped in pain as the small blade penetrated her shoulder. She flung Kroni to the right. Dagon saw a few straggling Devians and commanded them to attack the furious Nywolf.

Although Xena preferred to tear Dagon to pieces, she faced the more crucial threat. The Devians charged at the growling beast blindly with absolute faith in their leader. Xena chomped down on two of them, instantly breaking their backs, and tossed them to the side. The last Devian tried a jump attack. Xena caught it in the air and crunched down on it as well, ending its life. The unrelenting Nywolf quickly turned around to finish her business with the leader of the Devians, but Dagon was gone.

Darkness Rises

Aiden landed short of Magus when he leaped. He did, however, land on the stage.

Priya felt reinvigorated with her power since the necklace was off. She wheeled around to attack Magus. She charged up and shot a blast at the warlock, who was still a bit distracted, wondering why Herana hadn't awakened. He sensed the attack coming and blocked it with an energetic shield. The blast ricocheted into the wall, throwing shards of rock everywhere. Magus returned fire, slamming his fists on the ground. The action threw a turbulent wave forward, blowing Priya and Aiden off the platform.

"Aww, my most complicit follower. You have proven your worthiness. Let me take it from here," came a voice from behind the evil sorcerer. Intrigued, Magus turned around to see the mystifyingly beautiful Herana. She was standing in her coffin, alive and completely reborn.

Magus wasn't only Herana's most determined follower. He was in love with her. He had pursued this occasion for almost half his life and would do anything for her. At Herana's direction, Magus took a few steps back and motioned for her to take the lead. Herana had a middle-aged seduction about her that could make any man grovel at her empowered divine appearance. She had long flowing black hair and a beautiful face with a witchlike pointy nose. Her body was voluptuous and muscular. The Queen of evil glistened with unimaginable power. She walked to the front of the stage, eager to engage her enemies.

Aiden and Priya glanced at each other, giving a cautiously confident vibe. They now faced the once defeated but most revered enemy of Legends. They gave each other a subtle nod, then fearlessly charged and simultaneously launched themselves up onto the stage in an aerial assault. Aiden jumped, slashing with his sword, and Priya performed a cartwheel, then vaulted herself up high doing a backflip kick. Herana blocked both attacks with ease, using her arm guard to defend against Aiden's sword and parrying Priya's kick. The trio continued with a barrage of punches, kicks, dodges, and blocks at lightning speed. Aiden's limbs gradually increased and decreased in blue light as if they were charging up and expelling power while he fought. He threw a right cross, left roundhouse, right cross, left hook, ducked under a punch, and let loose an overhand right, while Priya hurled a right cross, left cross, dodged a punch, threw right and left hooks toward her stomach, and then delivered a hard left front kick. Herana was incredibly fast, blocking and dodging every strike, while retaliating with attacks. The fight progressed similarly. Herana continued to block and avoid all strikes until she connected with a right cross to Aiden's face, followed by a side-kick to Priya's stomach. They both flew backward, landed on their feet, and slid. Before Aiden reciprocated the gesture, he realized everyone was staring at him. Unsure why he glanced down at himself and saw his entire body glowing blue.

Exhilarated with power, Aiden sprinted at Herana and unleashed a furious flying knee. Herana looked unnerved but blocked Aiden's zipping knee before it hit her in the face. The impact knocked Herana into the vicinity of Priya. The Princess kicked the dark Queen's side, followed with a spinning elbow to her head, and continued rapidly throwing punch and kick combos. Herana recovered in time to block the rest of Priya's strikes, countering a punch and planting a fist in Priya's face. Aiden zoomed forward, again moving faster than the speed of sound, and threw more combos at blistering speeds. This time, Herana could not keep up with the two of them. Both Aiden and Priya, unprecedentedly, connected several times, cracking Herana in the face and body. Herana's legs wobbled after Priya nailed her in the chin with a left cross. Aiden finished a combo with a roundhouse kick, smacking Herana across her cheek. The once thought undefeatable sorceress spun in the air and landed on her side a few feet away. They each took one step forward, and the evil Queen unveiled one of her most overpowered attacks. Herana closed her eyes, and her body jerked forward, releasing a telekinetic wave that crippled both heroes.

They felt the impact vibrate within their cores and flew in two directions. Aiden crashed into the wall. Priya flew thirty feet and tumbled to a stop. When they attempted to move, piercing pains flooded their bodies internally, originating from inside their bones. It was horrific pain. They tried to stand and couldn't. Determined, they tried again. The two fought through the agony, forced themselves up, and managed to regain their composure.

Magus was tired of watching and vaulted himself in front of Aiden. Even though he was still trying to recover, Aiden was unafraid and stared the warlock in his eyes. Magus gripped his sceptre tightly. The dark magical weapon lit up with power. He whipped the sceptre around, but before he finished his attack, a turquoise blast of energy cracked him in the back. It saved Aiden from a devastating hit. The blast came from Priya. She let loose a few more blasts, switching her aim back and forth from Magus to Herana. The two evil wizards blocked the attacks, ricocheting the energy into the cave walls. Each blast crashed into the walls with authority, sending rocks and debris flying. While Magus was distracted, Aiden ran at him, but it seemed Herana was no longer toying around. She revealed another mythical power. The dark Queen released a telekinetic force that stopped both heroes mid-strike before fulfilling their assaults. Aiden and Priya tried to move, but they couldn't. There was nothing they could do.

Herena spoke in an intrigued yet condescending tone, "You two are impressive, but not good enough. Did you honestly think you could beat me? Hahaha! Did you forget who I am?"

Aiden hovered in the air, caught in the middle of a jump attack. Priya was frozen, midway through sending another blue blast. The hold Herana had on them was so tight they couldn't talk.

"What do you say we end this right now?" the evil Queen continued, "I could simply crush you two, and the war would be over. I think that's what I'll do." Her face contorted in devilish glee. She began tightening her grasp on the two.

Aiden and Priya felt the oxygen departing their lungs. They resisted with all their might. The strength of Herana's power seemed insurmountable.

At once, the dark Queen stopped, remembering something. "Wait!" she exclaimed, "I almost forgot the best part. I have something to show you! I'm sure you're going to love it!"

Five Against an Army

Melia was next to Aiden when he broke free from the Devians' grasp and dove to save Priya. She also tried lunging forward but was yanked back into the crowd. She fought for her life, and creatures dogpiled on top of her. She was being smothered. Jack, Cedric, and Gil stood close behind Melia and saw what was unfolding. They dropped the Gorger disguise to help her. Jack grabbed Cedric and Gil and launched them over the crowd to the top of the dogpile. The two started stabbing Devians in all directions. Jack bull-rushed his way through the evil army, sending them flailing, and made it to the pile. He began digging Melia out, throwing Devians across the cavern. Borak was in the crowd, watching, and saw Jack running toward the mound of creatures. He ran, jumped off a nearby Devian, and flipped through the air in Melia's direction. Borak followed Jack, performed a front flip over Jack once they reached the pile of creatures, landed on top of it, and stabbed a Devian about to cut down Gil. He worked his way down the pile, maiming wicked creatures, and found Melia's hand. Borak grabbed her hand, kicked a Devian off her, and lifted her to her feet. The five of them looked around and realized Herana's army now surrounded them.

Melia immediately threw her boomerang blade. It traveled around the inner circle, taking out all the enemies in front. While this occurred, Borak remembered he lost his bo-blade and thought this was as good a time as any to test the prophecy. It said that once a hero's weapon had forged a bond with its proper owner, the owner could call it, and it would come, as long as it wasn't too far away. Borak held his hand in the air and tried to focus on his weapon, but nothing happened. A few of the Devians looked at Borak, wondering what he was doing.

Melia caught her boomerang. The horrible creatures rushed the heroes within the circle. She began slicing up any Devians that came her way. Borak attempted one more time to call his weapon. This time, he visualized the weapon sitting out in the field where he lost it and immediately felt an invisible tug. Borak saw three Devians running at him, so he pulled on the unseeable force connected to his bo-blade. His weapon lifted off the ground and streaked through the air. It landed in his hands as the Devians reached him. The ninja hero slashed across all three of the enemies' necks, and they fell to the ground dead.

Jack fought using his usual hands-on wrestling and smash-mouth style, while Cedric and Gil covered his left and right sides. Jack chopped through a Devian with his newfound battle ax, then grabbed another one and threw it into the crowd. The flying Devian annihilated all who were in its line of flight. An evil Grandar charged Jack. He ducked under the creature's sword and drove his shoulder into its stomach. He picked up the wicked giant and slammed it hard onto the ground. Jack ferociously raised his ax in the air and sunk it into the giant's chest. A few creatures snuck past Jack on either side. They went after Cedric and Gil. Cedric leaned back, watching a sword whiff by his face, and spun in a 360, slicing the Devian across its arm. He followed by lunging at the creature, critically stabbing it, and turned to block another attack. Surprisingly, it was a Hairie. Cedric deflected the Hairie's strike and followed his momentum with a wheel kick that connected, beautifully, to its face. The evil Hairie wobbled, then fell, knocked out cold. Gil jumped over a sword strike, sliced down the Devian's chest as he landed, and tripped another with a back foot sweep. The Devian fell to the ground. Gil stuck the creature in the heart, ending its life.

Melia noticed her brother summon his weapon. She watched him curiously out of the corner of her eye. Borak's bo-blade began glowing gloriously again. He whipped it around, creating the effect of molten hot helicopter blades. The oblivious army rushed forward. Borak mowed them down in a gruesome defense, splattering blood everywhere and cutting many of them in half. He walked forward, destroying many enemies in front and on both sides of him. Numerous wicked Devians and Hairies lit on fire. The blades were so hot, anything they touched instantly caught aflame. Borak whipped the bo around a few more times and came to a stop in a ninja pose.

Melia muttered to herself, "Now, that's a knife."

The group of five persisted in their efforts to hold off the massive army surrounding them, but even though they had superb skills, their chances were slim. The side of the circle that Jack, Cedric, and Gil were holding broke down as irate Devians and Hairys rushed in. Jack slung his ax in all directions, taking out many hideous creatures. Cedric and Gil killed a few more as well. In the process, the creatures pushed the three back to Melia and Borak's position. Melia sliced through a few Devians, then had to take a defensive stance, blocking the overwhelming army with her shield. The situation was dire.

Borak knew he had to do something quickly. He whipped his bo-blade around and threw it in front of him. It spun like helicopter blades again. The molten hot weapon cut down all evil creatures in its way and opened a path to escape. The path lit up like a runway as every enemy it hit inflamed like living torches.

Borak yelled, "This way!"

The other heroes saw the lighted path and ran for it. Hope reemerged in their minds. They gained a little distance between them and the army. Then, a depressing sight stopped them. Geri and Freki leaped from the cliff where they had found Sen earlier and landed in front of them. The beasts blocked the lighted pathway. Regin sat on top of Geri, grinning diabolically.

Regin Joins the Fight

"Well, look what we have here! A bunch of wannabe heroes!" Regin scorned. He looked around at the situation, "Looks like there's no way out!"

Regin was right. The five warriors were entirely and utterly surrounded. Borak attempted to call back his weapon, but it didn't come. He realized he must be low on energy. He half-wished he hadn't thrown it, but then again, he had needed to do something. Slightly panicked, Borak looked over his shoulder and saw his team behind him, struggling severely to hold back the angry army. It didn't look good. Borak had no choice. It was time to act, even if that meant death. The ninja hero pulled a dagger and sprinted at Regin and the Nywolves.

Borak bellowed in courage, "We shall not surrenderrrrr!"

Borak and Regin eyed each other with contempt as Borak ran. The ninja prepared to leap, but before he did, something halted him in his tracks. An immense blast of energy zipped over his head and cracked the Nywolf on which Regin was sitting. Geri was thrown backward. Regin was flung off Geri and slammed into a wall close to Priya. His sword bounced out of his hand. A horn blared from the back of the cavern. Borak turned to see where the noise was coming from and caught a marvelous sight. The warriors from the Druid Kingdom stood there with the Druid Queen and Farley in front.

"Did somebody call for a magical army?" Farley shouted exuberantly.

Melia saw the arrival of her Druid friends. Reignited with new motivation, she pushed away from the Devians she shielded and attacked with her boomerang blade. She was low on energy, so she didn't toss it, afraid it wouldn't come back. She slashed savagely, cutting through anything around her, then spun to the side and stuck a Devian in the forehead. Thankfully, the onslaught of creatures lessened as some turned to fight the oncoming Druids.

Jack's battle ax was running out of juice, as well. Its gleam dulled as he whipped the heavy weapon around, continuing to lacerate enemies who dared come near him. The two Hairies used their quickness and agility to lunge forward and backward, stabbing creatures one-by-one repeatedly. They all were becoming achingly tired.

Freki stood in front of Borak. The Nywolf had its head lowered, staring him down like he was prey. Borak noticed his bo off to the side, laying on the ground. Brazenly, the ninja went for his weapon. Freki swiped at Borak. He performed a gainer over the Nywolf's paw. The paw zipped under him. Borak landed on a Devian's head and began to run across the top of the crowd of enemies. He leaped to a Grandar's shoulders, jumped over a sword slice, and landed on another creature's head. Freki dove at him. Borak took another step and leaped off an enemy's shield. He twisted, dodging right and left paw swipes, hung in the air, and the Nywolf's savage bite barely missed him. He landed on top of Freki while the beast was mid-dive and ran down the creature's back. Borak launched himself off Freki's hind end, flipped in the air, and landed next to his weapon. He picked up his bo blade and twirled it around. Freki tumbled into the crowd.

Unexpected Arrival

"Call him in!" Herana demanded.

Magus followed her order and commanded his soldiers, "Bring the boy!" He turned and stared Aiden in his eyes.

Aiden halted his struggle to free himself, perplexed at what Magus said. It was strange that Magus and Herana were staring at him, appearing to relish the moment.

While Aiden contemplated what could be happening, he heard, "Dad!"

The voice came from an opening in the cave behind the stage. Aiden immediately recognized it. It was his son. Chase appeared, being led by two Devians.

Aiden tried to shout but couldn't since Herana still had his throat practically squeezed shut with her telekinetic power. He could only make a muffled sound. Herana was enjoying herself now, so she released Aiden, looking forward to the show. She had another surprise up her sleeve about which Aiden didn't know.

Aiden fell to one knee but got up immediately and ran to embrace his son. He grabbed Chase tightly, picked him up, and kissed him on the cheek.

"I thought you were dead! Thank God, you're okay!" Aiden exclaimed, half-sobbing. He felt a mixture of happiness, sadness, and excitement, but something felt off, "You're okay, right?"

Chase only leered at his father oddly.

Aiden set him down and repeated himself, "Chase! Are you okay?

What's wrong?"

Suddenly, Chase pushed his Dad from him and screamed, "You killed my mother! You killed my mother!"

Aiden was caught entirely off guard and reacted, "Wait, What? Chase, I...!" but before Aiden could say anything else, Chase pulled a dagger and sliced his father across the cheek.

Chase stood there, mouth quivering.

Aiden felt his cheek. It was wet with blood. "Son, why? What are you...? I didn't! They did that!" he stammered in disbelief.

Herana and Magus watched, satisfied by what they saw. It was working out perfectly as planned. Chase appeared to think about what his Dad said for a split-second, then shook it off and raised the dagger to attack again.

"Son, noooo! Put it down! What have they done to you?" Aiden pleaded, putting his hands up in defense.

There was a loud crash. Regin rammed into a wall not far from them. Chase paused. Aiden heard someone shouting and flipped around to see Farley with the Druid warriors. Next, he saw the Druid warriors unleash a storm of aerial blasts, and Xena launch herself into the middle of the evil army. Quickly, Aiden whipped back around to look at Chase. Chase was standing in the same position. Seeing the unpleasant turn of events taking place, Herana snatched Aiden up again in her invisible grasp.

Herana yelled at Chase, "Kill him, boy! Remember what he did! Get your revenge!"

Chase stared at his father, confused and unstable, still holding the dagger in the air.

Herana now commanded Chase, "Kill him! He killed your mother! Kill him now or suffer the consequences!"

Chase's eyes never left his dad's. The boy was conflicted, trying to figure out what he should do.

Aiden tried to speak but couldn't. He saw his son was fighting within himself. Chase had been waiting a while to kill his dad, but it didn't feel right for some reason. The boy screamed in anguish and dropped the dagger.

Herana scolded him, "You little shit!" She glared at Aiden and spoke in a hateful tone, "You know what? I'd rather do it myself anyway!" The dark sorceress let out a sinister laugh as she charged up, "Hahahaha!" She fluctuated in gloomy yet powerful light and began telekinetically squeezing the two heroes in her grasp.

Aiden and Priya were being crushed alive. Aiden started to lose consciousness and heard a familiar woman's voice. It was the same voice he heard a few times before, during flashbacks and dream-like states, but this time, he knew it wasn't his wife. Out of the corner of his eye, he saw Sen standing at the cave entrance. The voice was......Sen.

Sen told him telepathically, "Aiden, call for the King's Sword! You must call for your sword!"

Aiden realized he felt something burning his side and remembered the enormous diamond the fairies had given him was in that pocket. He felt the bulkiness of it now. The fairy had said the diamond would bond him to Naru's sword, thus repairing the legendary King's Sword. This would make him the sword's new wielder. The fairy also said Aiden needed to call the sword when he needed it. It seemed the diamond was telling him it was time.

Aiden blocked out everything around him, including the fact he was being crushed alive. He closed his eyes and focused on the sword he'd once seen Naru using. Aiden could feel the gem's power burning his side while searching for the great weapon. He also felt the gem pulling his vision closer to the sword. Then, he saw it. He saw the sword glowing, stuck in the bottom of the river in which it had fallen. Aiden's entire body lit up blue. He used all his strength to concentrate on the sword. The sword began jerking back and forth. Aiden knew he was at his maximum effort, so he yanked on the connection he felt with the weapon. The sword raised from the river floor and fell to its side.

Herana sensed what Aiden was doing and smirked, "Good try, newbie. Now, it's time to die!"

Xena, the Druid Warriors, and Farley

Xena pounced into the crowd and mauled any evil creatures who were around her. She bit, kicked, and thrashed, ignoring many stabs and slices received at her legs and feet. The Druid Queen slung her ax around, releasing numerous discharges, while the rest of her warriors rushed into the cave and unloaded blasts of energy. The fifty Druid warriors had good armor and were competent in the art of magic. Colorful, energetic bursts struck the wicked army, taking out many surprised evil Devians, Hairies, and Grandars. The Druid warriors pushed forward and clashed with Herana's army. They commenced hand-to-hand combat, using magic to strengthen their attacks and durability. Every blow thrown by the warriors hit their enemy with a shocking impact that emitted dazzling sparks. Farley joined the action, zinging large balls of energy with finesse. The little Evo threw balls of energy up in the air, and they dropped into a targeted group of enemies, exploding on impact. BOOM! One blew up, sending Devians flying.

Upon seeing this, Hyra complimented, "Nice one!"

Farley saw his friends were still in the fight but needed his help. He worked his way forward toward them. He swung to the side of the battle and ran into Sen, who struggled to stand. He couldn't believe it.

"Holy cow!" Farley exclaimed. He noticed her condition.

The magical Evo swiftly took action, grabbed the weak, lone surviving Royal Mystic, placed his hand on her chest, and began charging her. He flashed in a pulsating fashion. Sen, instantly, perked up as she felt the incoming power. After several seconds, Farley released her. Extravagant blue light coursed through her body. She looked strong and confident now. The beautiful Mystic cracked her neck and knuckles, ready to fight.

Sen telepathically told Farley, "Thank you, little one."

"Glad I could help," Farley replied, "But if you'll excuse me..." He propelled himself into the middle of the crowd of creatures where the others were fighting.

The Evo landed and rolled to a kneeling position. He saw his friends wrestling with exhaustion and their weapons languishing. Jack was the closest to him. He quickly hopped in front of Jack and pounded the ground, knocking the Devians back. Farley placed a hand on Jack's ax and charged it.

"Thanks, mate!" Jack responded and went back to fighting.

The agile Evo flipped backward and grabbed both Hairies at the same time. Since their weapons didn't have gems, he held onto their arms and gave them a boost of energy. They instantly felt their vigor replenished. Farley felt his stomach turn and regretted what was about to happen. He let out a thunderous fart, "Brrrrrrrrrr!"

The two Hairies heard and erupted in collective laughter. "Hahaha, you could have warned us, guy!" Cedric teased, and even Farley laughed.

Farley leaped to the other side of the circle and rolled under a boomerang slice Melia threw at a Devian. He blasted a powerful attack and knocked back the Devians in the vicinity. The skilled Evo snatched Melia's weapon and charged it. The boomerang blade lit up beautifully.

Melia joked, "'Bout time you got here! You've been missing all the fun!"

Borak arrived next to Farley and said, "Hey, don't forget me!"

"Ah, there you are!" Farley excitedly responded, "I would never do that!" Farley placed his hand on Borak's bo-blade and charged it.

Sen Joins the Fight

Sen felt like herself again and jumped into action. Before the others found her, she was on the cross, on the edge of death. She was sure she would die at that time, but now, because Farley recharged her, she felt the best she had in months and was in prime condition to attack at full force. Sen placed her hands together, activating her powers. She moved her hands in a circular motion. A sideways whirlwind of energy appeared in front of her. She slung her hands forward and threw the whirlwind ahead of her into the massive crowd of raging Devians, Hairies, and Grandars. The sideways tornado-like formation cleared anything in its path, throwing creatures all over the cavern. Sen followed behind her attack and joined her friends in the battle.

The King's Sword

Aiden could feel the output of power Farley was exerting. It was a strange sensation.

As Aiden continued to be crushed alive, he remembered the purple crystals he had received at Druidia. The Druid in training who gave them to him said they could enhance focus. Aiden didn't know how to use the crystals, but it was apparent this was a good time since he needed superior focus in his current situation. He could see Priya's body gleaming a turquoise blue as she fought the ever-tightening squeeze Herana was imposing. The only chance Aiden had at saving them both was to call the sword. He closed his eyes and imagined grabbing the crystals from his front pocket. Almost as if planned, purple smoke seeped through the front of his gambeson and flowed into his head. He had activated the crystals. Instantaneously, he felt like he had taken a potent stimulant which increased his cognitive processing. It was all too real. Aiden would have sworn he was standing under the water, next to Naru's Sword, and simply needed to reach out and grab it. So, he did. In his mind, he reached for the sword and picked it up.

The King's Sword rose from the depths of the water and zipped through the air at tremendous speed. Within seconds, it reached the back entrance of the cave and whizzed toward its new owner. On its way, the sword decimated the limbs, torsos, and heads of many creatures in the dark army, who were battling with the other heroes. Evil Devians and Hairies fell, further weakening the wicked horde who had reduced to hundreds instead of thousands.

Herana knew time was running out and amplified her attack. She added a jolting shock of electricity while compressing the heroes. To her dismay, the most incredible sword in the world landed in Aiden's hand.

A bright blue electrical explosion caused both Magus and Herana to fly backward. Aiden's large gemstone floated in the air. It was connected to the sword with electrical currents. Aiden raised the sword. An electrical storm surrounded him as the gem attached itself to the handle. There was a bright flash and the electricity around Aiden collapsed inward, disappearing into the diamond. Residual energy traveled down the sword's handle and surged through Aiden's body. The bond was successful. The King's Sword was now bonded to him for life. As foretold, the Hero of Legends had become the wielder of the most powerful sword in the land. When Herana went up against it before, the sword forced her into the Spirit world.

Magus and Herana were bewildered by the drastic turn of events. The situation had completely flip-flopped. One second, they were on the verge of eliminating their most significant threat, and the next second, they were confronting the one weapon and hero prophesied to destroy them. Aiden quickly grabbed Chase and pulled his son behind him. The two villains didn't waste any time. They each released high-powered beams of energy in Aiden's direction. The sword Aiden held seemed to have a mind of its own and protected him. It attracted the rays to it and absorbed the light. Aiden felt the sword becoming more powerful as if the beams were charging it. He also felt invigorated. His body reignited in a brilliant incandescent blue aura. The sword began to vibrate, suggesting it was at full strength.

"Stop!" Herana commanded, "We're giving him more power!"

The two warlocks halted their attacks. Instinctively, Aiden whipped the sword in their direction and gave the evil sorcerers a dose of their own medicine. Instead of a beam, a giant ball of energy discharged from the sword's tip. Magus and Herana dove out of the way. The ball of energy crashed into the cave wall and cracked it, shaking the entire cavern.

Priya vs. Regin

Regin had been watching the events unfold. He was angered that Herana hadn't killed Aiden and Priya, and now Aiden was the wielder of the King's Sword. Priya had her back to him, distracted by Aiden's fight against the evil warlocks. Regin rose to his feet and dove into her. They tumbled over each other. Since neither had their weapons, they engaged in a duel of mixed martial arts.

Regin ended up on top, but the Princess kicked him off. They got to their feet. The Princess threw a right cross, then a roundhouse kick. Regin dodged the punch and blocked the kick. He countered with a straight left and right. Priya slipped both punches and threw another right cross. Regin side-stepped her strike and connected with a left jab to her face. He delivered another right, and Priya caught it in the air. She twisted around, and judo flipped him over her. He slammed to the ground. Regin tried to get up, but the graceful Princess side-kicked him in his stomach, causing him to slide back a few feet. He gave Priya a furious look, then quickly bounced up and rushed her. He jumped, performing a double kick. Priya blocked the kick to her face, but the other foot hit her chest and knocked her onto her back. Unfazed, the beautiful Princess flipped up to her feet, dusted herself off, displayed a powerful ninja stance, and prompted Regin to come at her again.

"So, the Princess knows how to fight, huh?" Regin commented sarcastically, "I don't believe it. I don't even have my necklace, and I will annihilate you. You don't have a chance!"

"You sure about that?" Priya replied, "I still have my powers, so I'd watch my mouth if I were you."

"Hahaha!" Regin laughed stubbornly and proceeded to berate the Princess, "You expect me to believe that? You have power from what? You are weaponless! You have nothing! You lying disgrace of a hero! It's just you and me, pretty lady. Mano-y-mano. My strength against your weakness! Hahaha! What could you possibly do?"

Priya was enjoying the moment and smiled slyly. It was apparent Regin was unaware of her internal gem.

The Princess raised her hand and yelled, "Glaive, come!" Her glaive flew into the room from the opening behind the stage and landed in her hand. She responded, "For one, here's my weapon." She stuck the glaive into the ground, "But I don't need it to beat your arrogant ass!" Priya immediately shot a blast of energy and nailed the powerless sorcerer.

Regin flipped over backward and landed on his stomach, knocking the breath out of him. Priya swiftly ran at him and performed a jumping ax kick to the back of his head, rendering the wizard unconscious.

Aiden vs. Herana and Magus

Herena stood up and commanded, "Come to me!"

A black staff with a blade on the bottom lifted out of the coffin where the evil Queen once lay and speedily flew into her hand. The staff had a wavy serpent-like design and an odd, dark-colored gem slightly under its top.

Herana glared savagely at Aiden and spoke, "I see you have more control than I thought. It's impressive that you achieved full potential. But, if you think you can beat me, let alone the two of us at the same time, then you're sadly mistaken. I defeated the world's fiercest warriors until Naru got lucky. I was seeking vengeance, but I don't feel his presence anymore. I guess you'll have to do. What do you say, Aiden? Are you ready to die?"

Aiden wasn't deterred in the slightest by what Herana said. If anything, her egotism only further motivated him to kill her.

He simply responded, "Go ahead and try. This should be fun."

The evil Queen's face contorted as if she was insulted. She glanced over at Magus, signaling to prepare himself. The two evil wizards raised their weapons in unison. A volt of energy connected the sceptre and the staff. The dark weapons energized magnificently in an intimidating display of power. Alarmed, Aiden bolted at the evil wizards, running faster than the speed of sound. He was moving so fast, he disappeared.

Herana quickly defended and slowed time so that she could see Aiden. She lowered her staff, disengaging it from its connection with Magus' weapon, and thrust it forward, releasing a blast. Magus followed suit, releasing more blasts. Although the sinister wizards were also moving rapidly, they weren't as fast as Aiden. Herana and Magus continued letting loose a torrent of energized assaults. Aiden easily slid under them and closed the distance on his enemies. The villains shot more blasts at Aiden as he slid. He whacked two blasts away with his sword before they hit him. Aiden slid within striking distance and sliced at Herana. She flipped over the strike. Aiden stopped, braced one hand on the ground to steady himself, and back-kicked Magus in his stomach. Aiden then proceeded in hand-to-hand combat with the two most powerful evil sorcerers Legends had ever seen.

Herana and Magus lit up with coursing electricity which meant they had reached full potential as Aiden had. They threw strikes so fast, the naked eye couldn't see them, and still, Aiden somehow moved quickly enough to block a strike from the staff, block another strike from the sceptre, jab Herana in the face, spin and elbow Magus on the chin, block a kick, and nail Herana with a straight right. The two warlocks resumed hurling lefts and rights combined with kicks and weapon strikes, but Aiden blocked and dodged every attack, followed by countering punches, kicks, and sword slashes. The sword slashes barely missed. Herana tried grabbing Aiden with her telekinetic power, but Aiden fought it off. Magus attempted to seize Aiden's arm and electrocute him, but Aiden reacted so fast; Magus was barely able to touch him before Aiden deflected the effort and throat-punched his nemesis. Aiden spun, blocked a front kick from Herana, and punched her in the stomach while ducking under a staff slash. He followed with a ferocious right uppercut and broke Herana's jaw. She flipped backward and hit the ground. Aiden swiftly thrust a wheel kick, cracking a throat-clutching Magus to the cheek. Magus flailed through the air and landed by Priya.

Priya vs. Magus

Having neutralized Regin, Priya turned her attention to a tumbling Magus, who rolled near her. She didn't allow him time to recover and jumped at him, swinging her glaive. Magus twisted, dodging the attack. The glaive fractured into the hard dirt. The evil sorcerer rose to one knee and shot an energy blast at her. Priya blocked the blast with her weapon. She swung her glaive again. Magus blocked her attack with his sceptre and countered with a powerful sceptre strike. It nailed Priya. She flew across the cavern into the remaining crowd of enemies.

Sibling Rivalry

Xena and her siblings had caught a glimpse of each other. They completely dismissed everything else that was happening. Even Freki wasn't concerned about his master, who had been tossed from his back when the Druid Queen's mighty blow hit Freki. Instead, revenge consumed him. Freki and Geri rushed their sister, charging their way through the dense collection of creatures between them. They stomped on top of unsuspecting Devians and launched themselves in a savage aerial attack. Xena waited patiently in her position, delighted her brothers were overzealously attacking. As the out-of-control Nywolves descended upon her, she rolled onto her back. Simultaneously, she kicked both of them over her, using their momentum to fling them farther than expected. Xena's brothers flew fifty feet past her and tumbled like rag dolls. Embarrassed, Geri and Freki rose to their feet. Xena silently laughed at them, grinning enthusiastically.

The brothers braced themselves, ready to pounce again, but before they did, several shots by some Druid warriors pelted them. Xena's siblings yelped in pain and ran out the cavern's back exit. The Druid warriors turned and resumed attacking the evil army, which had dwindled to only a few hundred. They bombarded the horrid army with more blasts while they moved forward, pinning their enemies between them and the other heroes.

Priya flew from across the cave and landed in the middle of the evil army. She disappeared. A second later, a few Devians flipped and fluttered up into the air. She leaped out of the crowd and landed next to Hyra.

Magical Weapons

Cedric yelled at Gil and Farley, "Are you guys seeing this?"

"Yeah, holy crap! Where are our weapons!" Gil remarked with a smirk.

"They are spectacular!" added Farley.

Borak, Melia, Jack, and Sen decimated enemies with their glowing special weapons. They pushed forward, mowing down the evil that stood in their way. Borak incinerated Devians with his molten hot bo-blade, who dared to advance on him. He sliced two in half on his left, then two more on his right. They all erupted in flames. He switched his attack to that of a flamethrower and scorched numerous creatures in front of him. Borak pulled his weapon in and punched out, sending a forceful burst of fiery energy forward. The Devians on fire in front of him flew backward into the crowd setting aflame more creatures.

Melia's boomerang blade shone bright green, beaming with power. She slung it into the crowd. It pierced through every creature in its path with ease. The weapon returned, and she caught it. A few Devians ran at her. She threw the boomerang at the ground next to their feet. The boomerang bounced off the dirt, and the dirt magically opened up and sucked the Devians' feet inside. The Devians' feet disappeared into the ground. They were stuck. Melia caught her boomerang again, lunged forward, and sliced their heads off.

"Jack's ax is ridiculous!" Gil added, pointing.

The battle-ax Jack picked up was remarkable. It gleamed in turquoise blue. He struck a Devian with it, and the creature froze in place. He chopped another Devian in half, and as the creature froze, the top half of it slid off its body and shattered on the ground. An evil Grandar jumped at Jack. He blocked the giant's strike with the ax. The villain's sword froze instantly. It had no choice but to drop the sword before its hands froze, as well. The sword shattered on the ground. The wicked Grandar was stunned by what it just saw. Jack chopped downward with the ax and stuck the creature in the top of its skull. Its head froze, but its body continued to walk as it slowly succumbed to the ice spreading into it. More Devians rushed him. Jack whipped the ax around and thrust a horizontal line of freezing energy forward. All the Devians froze in place.

Sen kept a weapon in a sheath inside her pant leg. Her weapon was chained blades. The blades were very large with gold handles, had Aire gems in the handles, and were connected by a long chain. She pulled out the chained blades and began slaughtering evil Devians. The blades lit up in an extravagant blue as she whipped them around in circles. She flung them left and right, cutting through a mass of creatures. The blades whisked around so smoothly, and fluently they seemed impossible to penetrate. She saw a group of Devians rushing Cedric, Gil, and Farley from behind. Sen slung her weapon downward, and a blade hit the ground in front of the vile creatures. The ground exploded, sending them flailing.

The Dark Queen's Secret Power

The Queen of Evil was hurt badly. It was time for her to unveil her final surprise. It was her last hope.

Herana jammed her staff into the ground and eerily spoke, "I summon the vile spirits from the Spirit World. I command you to take his soul!"

Aiden wasn't sure what to expect. Black smoke poured out from the gloomy gem in the staff. The smoke encircled the hero and began to suffocate him. He tried resisting, but even though Aiden was invigorated in a superbly high-powered state, the more he struggled, the tighter the smoke compressed on him. The smoke was dense. It felt like an anaconda was squeezing him.

Unfathomably, whispers and angry threats could be heard from the smoke, as it began asphyxiating him, "You're going to die," "You're ours now," "You have no chance," "Give up," "Join us."

Aiden fell to the ground, desperately fighting for a breath. He felt something pulling from within him as if his soul was ripping from his body. He fought with every ounce of energy he had, clutching onto his soul. Suddenly, he realized he was floating above himself. Aiden looked at himself from above, smothered in constricting wicked smoke. He didn't know what to do. He continued resisting the pull on his soul with all his strength. He felt his grip on himself slipping. Aiden's blue aura brightened. He yanked his soul back hard, and it returned to his core. Aiden sensed he was losing consciousness and had a dreadful thought that he would die anyway. He needed air.

Aiden's vision narrowed. The dark began creeping in. He was about to faint when he saw something. He thought it must be a delusion. Herana was wholly enraptured with killing her archenemy and hadn't noticed. An animal snuck up behind her. It zapped Herana with an extraordinary shock, rendering her incapacitated. The smoke around Aiden dispersed as soon as she fell. Aiden sucked in a lungful of air only seconds before passing out. He smiled appreciatively as the puma he'd once saved walked up to him and licked his face.

Chase watched in awe as everything happened. He couldn't believe his father had these powers. "What they told me must be true, right?" he thought, "I saw it with my own eyes, didn't I?" He swore Aiden stabbed his mother in the heart, as they said. He remembered it, but it was fuzzy.

Seeing what happened to Herana, Magus blasted Aiden with a fiery inferno. The puma bolted out the cave opening through which it entered. Aiden blocked the fire with an energetic shield, protecting his son and himself. Magus used the distraction to help a weakened Herana back to her feet. He decided it was best to make a getaway.

Magus halted the fire and yelled as he swung his sceptre around, "Raaaaahhh!"

The sceptre hit the ground with tremendous force. The ground began cracking and separating. The entire cave shook, mimicking an earthquake.

Earthquake

"Hi, Mom!" Priya greeted her mother, surprisingly upbeat for the situation. She was clutching her ribs.

"Hi, daughter! Are you okay?" Hyra replied, concerned.

"It's nothing. Let's finish these bastards off!" the Princess answered. She stepped in front of her mother, whipped her glaive around, and released an energetic tidal wave. The wave knocked down many enemies.

The brave warriors were on a roll. They continued moving forward and killing evil creatures. The evil army was trapped. They were being attacked from all directions. Although several Druid warriors had lost their lives, the battle was on the verge of being an epic success.

Hyra yelled, "Finish them off! Move-in!"

All the warriors shouted a battle cry and charged forward. One after another, more evil creatures ceased to exist. They were thriving on the indication of victory. Just as it seemed nothing could go wrong, the cavern started to shake. Chunks of the ceiling began to break apart. Everyone in the cave was instantly in peril.

"Son, we have to move!" Aiden shouted. He grabbed Chase by the collar and started running toward his friends.

Magus led Herana to the exit behind the stage, but she had one more thing she wanted to do before they escaped. Herana stopped Magus and grabbed Chase with her telekinesis. She ripped Chase out of Aiden's grasp, yanking him over to where she was.

"Noooo!" Aiden pleaded.

Chase cried back, "Dad!"

Magus and Herana disappeared with Chase into the exit.

Aiden was beside himself. He faced the most difficult decision in his life. Should he go after his son or save his friends? If he chose wrong, someone he loved would die. The cave was collapsing on the other heroes. They were all about to be crushed alive. Although Chase was in the enemy's hands, he was not in imminent danger. Chase was okay for the time being, and he couldn't save the worlds without his friends. Aiden made his decision.

Everyone had stopped fighting and turned their attention to the more crucial threat. The ground was splitting in several areas, creating significant gaps, which descended into unknown depths. If anyone fell down these newly formed crevices, they would surely die. At first, small rocks and dirt dropped from the ceiling and quickly changed into large rocks, boulders, and huge chunks of dirt. The ground split in two between the heroes. Jack, Cedric, and Gil were on one side. Borak, Melia, Farley, and Sen ended up on the other. The fracture between them grew in width and progressed the entire length of the cavern. It swallowed up several Devians.

The Druid warriors spun around and bolted out the back exit while more and more hunks of the ceiling fell violently. Two warriors were crushed. The rest made it out before the cavern completely caved in... all but one. Outside, Hyra noticed Priya wasn't with her. After realizing what her daughter must have done, the Queen of Druids prayed she would somehow survive.

Escaping didn't even cross Priya's mind as the others rushed out the back. She couldn't leave all her friends to die. Instead of running away from the danger, she rushed into it. The courageous Princess sprinted at the remaining creatures, which separated her from the other heroes, as hundreds of pounds of dirt and rock plummeted overhead. She dashed between the frantic Devians, preoccupied with their survival. She slid up to Melia, Borak, Farley, and Sen as a massive chunk of dirt was about to smash them. Priya threw her hands up, forming an energetic shield. The chunk of ceiling crashed into the shield, but it was so heavy, the Princess struggled to hold it up. The immense weight was overwhelming. She fell to her knees.

Sen reacted swiftly. She fired a stream of energy into Priya's magical shield, taking some of the load off before it was too late. The shield now had twice the strength, but it was still cumbersome. They both strained to summon up more power.

"Throw it over there!" Sen shouted telepathically into Priya's head.

The two pushed with everything they had and chucked the hunk of dirt off to the side. It hit the ground with a loud crash. Priya took a few breaths. She looked up and quickly realized everyone wasn't there. Immediately, she looked across the large crevice and saw Jack, Gil, and Cedric in practically the same situation as the one from which she saved the others.

Aiden snapped into action and slowed time again. He had learned somewhat how to control it. He saw Priya save the other group, but an enormous boulder was literally about to flatten Jack's head. He moved in a flash and arrived next to his friends. They looked defeated as they stared up at a boulder that was seconds from their demise. At once, Aiden activated a shield large enough to cover everyone. The boulder crashed on top of the shield and broke into chunks. The rest of the cavern ceiling imploded. A thunderous bang reverberated within the shield. It became dark except for a dull glow from the shield. A moment passed, and it was quiet. They weren't sure exactly what happened, but it felt like they were still alive. All they could see was rock and dirt magically surrounding them.

Cedric broke the silence, "I think we got 'em!" He looked at Gil.

Gil was peering around the collapsed cave in which they were encased. He responded, "Uh, yea! I'd say so."

Cedric asked a serious question, "So, what do we do now?"

Aiden was straining to hold up the tens of thousands of pounds on top of the shield. It was extremely heavy and draining. He hunched over, pulled his arms in, then stood up powerfully, throwing his arms outward.

Aiden yelled in exertion, "Aaaaaahhhhhhhh!"

The shield exploded with tremendous force, hurling everything on top of it miles away. They had closed their eyes but now felt the glorious warmth of sunlight on their skin. Everyone opened their eyes. Unbelievably, they were now outside in a wide-open circle, encompassed by boulders and dirt.

A Hero Goes Down

"Aww, that feels nice!" Melia said.

Suddenly, when it seemed all was well, Jack collapsed. He was lying on his back, shallowly breathing. Everyone ran over to him.

Reaching him first, Gil asked frantically, "What's wrong? What happened?"

"I, uh, I don't know, mate. It hit me all at once. I...I'm so tired. I can't feel anything," Jack answered in a weak voice.

Jack was bleeding from gashes all over his giant body. It was hard to tell where any critical injuries were.

Sen spoke into Aiden's head, "There! At his side. Do you see it?"

Aiden looked and saw it. There was a deep laceration partially concealed under Jack's arm from where a lot of blood was pouring.

"Lift your arm, Jack. Let me see," Aiden told him compassionately.

Jack lifted his arm, and everyone saw what they were dreading. Thick reddish-purple blood was oozing out of a significant cut in his side.

"That's organ blood," Melia informed, under her breath, "It probably got his lungs."

At that moment, Jack coughed up a tremendous amount of blood.

Hyra and a few warriors climbed to the top of the rubble. They saw those gathered around Jack. She didn't want to interrupt and only watched.

Jack knew it wasn't good by the looks on everyone's faces, plus how he felt. He spoke to his friends, "It's okay, fellas. We won, didn't we?"

Aiden responded sadly yet intensely, “Magus and Herana got away with my son.”

Jack’s eyes opened wide, and he replied, “Your son? He’s alive? Well, hell, what are we doing here! We gotta go get ’em!” Jack tried to get up, but a sharp pain shot through his body, and he fell back down. “Sorry, mate. It looks like I might have to sit this one out,” the giant confessed.

Aiden grabbed hold of Jack’s hand. He looked his friend in the eyes endearingly and responded, “Jack, you did good. You’re a good man.” A tear dropped from Aiden’s eye, “I love you, man. They won’t get away with this. I promise.”

They all closely surrounded Jack. Some placed their hands on him.

Jack smiled at Aiden and remarked, “I know they won’t, ya crazy bugga’. It was...” He coughed up more blood, “It was fun while it lasted.”

Aiden clenched Jack’s hand. He felt the giant losing his grip.

Jack solemnly stared at Aiden and struggled to force out more words, “I...I’ll see ya blokes lal...later.” His head laid back on a rock. The heroic Grandar took in one last breath and stopped moving.

They put their heads down in respect. Most shed tears, especially the Hairys. It was hard to believe. No one said a word. They all remained in silence. Hyra made her way down to them and placed her hand on Aiden’s shoulder. Aiden glanced over at her, enduring apparent emotional agony, but Hyra, for some reason, appeared optimistic.

The Druid Queen spoke, “Aiden, use the potion. Give him the potion.”

At first, Aiden wasn’t sure what she meant. Then he remembered the potion she gave him when he was leaving Druidia. The potion was supposed to bring someone back to life. Urgently, he pulled out the rejuvenating liquid and poured the whole vial into Jack’s mouth. Aiden waited nervously for many seconds. He looked over at Hyra, who was confidently watching Jack. After a couple of minutes, Aiden turned around and dropped his head. A few more seconds passed, and Hyra nudged him.

Aiden heard a voice behind him, “Why does everybody look so gloomy? Did somebody die?”

Aiden grinned gratefully. He turned around to see Jack alive and giving him a sarcastic look. He smothered the giant with a relieved hug.

Jack grimaced in pain, telling him, “Rrrgghh, careful, mate! I’m still injured here.”

Aiden replied, “Oh, sorry! I thought I lost you, man. I’m so glad you’re still with us. How do you feel?”

“Ahh, nothin’ I can’t handle. I’m in a little pain, that’s all,” Jack confessed, then added, “I think I can walk though.”

Aiden looked down at Jack’s previously fatal injury and saw it had stopped bleeding. The damage didn't look as bad as before, either. Whatever was in that potion must have partially healed him. Aiden gave the tough Grandar his hand to help him up. Jack grabbed it and got to his feet.

Not the End

As everyone turned to leave, Farley sensed something powerful coming from within the rubble. "Hold on," he told the group, "There's something here. Wait a moment."

Farley held his hand in the direction from which the sensation was coming. His hand flashed in white light. Some rocks and dirt began vibrating, then moved to the side, opening a hole. An item zipped out of the hole and landed in Farley's hand. It was the Necklace of Herana. He was pleased with his find and walked over to Aiden.

"Here you go, Master Aiden. I think you're going to need this," Farley told him. He handed Aiden the necklace.

Aiden took the necklace. It shimmered in his hand. He stared at it, thinking, "This necklace has caused a lot of problems." He wasn't sure why he would need it but figured Farley was probably right. He put it away, and the heroes left on their journey home.

It was a tiresome trek. Cedric reclaimed his dagger once they crossed over the Snake River bridge. The world-saving crew then stopped at Druidia for a day and received many amenities to help them heal and rest up. They didn't stay long out of concern for their home. The last time they had seen their home, a tidal wave explosion of dirt was annihilating it. With Magus and Herana still out there, the Kingdom of Heirstone needed to be rebuilt and refortified. They also needed to get back to bury the Royal Family. It was an unbearable thought. Nevertheless, the King, Queen, and Prince of Heirstone were beloved and respected, especially after dying warriors' deaths. The least they could do was ensure the Royal Mystics received an honorable ceremony.

The crew emerged from the woods and saw Heirstone. It was a terrible sight. It was unbelievable how much damage Magus had done. The only thing that remained was the battered castle. Everything else was destroyed. The natural moat, which previously flowed behind the back castle wall, was now mostly damned up by dirt and rock that Magus' attack had shifted. Only a small stream trickled through. The ground level was disrupted in its entirety. One area of the ground, out in the field, had lowered many feet. This uncovered two large similar-looking mysterious objects. Some of the residents were in the process of removing the odd, heavy artifacts. The heroes walked up to them.

"They're back! They're back!" shouted a female voice.

"What? Who?" replied a male voice.

"Look! Over there!" responded the first voice.

The rest of the residents all looked and saw the heroes. They ran to greet them.

"What happened? Did you kill that son-of-a-bitch?" asked a different Roak man.

"I'm afraid they got away," Aiden, disappointedly, answered.

The same Roak questioned again, "They? You mean Magus and his army?"

Aiden didn't want to tell them the bad news this soon, but since it came up, he explained, "Herana has been reincarnated." There were many gasps from the crowd, "And we barely got out with our lives. But we were victorious in killing off the evil Devian army..." The crew spent the next hour describing everything that happened. They then, subtly, made their way to the castle for some much-needed downtime. They were all injured and needed to heal.

The next day, the artifacts found in the field were brought into the courtyard and set close to where the burial ceremony would occur. The two conspicuous relics formed an L shape and were about ten feet tall. They were made of hardwood and had hand-carved wavy tribal-type designs that flowed from top to bottom. There was also ancient writing that no one understood in the center of each piece. Interestingly, when moved into the courtyard, they had been flipped upside down and placed together. The pieces fit together perfectly and formed a door frame.

Three days after their arrival, the heroes were well enough to attend the ceremony. The Royal Family's corpses had been ritualistically preserved, and all the preparations for the event had been made. It was time to bury

Naru, Carys, and Conrad.

Everyone gathered in the courtyard. The three deceased Mystics lay in decorated caskets covered with flowers and extravagant fluorescent gems. The coffins were on the stage in the courtyard's center where all events occurred. Crowded together in front of the caskets was a large gathering of surviving residents. The heroes sat on the other side of the coffins. Sensing the crowd becoming restless, Aiden stood up and began the interment.

"Ladies and gentlemen, everyone who has survived this tragedy. Today is a sad yet glorious day. We have lost our King and Queen and the Prince. They fought with courageous fortitude and almost defeated Magus. They gave their lives to protect their people. We will always remember and respect them for their bravery and conviction in their duty as our leaders. They succeeded in protecting those who are still alive. They succeeded in preventing the castle from destruction. We will NOT allow that effort to be FOR NOTHING!" Aiden shouted the last part of the sentence, and the gathering roared in agreement. Aiden continued, "From this day forward, we shall always celebrate this day. We shall celebrate the lives that they gave to protect us. We shall celebrate our survival. And we shall celebrate our victory!" The crowd cheered again, "But the responsibility now turns to us. These heroes, including myself, pledge to lead and always protect the citizens of Heirstone. You have our word, and that includes going after that SON-OF-A-BITCH!" The crowd cheered ecstatically. All the heroes stood, displaying their unity.

Once the cheering and applause died down, a resident walked out in the open in front of the coffins. It appeared to be an older person with a cane, wearing an old raggedy robe, but one couldn't be sure since the person's hood concealed the face. The discreet individual had a mystique aura and abruptly threw off the robe. It was an old human lady. Aiden recognized her. It was Thora! The woman who had accosted him at Druidia when trying to save Priya.

Thora addressed the entire assembly with earnestness, "Behold, your team of heroes! These are the ones who will save you from the tyranny of evil. They have surpassed what the Prophecy of Heroes foretold, and that which was written has come true, except for one last prediction. In its last few sentences, the Prophecy informs of a Mystic who must be summoned from the Spirit World...an essential addition that completes the team. That Mystic is one of the three that lay before you."

Initially, there was silence while everyone tried to process what was said. Then a low rumbling of unsure conversations began in the crowd.

"I remember you. You're the lady from the cabin," Aiden spoke loud and clear, "You told me you wrote the prophecies, and now you're telling me one of these corpses will come back to life and join us?"

The old lady smiled and answered, "Yes, Aiden. One of these brave Mystics will join your team and become a Hero of Legends."

Aiden glanced around to see if anyone else thought this woman was crazy. After confirmation that many others felt as he did, he questioned in disbelief, "And how is that supposed to happen?"

The apparent clairvoyant didn't have time to respond. The door-shaped artifact next to Aiden popped and flashed. The breakpoint where the two pieces joined sparked at the top and slowly worked its way down like a welding arc. The arc went out at the bottom of the break. Everyone heard fizzling and crackling sounds. A blue transparent screen appeared and disappeared off and on until it stabilized. A portal opened.

They could hear sounds of a battle coming from within the portal. Aiden looked over at where Thora stood and discovered she had vanished. All of a sudden, Captain Dunagan emerged, diving through the portal. He landed on the ground and rolled to his knees. Whiz kid materialized next, followed by an upgraded WAFU. WAFU shot his fifty cal minigun into the portal and stopped as soon as he realized he wasn't on Earth anymore.

"Where's Dozer...and Sherri?" Whiz kid implored, deeply concerned.

Instantaneously, a Devian soared through the portal. Sherri pursued it and shot it out of the air with her handgun. Dozer traveled through last, sliding on his back with a Devian on top of him. He jabbed the Devian up through the bottom of its chin with a buck knife and threw the creature off him. The portal closed, and everyone stared at each other awkwardly.

The situation teetered on whether to attack when Cedric broke the ice saying, "Who are these weird-looking creatures?"

Aiden smirked and sarcastically asked Cedric, "Are you saying I look weird?" He then joyously greeted his friends, "Captain! You guys! I wasn't sure if I'd ever see any of you again! What's happening on Earth?"

Dunagan rose to his feet and embraced his comrade to whom he owed his life, responding, "Aiden, so good to see you! I wish I could say everything's great, but obviously, that's not the case. Every time we see each other, it seems like the world's coming to an end. That ugly son-of-a-bitch has come back, and there's some other magical woman with him this time, calling the shots. We need your help!" Dunagan stared at Aiden soberly, then peered around and added, "By the way, where the heck are we?"

Gil understood what everything he heard meant. He disappointedly glanced over at his buddy to complain, "Not again! We just got back!"

Cedric's face lit up with a huge grin, and he remarked, "Just got back? We're just getting started!"

Glossary

Catapult - Large wooden mechanism used during battle to forcefully propel stones, spears, or other projectiles
Chewbacca - A fictional character from Star Wars films; Wookie
Cordage - Old ropes
Death water - Water that, if entered, will kill someone
Druidia - Magical town where creatures live and study to become Druids
Flank - Attack or pursue something from the side
Gainer - An acrobatic trick of performing a backward flip while still moving forward
Gambeson - A padded defensive jacket worn as armor separately or combined with mail or plate armor. The typical kind of armor worn on Legends
Hadouken - A special attack from Capcom's Street Fighter series of fighting games. The attack is an energetic blast through the air
Heirstone - King Naru's castle; the home of most of the heroes
Louches - Disgraceful or shady people; not reputable or decent
MREs - a Meal, Ready-to-Eat. It is a self-contained field ration in lightweight packaging.
Ope - Doofus, goofball, dork
Orb - Spherical body of energy
Parry - Ward off an attack followed with a countermove
Shaka - A hand gesture in which the thumb and little finger are extended outward from a closed fist; used when greeting or parting from someone or to express approval or solidarity
Stargate - A device consisting of a traversable portal that can send something or someone, nearly instantaneously, to another location light-years away
The Flash - Superhero who runs faster than the speed of light
Twerking - A sexualized dance move involving thrusting hip movements in a low, squatting stance
Wing Chun dummy - A wooden dummy used in martial arts as a practice dummy to train both offensive and defensive skills

Characters

Aiden - Human/Mystic; 6' 4", muscular, dark brown buzz-cut hair, unshaven facial hair; Marine background; Weapon is a Glock 21 and AR 15 on Earth and the King's Sword on Legends; Bonded with a huge Aire gem; Has an unknown, untapped potential of powers; Hero of Legends

Priya - Roak/Druidess; 5' 6", fit, athletically voluptuous body, beautiful, long brunette hair, amber eyes, tanned skin; Princess of Heirstone and Druidia; Weapon is a glaive; Bonded with a Watre gem; Skilled fighter and has strong powers; Hero of Legends

Borak - Roak; Melia's brother; 6' 2", muscular, long black hair typically kept in a ponytail, clean-shaven, body and facial tattoos; Top warrior of Heirstone; Weapon is the bo-blade; Bonded with a Fierna gem; Skilled ninja developing strong powers; Hero of Legends

Melia - Roak; Borak's sister; 5' 10", muscular, long black hair typically kept in a ponytail, body and facial tattoos; Top warrior of Heirstone; Weapon is the boomerang-blade; Bonded with a Dirte gem; Skilled ninja developing strong powers; Hero of Legends

Gil - Hairie; Cedric's best friend; 4' 2", long straggly hair covering the body and most of the face; Warrior of Heirstone; Weapons are a sword and daggers; Skilled fighter developing strong powers; Hero of Legends

Cedric - Hairie; Gil's best friend; 4' 1", long straggly hair covering the body and most of the face; Warrior of Heirstone; Weapon is a unique dagger also used as a key; Bonded with a Dirte gem; Skilled fighter developing strong powers; Hero of Legends

Jack - Grandar; 8' 4", muscular, semi-long blonde hair, bald on top, beard, many earrings; Warrior of Heirstone; Weapon is a battle-ax; Bonded with a Watre gem; Skilled fighter developing strong powers; Hero of Legends

Farley - Evo; 3'6", red fur; Warrior and magic-replenisher of Heirstone; Doesn't have a weapon; Skilled fighter and extremely powerful; Hero of Legends

Naru - Mystic; 6' 1", muscular, long curly gray hair, long beard; King of Heirstone; Weapon is the King's Sword; Bonded with a huge Aire gem; Skilled fighter and extremely powerful; Hero of Legends

Carys - Mystic; 5' 9", fit, long reddish blonde hair; Queen of Heirstone; Weapon is the Bow of Myrial; Bonded with an Aire gem; Skilled fighter and extremely powerful; Hero of Legends

Conrad - Mystic; 6' 3", muscular, short dirty blonde hair, clean-shaven; Prince of Heirstone; Weapon is a Halberd; Bonded with an Aire gem; Skilled fighter and extremely powerful; Hero of Legends

Sen - Mystic; 5' 10", fit, beautiful, long dirty blonde hair; Princess of Heirstone; Weapons are a sword and daggers; Bonded with an Aire gem; Skilled fighter and extremely powerful; Hero of Legends

Marvin - Mystic; Conrad's son; Short brown hair; Prince of Heirstone; Weapon is a small sword; Fighter in training

Thora - Human/Mystic; 5' 4", older lady, long gray hair; Writer of Legends; Weapon is a cane; Bonded with an Aire gem; Skilled fighter and extremely powerful

Hyra - Roak/Druidess; Priya's mother; 5' 8", muscular, beautiful, long brunette hair; Queen of Druidia; Weapon is a battle-ax; Bonded with a Watre gem; Skilled fighter and extremely powerful

Druid King - Roak/Druid; Priya's father; 6', muscular, long black hair, short beard, earrings; King of Druidia; Weapon is a scepter; Bonded gem unknown; Skilled fighter and extremely powerful

Cornelius - Bear; Larger than bears on Earth; 2000 pounds, muscular, short gray hair, long fangs, sharp claws; ability to speak because of Druidia's magical powers; Guardian of Druidia; Weapons are claws and teeth; Skilled fighter and extreme brute strength

Sasha - Human; Aiden's wife; 5' 4" average build, semi-long light brown hair; Weapon is a knife; Defensive fighter

Chase - Human; Aiden's son; Short brown hair; Weapon is a knife; Fighter in training

Captain Dunagan - Human; 6' 2", fit, black buzz-cut hair, clean-shaven; Marine; Weapons are a 1911 and M27 IAR; Skilled military fighter

Sherry - Human; 5' 10", fit, black hair in cornrows; Marine; Weapons are a Glock 19 and M4 carbine; Skilled military fighter

Dozer - Human; 6' 1", muscular, shaved black hair; Marine; Weapons are a Glock 19 and M16; Skilled military fighter

Whiz Kid - Human; 5' 8", fit, long dirty blonde hair, glasses; Marine; Weapon is a Glock 19; Skilled technology and medical expert

Pecko - Human; 6' 1", fit, light brown buzz-cut hair, clean-shaven; Marine; Weapons are a Sig Sauer M18 and WAFU; Skilled military fighter

Danny - Human; 5' 10", muscular, black buzz-cut hair, clean-shaven; Marine; Weapons are a Glock 19 and M27 IAR; Skilled military fighter

Missy - Human; Aiden's mother; 5' 6", fit, long blonde hair, glasses; Weapon is a knife; Defensive fighter

Xena - Nywolf; Sibling of Geri and Freki; Smaller than her brothers; 1500 plus pounds, muscular, long white and brown hair, massive head, huge fangs, large paws, sharp claws; Weapons are claws and teeth; Skilled fighter and extreme brute strength; Hero of Legends

Magus - Mystic; 6' 6", muscular, red stylish hair, beard, earrings, body tattoos; Leader of the evil army; Weapon is a scepter/naginata; Bonded with the largest Aire gem known to exist; Skilled fighter and extremely powerful

Herrana - Mystic; 5' 11", fit, athletically voluptuous body, beautiful, long black hair; Queen of the evil army; Weapon is a staff; Bonded with a rare black Aire gem; Skilled fighter and extremely powerful

Freki - Nywolf; Sibling of Geri and Zena; Largest Nywolf; 2000 plus pounds, very muscular, long brown and black hair, massive head, huge fangs, large paws, sharp claws; Soldier in the evil army; Weapons are claws and teeth; Skilled fighter and has extreme brute strength

Geri - Nywolf; Sibling of Freki and Zena; 2000 plus pounds, muscular, long brown and black hair, narrower in stature, massive head, huge fangs, large paws, sharp claws, long snout, and skinny eyes; Soldier in the evil army; Weapons are claws and teeth; Skilled fighter and has extreme brute strength

Regin - Roak/Druid; 6' 2", muscular, long black hair, body and facial tattoos, clean-shaven; General of the evil army; Weapons are a necklace and sword; Bonded with the Fierna gem; Skilled fighter and extremely powerful

Siren - Roak/Druid; 5' 10", fit, long black hair, body, and facial tattoos; General of the evil army; Weapons are a sword and daggers; Bonded with the Dirte gem; Skilled fighter and extremely powerful

Drakkar - Gorger; 14' 5", biggest Gorger known to exist, broad and muscular with a belly, sporadic straggly hair, missing teeth, greenish skin, many piercings; Leader of the evil army; Weapon is a spiked club; Skilled fighter and has extreme brute strength

Dagon - Devian; 6' 2", thin but muscular, sporadic straggly hair, a mixture of flat and fang-like teeth, reddish skin, piercings, and tattoos; Leader of the evil army; Weapons are a sword and daggers; Skilled fighter and has powerful strength

Kroni - Devian; 6', thin but muscular, sporadic straggly hair, a mixture of flat and fang-like teeth, reddish skin, piercings, and tattoos; Soldier in the evil army; Weapons are a sword and daggers; Skilled fighter

Juggy - Devian; 6', thin but muscular, sporadic straggly hair, a mixture of flat and fang-like teeth, reddish skin, piercings, and tattoos; Soldier in the evil army; Weapons are a sword and daggers; Skilled fighter

Benny - Hairie; 4' 1", long straggly hair covering the body and most of the face; Soldier in the evil army; Weapons are a sword and daggers; Skilled fighter

Sidekick - Hairie; 4’, long straggly hair covering the body and most of the face; Soldier in the evil army; Weapons are a sword and daggers; Skilled fighter

Creatures

Roak - Creature from Legends; Typically above average human height, human characteristics except more muscular and cut, pointy ears, long black hair kept in ponytails, are clean-shaven, and have many ritualistic tattoos including small face tattoos

Grandar - Creature from Legends; Typically eight-plus feet tall, significant human characteristics, a broad body structure including head and jawline, are muscular but not cut, have relatively long hair that hangs naturally, a beard, and numerous earrings in their ears

Hairie – Creature from Legends; Short, shaggy, dwarf-like creatures; 4 ft tall, human characteristics, large ears, long human-like straggly hair covering their body, facial hair that covers most of their face; feet similar to an ape which can use as hands

Evo - Creature from Legends; Around 3-1/2 feet tall with mixed human and canine characteristics (fox), human hands and feet, a tail, no snout but a canine nose, long red fur on body and tail, and short red fur on face and tops of hands and feet

Mystic - Creature from Legends; Typically above average human height, human characteristics except more muscular; Born with the ability to wield magic and can tap into their maximum potential; Strongest creatures on Legends

Druid - A state when a creature reaches the ability to wield magic; The title of a magic wielder

Druidess - Female Druid

Devian - Creature from Legends; Devilish-looking; Above average human height, a variety of mangled flat and fang-like teeth, thin but muscular, reddish skin, sporadic straggly hair, and piercings and tattoos

Gorger – Creature from Legends; Ogre-looking; 14 feet tall, missing teeth, broad and muscular but with a belly, greenish skin, sporadic straggly hair, and piercings

Nywolf - Animal from Legends; Wolf-looking; 1500 plus pounds, muscular, long black, brown, and white hair, massive heads, huge fangs, and overly sharp claws

Puma - Animal from Legends; Look like a large puma; 300 pounds, muscular, short tan and black fur, large heads, long fangs, and overly sharp claws; Possess power to electrocute prey and enemies

Bear - Animal from Legends; Looks like a large grizzly bear; 2000 pounds, muscular, short gray hair, long fangs, and overly sharp claws

Rock deer - Animal from Legends; Look like a rock when lying down; Similar to a mule deer; 150 pounds, short, stubby, sandy beige color and antlers look like tree branches

Fohawk - Animal from Legends; Colorful like a Macaw parrot but have the body structure of a predatory hawk; Size of a hawk; Feathers form a faux hawk hairstyle on their head; Eats desires fruit

Desires tree - Large tree on Legends; has pear-sized lavender fruit; tricks those who consume it with hallucinations of most wanted desires; Hallucinations usually end in the creatures death

Snake - Animal from Legends; A combination of cobra and rattlesnake; Same size as a cobra; bright multi-colored bands of pink, blue, and black, a cobra hood, and a rattle; Can hypnotize prey or enemies with its stare

Monkey - Animal from Legends; Look like a spider monkey; The size of a spider monkey; Have the third hand on their tail

Monigator - Animal from Legends; A cross between an alligator and monitor lizard; 500 pounds have black scales, rounded head, long fangs, long monitor-like tongue, overly sharp claws, and long legs; Makes sounds similar to the raptor from Jurassic Park; Live in desolate bodies of water

Scorpula - Animal from the tales of Legends; Looks like a colossal scorpion/ tarantula combo; 1000 pounds, have short black fur, huge fangs, and ten legs; Have super strong webbing; Can shoot purple acid from their mouths

Dragon - Animal from the tales of Legends; Looks like a giant dragon; Weight unknown, muscular, green and gray scales and spikes on the body, enormous head, massive fang-like teeth and claws, and serpent-like eyes; powerful; Can shoot fire from the mouth

Reever - Animal from the tales of Legends; Looks like a humongous pelican; 500 pounds, white, black, and gray feathers, huge beak, long legs, and a short neck; dragon's favorite food

Weapons & Tools

Bo blade - Borak's weapon; A bo staff with blades on each end, tribal designs, and a red gem

Bo staff - a Japanese martial art weapon made of usually red or white oak that is between 5.9 ft to 9ft. long, used to strike and block opponents and their weapons

Boomerang blade - Melia's weapon; A boomerang with retractable blades on each end that deploy when the weapon is thrown and retract on the return before the wielder catches it

Glaive - Priya's weapon; A weapon consisting of a large blade fixed on the end of a staff. The blade is curved, resembling a broadsword

Scepter - Magus' weapon; a mighty ornamented staff/wand that contains the largest Aire gem known to exist at its top.

Halberd - Conrad's weapon; A spear and a battle ax combined

Naginata - Similar to a glaive; A weapon consisting of a long skinny blade on the end of a staff. The blade is curved, resembling a samurai sword

Leupold scope - High-quality tactical scope on Aiden's AR 15

Hellfire trigger - A device that allows Aiden's AR 15 to fire at a rate approaching that of a fully automatic firearm

WAFU - Water, Ammunition, and Fire Unit; Virtual reality controlled weaponized robot that can attack with a water jet, minigun, and flamethrower
Magma bombs - Potion that, when thrown, explodes into a wave of lava

Healing shield - Orb of energy that protects and heals someone; it also initiates visions while encompassed by it

Fierna - Red gemstone found on Legends that contains energy from the element fire; similar to a ruby

Watre - Turquoise gemstone found on Legends that contains energy from the element water; similar to an aquamarine

Dirte - Green gemstone found on Legends that contains energy from the element water; similar to an emerald

Aire - Clear gemstone found on Legends that contains energy from all elements; similar to a diamond

About the Author

Russel Bush is a creator of fantasy, action, and comedy plotlines. In this, his first novel in a trilogy, his desire is to take readers on an unforgettable adventure away from any monotony and discord of daily life.

In the distant, mysterious world of Legends, Russel grants you the ability to immerse yourself in the folklore, romance, and family lives of an intricately imagined other world. Of particular interest to female readers, Russel has included strong, brave young women warriors, often missing from typical fantasy novels.

Originally from Los Angeles, Russel lived several years in Hawaii and now resides in Las Vegas where he spends as much time as possible with his son, Skyler, and his two dogs, Logan and Junior. Russel and his son are often caught entertaining each other with their sarcastic senses of humor. Russel spent some years as a special ed teacher and has always been an avid moviegoer and show streamer who can enjoy almost any genre. That being so, fantasy has always overly intrigued him. Russel also trained in mixed martial arts for several years which enhanced his ability to add the detail of the fight scenes. Currently enjoying a slower lifestyle, Russel looks forward to continuing the next volume of Legends.

Legends
The Prophecy of Heroes

www.ingramcontent.com/pod-product-compliance
Lightning Source LLC
Chambersburg PA
CBHW070643310726
48982CB00001B/401

9780988230774